TRYSTAN GUIDED MY FACE TO HIS

His hand slid upward and cupped the back of my head, so that I could not escape him if I tried. With savage and relentless force, he pressed his lips to mine and devoured them with the hunger of a starving creature. I was swept forward on a crest of passion, exhilarated by its power.

Could anything be more wonderful than this?

Could any price be too great to pay?

Telling myself the answer to both my questions was no, I gave myself up to him and returned his kiss with a passion I had not known existed in me. And in the middle of that torrent of need and abandonment, we clung to each other, two lost souls rocked by the storms that assaulted Wolfeburne Hall.

Also by Penelope Thomas

Master of Blackwood
*Passion's Child
Thief of Hearts

*written under the name P.J. Thomas

Available from
HarperPaperbacks

Harper
Monogram

The Secret

⊱ PENELOPE THOMAS ⊰

HarperPaperbacks
A Division of HarperCollinsPublishers

HarperPaperbacks *A Division of* HarperCollins*Publishers*
10 East 53rd Street, New York, N.Y. 10022

Copyright © 1993 by P. J. Thomas
All rights reserved. No part of this book may be used or reproduced in any manner whatsoever without written permission of the publisher, except in the case of brief quotations embodied in critical articles and reviews. For information address HarperCollins*Publishers*,
10 East 53rd Street, New York, N.Y. 10022.

Cover illustration by Diane Sivavec

First printing: October 1993

Printed in the United States of America

HarperPaperbacks, HarperMonogram, and colophon are trademarks of HarperCollins*Publishers*

❖ 10 9 8 7 6 5 4 3 2 1

1

When I was small I had a secret.

I did not speak of it to anyone. Dared not, lest they know me for what I was and put me from them in disgust.

I dreaded they would find out. Dreaded they would see past my meek and quiet facade to what lay hidden deep within. And yet they never did.

Silence was my only friend, but in that silence my secret tortured me. There was not one person to whom I could confess, no one who might have listened with an accepting or forgiving ear.

I was bad.

Evil.

Unworthy of the home that had been given me.

Knowing this, I held my tongue and took no one into my confidence. Whatever low conception they held of my person, I came to realize they could not see the beast in me.

It lived within my heart—the beast that urged me to steal one of Mr. Treadwell's carving knives from where it hung in the kitchen. I used to watch him every Monday evening, seated on the railback chair in the kitchen, sharpening the blades until they gleamed.

The beast in me watched covetously while he set each knife back into the wooden stand affixed to the wall, mere inches beyond the reach of an eight-year-old child. Its evil voice whispered in my ear, seductive and cajoling, telling me to wait until dark and then slip downstairs and do what must be done. I had only to fetch the stool that stood near the hearth, and whichever knife I chose would be mine, a grim reward for my stealth and cunning.

Prize in hand, I must stalk through the darkness again, up the long staircase with its creaking treads and cold banister, up to the second floor, to the bedroom of my worst enemy and greatest tormentor. She was a stocky child almost three years my senior, but, asleep and huddled beneath the satin counterpane, she would have been vulnerable to my attack.

It was all clear to me. My hand would raise high above my head, still gripping that awful weapon. Then downward it would thrust, burying the knife deep within her, spilling that rare blue blood of which she was so proud.

Henrietta was a Wolfeburne, and there had been Wolfeburnes in England as far back as anyone could recall. They had fought with William the Conqueror, followed Richard the Lionhearted to the Crusades, sailed with Drake when he vanquished the Armada, and rode with the entourage that accompanied Charles II on his triumphant return from Holland.

It would not have occurred to her that, had she gone back far enough, she might have found her ancestors grubbing about in the dirt for beetles or painting their bodies and dancing naked around huge standing stones. Doubtless, if the notion had occurred to her, she would have satisfied herself by assuming those ancient Wolfeburnes had owned that patch of dirt or had themselves caused the stones to be raised upright.

Then, too, they were probably all of them properly married, each couple having exchanged beetles or danced clockwise around the tallest stone, whichever was deemed to be the correct manner to bond them securely and acceptably in wedlock. I can see them stretching back in time, standing in pairs, husbands and wives, every one.

All of them properly married.

As her own parents had been.

And mine had not.

It was something Henrietta never let me forget. No more than she let me forget I was a commoner and she was a lady. Even now her jeering face returns to me, the stiff brown ringlets bumping against her chubby cheeks, her shrill childish voice screaming, "You are a bastard and your mother was a wh—"

"Mistress Henrietta!"

Mrs. Severne's plump and dimpled hands covered her charge's mouth, putting an immediate end to her outburst. Her quick actions left me in doubt as to what my mother was supposed to have been, but it was not for my sake she had stirred herself. "A *lady*," she informed Henrietta, "does not use such language."

"And I am a lady, am I not, Nanny?" Henrietta demanded as soon as she had struggled loose and could speak again. "Jessamy is only a vulgar, common street girl who ought not to have been brought to Wolfeburne House. Or given a Wolfeburne name."

The first Jessamy had been her great-grandmother, and the name had been bestowed upon me shortly after Lady Wolfeburne saw fit to take me into her home. It was not a name I much liked, but there was some pleasure to be had from anything that upset Henrietta.

Certainly, it was a prettier name than hers.

She had been named for her father—Henry Edward, Lord Wolfeburne—a stodgy man with a lethargic brain and body. A gentleman of mediocrity who did nothing that was not at once normal and ordinary, a dull little man who doted upon his daughter for the sole reason that she bore his name and he saw himself in her.

Whatever Henrietta had to say about my parentage, Mrs. Severne hastily agreed with her. Not to agree would be to invite a wild, uncontrollable tantrum that would go on until Lady Wolfeburne appeared, in all her slender perfection, demanding to know why Nanny couldn't control the antics of one small child. There was only her heightened color and tight smile to remind the three of us how much she hated to be bothered unless it was her own dear Annabelle who clamored for her attention.

To save herself from her mistress's wrath, Mrs. Severne always accused me of having provoked the quarrels, and I would be sent to my room until I could learn to behave in a manner suited to young ladies.

At this, Henrietta would announce, "She is not a lady. *That* is why she does not behave like one."

And the beast in me would whisper about the knives in the kitchen.

I cannot know what I might have done had our lives

continued in this fashion. Perhaps, one night, I should have gathered up my courage and braved the winding back stairs in the dark of night, determined to make my way to the kitchen. Had my anger carried me that far, I do not doubt that the beast would have leapt forth and done the foul deed before my reason returned.

Who knows what would have become of me had it not been for . . . ?

But I precede myself.

I did not always live at Wolfeburne House. I began my life in a single room above a butcher's shambles, a room that smelled of gin and the heavy scent of lavender, while underneath there was always the unbearable odor of rotting meat.

I lived there with my mother, of whom I have only the haziest recollection, although I can picture the street below our window simply by closing my eyes. It was a busy lane, one used by an endless array of carts and barrows, coaches and carriages, each leaving the mark of its passing in the broken cobbles and the litter that clogged the gutters.

I had a rag doll. Meg, as I remember, although it was so many years ago, I can no longer be certain if that was her name or my own. We used to sit on the doorstep when we were told to go outside, watching for the coaches and carriages with their shiny harnesses and the bright crests upon their lacquered doors. It became a game to see which of us would spot them first. Meg would always lose, although often I pretended her yellow button eyes had been quicker than my own.

Sometimes I grew bored and would stare out into the lane, thinking rather than seeing. Meg would lie quietly in my lap, knowing that I was not in the mood to play with her. It was on one such afternoon I caught sight of a copper penny, shining at me from atop the gray cobbles. I did not pause to think but ran headlong into the lane.

There was the ringing of iron horseshoes, an oath, and a startled cry. I looked up from my treasure to discover a carriage standing near enough to me that I could lift my hand and touch the fetlocks of the lead horses.

"Is she all right, Todd?" a woman's voice demanded, her tone harsh with fright.

"So far as I can see, milady," came the reply.

High above me on the driver's seat sat a gangly man with sad eyes and a long face. He regarded me from beneath the brim of his top hat.

"Bring her here," the woman in the carriage ordered.

Obediently, if unhappily, Todd descended, picked me up, and set me down in front of his mistress for her inspection.

She was exquisite. Pale gold ringlets peeked from beneath a feathered bonnet, and the face beneath the curls was a perfect oval. She had a retroussé nose, her eyes were deep blue, and the deep rose of her faintly curved lips was set off by the soft pinkness of her skin.

I wondered hopefully if she would add a second penny to the one I had found.

Instead, she clapped her hands together like a pleased child. "Goodness! What a pretty little thing."

I had never been called pretty by anyone and thought it behooved me to smile and curtsey, a trick my mother had taught me for her own amusement. Since I managed this without losing my balance as I often did, my smile broadened considerably.

"How cunning," the lady cried, clasping her hands to her bosom. "And what a place to find her. Do you think she has a mother and a father?"

The driver snorted. "A mother, leastwise."

The lady's eyes moistened, and she reached out a soft hand to touch my curls, which were only a shade darker than her own. "What kind of woman would allow a child of this age to run about in the streets?" She did not wait for his answer. "Such a creature does not deserve to be blessed with a daughter when there are those of us who—" She frowned. "Go and fetch the girl's mother, Todd. I would like to speak with her."

This required a little help on my part, which I gave by vaguely pointing in the direction of an upstairs window. Todd went off, shaking his head and muttering beneath his breath. His boots thudded a protest against the worn steps.

It was several minutes before he returned, my mother nearly stepping on his heels in her haste. This is the only image of her that remains in my memory, her chapped hands hurriedly fastening her apron over her dress to hide the grease stains, strands of gray hair slipping from the knot at her nape. Even to my young eyes she appeared shabby and mean compared to the golden and bejeweled lady in whose lap I now sat.

Hands wringing, my mother gave a short curtsey and asked, "'As the child been botherin'—"

The lady cut off her question with an impatient wave. "How dare you let a child of this age roam about the streets to be trampled? It would be nothing less than you deserved if I were to call the constables."

But that, I learned, was not at all what Lady

Wolfeburne had in mind. She had been married five years and borne no children, and she ached for a child to reflect her golden loveliness. There was Henrietta, of course, the child of her husband's first marriage. Dull, deliberate Henrietta who could endear herself to no one, least of all to this glamorous woman who had married her father and usurped her position.

It took but a few minutes for Lady Wolfeburne to convince my mother that she was far more able than she to provide for me—as indeed she was. Perhaps a few coins exchanged hands to ease my mother's loss. If so, I was spared being told of that ignomity.

In less time than it would have taken to choose fresh vegetables or a good cut of beef, I was given into her ladyship's care, lifted into the carriage to begin a new life. With but a single nod to the driver, we left my mother and my beginnings behind us in the street.

I did not even think to look back or wave good-bye.

Nor do I remember feeling despondent or suffering any loss, save for the rush of guilt that engulfed me when I remembered I had forgotten the faithful Meg, deserted her in the street to suffer the fate that had so nearly befallen me. Shamed by my appalling treachery, I could never bring myself to play with the porcelain dolls that were given me, but set them on the shelf in favor of other toys.

For six months I enjoyed an idyll of never-ending treats and surprises. There were printed muslin dresses trimmed with lace. A room of my own with papered walls, brocade bed hangings trimmed with a deep fringe, and two child-size walnut chairs with embroidered pillows. In between sumptuous meals, there were chocolates and cream-filled pastries and the golden lady to fuss over and cuddle me if I suffered a tummy ache from excessive eating.

Henrietta stalked through the corridors like a cat, watching and waiting for the day when all backs, save hers, should be turned. Her dull eyes gleamed with hatred as they had never gleamed with either life or intelligence. She refused to play with me or take the dolls I offered her.

Unable to understand her jealousy at the young age of five, I assumed that she, too, had left someone like Meg behind somewhere and did not care to be reminded of her faithlessness. And if she did not want to share my games, I was content to play alone. It would have taken more than her churlishness to upset my new and glorious world.

But that upset came, and all too quickly.

Six months after I was taken to the Wolfeburne House, the lady changed. She pushed me from her lap, and her ears tired of my endless prattle. Dirty nails that had once brought forth tinkling laughs earned me grave looks and sharp rebukes. Tangled hair brought a frown to her pretty brow. Over my head, speaking glances were exchanged between Lady Wolfeburne and Mrs. Severne, and my past, never before mentioned, became a subject of much discussion and concern.

One day, Lady Wolfeburne retired early to her suite, and I was taken from my pretty room with its papered walls and fringed hangings and given another in the attic. All my toys were neatly packed in a large sea chest that stood beside a small truckle bed. Mrs. Severne pushed me through the door, turned, and swept down the back stairs.

Seconds later, Henrietta appeared. She surveyed my new quarters, her upper lip curling in disdain. "You have become a b-burden." She struggled with a word she had overheard pass between her mother and Mrs. Severne.

Neither she nor I knew its meaning, but there was a menace in the sound. "I am not a burden," I declared. "I am not."

I pushed her aside and ran downstairs to the golden lady's bedroom. Somewhere within, I heard a baby's cry, but Mrs. Severne stopped me from entering. There was a hardness to her soft, plump hands that I had never noticed, and her mouth drew into a grim line.

"Lady Wolfeburne does not want to be disturbed."

The finality in her words dismayed me.

I had, indeed, become a burden. Replaced in the lady's favor by little Annabelle, a daughter of her own who reflected all her beauty. Overnight, I had sunk to a level lower than Henrietta's, lower even than the scullery maid's. I became what I had been, a base child of the streets who must not be trusted near the precious new baby.

And so all backs were turned.

And Henrietta pounced.

She broke my toys, snatching them from my hands to crush them beneath her feet. Again and again, she reminded me I had no father. She insisted I should not be called Wolfeburne, but Lane, since that was where I had been found. As I had not been properly adopted, and she was as persistent as she was malicious, the name stuck.

The golden lady shuddered to think of my being placed on a parity with her precious Annabelle in the minds of her friends. Even her stepdaughter was relegated to the rank of "my husband's child with his first wife." I could not hope to do better.

Thanks to Henrietta, I did much worse.

Invariably, when we three children were introduced to company, she followed up the use of that demeaning surname by announcing that I was "a charity girl." If she could have stripped me of her grandmother's name, she would have done that as well. But no one would trouble themselves to address me in a new fashion and, in that, she was defeated.

Henrietta did not suffer many defeats, and it was then that I first heard the beast's whisper. With each assault and cruel prank she played, he grew stronger, fed by a hatred and anger that had no outlet. She could move, when she liked, with great stealth, and I rarely had warning of her attacks.

Save once. I was standing on the back steps, looking out at the wintry courtyard, where the bushes and earth were all gray and withered. There was a slight noise directly behind me and the unavoidable click of the door latch. Needing no more warning, I promptly stepped aside.

Henrietta plunged past me, her arms outstretched, and hurtled down the steps to the paving stones. She landed with a loud cry and lifted her hands. Her palms were badly scraped, and tiny dots of blood trickled down her wrists.

I stood and gaped, not at her outraged expression but at those upturned palms. Her blood was red. Unmistakably and startlingly red. It was not even distinguished by a bluish or purplish tinge but was as red as my own was supposed to be, my common blood that had always been proof of my inferiority and tarnished ancestry.

I lifted my gaze to her face and laughed.

And laughed and laughed.

And when I was done laughing, the beast was gone.

Henrietta stared at her hands in horror, her mind as childishly literal as my own. With the blood pooling in her palms, she raised her head and let out a scream that fetched all the kitchen staff as well as Mrs. Severne and Lady Wolfeburne. I was dispatched to my room in disgrace, all of them believing I had knocked her down. Nor did I resist, for I no longer cared.

After that, Henrietta could do little to hurt me. Her taunts and slurs fell on deaf ears. Having been deceived once, utterly and intensely deceived, I questioned everything that was said—to me and about me. The nature of my birth. Her superiority. Even the goodness of the Wolfeburnes on whose charity I depended. And if I appeared obedient and tractable it was because, having won the war, there was no longer any need for me to fight.

Not long after the accident in the garden, his lordship's younger brother, Trystan Wolfeburne, came down from Oxford. He had written advising his brother of his coming. Lord Wolfeburne did not seem as enthused as should have been expected of a man who had not seen his brother in ten years, but it seemed to me that he hated to be bothered with matters that pertained to his Cornish family. He had not, in the three years I had lived beneath his roof, paid a single visit to his ancestral home, and he told anyone who cared to listen that he preferred to leave everything in the hands of his steward, Mr. Morrison.

There was a great deal of commotion that afternoon, maids bustling between the kitchen and the drawing room, fresh pastries being pulled from the oven, and Lady Wolfeburne sharply rebuking Mrs. Severne and her personal maid for the smallest of accidents.

Drawn by the delightful aromas, I wandered into the kitchen only to be shoved from behind and propelled into the coal cellar. Henrietta slammed and locked the door behind me before I could scream a protest.

No one thought to wonder at my absence. Locked in darkness, coal dust clogging my nostrils and burning my throat, I banged my small fists against the heavy wooden door. The noises were deadened by the thickness of the oak, and no one heard my muffled cries over the rattle of pans and the cook's short-tempered exclamations.

I remained there a long while. At last, realizing that I would get no help from the servants, I crawled over the heap of loose coal and rattled the door that let out onto the street. This was ill-fitting, and banged soundly, all the while showering me with a thick layer of soot. To my great relief, it could not have been more than fifteen minutes before the outer bar was lifted.

The door opened and a gray light, seemingly brighter than any summer sunlight, flooded the cellar and made me blink. Before my eyes had recovered, a strong hand pulled me from my black prison. I opened my eyes cautiously to see a dark man towering above me, a look of amazement on his handsome face.

Being only eight, I supposed he was quite old, but that did not stop me from liking him immediately. He had gentle eyes and a nicely shaped mouth, one that begged to be teased into a smile. His woolen frock coat fitted him with grace and flair, and his top hat was perched at an angle that Lord Wolfeburne would have called jaunty.

"Good Lord!" he exclaimed. "How came you to be down there?"

"I was locked in." I did not say by whom or suggest it was an accident, and he, tactful creature, forbore to ask.

Eyes puzzled, he regarded me. "Surely you are not Henrietta?"

"I am not!"

His eyebrows rose, and I suspected that my adamant reply had betrayed me. But whatever he thought, he said only, "I hope you were not imprisoned long."

"Since shortly after midday," I admitted, warm with pride.

His eyebrows rose again. "But you must have been there for nigh on an hour. It is a wonder you are not hysterical."

"I do not get hysterical," I replied, knowing full well the meaning of the word. It was the one Lord Wolfeburne used when his lady took to sobbing and wailing over some silliness.

My rescuer smiled. "How very wise of you. I have always thought ladies too easily affected by the least inconvenience. It is a pleasure to make the acquaintance of one who is not." He lifted his hat and bowed. "Trystan Wolfeburne, at your service."

He proffered his hand for mine. Dismayed, I stared at the polished nails and the long fingers that smelled faintly of soap. My own were covered in coal dust. Then, too, he wore a ring, a wolf's head carved in gold. Two small sapphire eyes glittered at me. I had seen its mate in his brother's possession, although it was not a piece of jewelry he wore.

Trystan Wolfeburne followed my gaze. "Interesting, is it not. It was designed for one of my ancestors, and copies are made for all the Wolfeburne men. They are interred with us when we die. A cheerful thought." He grinned at me, still waiting for me to give him my hand.

I hesitated, reluctant to soil any part of his perfection and thinking with dread of the punishment that would be meted out to me by Mrs. Severne if I did. Trystan Wolfeburne knew nothing of my thoughts. He waited calmly, refusing to withdraw.

Timidly, I complied.

His smile deepened.

Obviously, he was nothing like his brother. Of course, he had not yet finished with his schooling, while Lord Wolfeburne was in his early thirties, but it was more than the variance in their ages. There was a sharp difference in their temperaments and manners. Trystan Wolfeburne's dark eyes shone with intelligence and good humor, and something told me he was a real gentleman—not like his brother who concerned himself only with appearances.

Having shaken my hand, he asked, "And you would be?"

"Jessamy," I said, dispensing with the hated *Lane* without a qualm.

He frowned. "You must forgive me. My brother dislikes to write letters, and I know little about his life. What place do you have in his household?"

It occurred to me to tell the truth and say *None whatsoever*. But that would have necessitated even greater explanation, and pride would not allow me to admit my worthlessness to this towering man who treated me as though I were a lady.

"Lady Wolfeburne took me in when I was five," I said.

His puzzled frown promptly disappeared. "Then you would be his ward. I cannot think why he did not speak of you. He is not usually so reticent when it comes to expounding on his largesse." His dark eyes sparkled, and his voice dropped to a confidential murmur. "He has yet to let me forget that he pays every penny of my schooling."

He winked, making me feel as though we shared a jest at his brother's expense. By that one act, he endeared himself to me completely, and I gazed up at him with an adoration that left me tongue-tied.

"I have shocked you with my ingratitude," he said, mistaking the reason for my silence. I started to protest, but he held up his hands. "No. You are quite right. Whatever I think of Henry, I have no right to mock him. I only pray that you will not shame me by giving him an account of my rude manners."

He grinned again, and I knew he was teasing. Nevertheless, I solemnly agreed to be sworn to silence.

That done, he gave me a long look and shook his head. "What am I thinking of, keeping you here talking after your dreadful experience in the coal cellar? We had better get you inside and see that you are given a hot bath."

He took my hand and led me up the steps, not minding that his white cuffs were sprinkled with soot and his palms were now as black as mine. The footman opened the front door, and his stiff expression became a look of horror. Mrs. Severne was summoned immediately, and I was dispatched to the upper realms of the house to be scrubbed and scolded for my carelessness. Nor did I leave my attic room again that day.

It was the last I saw of Trystan Wolfeburne, for he never visited us again. There was, I believe, some argument between him and his brother, and I often wondered what had been behind their disagreement. On days when Henrietta was especially difficult, I liked to pretend he had championed my cause and advised his brother to show me greater kindness, but this was most unlikely. As I grew older, I heard rumors that it had been something to do with Lord Wolfeburne's disinterest in his ancestral estate, but this was never more than idle gossip that I disregarded, favoring my own interpretation.

Thereafter, my life fell into a dull routine, and no incident stood out above the rest. I took lessons with Henrietta, learned to play the piano, practiced my needlework, and was taught all the gracious manners necessary to a lady without ever being treated as though I belonged to that class.

My subdued and obedient manner convinced everyone I was less threat to Annabelle than they had first supposed, and she was often entrusted to my care. I became a kind of governess, a convenience for which they need pay nothing more than the room and board they already gave me.

I grew tall and slender, to the chagrin of Lady Wolfeburne, whose golden looks were fading. She insisted I pull back my hair in a plaited knot and dressed me in severe, dark dresses that were better suited to an elderly matron. Still, I learned to carry myself with a grace and composure that made her frown with annoyance whenever she glanced at me.

Henrietta left her teens behind her but remained in her father's house, having yet to find a husband. For this, she had only herself to blame. She never tried to be pleasant or amusing to the gentlemen who visited Wolfeburne House, and her vindictiveness showed in her voice and expression.

I, too, was unlikely to marry. Lord Wolfeburne did not feel obliged to provide me with a dowry, Lady Wolfeburne having assured him that no gentleman of decent family would want me for a wife. And because of my genteel upbringing, the thought of offering me in marriage to a rougher man offended their sensibilities.

"Nor can I think of anyone who would be willing to take her into their home as either a governess or companion," Lady Wolfeburne remarked to her husband at supper one evening, her words carrying over the long walnut table that stretched between them. "It really is most vexing."

She spoke as though I were not there, sitting across from their two daughters, taking slices of roast beef from the same platters that had been offered to everyone else. But I was long past the age when I would have asked myself what was wrong with me and wondered instead at their insensitivity and lack of manners.

Nor did I much care about their plight. I was reasonably content to remain where I was, secure in the knowledge that they cared too much for appearances to throw me out on the street, and free to fill my hours with reading or amusing Annabelle. She was pretty and spoiled, but not at all malicious.

In the end, it was Lord Wolfeburne who decided my fate. Not many months after my seventeenth birthday, he failed to rise from his bed. Within the hour, a surgeon had pronounced him dead. In the weeks that followed, there were letters to be written, funeral arrangements to be made, services to be attended, and a myriad of other details that demanded my attention, since much of the load fell upon my shoulders.

His brother, the new Lord Wolfeburne, did not attend the funeral or pay us a visit to offer his support or extend his condolences. In answer to his bereaved sister-in-law's letter, the only one she stirred herself to write, he sent a missive of his own. This I hand-delivered to her, taking it to her bedroom where she had prostrated herself in sorrow.

That evening, she descended to the dining room, pale in her black mourning dress, and regarded us with a solemn look. In her hands was his lordship's letter. Carefully, she smoothed out the folds in the page. "This concerns all of us," she said, "for it falls upon your uncle to provide for us now that your . . . your . . ."

"What does he intend?" I asked, thinking that if I did not speak she would surrender to tears.

She frowned at my rudeness, but her irritation gave her the strength to finish. "Annabelle, Henrietta, and I will remain here, in this place that has always been our home. But you"—she gave me a severe look—"are to go to Wolfeburne Hall. Lord . . . Trystan, Lord Wolfeburne is widowed with a young daughter who needs a governess."

I stared at her, resenting the way my movements were dictated without my having any say in the matter. Such arrogance was uncharacteristic of the young man I remembered, and I suspected the final decision had been made entirely by her ladyship.

She caught my glare and averted her gaze. "I have no choice but to agree, since our income will be drastically reduced. He means to keep us on a strict allowance, one that will demand much sacrifice on all of our parts."

It was, I supposed, a form of apology.

But despite her protestations, she seemed glad enough to be rid of me.

2

I made the journey from Paddington Station to Cornwall by train, a puffing, soot-belching monster that clanked and chugged through rolling green fields, wooded hills, and centuries-old hamlets. Grit slipped through my gloves and became ingrained in my fingernails. My skirts grew rumpled and my face grimy. Even my reflection in the glass appeared pale and anxious.

I quickly gave up the pretense of reading and, book open and forgotten on my lap, lapsed into daydreaming about my new home. And the new Lord Wolfeburne. Ten years ago, he had seemed old to me, but he could not have been more than twenty. Even now, he was still a young man. I hoped he was as pleasant as I remembered.

In Cornwall, we crossed a series of viaducts that spanned a stretch of deep valleys. Menheniot fell behind, then Liskeard, and I hastily gathered my belongings, fearing that Doublebois Station would be upon me whilst I was wool-gathering. I need not have worried, for there was little enough to collect, and the porter gave me ample warning. It was mid-afternoon when I disembarked, hastily searching my purse for a few coins to tip him for setting my portmanteau safely at my feet.

Wolfeburne Hall lay three miles to the north on the very edge of Bodmin Moor, and Lady Wolfeburne had written to her brother-in-law, warning of my arrival and asking that I be met.

It was disconcerting to find no likely looking person standing on the platform; nor did anyone approach me and ask my name. Overhead, the station clock bore a red third finger to mark London time, local time being behind by a full twenty minutes, and I wondered if the discrepancy had caused some confusion. But the extra minutes passed and I still found myself alone.

I decided I would have to manage on my own and tried to ignore the sense of foreboding that had already taken hold of me. Struggling with my portmanteau, I made my way to the dingy building that was perched at the edge of the rails, and asked the clerk how I might get to Wolfeburne Hall.

He looked up from the figures he had been scratching in his ledger and with ink-stained fingers pushed his spectacles squarely onto his nose. "What 'ee going there for, 'en?" he asked, with the air of someone who must have his own curiosity satisfied before there would be any help forthcoming.

"I am to be governess to Lord Wolfeburne's daughter," I replied.

"And the last'n, what happened to she, en?"

"I could not say. I suppose she gave notice and left."

He shook his head. "Her never left from here.

Could have left from Bodmin-Road or Liskeard, I s'pose, but that's a lot farther to go." He shook his head at the foolishness of the young gentlewoman I had never met, then frowned at me in a manner that suggested I probably had no greater sense than she. "And where do 'ee be coming from?" he demanded, as though that would tell him whether or not I had my head on my shoulders.

Deciding it would do no good to offend him, I kept my answers civil. Finally he nodded in the direction of one of the benches against the wall and told me to wait until he returned.

Five minutes later, he reappeared and said, "Young Bowden be going yer way. He's come delivering his taters."

Young Bowden proved to be a grizzled old man of nearly sixty, with two missing front teeth and a hacking cough. A tobacco pipe hung from the corner of his mouth, and a cloud of blue-gray smoke wafted about his head. He sat on the seat of his dray with his wrinkled hands resting upon the reins and peered at me suspiciously. "I went take 'ee no further than crossroads," he said. "From there 'ee be by yourself."

"How far is that from the Hall?" I asked, fearing he meant to leave me stranded in the middle of nowhere.

"Not more'n few minutes walk."

Reassured, I gave him my hand, and he helped me up onto the seat. The clerk threw my portmanteau onto the flatbed with the sacks and bid us farewell. The narrow streets of the tiny village, with its Norman French name the locals pronounced *Doubleboys*, quickly fell behind. For over half an hour we plodded down a country lane, through scattered stone-hedged farms, following the swishing tail of a tired, one-eared nag who must have been much of an age as myself. The farmer said nary a word to me, save to grunt at my polite remarks, and I contented myself with admiring the rocky farms and staring ahead at the gentle hill rising out of the low-lying lands to the west.

It was early summer. The breezes were warm and the sky shimmered overhead, a clear stretch of azure blue. Between the rocking of the dray, the late afternoon heat, and my own weariness, I was lulled into a drowsiness from which I did not emerge until an abrupt jolt shook me awake.

"This be as far as I go," Mr. Bowden informed me, with a dark glance for the moorlands to the north.

I turned my eyes in the same direction, and my gaze swept over a wild sea of gorse and heather and tufts of coarse grasses until at last it came upon Wolfeburne Hall. Bleak and grim, with a glowering granite face, it rose from that feathery green sea as though some giant hand had thrust the stones upward and let them cascade into a monstrous dwelling.

Those stones were falling still. The westernmost towers had crumbled beneath the weight of their years, and huge sections of the walls had already been reclaimed by the moors. But the eastern half of the Hall stood firm. Stolid and squat, with a line of chimneys poking from the slate roof and sunlight glancing off the mullioned windows, it stared back at me with a cold arrogance that spoke little of warmth and comfort, and nothing at all of welcome.

I took a deep breath and jumped down from the wooden seat.

"Stick to the path," the farmer advised me as he tossed down my portmanteau. "'Twill be dark soon. Thee's dussn't want to be out on moor after dark."

Something in his tone made me glance up at him again, but he had already taken his seat. Then a thought seemed to strike him. "Thee'll be talking to his lordship, will 'ee? Tell him Young Bowden be saying another sheep 'as been killed."

With a grunt for emphasis, he picked up his reins and clucked to his horse. The axles creaked and the dray began rolling again. I watched him until the eddies of dust had settled, wondering about his odd remark. Finding no explanation, I turned my thoughts to what lay ahead.

From what I could surmise, his "few minutes walk" demanded that I set off on a brisk hike that would have taken all of fifteen minutes had I been unencumbered. Laden with the weight of my belongings, it promised to take twice as long.

I struggled along for a short distance, hampered by my voluminous serge skirt and the deep ruts in the path. My muscles ached and, though I changed hands frequently, my palms stung where the leather handle cut into them. A stone turned beneath my shoe and I stumbled, almost twisting my ankle.

Fearing that I might do myself some harm if I continued in this fashion, I left the portmanteau in the grass by the side of the road where it could be collected later. That done, I set off at a happier and faster pace and soon came to the towering gateposts flanking the white gravel driveway. Stones crunching beneath my shoes and the early evening breeze buffeting the brim of my hat, I made my way to the marble portico with as much resolution as could be mustered under those rather ignominious circumstances.

The front door swung open almost before I could release the brass doorknocker, and a young maidservant stared at me from a gloomy hall, a feather duster still upraised in her hand. She regarded me with some surprise—not unwarranted, I realized—dropped a quick curtsey, and inquired as to the nature of my business there.

Upon learning I was the new governess, sent for by Lord Wolfeburne, she became even more curious, and forgot herself long enough to say, "'Ee, Miss?"

The question emphasized my extreme youth, my disheveled state, my lack of luggage, and the curious manner of my arrival. Feeling that some explanation was called for, I said, "Lady Wolfeburne wrote a letter, notifying his lordship that I would be here today. Apparently, it has not preceded me."

This was sufficient to persuade her to admit me to the Hall. She indicated a caned chair where I might wait until she had fetched Mrs. Pendarves, the housekeeper, and disappeared down a dimly lit corridor. Left to myself, I made a quick survey of my surroundings.

They were as bleak and uncompromising as the exterior. The deep-set windows foreshortened the light and kept much of the hall in a gloomy twilight. The sun's heat also failed to seep through the thick walls, and the air was unnaturally cool. Nor did the darkness and discoloration of the portraits hanging on the walls do anything to brighten the somber mood.

I shivered and looked upward, at a long curving stairway that rose to a second-floor gallery. Just as my gaze reached the top, there was a slight movement at the rails, and I caught a glimpse of a ghostly face. I choked back a gasp, then silently reproached myself for my foolishness. It was a child's face, no doubt the very child I had been hired to teach.

"Why don't you come down and say hello?" I asked softly, not meaning to frighten her.

She stood, bringing her face into view above the banister. It was a pretty face, with luminous dark eyes and a cupid's-bow mouth. Her dark ringlets were caught up with an enormous sapphire bow, and the full sleeves of her dress were edged with double layers of delicate lace. She looked to be about eight or nine, small for her age and, despite the appearance of being well-tended, touched by an air of what looked horribly like desperation.

"Are you real?" she demanded in an intense voice that was all the more disturbing for its high childish pitch.

It was a day for curious questions. "Of course I am real," I replied. "Why ever would you ask such a thing?"

"You were sitting so still and silent, I was not certain."

"Do you mean to say you thought I was a ghost?"

"That. Or something near to one."

It was an odd answer. "And what is near to a ghost?" I asked.

She hesitated. "I . . . I truly cannot say, but there is . . . something."

"You believe this?"

She nodded again. "That is the reason my mother left me, and all of my governesses. You will leave, too," she said in a tone that was resigned and profoundly sad.

It convinced me, as nothing else had yet succeeded in doing, that I wanted to be there. "If I do," I told her, "it will not be because I have been chased away by something as fanciful as spirits."

"Then you think I am imagining things."

Her voice sounded sadder still, and I wondered at the depth of her unhappiness. Had she been ridiculed for her fears? If so, she need not have thought I would do the same. But nor could I allow her to hold on to a notion that was clearly upsetting to her.

"I do not believe in ghosts. Or anything like them. Although there are many reasons for people to think they have seen them. Particularly in old houses that abound with strange noises. After awhile, one becomes accustomed to the oddities and ceases to notice them."

"That is what my father says. But . . ."

Her brow puckered in thought, and some war waged within her, visible only in the strain upon her face. At last, she said, "It is wrong to lie."

"Indeed, it is."

"And my father is a good man."

Since that opinion fitted my brief memory of him, I was quick to agree. "By your own words, there seems to be little reason for concern."

She nodded slowly. "But . . ."

But she remained doubtful. And while she could not bring herself to accuse her father of lying, something in his manner must have persuaded her that she had been fobbed off with a false explanation.

At the end of the corridor, a door opened and there was the sound of footsteps. Not a woman's light step but a firm, masculine tread that crossed the flagging with quick, broad strides. My attention wavered. When I glanced up again the child was gone.

My gaze returned to the corridor in time to see a man emerge from the shadows and bear down upon me as he would an intruder in his home. He was an odd rendering of the young man I remembered. His hair was shaggy and unkempt, and he wore neither coat nor waistcoat. His cotton shirt was badly rumpled. It fell open at the neck, one of the collar buttons dangling precariously from a thread, and the ends of his satin neckcloth flapped against him as he walked.

Nor did his attire account for all of the changes in him. His handsome face was drawn, his cheekbones stood in sharp relief above dark hollows, and his jawline was shadowed with stubble. Then, too, there was a derisive set to his mouth that I did not recall from his youth, and a bitter, knowing look in his dark eyes.

"So, it is you, then," he said. "Your precipitous arrival has forestalled me from rescinding an offer that was carelessly and hastily made. I was this very moment composing a letter, advising my sister you were not wanted."

I flinched. He did not say that I was not *needed*, nor that my *services* were not wanted, but that *I* was not wanted. He could not have known but, had he kicked or struck me, the pain he caused would not have been as great. Again, I was to be dragged from my home—such as it was—only to be rebuffed.

I lifted my chin. "I did not ask to come here. It was your letter that brought me."

He recoiled and adopted a disdainful pose. "Ah, that voice," he said, regarding me down the length of his nose. "It is one I have never forgotten. Such equanimity in the face of adversity, even as a child. I do believe I would have recognized you anywhere. You retain that same obstinacy of manner, that cool autonomy and stern gaze."

Even had his words been complimentary, the mockery in his eyes would have twisted their meaning. I dearly wanted to turn upon my heel and stalk from his door. But only minutes ago, the child had said I would desert her. In good conscience, I could not permit her prophecy to be so easily and quickly fulfilled.

"If you regretted your invitation, sir," I admonished, "you would have been wiser to make your reply sometime before the afternoon of my intended arrival."

"Sheer impudence. How was I to know you meant to descend upon me all in a rush?"

"You were advised."

"Advised? By whom and what?"

"Lady Wolfeburne wrote a lengthy letter, one that I posted myself a fortnight ago."

"What letter? There has been no letter. What the devil is she talking about, Mrs. Pendarves?" He turned to a small woman who hovered at his side.

His presence was so strong that I had not noticed her standing there. She was small—a full head shorter than myself—and her dark gown blended into the dusky gloom. From her hair, which was coiled around her head in a silver braid, I gauged her to be fifty or more, but she had few wrinkles and her black eyes were as bright and attentive as those of a magpie. I felt confident she was a most capable housekeeper.

Providing the final proof that my assessment was correct, she replied, "It arrived a week ago Thursday, milord. I gave it you with the others that came that same day." Her voice was calm in the face of her employer's irritation.

He scowled at her, then shrugged. "If you say so, then no doubt it is true."

He threw back his head and let out a reckless laugh, but there was more posture than amusement to his mirth, and the sound died almost as it left his lips. He stopped abruptly and regarded me with yet greater mockery.

"It appears I am to blame for this muddle. I have paid little attention to my correspondence of late. It bores me and I have grown impatient with all that is dull and tedious. Come into the study and we will decide what is to be done with you, for you cannot stay here."

He turned and made his way back down the corridor, not looking to see whether or not I followed. This, I did, having no other choice, although I was not yet resigned to returning to London. My hopes were encouraged by Mrs. Pendarves's friendly smile and the nod of approval she bestowed upon me.

Lord Wolfeburne led me to his study, a cramped room, made smaller still by the drawn curtains and dimly burning oil lamp. His desk overflowed with clutter— pens, an overturned brandy snifter, ledgers, and a mound of letters, some unopened, some crumpled into balls.

There was a warning growl, and two Irish wolfhounds, enormous dogs with wiry hair and square muzzles, raised their heads from the hearth and bared their teeth at me. At a sign from their master, they quieted and rested their heads on their paws, but their eyes still watched me. Although I had always liked dogs, I would not have dared approach these two.

Lord Wolfeburne swept aside a pile of newspapers that was scattered across the brocade settee and motioned for me to sit down. I did so gingerly, wondering what manner of debris lay beneath the cushions. He took his place behind the desk, leaned back in his chair, and placed his boots upon the oaken surface in complete disregard for the papers that were strewn there.

He lifted the pile nearest his hand and rifled through them. Not finding what he wanted, he took a second and then a third. Here, he had some success for he pulled an envelope from their midst. After a cursory look at the handwriting, he tore open the letter.

"Let us see what my dear sister has to say." He scanned the page, then quoted, "She has been well educated and has given my darling Annabelle her lessons for nigh on two years. One cannot fault her intelligence, but it would not do to trust her completely. She is of low birth with tainted blood in her veins, blood that would keep her from finding a position elsewhere, and I would not like to think of your dear Clarissa coming to some harm."

"What a fool my brother married," he cried, oblivious to the hot flush that burned my cheeks. "Did she but know the truth—"

He flung back his head and released a second torrent of wild laughter that was even greater than the first. This, too, stopped abruptly, and his gaze raked my warm face.

"What?" he demanded. "Do you give credit to her nonsense?"

"Indeed, I do not."

"But you are wounded by her insensitivity, nonetheless. Do not be. Good manners might demand that you overlook rampant ignorance, but nothing compels you to take her words to heart. It should be a simple enough matter to find you a post among my acquaintances, and I see no need to hide anything from them."

His kindness was as unexpected as it was welcome, like a spring of cool water gushing from barren rock. But he was still determined that I should go. That, however, could not be accomplished immediately.

"If that is what you wish," I said, mustering an outward complacency. "And until that time you can find me a post, I will teach your daughter what little I am able."

"You have a talent for deceit, Miss Lane. No, you must leave tomorrow morning and return to London. I shall contact you there."

"But what of the child? Am I wrong in thinking she is still without a governess?"

"You are not. But I have decided to dispense with them and leave her education to the local parson's daughter. Miss Worsley can return each night to the parsonage, and Mrs. Pendarves can take care of Clarissa during those hours when she is absent."

"I should think Mrs. Pendarves's hours were filled with enough tasks. You cannot expect her to play both roles."

"Can I not?" he demanded, arching a brow. "Either way, it is no concern of yours. But your presence here threatens to be a nuisance."

"Three weeks ago you would not have said so."

"Three weeks ago I had drunk too much brandy and was incapable of making a sensible decision. I remembered a small child who was not frightened after having endured an hour or more in a locked coal cellar and supposed she would not fall prey to the same fancies that have plagued the string of foolish women who have passed in and out my doors."

So that was his reasoning. It seemed ludicrous that our chance meeting should have been the cause of my presence there, but I was not one to overlook any opening, no matter how small. "And what caused you to change your mind? You had no reason to believe me any different."

"I realized that you could not be more than eighteen, at most. Too young to be subjected to . . . to the horrors of my rude company."

"Seventeen," I said, correcting him, and was rewarded with a glare that chastened me not at all.

He regarded me severely for a long minute. I lifted my chin and faced him squarely, struggling through expression to show him the reproach I could not voice in words. A silent war waged between us, and then his shoulders dropped, and he seemed to slump in his seat.

"It's no good. I refuse to have Clarissa upset again. You must be gone before she discovers you."

"Then you are already too late. We have met and spoken. Nor do I think I exaggerate in saying she has taken a fancy to me," I added, determined to make a strong case for myself.

He swore heartily, then suddenly remembered he was not alone. "Do not expect courtesy in my presence. It is a social art with which I have long since dispensed."

"If you mean that by way of an apology then, by all means, you are forgiven."

"An apolog— Good God. I do not make apologies to any man, least of all to some wide-eyed innocent who has had the impudence to rebuke me beneath my own roof twice inside of one hour."

"Then I shall not fault you for your discourtesy but assume that, having spent too many years in your own company, you have fallen into the habit of speaking without thinking."

"And that's thrice," he retorted. "No matter. You may do as you please—as I will do. In the meantime, we must think of how to unravel this confounded mess."

"I can think of only one solution. I must remain." Before he could object, I added, "It was, after all, your intention to hire me, and I cannot see that matters have changed. Nor am I likely to run away for, unless you give me references, I have nowhere to go. Certainly, Lady Wolfeburne does not desire my return."

He scowled at me. "I begin to wonder which of us is master in this house. You seem determined to stay, even over my objections."

"Indeed, I am. You may think it arrogant of me, but I am certain it is within my power to do Clarissa some good."

"Do you, indeed?"

He threw his legs down from the desk and rose in one fell move. In two strides he had covered the distance that separated us, and he yanked me to my feet. Ignoring my cry of surprise and the dogs' sudden growl, he dragged me to the window and threw back the curtains.

Bodmin Moor spread away to the north, a wild stretch of windswept moorlands, broken by granite outcroppings. It was like looking out upon a foreign land, a land that belonged to a time long past. A heavy fog swirled within its depths and spread toward us with preternatural haste, and the gentle breezes had grown into a strong wind that shuddered through the gorse and heather.

Lord Wolfeburne held me in front of him and his fingers tightened on my upper arms, making it impossible for me to escape. I could hear the rough intake of air entering his lungs, could feel the warmth of his breath upon my brow, and caught the whiff of brandy that clung to him as shaving soap might linger upon another man.

In a low voice he murmured in my ear, "And when the dogs howl in the night, and the fog twists their furious cries into screeches that sound more human than animal, more demonic than anything you think could have been created by nature, will you still wish to remain? When the fog creeps and crawls outside the door, and appears like a misshapen face at the window, what will you do then, Miss Lane?"

"I shall close the curtains and put more coals upon the fire," I replied evenly, but my heart thumped against my ribs.

He brought his head closer until I could almost feel the rough stubble on his jaw against my cheek. "I shall remind you of what you have said to me."

"There will be no need."

"I wonder."

With a short laugh he released me, dropping my arm as suddenly as he had jerked me from my seat, and he drew the curtains shut with a snap. When the room was cloaked in gloom once again, he stood with his back to me, staring in front of him as though he could still see the moors and was haunted by them.

Just as I had begun to wonder if he had forgotten me,

he said, "You must not, at any time or for any reason, leave this house at night. I release the dogs and let them roam free. You would not like to come upon them."

My gaze wandered hesitantly to those large jaws. "Indeed, I would not."

"Nor are you to wander about the ruins. The walls are crumbling and could collapse."

"You have my word I shall attempt no such foolishness."

"And, on occasion, I shall expect you to dine with me. I am not always fond of eating alone."

"If that is your wish."

His last demand had startled me, and my answer was neither enthusiastic nor grateful. But I felt incapable of pretending that I would enjoy his company. He was not, in any way, the young man I remembered.

"Well, then?" he demanded, turning abruptly and looking at me as though he were surprised to find me standing there. "Go and tell Mrs. Pendarves to prepare you a room."

"There . . . there is the matter of my belongings. I left them in the grass, not far from the crossroads."

He frowned. "She will give you what you need for tonight. It is almost dark, and I will not send someone to fetch them at this hour. Don't stand there gaping!" he cried when I stared at him dumbfounded. "You have my assurance, they will be safe enough."

I found his reluctance to send someone for my belongings most curious, for surely if he kept the dogs inside, they could take a lantern and follow the road. But then I remembered the approaching fog, and supposed it was an easy matter to wander astray. It would have dismayed me to have been the cause of an accident.

Nor did I wish to incur his anger by protesting. I'd had enough battles for one day.

3

Troubled and confused, my thoughts still possessed by Lord Wolfeburne's inexplicable behavior, I set off in search of the housekeeper. Almost nothing remained of the pleasant and sympathetic young man I had met as a child. What could have caused the drastic change?

I found Mrs. Pendarves seated in the caned chair in the hall, her small hands folded patiently in her lap. She rose, her sharp eyes searching my face, and her hands reached out to me. Then, as if abruptly aware of the supplication in her gesture, she dropped them and straightened her back.

"You will be needing a room for the night," she said in a sharp voice that I suspected was meant to disguise her momentary lapse. "It is being prepared."

"I shall be here a good deal longer than one night. Lord Wolfeburne has agreed to let me stay."

Her face brightened slightly, but having betrayed her feelings once, she was not willing to do so a second time.

"Will your luggage be arriving soon?" she asked, as though that were the only matter that deserved remark.

I admitted that my one and only bag lay near the crossroads.

She glanced upward to where the darkening skies pressed at the transom, and nodded. "Lord Wolfeburne doesn't like anyone leaving the Hall at night if it can be avoided. We're too near the moor, and there's no reason to take chances. Your belongings will be safe until morning, and I can let you have the few things you will need for tonight."

Her calm response convinced me I had read mystery into a situation where none existed. I doubted it would be the last of their habits that I questioned, nor even the strangest.

Mrs. Pendarves led me up the stairs to the broad gallery that overlooked the hall. Two brocade settees with carved walnut legs and high curved backs stood against the wall, set below rows of mullioned windows that stretched from waist height all the way to the high ceiling.

One of the maids, garbed in sedate dress with a white apron and frilled cap, was drawing the curtains. She paused to bob a flustered curtsey, but her gaze flickered from my face to those tall windows that had yet to be cloaked by the heavy velvet draperies.

"This is Miss Lane," Mrs. Pendarves said, commanding her full attention. "She is Lord Wolfeburne's ward."

It startled me to hear myself referred to in so benign a light, and I was shaken by a wave of awkwardness that I supposed could only have been due to the thought of the humiliation I would suffer when they learned the truth. But neither woman noticed my discomfort.

"She has come to be governess to Miss . . . to Lady Clarissa." Mrs. Pendarves turned to me. "If you need anything, you have only to ring for Mary." She glanced about the gallery, frowning. "You are late in finishing this evening."

"Had to make up young lady's rooms," Mary said. "'Twas dark afore I was done."

"You had only to ask if you needed help."

"Yes, mum. Won't happen again."

"See that it doesn't."

We left the gallery and walked briskly down a long corridor that stretched the length of the west wing. Mrs. Pendarves's taffeta skirts rustled pleasantly, and our footsteps were muffled by a long carpet that covered the oak flooring.

There were several doors set in the walls. Every one of them was firmly shut, their faces blank and forbidding, but the housekeeper advised me of the purpose to which each had been put. The first was the nursery, now empty. The next, Lady Clarissa's bedroom. If she was inside, she did not peep out to watch our passing. Then came the schoolroom, but we did not pause there. At the end of the wing, Mrs. Pendarves ushered me into a small suite.

I stepped inside and barely succeeded in stifling the gasp that threatened to burst from me. I had expected rooms built with the modest intention of housing the Hall's succession of governesses. But not many years ago, someone had evidently refurbished them with a lavish hand.

My gaze went first to the bed, a massive affair that reached from ceiling to floor. There was intricate scrollwork on the carved, gilt headboard; the tester was draped in scalloped, rose brocade and trimmed with a deep fringe; and the matching bed curtains were drawn back to reveal plump feather pillows and a satin counterpane.

Against the wall stood a mahogany wardrobe and dressing table, and a marble-topped washing stand had been set in the far corner. A fire burned in the marble fireplace and, through the connecting door, I could see an adjoining sitting room. That was equally lush, if I was to judge by the profusion of color and the delicate corner of a French Provincial writing desk that was visible through the open doorway.

"Surely there is some mistake." I was aghast at the impropriety of my living in such luxury. "Lord Wolfeburne cannot mean me to have these rooms."

"They are intended for Clarissa's governess," Mrs. Pendarves said. "Nor are there any other rooms in this wing to give you, unless you were to move into the nursery, and that would hardly fit your needs. Besides, it would be unthinkable to regard you only as his daughter's governess, since you are both his ward and a member of the Wolfeburne family."

I trembled. "I fear you overestimate my importance. Lady Wolfeburne took me into her home on a whim." I could not bring myself to say out of charity, for she meant only to satisfy her own needs. "We share no common blood, and my family was of a much lower station."

Mrs. Pendarves's black eyes studied me soberly, and within their depths I could not discover even a hint of the horror I expected to see there. Determined to stumble through my confession to the end, I added, "Lord Wolfeburne could not possibly regard me as his ward but more as one of the many responsibilities he was forced to shoulder upon the death of his brother."

"Nonsense," she said with a smile. "It was he who advised me you were his ward. My dear life. Such a fuss over a small suite, when even the guest bedrooms in the east wing haven't been used in over forty years."

"Not used?"

"Nobody comes to the Hall. Lord Wolfeburne's father always discouraged visitors, and he himself . . . well . . . he doesn't have many friends in Cornwall."

"He is much changed from the young man I remember." Suspecting some of the cause could be due to the loss of Clarissa's mother, I added, "His wife's death must have come as a severe blow."

"As it did to all of us."

If I was hoping for answers, I was disappointed. Mrs. Pendarves's face smoothed into a polite mask and those small hands, still and proper, remained clasped. Nothing in her expression invited further questions.

She excused herself soon afterward, leaving me to gape at my surroundings. The curtains had been drawn over the windows, and I drew them back to stare out at the moor. To my disappointment the fog had reached the estate. It hovered at the windows, throwing back the light from the oil lamps.

There was a soft tap on the door, and Mary entered, her arms filled with flannel towels and an assortment of smaller articles that threatened to slip from her grasp. Her gaze moved beyond me to the window, and she stopped abruptly. The color drained from her face, and she dropped her armload on the edge of the bed and hurried to draw the curtains.

"Whatever is the matter?" I asked, completely bewildered.

"Damp gets in. And Lady Clarissa's health tedn' what it belongs to be." She nodded at the bed. "Mrs. Pendarves said I was to bring 'ee towels and nightclothes. Need summat else'n, do 'ee?"

I sorted through the pile and found, among the flannels and towels, a bar of soap, a nightdress, knitted slippers, and a striped cotton dressing jacket that had been trimmed with lace. They were freshly laundered, and each item was well stitched from fabric that was better than anything Mary would have owned. Still, they were not fine enough to have belonged to the deceased lady of the house. I wondered if I had Mrs. Pendarves to thank, then decided the garments had been made for someone who was both taller and heavier than I, whereas she was considerably smaller.

"This will be fine," I told Mary with a smile. "It will be a relief to wash and get out of this dusty dress."

Satisfied, she left me to my toilette, but returned twice more that evening. Once, to bring my supper on a tray, and then again to remove the empty platters. Shortly thereafter, I crawled into bed, my eyelids drooping. I drew the counterpane up around my chin, settled into the heavy warmth with a satisfied yawn, and shut my eyes.

Immediately, they opened again.

I had forgotten to deliver Young Bowden's message.

With a shrug, I decided it could wait until tomorrow. The sheep was dead, not ill, and unlikely to suffer any discomfort due to my lapse of memory.

I fell asleep and did not wake until Mary knocked on my door the next morning. My dreams vanished even as I opened my eyes, but they left me feeling vaguely troubled and unsettled.

The odd sensations faded beneath the warmth of Mary's bright smile. She set down my breakfast tray. "'Ee was comfy, were 'ee?" She waited anxiously for my answer.

I nodded. "I slept the night through, and the counterpane makes the fire quite unnecessary."

This satisfied her, and she set about her tasks. In a few minutes the curtains were pulled back, and the morning sunlight flooded into the bedroom. It chased away the shadows and wiped the last vestiges of sleep from my eyes.

I rose, pulled on the dressing jacket and the knitted slippers that were loose on my feet, and hastened to the window. Outside, the rough moorland drifted northward to the horizon. Compelling yet foreboding, it captivated me even as it filled me with trepidation. There was a magic to the place, but it was a dark and dangerous magic.

I pulled my gaze back from the green depths that stretched from the hedge that ran around the back of the Hall, and found myself staring at the ruins. They were not, as I had supposed, adjoined to the newer structure, but lay a short distance to the east. Mossy mounds encircled them, remnants of what must once have been outer walls.

Of the castle itself, all that was left standing were the walls of a main hall and a gray tower, where dark slits had been cut into the sheer, rock face. Rooks and curlews, black wings fluttering, flew through the collapsed roof to hidden nests or perched on the stone ledges.

My stomach growled, and thoughts of my waiting breakfast distracted me. I washed my face and hands, then sat down to eat, hoping that my portmanteau would shortly be recovered. Mary reappeared before I finished, carrying with her a brown merino dress that was not my own but was nevertheless appropriate to my position.

"Davey'll fetch your belongings, but wheel's off cart and wants fixin'," she said. "Mrs. Pendarves says 'ee can wear this'n today."

I accepted the offering gladly.

The dress, a simple affair, had apparently been owned by the same person whose nightgown I had borrowed. It was an inch too long for me and had been cut for a heavier or larger-boned woman. Like the night garments, it was well made, but the cuffs had been carefully turned. The seams had been meticulously stitched, with a hand that was far more exacting than mine.

Wondering to whom I owed my gratitude, I dressed and plaited my hair into its usual knot. When Mrs. Pendarves appeared she found a suitably sedate and modest young woman waiting to be introduced to her pupil.

The schoolroom was singularly gray and drab. Clarissa was the one splash of color in that gloomy setting. She wore a dress of stiffened muslin trimmed with violet satin ribbons, a pale shade that only emphasized her fragility and drew attention to the unnatural size and brightness of her eyes.

As we entered she jumped down from her chair to make a polite curtsey. Mrs. Pendarves nodded her approval, her eyes soft with some emotion that looked like pity. The look vanished from her face the instant she became aware of my curiosity, replaced by that quietly respectful mask that could have hidden a thousand secrets.

The elderly woman remained long enough to introduce us, although I insisted on Clarissa's using my first name. She seemed to need a friend more than a governess, and I was determined to break down the usual barriers that stood between teacher and pupil.

Seeing that we were comfortable together, Mrs. Pendarves quietly excused herself, and we were alone. I regarded Clarissa with concern. Dark rings encircled her eyes, and her face appeared paler in the sunlight than it had on the dimly lit stair.

"Did you sleep poorly?" I asked, bothered that a young girl should be subject to restless nights.

She gazed back at me, her face clouded with a melancholy that disturbed me all the more for its air of resignation. "I always sleep poorly," she admitted. "Just like my mother, before she died." There was a conviction in her voice that said she, too, would suffer the same fate.

"There are a lot of reasons for sleeping poorly," I said in my firmest voice. "A lack of exercise and fresh air will destroy the best of health. Eating rich foods will also keep you awake. Your cousin Annabelle often suffered from nightmares after eating too many sweets, but nobody told her she was a nervous child."

This garnered me a wan smile. "I'm glad you didn't let Papa send you away," she said.

"And how did you know he would try?"

"I've had so many governesses, and he worries more and more each time one leaves. They always leave, and I knew that soon he would not let them come at all. I thought Miss Osborne would be the last. I saw it in his face. But you must have done something to him to make him let you come. And to convince him you should stay. So you will be the last instead of her." She lifted her face to mine. "I'm glad it will be you, Jessamy. You will be my favorite of them all."

"That is a very good thing," I answered. "For I expect to be here for many years."

She nodded politely but said nothing.

"Perhaps it would be a good idea if we forgot about your studies for today," I said. "We can use the day to become better acquainted. Do you mind if I ask you questions about yourself?"

She shook her head.

"Good. And, in return, you may do the same of me."

Her smile broadened. "Miss Osborne only liked to discuss our lessons. Tell me, why are you wearing her dress? Do you have none of your own?"

At learning the solution to the mystery of the dress's original owner, I was slow to regain the use of my tongue. "Mrs. Pendarves lent this to me until my portmanteau arrived," I said at last. "I did not suspect that it belonged to my predecessor."

"Then you *do* have dresses of your own?" she said seriously. "For I shall ask Papa to buy you some if you do not. He gives me everything I want."

My cheeks grew warm at the highly improper suggestion. "Indeed, I do," I told her. "But thank you kindly for your offer."

She dismissed my thanks with a quick wave. "Papa

likes to buy me material for dresses. He likes to see me smile."

"No doubt he loves you dearly. But you must not prevail upon him to do the same for me. I have more than enough for a young gentlewoman of my modest position."

Again, her look was doubtful. "Miss Osborne was poor and had only a few dresses."

"Then I am surprised she left this one behind, for it is well made and would survive several more years of wear."

Clarissa's eyes widened. "She left *all* her belongings. She didn't come to the schoolroom one morning, and when I went to see if she was sick, her room was empty. Papa was most annoyed. Mrs. Pendarves said that no decent lady would behave in such a scandalous manner, and it was just as well that she left before she did me any harm." Her brow puckered. "But only the week before, Mrs. Pendarves had said she was serious-minded and better educated than any of my previous governesses. Although I am certain she thinks you are serious-minded, too," she added quickly to save my feelings.

I smiled, but my thoughts remained with the curious Miss Osborne. "Did no one see her leave?"

"No. Mary was the last to talk to her when she collected her supper tray. What do *you* think of Miss Osborne's odd leavetaking?"

"I think it was most unreasonable of her not to inform your father."

"Perhaps she was afraid of him. The other governesses stammered when they talked to him, and some of them burst into tears when Mrs. Pendarves told them he wanted to see them."

I could well appreciate those ladies' fears. Lord Wolfeburne, with his mad laughter, could have made a stout-hearted gentleman quake. A sheltered young maiden would have been at a complete loss in his presence.

"I fear we may never learn her reasons for leaving," I said aloud. "But it is, indeed, most curious."

Satisfied that the subject had been exhausted, she reached down and picked up a golden-haired doll that had been sitting beside her. "This is Matilda," she said. "You must teach her as well as me, for she would not like it if I were to become smarter than she. She worries I would find another playmate if that should happen, although I have told her that I never would."

I smiled, remembering Meg with a pang of guilt. "Matilda is a lucky doll to have so thoughtful a young mistress. Certainly, she may join you. And she may whisper the answers to you so that you may tell me if she likes."

"She would like that very much."

My words had the effect I had been seeking all morning. A glow illuminated Clarissa's face, and the shadows and tension vanished. She was, I realized, an exceptionally pretty child. Only her solemn expression and the anxious look in her eyes detracted from her appearance.

I spent the rest of the morning discovering how advanced she was in her schooling. She was bright, and read as well as she spoke, and her governesses had been most thorough in teaching her French, needlework, art, and music. But her mathematical skills were rudimentary, and her geography was not much better. Surprisingly, her knowledge of history was extensive for someone of her age.

"Miss Osborne loved history," she explained. "Her father was an archaeologist, and she traveled with him and kept his notes until he died. That was why she came to Cornwall. She was fascinated by the standing stones and the beehive huts, and it caused her great distress that Papa refused to let her explore the ruins."

"Is the castle very old?" I asked, more than a little curious myself.

She nodded, taking great delight in being able to instruct me. "It was built in the thirteenth century by Edmund Wolfeburne," she said, speaking in a manner that suggested she was quoting something that had been told to her. "The Hall itself is relatively new, built during the late sixteenth century, updated on numerous occasions, and hardly worth the notice of a true historian."

The disparagement in her voice was noticeable and unmistakably belonged to an adult voice. I suspected the recently departed Miss Osborne. Clearly, she had thought herself above the level of the ordinary scholar and had not bothered making even a pretense at humility.

Clarissa grinned, and her manner became that of a child again. "Miss Osborne was terribly disappointed in the Hall. But the castle has a dungeon and a chamber that has no floor that she desperately wanted to see."

"Without a floor? Why would such a room be built?"

"Oh, there is an excellent reason, truly."

With great excitement, she took my hand and pulled me to the windows. Her finger pointed at the tower. "There are sleeping chambers in there, but one of the doors lets onto a room that opens onto a deep pit. That is how my ancestor rid himself of his enemies. He invited them to feasts and plied them with mead or ale. Then, when they had drunk and eaten themselves into a stupor, he led them up the stairs and opened the door. They had only to step into the room, and they would fall to their death."

"Not what one would call hospitable."

She giggled. "Miss Osborne said the early Wolfeburnes were terrible people. But we're not like that now."

"Certainly, *you* are not," I said. Although privately I wondered how she would feel if she ever met Henrietta.

Clarissa turned to me. "And Papa? He is not like that either?"

"Of course, he is not," I answered hastily, realizing she had misinterpreted my reservation.

"He is a handsome man, is he not?"

"Indeed, he is," I said, anxious to make amends.

Satisfied, she allowed me to guide her back to safer topics, and the morning passed with such swiftness that we were surprised when Mary interrupted us with our luncheon tray. As we ate together in the schoolroom, I supervised Clarissa's table manners. They were, for the most part, above reproach. Only her tendency to burst into conversation before she had swallowed everything in her mouth needed correction.

Afterward, I sent her to her room to wash her face and hands, and I retired to my own suite to do the same. Lavender pomanders had been laid in the drawers, their fragrance seeping into the bedroom, and all the tabletops had been dusted. I opened the door of the wardrobe to find my dresses, neatly pressed and hung.

The black mourning dresses gave me no feeling of pleasure. Lady Wolfeburne had seen fit to have three made up for me. One was of fustian, the second cut from twilled wool, and the last was taffeta. None of them was attractive, but all were undeniably suitable.

My gaze went to the bottom of the wardrobe, but my portmanteau was nowhere to be seen.

On the way back to the schoolroom, I came upon Mary and thanked her for attending to my belongings. "But where did you put my case?" I inquired.

She glanced down at the feather duster in her hands and mumbled, "Mrs. Pendarves said 'ee don't need'n anymore and to take'n up to attic."

"She is quite right," I said, wondering why the question distressed her.

Mary nodded and hastily excused herself, thereby adding to my conviction that there was something odd about her behavior.

I expected, upon reaching the schoolroom, to find Clarissa waiting for me. Instead, the solemn figure of Lord Wolfeburne met my gaze. He stood at the window, his shoulders and jaw set in a stiff line, looking intently toward the ruins. But whatever the spell that had been cast upon him to make him so silent and still, it broke upon his hearing my approach. He turned and stepped forward to stand directly in my path.

The savagery I had seen upon his face the previous evening had faded, but some vestiges still lingered in the brightness of his eyes and the sardonic twist to his mouth. His clothes were the same he had worn the day before, and his hair still tumbled raggedly about his face, although he had seen fit to make use of a comb. Still, there was a magnetism and force about him that made the carelessness of his attire unimportant.

"And are you satisfied with your pupil?" he demanded, not bothering to wish me a good day or address me by name.

"I am. She is intelligent and there are but few gaps in her education."

"Then it is to be hoped you will not find your duties here too difficult."

"Not difficult, at all."

"Nor unpleasant?"

"On the contrary, she is an endearing child."

He nodded, as if this opinion concurred with his own. "And what of you? Are you satisfied with your rooms?"

"I am wholly overwhelmed by your generosity."

He shrugged. "You must thank Mrs. Pendarves. I leave those matters in her capable hands and must be absolved of any guilt and denied any credit."

"I already have done. But there is a small matter that concerns me. She seems determined to regard me as a member of your family, and I believe you are, in part, to blame for the misunderstanding."

"And how else should I regard you?" he asked sharply, seeming somehow offended.

My stomach fluttered with anxiety, although I had faced greater condemnation than what I now saw there. "I am merely your daughter's governess," I said, trying not to let my words falter and betray the emotions that struggled within me. "We are not related, neither legally nor by blood." I studied him, watching for his reaction and wondering if he mistakenly supposed that his brother had made formal adoption arrangements.

To my surprise, he gave a rude snort. "Had you been my brother's natural child, you would not have been invited here, though it was your ancestral home."

He rubbed his stubbled jaw with the back of his hand and fixed his gaze upon me. In a softer voice, he murmured, "Nor would I have held you in any esteem. He was cruelly self-indulgent and encouraged the same in his wife and his two daughters. That you escaped such spoiling was mere good fortune."

There was an intimacy to his tone and a look in his eyes that gave greater meaning to his words. As though he also benefited—or expected to benefit—from his family's neglect of me.

I stiffened. "As a child, I would not have agreed with you." Still, his remark offered some explanation for his harsh treatment of his brother's widow. "Is that why—?" I stopped, realizing my question was rude in the extreme.

"You were about to ask?"

"Forgive me. I spoke without thinking, and my question would have been both forward and impertinent."

"Would it, indeed?" The bitter twist to his lips vanished, replaced by a rakish grin that could have broken hearts from Cornwall to Scotland. "Then I admit to a greater interest in what you were going to say than I have felt for anything that has gone before. Finish."

His command robbed me of any hesitance I might have felt. "I wondered if your dislike for your brother's family was your reason for reducing Lady Wolfeburne's income."

"Who the devil told you I had done that?"

"She said so herself. It was the reason she sent me here."

"Utter nonsense. I have agreed to pay for all her expenditures and grant her the same allowance she enjoyed from her husband." He frowned at my gasp of dismay. "I suppose you think I should have left you in sublime ignorance? Well, I do not. Only fools hide from the truth, or demand that others conceal an unpleasantness from them. If you wish to remain here, I expect nothing less than that strength I once saw in you."

"I shall do my best not to disappoint you," I managed to reply.

"See that you do."

If he intended to make a lengthier response he was halted by the appearance of his daughter. She ran into the room, more cheerful than I had yet seen her, and gave a cry of delight. "Papa. Do you intend to listen to my lessons?"

The interruption sent a flash of annoyance across his dark face. "I most certainly do not," he retorted, then smiled to remove the sting from his words. "I would not force my company upon two such charming ladies," he added, with a quick glance at me.

I quickly averted my gaze.

"But I want you to stay," Clarissa said. "And Jessamy would not mind. She thinks you are handsome and good."

Lord Wolfeburne's eyebrows rose, and my cheeks suffused with warmth. "And how did she elicit that admission?" he asked, greatly amused by my discomfiture.

"They were her own statements, and I could hardly protest," I mumbled.

He regarded me for several long seconds, taking enormous pleasure out of my growing embarrassment. At last, he took pity on me and said, "Had you done so, it might have saved you from an awkward moment."

"Or added to my humiliation."

"Will you stay, Papa?" Clarissa demanded again.

He shook his head. "I have done with lessons, at least those lessons that can be taught in schoolrooms."

"What other kind are there?" she asked.

"You will learn soon enough."

He bent over and gave her a kiss, the amusement still obvious in his dark eyes. Clarissa threw her arms about his neck and hugged him, determined that he should not leave, and I was struck by the intensity of her affection for him.

Murmuring a soft protest, he disentangled himself and straightened. It was then I remembered we had another matter to discuss. "Young Bowden asked me to tell you that there was another sheep found dead on the moor."

Lord Wolfeburne flinched, and his face suddenly looked haggard. Then he caught sight of his daughter's upturned face and forced a smile. "That is one of the reasons my brother chose to live in London. Matters of estate are tedious in the extreme. It is hardly worth the title and the income. Although I admit to an unwillingness to relinquish them now that they have come into my possession."

Laughing at his own jest, he strolled into the corridor.

I waited until he had gone, then wandered to the window. There, I paused at the exact spot where he had been standing, and looked out, searching for whatever had captured his attention.

But there was nothing.

Nothing but the ruins themselves.

4

The soft touch of Clarissa's hand upon mine drew my thoughts back to the schoolroom and to her. "Are you all right, miss?" she asked, her eyes wide and dark.

"I am," I said in a bright, cheery voice. "And did I not tell you to call me Jessamy?"

She smiled and her doubts were quickly forgotten. "I am unused to calling my governesses by their first names," she confessed, and her fingers tightened on my own. "I cannot promise always to remember, but I will do my best."

"It will soon come naturally," I told her. "And you have a right to call me by my first name for there is a connection between us that you did not share with the others."

Although it had not been my intention, I realized that, by insisting upon this familiarity, I had opened the door to a trust that might otherwise have taken a long while to inspire. It was a lot to be gained so easily.

"I think we have had enough of lessons for today," I announced. "Do you agree?"

In response she ran to the straightback chair where Matilda was perched, her blue eyes staring vacantly into the schoolroom. Clarissa bent down and, face shielded by her long ringlets, whispered into the doll's ear. I dared not smile lest she suppose I was laughing at her.

After a short consultation, Clarissa lifted her head, a broad smile on her face. "Yes," she said. "It would not do to become idle but, as Matilda says, this is our *first* day together."

"My thought exactly. And did she say also that an active body makes for an active mind? I think a walk in the garden would do us both good."

"Both?" Her lower lip quivered. "But Matilda will not want to stay here by herself. She . . . she is easily frightened."

"Did I say both? I meant all of us." My quick amendment was rewarded with the return of her smile.

It was a warm day. The early morning haze and the drift of clouds had blown northward, leaving an unbroken stretch of blue sky above the moors and the Hall. But having been warned that Clarissa's health was fragile, I insisted she fetch her jacket and put on her walking boots.

In the garden, she kept one arm wrapped around the flaxen-haired doll, tucked her free hand within my own, and tugged me down the flagstone walk. To our left, a thick hedge of rosebushes separated the path from the outer walls of the Hall, giving a splash of gay color to the dreary stones that towered above our heads. To our right, the lawns rolled away from us, a green expanse cut by a precise layout of rectangular flowerbeds that swelled with rhododendrons, camellias, and Chinese magnolias.

After London's gray streets and sooty buildings, the brightness of my surroundings enchanted me, but Clarissa hurried onward, looking straight ahead, intent upon some destination of her own choosing. She was abetted by the wind that swept off the moor and buffeted against the full skirt of my dress, shoving me forward with a strong hand. We rounded the corner of the house in a rush, and I found myself face to face with those same ruins I had glimpsed from the schoolroom window.

"There!" Clarissa pointed proudly. "That is where the Wolfeburnes once lived."

Seen from my suite, the crumbling castle had looked smaller and decidedly less imposing, but the view from that angle had been misleading. The massive stone structure sat atop a small knoll, and there was a sizable section to the west that had been untouched by the years. Even the great hall, with its crumbled roof, appeared from below to be intact, although I knew this to be untrue.

"It's awesome," I said, holding her hand firmly and bracing my weight to prevent her from dragging me nearer. "But we must stay at a safe distance. I made a promise to your father."

She sighed. "Now you sound just like Miss Osborne. I thought you would be different."

"Not entirely." I felt chagrined by how quickly I had fallen short of her expectations. Likely, it would only be the first of many times. "I imagine your father did not want to see you come to harm when you were in Miss

Osborne's care any more than he does now that you are in mine," I said, hoping to restore myself to her good graces.

She agreed to this willingly enough, but her gaze remained fixed on the ruins.

"And did you bring Miss Osborne here, as well? And try to coax her into taking you inside?"

Clarissa shook her ringlets emphatically. "She always chose to walk this way, but she never dared leave the path. Isn't it silly to come this far, again and again, and then stop?"

"Perhaps. But even we must not go farther than the outer ring of fallen stones. Only think what might happen if the uppermost stones toppled while we were inside the castle walls. You would not want to see Matilda harmed by your carelessness."

"No." She gave her doll a fond glance, and we strolled across the spongy grass. "But if we were careful—"

There was a flutter of movement within the castle, and the rooks burst from the collapsed roof and took wing. They spread upward like a swift-moving storm, a good twenty or more, their raucous cries shattering the silence, their black wings marring the blue sky. Once aloft, they circled the tower in an ominous cloud of harsh sound and darkness.

"Whatever could have startled them?" I asked.

My question was answered almost immediately. A man emerged from the depths of the ruins, his eyes squinting into the sunlight that shone at our backs. From his thinning hair and graying sideburns, I guessed he was in his forties. He did not appear to be a gentleman, for he lacked the proper bearing. Nor was he wearing a coat or hat, although he was respectably attired in dark trousers and waistcoat. His shirt sleeves had been rolled back over large, fleshy forearms, and a farmer's pitchfork bounced on his shoulder.

The sharp prongs glinted in the sunlight, and I drew Clarissa closer to me. "Perhaps you should run and tell your father," I advised, intending to remain where I was to assure myself that the fellow was up to no mischief.

She lifted her face to mine. "It's only Wilkins. He's my father's steward."

Although his eyes were temporarily blinded by the light, Wilkins's head turned to the sound of our voices. He raised his hand to shade his eyes and squinted again. I did not care to be the subject of such intense scrutiny, but forced myself to stare back. This time, he saw us standing in the shadow of the Hall, directly in his path.

"Good afternoon," I said politely.

His mouth set in a grim line, and he gave a brusque nod of his head that was more of a dismissal than an acknowledgment. I gripped Clarissa's hand more firmly and refused to step aside. "There is no need for incivility," I said in a stern voice.

Clarissa tugged on my hand. "He can't speak," she whispered when I glanced down.

Dismayed, I stared at the man, and my cheeks flushed with a prickly warmth. "Please forgive me," I said. "I had no idea."

My apology might just as well have been left unsaid. He gestured at us to move out of his way, and the pitchfork bounced angrily on his shoulder.

I stared at him. He had the most disconcerting

eyes. They were a pale blue, almost colorless, and he blinked excessively. His sensitivity to the sunlight explained his inability to see us so soon after having stepped from the shadows of the ruins. Recalling where he had been gave me the strength I needed to gain control of myself.

"You had better mind your manners," I told him. "It would serve you right if I advised his lordship that you have been poking about the ruins. Come along, Clarissa."

With a protective arm around her shoulder, I attempted to lead her around the man. Wilkins glared at me. Blinking rapidly, he yanked the pitchfork off his shoulder and thrust the prongs at us.

"Just what do you think you're doing?" I demanded. "Put that down and let us pass."

Instead, he stepped forward menacingly, bringing the iron points to within a foot of my nose. I gasped and drew back, carrying Clarissa with me. Wilkins advanced upon us, driving us backward until our heels brushed the flagstone path. Then, with a guttural snarl, he turned abruptly and stalked off. I watched him leave with enormous relief.

Had he thought we meant to go into the ruins? If so, his method of warning us off left a great deal to be desired. "What a disagreeable man," I said to Clarissa when he had disappeared behind the Hall. "I cannot think why your father would employ him."

She shrugged, but her attention had already returned to the ruins. What kind of life had she led that she could dismiss the steward's behavior without a moment's thought?

With that question on my mind, we continued our

stroll. Thereafter, we were uninterrupted by anything save the cries of the rooks and curlews, and the sound of the wind upon the moor. It rustled through the gorse, whispering and murmuring, reminding me of the harsh, dry voices of old women intent on their gossip. There was something hypnotic in the sound, and I was lulled into drowsiness until Clarissa spoke and broke the spell.

"Do you think it hurts?" she demanded.

I glanced down at her curious face. "Do I think what hurts?"

"Not being able to speak."

"The word is mute," I told her. "Wilkins is a mute. And, no, physically I do not think he suffers. But perhaps in other ways."

"How, then?"

I frowned, thinking of the many occasions I had been forced to sit silently on the sofa while Annabelle and Henrietta prattled to their parents. "It cannot be pleasant never being able to say what one thinks or feels."

Clarissa nodded, and her teeth pulled at her lower lip. "I suppose that is why he always seems angry. Next time I shall smile at him, even though I don't like him very much."

"That is a very good idea," I said, although I was not convinced the blame for the man's bad manners could be laid entirely at the feet of his disability.

By the time we had returned to the Hall, Clarissa's cheeks were a bright pink, and her eyes glowed. The lilac hue of her dress, which had seemed too bright for her sallow skin that morning, now seemed pale and understated. I took a complacent satisfaction in the changes I saw in her, even in this short a period, and told myself it would not be long before I had transformed her into a happy, noisy nine-year-old. Thinking a brief nap before supper would do her good, I told her to go and lie down and retired to my sitting room.

It was a pleasant place. The gilt and rose flamboyance of the bedroom flowed into the sitting room where, beside the writing desk, there was a worktable fitted with fluted silk drawers and two tufted armchairs complete with gathered skirts. Light flooded through the tall windows and sparkled across polished walnut occasional tables.

I stretched out on the settee and let my head fall back upon the embroidered cushions. There was much about Wolfeburne Hall to engage my thoughts: the odd customs; the dead sheep; the succession of governesses—one of whom, at least, had departed without any explanation; Clarissa's fears; and the startling change in his lordship's personality. I could not help but wonder what storms raged beneath all those dark clouds.

Long before I came to any satisfactory conclusion, there was a knock on the door. At my bidding Mrs. Pendarves entered. She carried a large vase filled with roses. The profusion of blooms and leaves concealed the upper half of her petite torso, and the scent wafted through the room.

I gaped at them. It was an extravagant display that would have been better suited to the mistress's suite, not the rooms of the lowly governess—ornate as they might be.

To my bewilderment, Mrs. Pendarves set them on the occasional table nearest the window and stood back to admire her handiwork. "The rooms smelled a bit musty to me," she explained. "I thought this might help."

"That's very thoughtful of you," I stammered. "They're lovely. But you must not go to such trouble on my account."

"Nonsense. You do like roses, don't you?"

"Indeed, I do. As it happens, only an hour ago, I was admiring those very blooms."

Her smooth face crinkled into a deep smile. "I thought I heard you go outside. Did you have a nice walk?"

"For the most part," I replied. "Although we had an uncomfortable few minutes when we met up with his lordship's steward."

"Wilkins? Oh, don't fret about him. His manners are rough, but that's from having worked in the mines. He won't do you any harm."

"Perhaps not. But I was not much impressed with him. Has he been employed by the Wolfeburne family for many years?" I asked, thinking there could be no other reason for his lordship to suffer the man's surly behavior.

Mrs. Pendarves shook her head. "No, not long at all. Mr. Trystan—Lord Wolfeburne," she corrected herself, "hired him after old Mr. Morrison died." Her brow puckered. "That would have been right after he left Oxford—about nine years ago."

Her words struck a chord in my memory. It was nine years ago that the two of us had met. Had the steward's death been the reason that brought him to London? He and his brother had supposedly argued over some matter of estate. It was something else to pique my curiosity.

"My dear life," Mrs. Pendarves went on. "That does

bring back memories. I haven't thought of old Mr. Morrison in years. Now, he was a good-natured man. Properly educated. Not like Wilkins, who can't read or write. And never a bad word for anyone. Never complaining. Honest as the day was long. He ran this estate as well as if it were his own. Of course, he was always rather sad. Melancholic, I would have called him. I never could see the reason for it myself, but some people are just like that. Can't see the sunshine for the clouds. Well, mustn't speak ill of the dead."

She gave the roses a last critical look and, taking brisk, short steps, walked across the room. Her hand rested on the doorknob, and she looked over her shoulder at me. "Mary will be up in a couple of hours with your supper. Will you be needing anything before then?"

I hesitated. Why had Wilkins been wandering about the ruins when Lord Wolfeburne had declared them unsound? "I did have a question," I finally said, deciding to judge the seriousness of the situation with a few careful remarks. "His lordship warned me to avoid the castle. I suppose no one ever goes there."

"Only himself," she answered promptly. "And Wilkins. He looks over the place now and then, and knocks down the stones that are loose and likely to fall."

Her answer was matter-of-fact, and I was convinced she was telling the truth. Certainly, it explained the man's presence there and his need for a pitchfork. I felt vaguely disappointed. The mystery was no mystery at all. If I wanted to discover what dark currents lurked beneath the surface at the Hall, I would have to look elsewhere.

Mrs. Pendarves bustled out the door, leaving me to

wonder why a man as unlikely as Wilkins had been hired to be steward to a large estate. It seemed he did not even warrant a respectful "mister" as the late Mr. Morrison had done. It made little sense to me. But it was, I supposed, none of my business.

I picked up the novel I had been reading on the train, thinking I could finish a chapter before it was time for supper. But I had not read more than a few pages before there was a second knock on my door, a hard, commanding rap that I could not possibly have mistaken for Mary's meek tap. I sat up and smoothed my dress around me before telling Lord Wolfeburne to enter, for I had no doubt it was he.

His tall figure filled the doorway, blocking out the corridor behind him, and he gave his surroundings a quick glance. His gaze fell upon the roses. With an amused chuckle, he strode into my sitting room. The door banged shut behind him.

He had taken the time to pull on his coat, although it was unbuttoned and the sleeves badly creased. Nor had he bothered with a neckcloth, but let his shirt hang open, and the shadow across his jaw had darkened.

He took the tufted armchair across from me, stretched out his legs, and studied me with a lazy smile. "It occurred to me we had not finished our conversation. You do not, I trust, object to this interruption?"

I took a deep breath and caught the faint smell of brandy. Goodness—the man was drunk. The knowledge was hardly reassuring.

"It is not my place to object," I said, putting my book to one side and giving him my full, and wary, attention.

"Oh come now." His dark eyes flashed with impatience.

"Would you have either of us believe that, should I fail to measure up to your standards, you would not promptly instruct me as to the appropriate behavior that gentlemen need display toward young ladies in their employ?"

"Since I have never before been a governess, I cannot profess to know what behavior is, or is not, appropriate."

He snorted. "And I am to think that you have no opinions on the subject? None whatsoever?"

"Perhaps a few."

In truth, I had strong notions of what was and was not acceptable, and he fell short on every count. Up to and including his habitual state of semi-undress. My gaze lingered on the tuft of dark hair that could be glimpsed in the open vee of his shirt.

One corner of his mouth lifted, and there was a knowing glint in his eyes. "At last, we are getting somewhere. Pray, enlighten me."

"I would rather not."

He feigned a look of amazement. "Why so reticent? I would not have thought you slow to express an opinion."

"Nor am I. But I doubt you would find those opinions to your liking."

"You think they would expose my failings?"

"Indeed, they would."

His tongue flickered over his lips. "I am intrigued. I have always thought myself the most charming of men. Cheerful to a fault. Attentive to all. Both amusing and easily amused. And yet you find fault with such a disarming character." He tossed back the mop of black hair that had fallen across his brow and gave voice to that disconcerting wild laughter.

"It is a poor mind that finds amusement where none is to be had," I said.

"I disagree. Any fool can laugh at a good jest. That takes no talent whatsoever. It is the rare man who grabs at laughter where no cause for mirth exists."

"And yet any village idiot can be found smiling and chuckling to himself."

"What effrontery!" Appearing more entertained than annoyed, he demanded, "Do you compare your employer to some mindless fool?"

"By your own behavior, you invite comparison."

He laughed again, and there were strains of real enjoyment in the sound. "What a sharp-tongued little beast you are."

His casual remark cut me in a manner that his earlier attempts had failed to do. Unaware of my sudden discomfort, he gave a royal wave of his hand. "Tell me, how would you have me behave?"

I glanced down at my own hands, still sedately folded in my lap. A demure, ladylike pose for someone who was neither demure nor a lady. It was almost as though I were an observer and not an actor in this little scene. "As I recall," I said slowly, "I greatly admired a young man who once rescued me from a coal cellar."

"What? That child? That naive pup? You cannot mean to tell me you were enamored of him?"

"That is not the word I would use," I said in protest, my cheeks prickling with warmth. "But only a true gentleman would treat a dirty child like a lady." I tried to look at him but could not.

He cleared his throat. "You must find my real character a severe disappointment."

His voice was faintly wistful. I lifted my chin and stared at him. "I am not convinced that what I see before me is a true example of your character," I blurted out, more bluntly than I had intended.

His lips twisted into that mockery of a smile. "Are you not? Well, we must spend more time together and I will convince you of your error."

"It was not for that reason you brought me here. My concern is with Clarissa's character, not yours."

He shrugged. "Then if that is your wish, let us discuss my daughter. That is, if you have anything to add to your earlier statements."

I swallowed. Clearly, he had no intention of leaving my suite until he had found the amusement he sought. And if I could think of nothing to say about Clarissa, then his attention would return to me. That was to be avoided at all costs.

"She is an intelligent child," I said. "Although, as I mentioned, there are gaps in her education."

He brushed my words aside impatiently. "I am well aware of the condition of her education. It is the fault of all these blasted governesses. I wanted your opinion of *her*." He leveled an intent gaze upon me, and it took all my willpower not to squirm beneath its force.

I took a deep breath and began again. "As I said, she is intelligent, and I think she has a good heart. But she seems a lonely child, both sensitive and imaginative. Old, dark houses, isolated from their neighbors by long stretches of moorland, are not the most ideal surroundings for such children. Perhaps, if her mother had not died . . ." I hesitated, wondering if I opened a wound, but his expression was detached and tolerant.

Reassured, I continued. "If she had not lost her mother, she might have had the love and support she needed to fight those fears. Instead, there has only been the repeated changeover of governesses, and their steady coming and going seems to have worked to her detriment." I stopped there, not willing to add that, in some way, he had failed to give her a much-needed reassurance.

"What?" he demanded, seeing I had finished. "No word of rebuke for the child's father? Surely you do not mean me to conclude that you approve of my part in this?"

"I have seen you together but once," I retorted, nettled by his ability to discern my thoughts and use them against me. "As yet, I'm hardly qualified to offer an opinion. But if you insist upon one—"

"I do."

"—you seem an indulgent parent, and she dotes on you."

He scratched his thumbnail across his stubbled jaw, all the while fixing me beneath his gaze like a hawk marking the field mouse it means to have for dinner. To my dismay, he seemed to know how greatly he disconcerted me, for he smiled and lazily shifted his long legs, setting one boot across the other. While I sat with rigid back and clenched hands, he appeared wholly and pleasantly at ease.

"Then you do not find me lacking," he said, surprising me by speaking after a lengthy pause. "Let me qualify that statement—you do not find me lacking *in this one instance?*"

I frowned. Provoking man. He deserved to be served nothing kinder than the whole truth. "You mean well.

But I think you may encourage her fears in ways you do not fully realize."

He leaned forward, apparently desirous of catching my every word. With a start, I realized his interest was genuine. Nor was he drunk as I had first concluded.

"And in what way am I guilty?" he asked, his face grave.

"I do not accuse you of guilt. Merely of ignorance."

"And if a parent is ignorant of his child's needs, does that not also make him guilty?"

"Only if he is willfully blind. I do not believe that is the case."

"Then I have been judged and found innocent but wanting."

"I do not wish to judge you."

"Then you are alone in that."

He slumped in the armchair and stared at me morosely. His face darkened, as though the sun had dropped below the horizon and left him in shadow. But the wall behind him was ablaze with afternoon sunlight. I waited for him to explain himself, but he dismissed his statement with a shrug.

"Tell me what I am doing wrong."

"Clarissa believes in ghosts."

"I have told her she is mistaken."

"You seem to have told her in such a manner as to convince her there is some basis for her fears," I countered. "She cannot bring herself to accuse you of lying. Nor can she make herself believe you."

The crease between his brows deepened. "And what would you have me do?"

Seeing his distress, I reached out and touched his

sleeve. His gaze traveled from my hand to my face, and his eyebrows lifted with rude amusement. Worse, there was a wolfish look in his eyes that could not be mistaken.

Stung by the assumption he had made, I drew back and said stiffly, "You must be more convincing in your arguments. Do not dismiss her fears with a light word and send her off to bed as though you have not heard her."

"And that is all you wish of me?" he asked, his manner as formal as my own.

"No."

"Then there is more." He sighed theatrically. "I thought as much."

I ignored his attempts to fluster me. "I think you would be well advised to spend more time with her. She seems to need attention."

"I expect *you* to give her that attention."

"I am her governess, not her father. She needs to know she has your love."

"And do you think for one instant she does not?"

"I think adults assume certain facts as self-evident. Children make no such assumptions."

He glared at me. I met that glare with complete equanimity, finding his anger vastly preferable to either his mockery or his rakish smiles. But my composure served only to annoy him further.

His fingers drummed against the arm of his chair. "For someone who admits she has never had the care of children before, you are vastly opinionated, Miss Lane."

"I said I was never employed as a governess before. I

had the care of Annabelle for a good two years. And my own experiences have taught me a great deal about the needs of children."

He leaned toward me, fastening upon my words, and I knew I should have weighed them more carefully before speaking them. "I cannot imagine that you received much love from either my brother or sister-in-law," he said. "Was there someone else who cared for you?"

"No one," I admitted warily.

"Not a single person?"

"At the start, Lady Wolfeburne found me amusing, and I may have supposed myself loved during that time. But I soon came to learn otherwise."

He studied my face. "A harsh situation. But you seem all the stronger for the experience."

"You may be right. But Clarissa is a very different child than I was," I said, determined to return the conversation to our original discussion. "What strengthened me would destroy someone of her sensitivity."

"She is like her mother. She, too, was given to dark fancies. I have great hopes that you will be able to rid Clarissa of them."

"With your help, it is my intention to do so."

"You have no self-doubt, then? No fears of failure?"

"None."

His eyebrows rose. "You are decidedly lacking in humility for someone of your species."

"False humility is worse than no humility at all," I retorted. "And as for my talents, I would hardly think it admirable if I, as an adult, could not offer guidance and support to a child."

The corners of his lips flickered upward. "Or correction to her wayward father?"

"I said nothing of the kind."

"And I am mistaken, then?" It was plain that he knew full well he was not.

I hesitated while I sought for words. "I think we can all benefit from the advice of others."

He laughed. "What a sly creature you are, Miss Lane. If you are not rapping me across the knuckles, you are employing the tact of a diplomat. Do you expect me to fail to recognize that the essence of both approaches is the same?"

"I expect you to consider what I have to say. And in a reasonable fashion. If you did not trust me to do my best for your daughter, you would not have brought me here."

"And I have had reason to regret that impulse," he said, but in an amiable fashion. "Is there nothing else, or am I permitted to go and bind my wounds?"

"I could hardly stop you if I tried."

"Of that, I am not convinced." He rose to leave. At the door, he glanced back at me as though struck by a sudden thought. "In the future, when you are given a message for me, I expect to receive it at the first possible opportunity."

Following so abruptly on the heels of his friendliness, the rebuke stung. "Normally, I would have done so," I said. "But given the disruption caused by my arrival, there was so much to occupy my mind, I did not remember until after I had gone to bed. I did not think the matter important enough to disturb either your rest or my own."

"That is hardly for you to decide."

"It will not happen again."

"See that it does not."

With that, he departed.

5

For the rest of that day, Lord Wolfeburne closeted himself in his study—much to my relief. I was beginning to approach our confrontations with a mixture of dread and fascination. Certainly, he stimulated me, but it was a disquieting stimulation, rather like finding oneself prone on a bed of nails. With care, one would survive unscathed, but it was not a matter to be treated lightly.

That evening, Clarissa and I ate supper in the schoolroom. With the onset of night, she had grown quieter, and her gaze lifted again and again to the windows and the tightly drawn curtains. Matilda was perched on the railback chair between us, regarding me with knowing eyes. I fancied her a sterner judge than Lord Wolfeburne. He, for all his harshness, seemed to have faith in me.

I wondered which of them would prove to be correct.

Then I rebuked myself for my silliness.

Clearly, it was my own self-doubt I read in the doll's dispassionate gaze. A self-doubt fed by Wolfeburne Hall's gloom and the odd behavior of its occupants. But, no matter what my feelings, I was determined Clarissa's demons would find me more than a match for them.

"If you're finished, we can read some fairy tales until bedtime," I said, thinking a story might capture her wandering attention.

She nodded willingly enough, but her smile was merely polite. Nor did she display much interest until I finished the last tale and said it was time for bed.

"Just one more," she pleaded. "It's still early."

Her eyelids were heavy, and she struggled to keep from yawning. But in her face I saw a feverish brightness that was inconsistent with her weariness.

"Would you like me to sit with you until you fall asleep?" I offered.

Some of the anxiety faded from her eyes, and she nodded, but still she dawdled, rising from her chair slowly and insisting upon straightening the cushions. At last, she picked up Matilda and, cradling her doll protectively, she allowed me to put them both to bed.

Despite her fears, she fell asleep quickly. It seemed that the walk and the fresh air had done as I had hoped. Nor had I escaped their effects and, surrendering to my own drowsiness, I also retired.

The howls of the dogs awakened me. They issued through the night, like the haunted cries of wolves baying at a full moon. There was something strangely human in their voices, an emotion I recognized but could not quite identify.

I shivered beneath my heavy blankets, unnerved by what I did not understand. Was this their hunting cry? Were they in pursuit of some rabbit? I thought of the dogs' large jaws and pitied the hapless creature that had drawn their attention.

Or had they found human prey? What if someone had mistakenly entered the estate? I rose, hurried to the windows, and drew back the curtains. A heavy fog blanketed the Hall and swirled before my gaze. It was impossible to see beyond the window casement, or even to discern the direction of the howls.

I opened my window and leaned out, hoping for a better view of the grounds.

Abruptly, the noise ceased.

And thereby ended any hope I might have had of locating the dogs. I supposed that they had caught their prey, if they had been hunting. Or, if someone had been trespassing, they had frightened off the intruder. That was, after all, their duty.

As mine was Clarissa.

I wondered if her sleep had also been disturbed. She would be well accustomed to the dogs, but it did no harm to check on her before returning to bed. I lit the oil lamp and reached for my night jacket.

Outside in the hall, all was quiet. The carpet muffled the sound of my footsteps, and the flickering light from my lamp cast mute, wavering shadows on the papered walls. I paused outside her door and quietly turned the knob.

Clarissa was sitting upright in bed, braced by a mound of pillows. The blankets bunched about her waist, and, caught in the light of my lamp, her face was a pale circle of white.

She turned toward me. "J-Jessamy?"

"It is I. There is no need for fear."

"Did you hear them?"

"I did. But it is only Castor and Pollux. Surely you have no fear of them."

"No," she said. "But the howls were so fearsome. What do you think disturbed them?"

"Likely, they have taken after a rabbit." I assured her with more conviction than I felt.

"Are you certain?"

I shook my head. "It is only a guess. But I think it a good one."

"But suppose it was not a rabbit?"

"A badger, then."

"Suppose it was something else? Something . . . bigger. Do you think the dogs would harm . . . would harm . . ." She gulped back a sob.

"Goodness, there is no need for you to be concerned. The dogs are well trained, your father promised me, and they would do nothing that was not expected or demanded of them."

"It was Papa who trained them."

"And I am certain they do him credit."

"It is just that they sounded so . . . so odd."

"That is because of the fog. Your father warned me it distorts sounds." Here, I stood on stronger ground.

She searched my face. But if she supposed I was only placating her, she was mistaken. At last, she sighed. "Will you stay with me until I fall asleep again?" she asked, her voice faltering.

I smiled. "That was precisely my intention."

I covered her up with the blankets, then sat down on the edge of her bed. But this time Clarissa did not fall asleep easily. She tossed and turned, and her eyes opened at regular intervals to make certain I had kept my promise.

Once she stirred and, finding I had still not left her side, said, "I am glad you have come to be my governess, Jessamy. None of the others would sit with me. They did not leave their beds at night."

"And why is that?"

"I think they were afraid, too. Except for Miss Osborne. And she said she would tell Papa if I made a fuss and disturbed her rest."

Her plaintive remark gave me a greater insight into my predecessor, a woman who already stirred my curiosity. She did not seem the kind of person I would have liked.

Clarissa did not speak again, but more than an hour passed before her breathing deepened and I dared return to my own room.

It was a different Clarissa who entered the schoolroom the next morning. The shadows under her eyes were darker, and her movements were slow and listless. The lessons proceeded slowly, and twice I had to draw her wandering attention back to her studies. By midday, we were both glad to put the books aside.

"Perhaps we would do better to spend the day out on the moor," I said. "Neither of us slept well last night, and lessons don't sit well on a tired mind."

But in the end, we were forced to remain in the garden. Clarissa's lacy dresses were more suitable for sitting quietly in the drawing room than energetic tramping through the gorse and heather. Still, I insisted we remain on the lawns rather than return to the edge of the ruins as she would have preferred. The miserable heap of stones could only add to her dark fancies, and I did not care to chance a second meeting with the surly Wilkins.

It was, perforce, a quiet day, and I imagined it would come to a quiet close. But that expectation was dashed by his lordship. We returned to the schoolroom to find the table set for one. Before I could ask questions, Mrs. Pendarves knocked on the door and informed me I was to dine with Lord Wolfeburne that evening.

Leaving Clarissa to her care, I retired to my rooms to attend to my toilette. There was little enough to do but change into yet another black gown, this one of taffeta, and return any straying wisps of hair to the braid knotted about my nape.

I left my room, just as the clock was striking seven— the appointed hour. But I could not go downstairs without first looking in on Clarissa and assuring myself that she was all right. To my relief, she was curled up on the settee with Mrs. Pendarves, chattering to her about the names of the flowers she had learned that day.

Apparently, my uneasiness was unfounded. With a smile for Clarissa, I bade them both a good evening and left. Lord Wolfeburne would be waiting, and I could not postpone our meeting any longer. But no matter what his behavior nor how he provoked me, I was determined to be pleasant and agreeable.

He was ensconced in the dining room, a glass of claret at his hand. It appeared not to be his first, but having already discovered that some of his drunkenness was mere posturing, I hated to make assumptions.

To his favor, he was suitably attired; his shirt was spotless and his coat and waistcoat in place. Yet his cravat was carelessly tied, and he sprawled in his chair with an utter contempt for the demands of good posture. His air, too, was dissolute. I could almost have believed it was ingrained in him, like a dark stain beneath the fingernails that could not be removed.

I hovered at the end of the table, wondering if I should seat myself or wait for him to help me with my chair. He scowled and pointedly took out his pocket watch and noted the time.

"I hope you will excuse my tardiness," I said, remembering my intention to placate him whenever possible. "I did not like to come downstairs without first seeing that Clarissa was happily settled."

He fixed me with an imperious stare. "Are you questioning Mrs. Pendarves's capabilities? I assure you she has managed well enough in the past."

"Not at all. But Clarissa did not sleep well last night, and I wanted to set my own mind at rest."

"And what, pray tell, disturbed her?" he asked with no less belligerence.

"The dogs and their howls."

"They have never upset her before."

"On the contrary. I think they have frightened her on many occasions."

There was a startled flash in his eyes, a crack to his veneer of indifference. "Why was I not informed?" he demanded, straightening in his chair.

It was not the first glimpse I'd been given of the depth of his feeling for his daughter. His character was not as wild and heedless as he wanted me to think. But further speculation was impossible while he leveled his angry gaze upon me.

"It would seem," I said, "of all her governesses, only Miss Osborne had the courage to leave her bed at night."

He muttered a curse that I pretended not to hear. "Stupid women. I was a fool to bring them here, and a greater fool to let them stay. What of Miss Osborne?" he demanded as though the fault was mine. "Why had I no report from her?"

"She threatened to tell you only if Clarissa disturbed her nights. And your daughter did not . . . does not"—I corrected myself—"want you to know of her fears. The dogs gave *me* a jolt. We can hardly blame her for being unnerved."

He glowered at me. "I do not recall *saying* that I blamed her."

"Indeed, you did not. Forgive me. Obviously, I was making excuses for her where none was needed."

"Indeed you were. I shall speak to her tomorrow and set her mind at rest." Forgetting me for an instant, he took a swallow of claret and swilled it around in his mouth. Still staring at me, he grimaced and swallowed.

I wondered which of us was not to his taste.

"Do you intend to sit down?" he asked. "Or am I to be obliged to crane my head to talk to you the entire evening."

"Of course not, milord." I pulled out the chair.

He nodded at one of the decanters on the table. "Some wine?"

I hesitated. I wanted all my wits about me.

"It is only Mrs. Pendarves's elderflower wine," he added, guessing the reason for my hesitation with an ease that annoyed me as much as it seemed to please him.

"Perhaps a small glass."

He poured the yellow liquid from the decanter into a long-stemmed glass. When it was two-thirds full, he paused. He shot me a questioning look and I nodded. With a shrug, he returned the stopper to the decanter. "Are you always this temperate?"

"I've never had any other choice."

He leaned forward and gave me the glass. For one instant, his wolf's-head ring flashed in the candlelight, and the dark hairs across the back of his hand stood out in sharp relief. By that single action, he intruded into my thoughts, making me doubly aware of his person. Just when I became convinced that was his intention, he withdrew.

"And were you to be given that choice?" he asked, drawing me back into the conversation.

"It would hardly be suitable for me to be otherwise."

"You disappoint me."

"Milord?"

"Such a dreary attitude." He feigned a yawn. "One would almost think you were raised by the village parson."

"Were I to behave otherwise, you would not want to give me charge of Clarissa."

He leaned back in his chair and regarded me. "But you are not in charge of my daughter this evening, are you?" he asked in a sly voice. "It would be more accurate to say you are in charge of me."

"I hardly think that is a proper assessment of the situation."

His smile broadened. "Have I shocked you, Miss Lane?"

"You have not."

"Really? I thought otherwise, but perhaps I am not as astute as I supposed."

"Indeed, you are not."

He stroked the curve of his glass with his forefinger, but all the while his gaze wandered over me. "Perhaps you should be shocked. I am told my behavior dismays all the proper young ladies in Cornish society. There is not one mother who wishes to see her daughter wed to me."

"You seem to take great pleasure in that knowledge." As much pleasure as he took in baiting me.

Dinner came as a respite. The few remarks he made were not challenging but pertained more to simple matters, such as my journey from London and my general comfort. But as soon as the plates were cleared, he looked at me again with greater interest.

"It is still early. You are not, I hope, of a mind to retire?"

Nothing would have pleased me more, but I acquiesced with a polite murmur.

"Good."

His dark eyes were bright with amusement and, again, I was convinced he knew exactly how I felt. If so, he was indifferent to my wishes. He settled back in his chair and stretched his legs beneath the table. He seemed to delight in each movement, taking a sensuous pleasure out of his own physicality, well aware that others could not or would not take the same pleasure.

"Perhaps you would be so good as to tell me something about yourself." He spoke in a deceptively polite manner, as though we were old friends taking tea together. "For all I know of you, you might well be a stranger and not a member of my own family."

For some odd reason, that remark unsettled me as his earlier assaults had not. "We are not related," I said, my back stiffening.

I might just as well have said nothing for all the attention he paid my words. He pressed his palms together and stared at me from across the tops of his fingers. "I am waiting."

"There is nothing to tell that you do not already know, milord." Even the thought of recounting my childhood memories for his ears made my throat tighten. I managed a half-hearted laugh. "I cannot imagine your wanting me to dwell on events that are of no interest to anyone other than me."

Something of my embarrassment must have been conveyed to him, and he dismissed the subject with a light wave. "Then you may talk of other matters."

Goodness. Did he expect me to expound upon a topic for his benefit, while he lounged in his chair and judged my arguments? Then he would be disappointed. I had learned to keep my opinions to myself. He might just as well have demanded that I stand up and remove each and every one of my garments. I flushed at the thought.

"Do you like the theater?" he asked when I did not speak.

"I have read plays, milord, but never seen any performed."

"Operas? Symphonies?"

"None that impressed me enough to expound upon them."

"Really, Miss Lane. You are a dull conversationalist."

"I am unused to delivering speeches. Nor do I wish to bore you. Perhaps, it would be better if I retired."

He stiffened and fixed me with a glare. "I have not dismissed you."

"Forgive me, milord. I had supposed—"

"It is not your place to suppose. Am I to expect that you will run from the room whenever I say something that upsets you?"

"Of course not, milord."

"Let us hope not, for it would do you no good. Very likely I would follow you to whatever sanctuary you sought and finish what I had begun."

"In the future, I shall wait until I am excused."

Reminding myself that I had determined not to provoke him that evening, I bent my head and clasped my hands neatly in my lap. In that pose, I waited.

"Good Lord!" he exclaimed. "Whatever faults you possess, I had not supposed you to be either meek or self-effacing. Am I mistaken? Have those loathsome traits been instilled in you?"

"Not to my knowledge," I retorted.

He swallowed the remains of his claret and banged the glass on the table. "What is the use of protestation? You sit at my table with your hands folded in your lap like some respectful schoolgirl. You dress in black—a color that in no way flatters your coloring—and pull back your hair with such determination that I can only suppose you wish to deny your youth and femininity. Those few sparks of temper you display on occasion are merely the dying embers of the child you once were. Soon, even they will be gone."

I gasped. "How dare you?"

"This is my home, and there is little I will not dare."

Any hope I'd had of holding my tongue vanished. "Good manners are completely wasted on you!" I cried. "But while I will suffer your rudeness, I will not endure attacks upon my person."

"I only speak the truth as I see it."

"What do you know of the truth? You know nothing of me, and you have no right to judge me. Especially not for my attire which was none of my choosing."

"Would you have me believe you did not order your own gowns?"

"I did not. Lady Wolfeburne had mourning clothes made up for all of us. Nor did she feel the need to include less somber gowns, given the position I was to assume."

"And did you bother to object? Or does gratitude for my brother's charity compel you to meek and unquestioning obedience?"

"If I saw signs of charity during my years at Wolfeburne House, then it was a mockery of that sentiment. Nor can I recall that I thought aught of your brother but that he was a foolish man given to indulging his wife and daughters for the sake of his own comfort."

At the end of this tirade, I became aware of the admission he had wrung from me and flushed. Lord Wolfeburne threw back his head and laughed, not with the reckless abandon that I had come to recognize, but with genuine amusement. It was the happiest I'd yet seen him.

"Poor Henry. He would be most offended to learn how little his largesse was appreciated."

"You had no right to provoke me," I muttered, unable

to lift my gaze from the tablecloth. "I would not have made those statements otherwise."

"But you did," he countered. "Selfish and stupid. Not your exact words, but certainly your sentiments. Or do you wish to retract them?"

I dared to glance at him. Apparently, he cared not at all that I had insulted his brother. Indeed, he seemed pleased. The darkness that hovered over him had faded, and he looked younger and decidedly more genial, as though his own troubles had been momentarily swept aside and forgotten.

Was that what he wanted?

At that instant, I became utterly convinced he had attacked me for no other reason than to stir me into a response. Any response as long as it distracted him from his own thoughts. He was watching me, like a cat waiting to see which way its prey would dart, enjoying the game without any need to make the kill. I felt the first warmth of outrage burning within me.

"That was cruel and unnecessary, milord. I felt no love for your brother or his family, but I had not intended to share those feelings with you."

"I see no reason why you should not. After all, I, more than anyone else, am likely to agree with you. Shall I assume, then, that you wear mourning clothes solely out of respect for convention?"

"If you wish."

"That is no answer."

And likely, if I did not give him one, he would return to his attack. I gave the matter a moment of serious consideration. "Given the choice, I find scandalous behavior preferable to hypocrisy."

"Be careful, Miss Lane. You will find you, too, are ousted from society."

"I would first have to be admitted."

His eyebrows lifted with genuine surprise. It seemed, despite his baiting, he held me in greater regard than had any member of his brother's family. That should have given me some comfort, but it did not. Instead, I grew increasingly uncomfortable, and would have been glad of the opportunity to resume the relatively unimportant role that had always been assigned me.

It was fortunate that an unrelated thought flashed into my mind and distracted me with a different concern. My gaze returned to his lordship. "I have been meaning to ask you a favor. Could you arrange for Clarissa to have some simpler gowns made up—some that would be suitable for walking on the moor?"

"You have only to instruct Mrs. Pendarves as to your wishes. You are in complete authority."

"Subject to your own, of course."

"I suspect my objections would carry little weight, should you choose to ignore them."

"You are mistaken."

"Am I? It was my impression that you meant to save my daughter." He paused, then added, "And to restore me to my former, insipid self."

I stifled another gasp. He was right in thinking I wanted to help Clarissa, but his second claim was outrageous. "You suspect me of too great an audacity. Besides, you were hardly insipid."

"Insipid, naive, and horribly boring."

"Nonsense, you were—" I broke off. Once again, he had been baiting me.

He lifted his knife and studied his own reflection. "What? No praise for my youthful charm. No hurled roses for my heroism?"

"The time when you deserved them is long past. And if it is your intention to spend the rest of the evening provoking me, I shall retire without your permission." I rose to leave.

He dropped the knife, and it clattered onto his side plate. "Please, stay." The mockery was gone from his voice, replaced by desperation. Again, I studied him, more certain than ever that he needed to be distracted.

"Am I to assume that I may expect kinder treatment at your hands than I have thus far received?"

He nodded and straightened in his chair, the image of the recalcitrant schoolboy. Only his guarded look and ever-watchful eyes warned me not to trust him. Warily, I settled back into my chair.

"And what shall we discuss?" he demanded. "Only refrain from boring me and I give you free rein to speak as you choose."

"There are two matters that confuse me," I said, watching him lest something in his face warn me to hold my tongue.

"And what are they?"

"First, there is the matter of Clarissa's last governess. Is it possible Miss Osborne could have met with some accident?"

To my relief, his expression remained the same, save perhaps for the thoughtful look in his eyes. "It is unlikely," he said after a slight pause. "She has been gone a month. If something unfortunate had occurred, surely it would have come to light."

"And yet the stationmaster said she did not take the train from Doublebois."

He shrugged. "She could have left from Liskeard, presuming she left by train. She may have met one of the local farmers and paid him to take her to Bodmin by cart."

"But she gave no notice."

"I made it plain upon hiring her that she would incur my utmost displeasure if she took it in her head to leave for any but the most dire circumstances."

"Nevertheless, I find it odd she left her belongings."

"Really, Miss Lane." His expression had grown bored. "Are you suggesting that she met with foul play and I disposed of her body?"

"Of course not."

"Good. For had I done so, I should certainly have had the foresight to dispose of her clothes at the same time. Take me for a murderer if you wish. But I shall trounce anyone who attempts to call me a fool."

"Neither was my intention," I said crossly. "But you cannot help but think her behavior odd."

"Again, I must disappoint you. More than one of Clarissa's governesses has slipped off without warning. To forestall just such an act, Mrs. Pendarves hid the poor woman's case in the attic. Had she wanted to take her wardrobe, she would have had to inform someone of her desire to leave."

"So that is why my portmanteau disappeared so promptly." I tried to fight back a smile and failed.

"And also why my daughter's last few governesses have enjoyed a luxurious suite and excellent care."

"A devious woman, your Mrs. Pendarves."

"But well-intentioned, you'll agree. As for the delinquent Miss Osborne, I fully expect her to send for her clothes when she has the courage to write. Are you satisfied?"

I nodded. "It seems I am more fanciful than I supposed."

"Wolfeburne Hall invites fancies," he responded in a more somber voice than I had heard that evening. His face darkened, but he threw off whatever memories had disturbed him and focused his attention on me again. "And what other matter confuses you? You referred to Miss Osborne as the first."

"It is presumptuous of me to ask."

"Delightful." There was a hint of that rakish grin I had seen earlier. "Should I agree, you must expect to be soundly and severely put in your place."

And with great enjoyment, no doubt. He took as much pleasure in reprimanding me as he did in baiting me. I hesitated, but curiosity compelled me to speak.

"It is the matter of the sheep." He stiffened, and I hurried on. "You were most upset that I delayed giving you the message. Of course, it may be none of my business, but is there some danger of which I should be aware?"

"You are quite right. It is none of your business."

He contemplated his glass, rapidly swilling the contents around and around. The red liquid rose nearer and nearer the brim, threatening to spill on to the pristine tablecloth. He seemed too absorbed or too disgruntled to care. I watched in fascination, not daring to speak.

At last, he set down his glass and lifted his head. "If there was any danger, I would be the first to inform you. But rather than give rise to more nonsensical notions, I will explain."

He pushed his dark hair back from his forehead, making me doubly aware of the deep furrows of his brow. "Over the years, the locals have lost a number of sheep. Most of the carcasses have been found in the vicinity of Wolfeburne Hall, and the farmers blame my dogs. The charge is ridiculous. But I would rather make restitution than awaken one morning to find the dogs poisoned by some malicious hand."

"Would anyone do such a thing?"

He sighed. "Some would. The sheep are, after all, necessary to their livelihood."

"But what of the animal that is truly doing the killing?" I demanded, outraged in his behalf.

He smiled faintly. "You must be more careful whom you champion, Miss Lane. You will find me a disappointing cause. But as to your question, the answer is simple enough. A wild dog. Or a sheepdog gone bad. I imagine the mystery will be solved eventually."

"And you are certain it could not be Castor or Pollux?"

"As certain as I am that I did not commit the act myself. More certain, since I am given to the unfortunate habit of drunkenness." He lifted the glass in his hand, but there was more braggadocio than apology in his smile. "So, have I answered your questions, or do you have more?"

"None. At least at the moment."

"Ah! I can look forward to others when your agile mind chances upon some other peculiarity in our day-to-day lives. You will find many. I am often accused of behaving in a contrary fashion."

"No doubt deliberately."

"Of what do you accuse me?"

"Merely of taking great delight in unsettling people. Am I mistaken?"

His eyes narrowed. "I wonder, Miss Lane. Are you always so astute? I see I shall have to be on my mettle when we talk."

"And I on mine. Since I seem to bear the brunt of your attacks and not the reverse."

"Do not underestimate your skill."

"I do not. I have learned to defend myself."

"Then there shall be no quarter needed?"

"Nor given?"

He grinned.

6

That night I awakened again to the sound of howls. I rose and ran to the window, although what I hoped to see I could not have said. Thin drifts of fog swirled past the window. The ruins were a gray blur in the moonlight, and the hedges that bordered the lawns a thick, charcoal colored line. I pressed my nose against the cold glass and squinted into the darkness, but saw nothing.

I shuddered and let the curtains fall. The misty night vanished behind folds of swaying velvet. But the sound of the dogs cut through their thickness and echoed off the walls, adding their strength to the shadows that lurked in the corners of my room.

Lord Wolfeburne was right. The Hall did give rise to dark fancies, and I had to be stern with myself if I did not want to add to Clarissa's fears. Convinced that she, too, would have been awakened, I lit my lamp and crossed the corridor to her room.

She was sitting up in bed, her large eyes wide with fright.

"Clarissa, you will catch cold if you keep throwing off your blankets in the middle of the night."

I stepped into the room, closing the door behind me in hopes of muffling the clamor. I might just as well have drawn a thin veil across an open doorway to keep out a chill wind.

"Is it another rabbit?" she asked, with a plaintive note.

I nodded and smiled. "Yes. They are chasing another rabbit. Come, now. Lie down and try to go to sleep."

"Did you see them?"

I wondered if I should tell her I had, then decided that would do more harm than good. Children had an uncanny knack for recognizing lies. "No, I did not. They must be around the far side of the Hall."

"But you are certain, nonetheless?"

"I am."

That seemed to satisfy her. With a sigh, she lay down and let me tuck the blankets around her chin, all the while watching me, searching my face for signs of any secrets that might have been hidden there.

I tried to make my actions natural and soothing, but my efforts were hampered by the rise and fall of those incessant howls. It was a wonder that anyone at the Hall managed to sleep at night. Surely there was something that could be done to keep the dogs quiet. That or they should have been banished, a notion that grew steadily in my favor.

After an interminable period, the racket stopped with an abruptness that startled me. Still, something seemed to linger in the silence. A feeling that something was amiss.

And who was to blame? Who allowed the dogs to run wild on their unholy hunts?

There was only one possible answer. Only one man whose word was law at the Hall.

By the time I had finished making Clarissa comfortable, I was furious with Lord Wolfeburne. How dare he allow this situation to continue? It was hardly surprising that the governesses in his employ departed in quick succession. More to the question was how had he managed to keep any servant for longer than a week—unless he chained them to their beds each night. I was of half a mind to rouse him from his sleep, drunken or otherwise, and demand that he give an accounting of himself and an explanation for his unconscionable disregard of his daughter.

There was a soft knock, and I glanced behind me to see the object of my fury. Lord Wolfeburne, clad only in his shirt and trousers, stood in the doorway. His gaze traveled beyond me to his daughter, and I was somewhat mollified by his obvious concern—although he had been a long while in making his appearance.

"Are you all right?" he asked her.

Clarissa smiled bravely. "Yes, Papa."

"Miss Lane told me the dogs have been disturbing you."

She glanced at me, then said, "I was not really afraid, Papa. But I could not help waking. They are so loud."

"Of course you could not. But why have I not heard of this before?"

"I did not want you to worry. I am much braver than . . . than Mama."

Her faltering words brought tears to my eyes, and Lord Wolfeburne was forced to swallow hard before he could speak. "I am proud of you. But in the future, if something upsets you, you must tell me or Miss Lane."

"But you have so many things to worry about."

"Promise me, Clarissa."

"Yes, Papa."

I wondered if she would keep her promise. It was so obvious that she wanted him to be proud of her. Her eyes shone with love and childish worship. I was reminded of the feelings of admiration I had once held for this same man. Was it only to children that he could be a hero? With whom he could be gentle and understanding? And did he know that, to more experienced eyes, he would be found lacking?

Certainly, I was not as willing as she to forgive him. "Do you have any control whatsoever over those animals?" I demanded.

He turned to me. "I roused Wilkins and advised him to attend to the matter before coming upstairs." Instead of rebuking me for my rudeness as I deserved, his eyes silently pleaded for forgiveness.

Abruptly, our gazes met. I realized I was wearing nothing more than my dressing gown, and my braids were falling about my shoulders like those of a schoolgirl. I crossed my arms over my chest protectively and delivered him a look that I hoped would have chastened the worst scoundrel.

"I will sit with Clarissa until she falls asleep," I announced. "There is no need for you to stay."

"And that will make two nights that you have gone without your rest."

"You need not waste your concern on me."

"I can hardly leave you to make amends for my own failures, Miss Lane."

"Clarissa is my responsibility."

"She is *my* daughter."

There was a finality to his tone that forbade further argument. He gave me no choice but to do as he had ordered, although that would necessitate my walking nearer to him than I would have liked, given my state of undress.

Reluctantly, I bade Clarissa good-night and forced myself to walk toward the door. If Lord Wolfeburne was aware of my discomfort, he feigned ignorance. Nor did he seem in a hurry to let me pass. I halted and looked at him pointedly.

His gaze rested upon my face, and a hint of a smile played about his lips. "Was there something else, Miss Lane?"

"There is not," I answered. "But if it is your intention to continue standing in the doorway, I shall have no choice but to remain."

"Forgive me, my thoughts were elsewhere."

He stepped aside to let me withdraw. In doing so, his sleeve brushed across my hand, sending a jolt up my arm that made me flinch. I scanned his face to discover if the act had been deliberate. My expression must have reflected my inner tumult, for his smile deepened.

If the act was not intentional, certainly he took great pleasure in seeing me lose my composure. I supposed he meant to make me suffer a little of the humiliation that he had suffered at my hands but a short while ago. That he might have had another motive, I would not allow. Even he could not be such a scoundrel as to flirt with me in his daughter's bedroom.

I escaped into the corridor, and only a sense of dignity kept me from running back to the safety of my own room. Upon reaching my door, I glanced back to find him watching me. There was an odd look in his eyes that I could not decipher.

Nor did I waste time in trying, but hurried inside. A moment before the door latched, he murmured something, but the words escaped me. I thought for a moment he had said, "Good-night, *Jessamy*."

But surely I was mistaken.

I lingered at my looking glass the next morning, attempting to coil my hair into a loose chignon. Three times I wound the chignon, and three times I pulled out the pins immediately upon seeing my reflection. The result was flattering, but unfamiliar and oddly disconcerting. At last, with a soft cry of exasperation, I braided my hair and coiled the braid into a tight knot. Only then, did I feel ready to leave my suite.

Clarissa skipped into the schoolroom. The circles beneath her eyes were darker, but she was smiling and her movements were less hesitant. Her father's attentiveness had made a noticeable improvement in her mood, and it pained me to see how eagerly she had responded to that simple show of parental patience and goodwill.

I soon realized that his presence had also instilled in her a desire to excel at her lessons. She struggled through the morning with a dedication that at first startled and later dismayed me. There was a feverish intensity to her determination that allowed for nothing less than perfection.

"Everyone makes mistakes when they learn something

new," I said, fearing she would exhaust herself if she continued in this manner.

She nodded dutifully, but her gaze remained fixed to her book.

At last, the clock struck noon, and I insisted she leave her studies. "That is more than enough work for one day. At this rate, I shall soon have nothing to teach you."

Her ringlets bounced about her face, and she gave Matilda a squeeze. "And will you tell that to Papa?" she asked.

"If that is what you wish."

She nodded happily.

I did not share her feelings. The man was entirely undeserving of her adoration. But perhaps the experience of the previous night would persuade him that something must be done about Castor and Pollux. I was determined to speak with him on the matter before the day was out, although it would have to wait until after Clarissa and I had taken our afternoon walk.

I had that morning spoken to the housekeeper about having a couple of sturdy dresses made up for her, but it would be some while before that could be accomplished. In the meantime, I supposed a stroll down the lane could be managed without undue difficulty.

Mrs. Pendarves nodded to us in the entry hall. Her gaze strayed to Clarissa's too bright face, and her brows knitted together in a frown.

"I thought a walk to the crossroads might be good for both of us," I said cheerfully, not wanting her to make her concerns obvious.

Mrs. Pendarves turned her attention to me. "Have you tired of the garden already, then?"

"No. But Clarissa has seen much more of them than I, and young minds soon grow restless if they are not stimulated."

This was not the entire truth. It was my wish to remove her, at least temporarily, from the influence of the Hall. Nor did I want to remain in the garden where her gaze would wander again and again to the ruins. There was something menacing in that solitary tower and the ominous shadow it cast.

If Mrs. Pendarves suspected me of prevarication, she did not attempt to probe for the truth. She wished us a pleasant afternoon and went about her business, leaving me to wonder if she suspected and approved of my motives.

Outside, a light breeze blew off the moor and tantalized our nostrils with the fragrance of gorse and heather. There was a wildness to the land that made me think of times long past, when Cornwall belonged to the early peoples who built the strange beehive huts and buried their dead beneath the stone quoits. I had the strangest feeling that, had my feet carried me but a short distance down the winding sheep and rabbit trails, I should have found myself returned to those ancient days.

I shook off my odd thoughts and bent my energies to interesting Clarissa in the bright flowers we passed along the sides of the lane—the buttercups, hairbells, red campions, and purple knapweed. This last, I assured her, was not a thistle, despite its prickly appearance. By the time we reached the crossroads, she was gripping a colorful bouquet in both hands, and the ever-present Matilda had been entrusted to my care.

Our nature lesson was interrupted by the sight of a black carriage pulled by a chestnut gelding. An austere gentleman and an attractive young woman sat inside the buggy, the latter chattering with all the animation that her companion lacked, although we could not hear her words.

We smiled and stood to one side to let them pass but, upon seeing us, the gentleman tapped his driver with his cane and ordered him to pull up on the reins. The carriage rolled to a halt directly across from us, and the gentleman leaned forward to peer at us from behind his spectacles.

"Lady Clarissa." He tipped his hat to her.

His companion's gaze went directly to me. She was slight and fair, with well-shaped features and the thickest lashes I had ever seen on a woman. "And are you the new governess?" she inquired without preliminaries. Her voice and expression were curious, but not brusque or unfriendly.

"This is Jessamy," Clarissa said. "She is more than just my governess. We are almost cousins."

I blanched, embarrassed that she should cast me in so important and false a light. "I was raised by Lord Wolfeburne's brother," I said quickly. "And I have come to take care of Clarissa."

The gentleman studied me, his gaze wandering from my face to my sober gown. Apparently, my appearance met with some approval, for he nodded and his lips spread in a grimace that may have been intended as a smile. "And a very good thing, too. Lady Clarissa needs someone in her life who possesses some sense of responsibility."

"Yes. Lord Wolfeburne has had the most unfortunate luck with governesses," I said.

He snorted and started to speak, but the young woman laid a slender hand upon his sleeve. "Really, Father. Don't you think you should introduce us?" Without waiting for him to reply, she leaned forward and offered me her hand. "I am Sarah Pengelley, and this is my father, Sir Ronald. We are your nearest neighbors. Pengelley Manor lies off to the east, less than five miles distant."

Her father snorted again, but his daughter nudged him and he pretended he was only clearing his throat.

Miss Pengelley continued in spite of him. "You must come to tea on Sunday. And Lord Wolfeburne with you. He has always been rather solitary, but I think his elevated position will place greater demands on him. It would be our pleasure to offer our support."

She glanced at her father's face, and he returned a scowl. Nevertheless, whatever his objections, she had committed them both. In a firmer voice than I would have expected someone of her size and demeanor to possess, she concluded, "We shall expect you at three."

"It is hardly my place to accept invitations for his lordship," I said.

"Naturally I shall send a more formal invitation by post."

"And I will advise him of your kindness. Doubtless, he will send a note to let you know if he is able to join you."

Sir Ronald gave his daughter a speaking glance, which she ignored. "If he cannot attend, then the two of you must come alone. I would consider it a kindness, for there are too few ladies of my own age in the neighborhood, and I would dearly like a friend."

"If his lordship gives his permission, it would be our pleasure to join you."

There seemed no reason why he would not, and yet already I knew Lord Wolfeburne well enough not to suppose he would always act in a reasonable fashion. Nevertheless, I intended to use all my strength to prevail upon him to let us go, for it would do Clarissa good to be away from the Hall.

Sir Ronald and his daughter bade us good afternoon and their carriage veered to the east. We watched them leave, then turned and set off homeward. Clarissa trotted at my side, chattering about what she would wear and wishing aloud that Sir Ronald had a daughter nearer her own age.

Upon reaching the Hall, I sent her off to ask Mrs. Pendarves or Mary for a vase for her wildflowers. I went in search of Lord Wolfeburne. The invitation from Sir Ronald gave me an excuse to approach him, and I intended to use the opportunity to bring up the subject of the dogs.

I was tensed for a difficult confrontation. But having set myself upon that path, I forced my reluctant feet to carry me to the study. My soft rap echoed through the corridor, making my intrusion and impertinence seem all the greater.

Several seconds passed, but there was no answer. I started to leave, but a sudden flash of insight made me try again. It was well within Lord Wolfeburne's character to ignore an interruption if he did not wish to be disturbed. If that was his intent, then he would find me harder to dismiss than one of his maids.

I let my hand drop to the doorknob. It turned easily.

Taking a deep breath, I pushed the door ajar. A few words escaped the room, but immediately broke off. I recognized the voice as belonging to his lordship, although the sentence fragment spoken was too brief to be anything but meaningless.

Without even poking my head inside, I called, "Lord Wolfeburne, are you there? I must speak with you."

There was an impatient growl that I tried to convince myself had come from the dogs.

"Milord?"

"Don't stand there dithering in the corridor," he replied. "Either come in or go away."

"I have not been invited."

"That fact did not restrain you from opening my door," he retorted.

I stepped inside. The curtains had been pulled open, and the study was lit with sunshine. My gaze went immediately to the windows. With an odd sense of shock I realized that from this angle one could see the ruins. Although why that should have startled me, I wasn't certain. Perhaps it was simply their grim nature.

Or was it because I had always supposed that, when Lord Wolfeburne stared out into the mist, it was the gardens or the moors he was envisioning?

"Is there a reason for this interruption?" he demanded, drawing my thoughts back to him.

It was then that I noticed he was not alone. The grim-faced Wilkins stood at the side of his desk, his brows drawn together and his lips twisted into a scowl.

Refusing to surrender to a similar feeling of ill will, I smiled at him pleasantly and turned to his lordship. "Please forgive me for disturbing you. But you did insist that I immediately convey any messages I was given."

Lord Wolfeburne stiffened, and his face looked suddenly haggard.

"It is an invitation to tea," I added. "From Sir Ronald Pengelley and his daughter."

"Is that all?"

He straightened immediately, and I realized he had taken greater care with his appearance that day. His shirt was clean and pressed, his neckcloth properly tied, and his black hair had been neatly combed. He had the look, if not the spirit, of the young man I remembered.

Lord Wolfeburne glanced at Wilkins, then back to me, and folded his arms across his chest. "And must we discuss this now?"

"Was I wrong in coming to you directly?" I asked, feigning complete innocence.

He snorted. "And there you have me, do you not? For if I dare to say yes, you will use my words against me on some other occasion when it pleases you to ignore my dictates. Wilkins, it seems we must finish our business later."

The steward made a low grunt in his throat and nodded stiffly. After shooting me one last glare, he shuffled out.

"What a singularly unpleasant fellow," I remarked when we were alone.

The hint of a smile flickered about his lordship's lips. "He is useful in his own fashion. But you had something to tell me, did you not?"

"Of course. Sir Ronald and his daughter would like us to join them Sunday at three, if you are able." I took a breath, but dared not pause lest he refuse out of hand.

"But should it be inconvenient, they insist that Clarissa and I go anyway. It would be good for her to get away, and the Pengelleys seem pleasant people—"

"Good Lord. Am I to be allowed an opportunity to answer, or have you already accepted for all of us?"

"Of course not. I only thought—"

"Enough. I shall consider the matter. But that is not what I meant when I asked you if you had something to tell me."

"Milord?"

"Oh, come now, Miss Lane. Do you think me foolish enough to believe that an invitation from Sir Ronald sent you rushing into my study. What is the real reason for your visit?"

"There *was* another matter," I said.

He gave a short laugh. "Well, then, Miss Lane. What is this latest complaint?"

"Hardly a complaint. More of a concern."

"Mere quibbling, Miss Lane. That is beneath you."

"Do you wish to hear me out or not?" I demanded.

"Perhaps we should sit down. I find conversations with you always drain me of my usual strength."

His dark eyes mocked me, and I questioned how I could have thought him, even for a brief moment, anything like his youthful self. The gentlemanly demeanor was but a brittle veneer, ready to shatter at the slightest touch. Nevertheless, I took my seat on the settee and waited until he made himself comfortable in the wing chair.

He pressed his fingers together and stared at me from across them. "Shall we proceed?"

I nodded. "For two nights following, Clarissa's sleep

has been disturbed. Moreover, the dogs frighten her in a way I do not understand."

"What exactly do you mean?" he demanded, leaning forward with increased interest.

"I cannot explain, for it makes no sense to me."

He relaxed back into his chair with studied casualness. "And what would you have me do?"

There was a false ring to his pleasantly asked question. Knowing I treaded on dangerous ground, I suggested, "Perhaps they could remain indoors at night."

"Then you are not insisting I sell them?"

"It is not my place to insist anything."

"That has always been my contention, but I am not convinced it is also yours."

"Good heavens. You cannot expect me to remain silent when Clarissa's health is jeopardized. Nor would I, if that was your wish."

"Your concern for her could not possibly exceed my own."

"Indeed, it *should* not."

He glared at me, a hard stare that allowed him to pierce my defenses while maintaining his own. His silence and the intensity of that stare accomplished what his words had failed to do. I was wholly discomfited.

It occurred to me that I was vulnerable to whatever moods should possess him. My unease was exacerbated by the memory of his whispered good-night the previous evening. In those moments we sat there, I became convinced that I had heard correctly. This wasn't a man who allowed himself to be inhibited by the morals and standards of others of his rank. My throat constricted, and my cheeks grew warm.

At last, he took pity on me and said, "Tell me, Miss Lane. What is the good of having dogs to guard the estate if they are locked indoors at night?"

I forced myself to assume a natural tone. "This is not London, milord. The countryside hereabouts seems quiet enough and the people honest."

"What of the animal savaging the sheep?"

"You do not keep sheep at the Hall. And even if you did, surely Clarissa's well-being is more important than that of mere livestock."

He rose and stared down at me. "It would be wiser for you to attend to your duties and teach my daughter the difference between fantasy and reality."

His autocratic manner infuriated me. "She is only nine years old. And in some ways, young for her age. It is too soon to expect her to show the discernment of an adult."

"In some cases, perhaps. But not in this one. It is important that she learn to control her imagination."

"And why is that?"

"Because she is *my* daughter."

"That is nothing more than arrogant nonsense." I rose to leave. But my anger did not allow me to depart without a final thrust. I fixed him with my most withering stare. "I had supposed that you, as her father, would be more sympathetic."

His eyes narrowed. "Do not try my temper too far, Miss Lane. I may find your effrontery amusing, but there are times when I do not like to be crossed."

"Is there nothing I can say that will make you reconsider?"

"The dogs are to remain on guard at night. That is

their job. But if it in any way consoles you, I have advised Wilkins that he is to leave his bed and silence them whenever they give vent to that awful racket."

His announcement deflated me as he had no doubt intended. He had already dealt with the matter, yet allowed me to labor under the assumption that there was a problem that needed attention. Had I been a lady, and on equal footing with his lordship, I would have soundly given him my opinion of his perversity.

"You might have told me," I said.

"And you might have assumed I would recognize the problem for myself. And act accordingly. Nor was I aware that it was my duty to report my decisions to you."

"Of all the high-handed—" I broke off and struggled to regain my self-control. "I am only concerned about Clarissa's welfare. And if I behaved presumptuously, you should have rebuked me at the onset of this conversation and saved me greater embarrassment."

A lazy smile spread across his face. "But then I would have been denied the enjoyment of your company. And of watching your temper flare. Do you know that your face becomes quite animated when you are angry? And your eyes and cheeks suffuse with color. Most becoming. Truly." He lifted his hand and brushed his finger across my cheek.

Tiny shocks coursed through me. I jerked my head away as though I had been struck. "It is unkind of you to mock me, and unbefitting a gentleman."

With some sadness, he let his hand drop. "It is a long while since I have been accused of being a gentleman. Did Sir Ronald fail to give you a description of my character?"

Still reeling from the shock he had given me, I answered stiffly. "You are mistaken. He said nothing untoward." And I could hardly be expected to presume disparaging remarks from what he had merely intimated.

Lord Wolfeburne chuckled. "How remiss of him. Nonetheless, I assume the invitation came from Miss Pengelley and not her father."

"You may assume whatever you wish."

"You are being childish."

"If so, it is because you have reduced me to your level."

He shook his head. "I refuse to take the blame for any behavior other than my own. That is burden enough for any man to bear."

I could not help but smile, and my good humor seemed to restore his geniality. I took the opportunity to press him to accept the Pengelleys' invitation. "It will be good for Clarissa."

He shrugged. "As you wish. And now, if there is nothing else . . . ?"

"No, milord."

I started to leave—rather to escape, for that was how it seemed to me. I had no sooner taken a step when I stopped abruptly, hit by a realization that had previously eluded me. "Good heavens," I blurted out.

"Is something wrong?"

"The dogs. Good heavens, the dogs. How could Miss Osborne have disappeared from the estate at night with Castor and Pollux on guard?"

To my surprise, instead of being startled by my revelation, he shook his head and chuckled softly. "I shall leave you to discover the solution on your own. You have an agile mind, one that appears to need puzzles to unravel."

"What nonsense."

"If you grow impatient"—he continued, as if I had not spoken—"or find this too difficult a challenge, I suggest you question your pupil. You will find, as I have discovered, she can be quite enlightening."

7

Lord Wolfeburne's cryptic remark left me in a quandary. I thought it foolish to reveal to Clarissa my doubts regarding Miss Osborne's fate, even if she could provide me with some answers. Then, again, his lordship did not think the matter would be upsetting or he would not have directed me to her. But did he know his daughter as well as he should? He had failed to note how the dogs' howls upset her.

Caught up in my thoughts, I climbed the stairs and wandered through the gallery. The curtains had been drawn, telling me the hour was growing late. Another evening would soon be upon us. I shivered. Already, I looked forward to the nights at Wolfeburne Hall with foreboding.

In my sitting room, the curtains had also been drawn, and Mary had not yet departed. With her back to me, she was bending over one of the lamps. She jumped at the sound of my door shutting, and the lamp wobbled on the table.

She turned around and gave a sigh of relief. "Oh, it's only 'ee, miss."

"And who did you think it would be?" I regarded her startled face with some amusement.

She flushed and managed a sheepish smile. "Only 'ee or Missus Pendarves. But I does get queasy. Working up here, all by myself."

"And why is that?"

She shrugged, and a frown creased her pleasant face. "Couldn't say, miss. Could be the emptiness. In servants' wing, someone's allus about, chattering or complaining. And at night, I shares a room with Alice. She'm sister and works in kitchen."

"I suppose that makes living at the Hall a pleasanter proposition. I could not help wondering why you would stay somewhere where you weren't comfortable."

"Oh, it's wages, miss." Her frown disappeared. "His lordship pays better'n anyone herebouts, and there's six other chillun to home."

So it was necessity then that kept her there. I supposed it was the same with the rest of the servants. "You are not put off by the howls of the dogs?"

She shuddered, but there was more theatrics than actual fear in her face. "They does make an awful racket. But it's harder to hear them from servants' wing. And Alice and I stuff our ears with batting. To help us sleep. I could bring you some, if 'twould help."

I smiled. However much I disliked the dogs' noise, I was not yet reduced to quivering beneath the blankets of my bed. "Thank you, but no. It would make it difficult to hear Clarissa if she called for me."

Mary nodded. "That's good of 'ee. Didn't bother

Miss Osborne to ask for summat. Said her couldn't get any rest of a night. And her weren't first to ask, I assure 'ee. Though others didn't mind telling they was scared. Not like Miss Osborne," she added in a scoffing tone.

I seized the opening she had given me. "I wonder why she left as she did, if she was telling the truth. If she was well paid, then it could not have been for money. Perhaps there was a man she wanted to marry?"

Mary snorted. "Not she, miss. Oh, her might have fallen in love, but her weren't kind of woman that'd make a man take notice. Her weren't pretty like 'ee. Her was bookish, and awful plain. 'Ee knows sort. Spectacles, and face that'd curdle milk. God forgive me for plain speaking, but her'll go to grave a spinster, I'd say."

"Then what could have possessed her to disappear as she did?" I said, more to myself than to Mary. I was at a loss to understand the woman's actions.

Mary leaned toward me, and her voice dropped to a confidential whisper. "I think her took to looking out at fog of a night. Tedn' good for a body." She gave me a knowing nod.

I looked at her, completely perplexed. "And what is there about the fog that would have bothered her?"

"Can do odd things to a mind. And fog that blows off moor round Wolfeburne Hall ain't like no other. There are things in't."

"What kind of things?"

"Unnatural things."

"But what kind of unnatural things?"

She shivered again. "I wouldn't know, miss. I don't

look out windows. Not less sun's shining and 'ee can see clear across moor."

"But then has somebody seen something to make you feel this way?" I was determined to have some answer.

She shook her head. "Ain't nobody foolish enough to try. Save maybe Miss Osborne. 'Ee take my advice and don't go looking about at night. Won't do 'ee no good and might do 'ee a deal of harm."

"Thank you, Mary," I said, trying to match her earnestness with my own. "I shall remember what you have said."

But despite her sincerity, the advice left me more amused than dismayed. Mary had seen and heard nothing untoward, but merely feared she might. Her speculation that Miss Osborne had been frightened away was nothing more than a projection of her own fears. The only new piece of information I had gained was that Lord Wolfeburne paid dearly to keep his help. Given his behavior, and the gloomy atmosphere of the Hall, I was not much surprised.

Nevertheless, convinced that she had advised me well, Mary returned to her tasks with a lighter step. Just when I thought she had done, her tongue clucked with annoyance.

"Is something wrong?" I asked.

She shook her head. "Just my forgetting again. I meant to bring 'ee up another lamp from kitchen. One gone from table by door. 'Twas real nice. Rose-colored with brass fittings. I looked all round last evening and couldn't find it anywhere."

I glanced at the gate-leg table. It was bare, save for a tatted doily, but nothing seemed amiss. "I do not recall ever seeing a lamp on that table."

"Maybe Missus Pendarves put it in one of t'other rooms afore 'ee comed. Though why her'd do that, I wouldn't know. Never mind. I'll bring one up when I'm done. The corner needs lightening."

She bobbed her head politely and hurried off. I walked slowly into the bedroom, still contemplating her words, and wandered to the wardrobe to put away my walking boots. To my surprise, I discovered my portmanteau perched atop the wardrobe. Had Mary placed it there? And why?

Hoping she had not yet gone downstairs, I hurried into the corridor and called for her. A moment later, coal scuttle clutched in her hands, Mary stepped out of Clarissa's bedroom.

"Was there something else 'ee needed, miss?"

"Just a question to ask. I wondered why my bag had been brought down from the attic."

"Lord Wolfeburne said 'twas to be brought down to 'ee."

That was the last answer I would have expected. "And did he say why?"

"No, miss." She shrugged. "I'd supposed 'ee had asked him for it."

"No, I did not."

"That's queer, 'en. 'Ee'd better ask *him*, miss. Him is kind of man who do keep his own counsel."

"Indeed, he is."

Had Lord Wolfeburne invited me to share his supper again that evening, I would have taken her advice, but apparently he was content to dine alone. Clarissa and I ate supper in the schoolroom with only Matilda for company.

It was a quiet meal. She bent her dark head over her food with the absorption she displayed toward her books, and she chewed each bite carefully and thoroughly. Matilda stared at her from the railback chair, her bisque face politely interested, and I did the same from across the heavy deal table.

I had no awareness of what I ate, for my thoughts were fully devoted to deciding how best to fashion the question I wanted to ask. At last, I set down my fork and smiled brightly. "Your father has promised me your sleep will not be disrupted tonight. He has put his steward to the task of silencing the dogs. I'm certain the formidable Wilkins is more than their match."

She smiled wanly, but did not appear greatly cheered, so I went on.

"He was quite cross with Miss Osborne when he heard of her behavior. But perhaps she did not want to tell him how Castor and Pollux upset you lest he realize that she, too, was frightened by their howls."

Clarissa looked up from her plate and laughed. "But that's silly." Her brow puckered. "It seemed she did not like them much at first. Indeed, she told me dogs were dirty creatures and should not be brought into a decent house. But it was not long before she took a great liking to Castor and Pollux."

"And why was that?"

"They are sweet animals when you come to know them. I suppose she could not help herself. She used to save bits of meat from her plate and give them to Castor and Pollux when Papa was not looking. It was a secret between us, for she knew he would disapprove. She made me promise to say nothing. Was it wrong of me not to tell Papa?"

My attention left the odd habits of Miss Osborne to consider this philosophical question. "It is not nice to tell tales," I said. "But if you think someone is doing something wrong or harmful, it would be worse to keep that a secret."

"Feeding Castor and Pollux didn't hurt them."

"No, indeed it did not."

But perhaps the woman had deliberately made friends with the dogs with the intention of slipping away secretly one night. Her decision to leave the Hall must have been made well in advance of her actual departure. I wondered that she had not also thought of some way to retrieve her cases from the attic.

But this was why the dogs had not forestalled her escape. I regarded Clarissa again. "I wonder how your father came to learn of this? For surely he must have known."

She nodded. "I did not mean to tattle, but he was so worried when she disappeared. No one could find her, and he did not think she could have left the Hall with the dogs on guard. I had to tell him they would not have stopped her." She gave me a look that begged for reassurance.

"You were exactly right in speaking up," I told her. "It would have been unfair to continue to keep a secret when everyone was worried. And with Miss Osborne gone, you did her no disservice."

Clarissa smiled. "That was what I thought."

Still, there was a darkness to her face that was not relieved by my praise, and she attacked the last of her trifle with such determination, I suspected there was more she was not saying.

"I can also keep a secret," I told her. "If ever you need to speak in confidence."

She lifted her face and studied mine. Her lips quivered, but no words came forth. Somewhere behind her eyes, there was a war being waged, and her fork twitched between her fingers.

Worried that she would make herself ill, I reached out my hand to hers. "You do not have to tell me anything. But if ever that is what you wish, I am always willing to listen."

She took a deep breath and some of the tension dissipated.

I wished I could have shared in her relief. More and more I grew concerned about her. What secrets did she hold?

And what damage did they do her?

That night passed in silence, and Clarissa returned to the schoolroom the next day looking well rested and decidedly more cheerful. Once again, she attacked her lessons with a passion. Her questions, too, were intelligent and discerning, and I realized she had a mind that needed to be kept occupied lest it be turned to darker thoughts.

Not long after we had begun, the housekeeper knocked at the door. Behind her stood a tall, reedy woman, well dressed, with a no-nonsense look that suggested she was both capable and well aware of her competence.

Mrs. Pendarves ushered her into the room and announced, "This is Miss Reager. I hope you will forgive the interruption, but she has come to take Clarissa's measurements. And yours," she added in a softer voice.

"*Mine?*" I rose from my chair.

"His lordship says you are to have some suitable dresses made up at the same time."

"B-but I have more than enough dresses to keep me," I stammered. "And when I need more, it is my responsibility to purchase them out of my own earnings."

Looking every bit the obedient schoolgirl, Mrs. Pendarves folded her hands and nodded. "Of course, you must do as you think best. But it might be advisable to go and tell his lordship. He does not like his orders to be countermanded."

From the slight smile on her lips, I knew she expected me to surrender at the mere thought of confronting him. "I will speak to him immediately," I said. "Is he in his study?"

She nodded. "Miss Reager can begin with Clarissa. There's enough light in the schoolroom for her needs."

Clearly, she expected me to return in defeat. I lifted my chin, determined she would be both surprised and disappointed.

The door to the study stood open. I raised my hand to knock, but before that was managed, Lord Wolfeburne ordered me to enter.

He sat behind his desk, his feet on its cluttered surface and a mocking smile on his lips. "Ah! Miss Lane. I've been expecting you. Mrs. Pendarves advised me the seamstress had arrived." His dark eyes were bright with laughter.

My annoyance deepened. Once again, he was deliberately provoking me. "You are entirely without conscience or sense of propriety."

"Without conscience? I have never thought otherwise. It has always been your contention I was less disreputable than I appeared. But improper? For wishing to see my ward *properly* clothed?" His odd emphasis suggested that his true intentions were very different.

Strangely, it was not that portion of his statement that scraped on my nerves. "It is time we ended this playacting," I said. "I am hardly your ward. I am nothing more than a young woman from a questionable background who was raised in charity. I doubt my antecedents are any more respectable than Mary's. Probably less. I ask nothing more than the salary that would normally be paid to someone in my position. Out of that, I shall arrange for my own dresses, if and when there is a need for them."

To my dismay, he swung his legs off the desk and rose. I was reminded again of the first time we spoke in his study, for his movements were every bit as quick and decisive. He was hardly recognizable as the same person who lounged in chairs and swallowed down spirits as though they were nothing more than weak tea.

In less time than it took for me to catch my breath, he had circumnavigated his desk and now stood before me, so near that I could see the faint shadow of his beard upon his jaw. He contemplated me with the fierceness of some barbarian warrior, and it took all my courage not to shrink back against the settee.

"As you say, Miss Lane. Let us be done with games. Perhaps my offer does not satisfy the demands of propriety. If so, then all the better. I have scorned propriety for many years and found myself none the worse for its loss." There was a firmness in his voice I would have admired, had he directed his authority to more appropriate matters. "However," he continued, "I do consider you my ward. And, as such, feel it well within my rights—indeed, my responsibility—to provide for you."

"But—"

"As for salary, I intended to provide you with an allowance. A fact I had not yet mentioned for, at the moment, you have no need for money."

I gaped at him. "An allowance?"

"It is more in keeping with your position here."

"On the contrary. It is not."

His face darkened and his body grew taut. I could sense the hardness of the muscles hidden beneath his gentlemanly attire, and was horribly conscious of the power he exerted to control himself.

In a voice that was dangerously soft, he said, "I will not have you confuse me with my brother, Miss Lane. On the whole, I found his behavior deplorable, and nothing that you have said of him persuades me to alter that opinion."

My palms felt excessively moist, and my heartbeat raced. I was suffused with a desperate need to flee. Only the knowledge that it would do me no good—and the prohibitive positioning of his solid frame—kept me seated.

I swallowed and forced myself to consider what he had

said about his brother. Some distraction could be had there. Lord Wolfeburne was, I concluded, justified in speaking as he did. I had allowed him to believe the worst.

"I have spoken out of turn," I said, my mouth horribly dry. "I had no right to criticize." I dropped my gaze, convinced that my apology and shame would bring an abrupt end to our argument.

But his lordship had no such compunction. "Am I to believe you have lied to me?" he demanded.

Anger replaced shame and my chin jerked upward again. "Of course not."

Our gazes met. Instead of reproach and disgust, I read compassion in his eyes. That and an awareness beyond anything I would have expected from him. He seemed to have known that, had he offered sympathy, I might have given way to tears. Instead he had deliberately aroused my temper.

If he guessed the direction of my thoughts, he did not let me contemplate them for long. "Then every word was the truth?" he asked.

I gathered the shreds of my self-composure about me. "The truth, perhaps. But not a truth that managed to make clear that it was your brother who fed and clothed me, who provided for my education, and whose roof sheltered me."

He chuckled and his expression softened. "As it happens, I myself must offer him the same gratitude. Until his death the Hall was his. I lived beneath his roof with my family, and fed them with monies he paid me. But I assure you, he did not act out of love or charity. It served his purposes to have me here, and the only sacrifices made were made by me. And by my poor wife who had a dread of the place," he muttered, almost to himself.

He shook off the unpleasant memory, and his voice gained strength again. "It also served his purposes to take you into his home, and only the need to maintain appearances prevented him from casting you back into the streets when Annabelle's birth made your presence unnecessary."

"But if that is your opinion, then you can hardly look upon me as your ward." As I pointed this out, I felt myself on safer ground, although he was still too near to me for any real comfort.

His annoying smile returned. "You think you have won your point, do you not? It is my pleasure to disappoint you. I may have no legal cause to refer to you as my ward. And, admittedly, I demand services that would not be expected of you under more usual circumstances. Nevertheless, I still regard you as being under my care and, in some fashion, a part of the Wolfeburne family."

Again I felt that odd need to rebel, to push him from me or surrender to absolute panic. He straightened, as though aware of my distress, and stepped to the edge of the hearth where he regarded me with a look of speculation. The clock on the mantel ticked loudly in the silence, while he twisted thoughtfully at the ring on his finger.

At last, he said, "But if you prefer to believe yourself merely a hireling, then you will do as everyone else in my employ does and obey my orders. Either way, you are to submit to being measured for a few decent dresses."

"I may be required to obey orders," I retorted, bracing myself for the fight to come, "but only if those orders fall within the realms of accepted behavior. Certainly you cannot demand I act in a fashion that would force everyone to question the true nature of our relationship."

He contemplated this remark, appearing to savor the possibilities. The look in his eyes seemed unduly warm and familiar. I struggled to catch my breath. Around me, the air in the room had grown thick and the walls too close.

Then he shrugged. "There is unlikely to be any questions asked, as you are the only person who fails to regard yourself as my ward."

With that announcement, he turned his back on me and strolled to the windows. There, he clasped his hands behind him and rocked back on his heels, apparently satisfied that the matter had been settled. His utter arrogance, abetted by the irrational fears he had roused, infuriated me.

"Certainly, milord, you must think as you wish. I suppose I should be flattered and appreciative." Although I felt only a sense of extreme disquiet. "But do not think for one instant that your generosity permits you to dictate to me. I will not have it. Nor will I submit to your flagrant abuse of your authority." I rose to leave.

He turned. The haggard expression had returned to his eyes, and his gaze sought mine with a desperation that undid me as his arrogance had not. I wanted to reach out to him, but there was something in his manner that refused either comfort or pity.

In a strained voice, he asked, "If you will not do as I bid, then will you agree to a humble request? There is already too much darkness in this damned Hall, and Clarissa has seen enough of mourning dress. Your persistence in this matter will only present her with a daily reminder of her mother's death. Had you strong feelings for my brother, I would not ask this of you. But as you do not, only social convention is offended."

Refusal would have been impossible; nor would I have tried. "Why did you not say this before?" I asked. "Did you think I am so heartless as to disregard her feelings?"

"No, I did not," he admitted with a sigh.

"Then why must you make a battle of something that required nothing more than a few words of explanation? Surely not for your own entertainment, for you seem to have derived no more enjoyment from this particular confrontation than I."

There was a darkness behind his eyes but, outwardly, his composure did not falter. Only his chest rose with a deeper, and more marked, swell. And when he spoke, his voice was softer than I had ever known it to be.

"It is not easy for me to ask a favor of anyone, Miss Lane."

"Not even when it is not for yourself you ask?"

"Not ever."

I took a step toward him, then caught myself and stopped. "But that is nothing but foolish pride," I said quickly, trying to hide my embarrassment. "We all need someone at some time. Surely, we have the right to expect something from one another. Some compassion and support."

Abruptly, he turned away from me again. Just when I supposed he wished me to leave, he murmured, "It is not pride."

"What then?"

"*It is fear. Total and abject fear.*"

I gaped at his broad back, thinking I must have misheard him. The notion that he could be afraid of anything seemed ludicrous. But surely that was what he had said.

"Of what?" I asked.

There was a long pause, and I became convinced he would not speak any more on the subject. Then, in a soft voice, he answered, "Of the consequences."

I was completely bewildered. Clearly, we had ceased to speak of dresses and favors and spoke of something else entirely, something completely beyond my comprehension. I was at a loss to know how to respond.

After much thought, I said, "I do not fully understand you. I only know that if it is within my power to help you in some manner, it would be my pleasure to do so."

He laughed softly. Not at me, it seemed, but more at some private jest that only he enjoyed. Then he drew back from the windows and, resting his arms on the back of his chair, he contemplated me. There was a wry smile on his lips, and his eyes were neither mocking nor angry. Only utterly and unbearably sad.

"You have no notion of what you would be inviting."

"I beg your pardon?"

"No matter. Only know you will have earned my gratitude in accepting these dresses. Although it was not an admission I intended to make."

"Again, you confuse me."

"Come now, Miss Lane. What kind of combatants will we make once we admit to being friends and allies. Will you rob from me the only pleasure I have taken in life for several long years?"

He was teasing me again. "There is no fear in that," I retorted. "I cannot remain two minutes in your company without becoming exasperated, enraged, or embarrassed."

"Then I may yet rest easy."

He made a deep and mocking bow.

I paid his foolishness little attention. Like his drunkenness, his mockery and teasing were merely part of the mask he wore. True, he was not the young man I remembered, but nor was he this disreputable caricature of a man he pretended to be. I had caught enough glimpses of his real self to know he possessed a character that was both serious and troubled.

He caught me studying him. "Is there anything else, Miss Lane? If not, Miss Reager is waiting."

As it happened there was. "A question, milord."

"And that would be?"

"I could not help but wonder why you had my portmanteau returned to me."

All traces of mockery vanished, abruptly replaced by an awful intensity. He moved from behind his chair and strode to my side. Clasping me by the shoulders, he pulled me against him until our faces were scant inches apart. His fingers bit into my flesh, and his breathing sounded forced and labored to my ears.

Then, too, there was a feverish brightness in his eyes that frightened me. I could scarcely credit the transformation. No part of him resembled either the drunken ne'er-do-well or the mocking combatant who took pleasure in taunting me. The man who held me captive was a complete stranger to me. There was a madness about him that was not affectation. Unable to hide my fear, I trembled in his grip.

In a voice thick with emotion, he said, "Promise me something."

I nodded mutely.

"Remember that, if you wish to leave this place, you have only to pack your belongings and summon the carriage. *You* are not a prisoner here."

I wondered at the strange emphasis, but could only stare at him.

His fingers tightened on my shoulders. "For some, this can be a dreadful place. I will not let it destroy you as it destroyed my wife. Or rob your youth and innocence as it has robbed me of mine. You only have to speak and you are free to leave."

"B-but I have no wish to leave, milord."

"Not now, perhaps. But you may. I will not have you sneaking off in the night, believing yourself alone and friendless. No matter whether you leave or stay, you will always be able to turn to me, Jessamy."

My name came to his lips as though it belonged there, as though he had used it often. Coming from his mouth, it sounded less like a name than an endearment, and I knew it would never sound the same to me again.

I gazed up at him, confused by the feelings that he stirred within me. It was as if I stood beside a precipice, and a power greater than anything I had ever known invited me to plunge over the edge. But to what? A kind of death, or something more terrifying? I shivered. Would I never feel comfortable in his presence?

His grip on me loosened. "Forgive me. I am frightening you."

"Not at all."

He shook his head. "I fear you have found yourself in a different kind of coal cellar. Just remember, for you, the door is open. I am the one who is unable to escape."

"Then I must help you as you once did me."

"Would that you could, Miss Lane."

And so we were back on formal terms yet again. Perhaps he had called me Jessamy without realizing what he had done. I felt a mixture of disappointment and relief, but knew it was for the best. Thinking this a good time to take my leave, I reminded him that Miss Reager would be waiting. Still, he did not let me go without first hearing my promise that I would remember what he had said to me.

Indeed, it would have been impossible for me to forget.

Miss Reager had finished with Clarissa and was waiting impatiently for my return. I apologized for the delay and submitted to her attentions. There was not only the measurements to be taken, but fabrics to be chosen— both for myself and Clarissa, since her dresses were to be made up to my instructions. Lastly, there were styles to be discussed. Long before we finished, Clarissa grew weary and asked if she and Matilda might go outside and play. I agreed, but told her she must not go beyond the gardens.

It was yet another hour before Miss Reager finished. His lordship had instructed her to make up five dresses for me, of various colors so long as they were not drab. By the time she had satisfied his request, she would have me looking quite the young lady. I did not know which I felt more, excited or dismayed.

Alone, at last, I put on my walking boots and went in search of Clarissa. The gardens were empty, save for a quiet young man cutting off the dead flowers, and he claimed he had not seen anyone other than the head groundskeeper. I strolled across the lawns, searching for likely niches where she might have secluded herself with Matilda.

It was not until I neared the ruins that I caught sight of her. She was perched on one of the massive fallen stones, humming a monotonous tune to herself, Matilda cradled in her arms. Her face was turned from me, her gaze fixed on the tower, and she stared with the kind of fascination that I had seen upon her father's face when he stared out of the study window into the fog.

"Clarissa," I called.

She did not answer. Nor did she move.

I hurried toward her, convinced that she had been frightened and suffered from some kind of shock. But the second I touched her shoulder, she started and glanced up at me.

"Oh, Jessamy. It is you."

Her face was a shade brighter than its normal color, and her eyes had a kind of sheen to them that I had not seen before, but other than that, she appeared unharmed.

"Are you all right?" I asked, not fully convinced.

After a second, she nodded. "I did not go too near," she added. "But Miss Osborne and I often used to sit on this stone after luncheon. She said we should not work until after our food had digested."

I frowned. Looking out upon the ruins was more likely to harm than help the digestion. I was beginning to hold grave doubts about whether Miss Osborne truly possessed the good sense that had been credited her. It seemed she had instilled her own fascination with the ruins in Clarissa—a fascination that did the girl no good whatsoever.

Thinking it unwise to linger, I said, "Speaking of luncheon, it is well past midday. I think we had better go and tell Mrs. Pendarves we are ready to eat."

She glanced back at the ruins.

I followed her gaze, but saw nothing.

"Is there something you would like to tell me, Clarissa? You know you can trust me."

After a doubtful pause, she managed a slight inclination of her head.

"Perhaps I can help," I said.

At last, she turned to me. "Have you . . . have you heard of changelings? Mrs. Pendarves used to tell me about them when I was small."

I nodded. "They are babies who are stolen by fairies at birth, are they not? And in place of the child, they leave old, wizened fairies who are bad-tempered and wicked."

"I am too big to believe in fairies anymore, but do you think there are places that change people?"

"In what way?"

"Like my mother was changed. Mrs. Pendarves said that when she first came to the Hall, she was gay and happy. But I only remember her as sad and frightened. It was living at the Hall that made her different."

"But there could be many reasons for her altered personality," I protested. "Reasons you or I could not possibly understand."

Her lower lip jutted out. "It made her sick. I know it did. So could there be other places, worse than the Hall, places that could change someone into . . ." She stopped and struggled for a word that was apparently not in her vocabulary. ". . . into something that looked like that person, yet was not them."

Had her face been less earnest, and had we been talking somewhere other than in the shadow of the ruins, I might have laughed. Instead, her fervor worried me.

"I have never heard of anything like that," I said. "Do you think the ruins is such a place?"

She gave no answer.

"But we have seen Wilkins come from there, and nothing has ever happened to him." I put my arm about her shoulder. "Really, there is nothing to worry about. Let us go inside and get something to eat. If we are much later, Mrs. Pendarves will make us go without our luncheon."

Another time, she might have laughed at the notion, but today she only nodded. Of what was she thinking? Of her father? Had she also watched him change? And why did she blame the ruins?

I led her away, eager to remove her from the disturbing site. Together, neither one of us speaking, we walked across the lawn to the Hall. Behind us the tower remained, an ominous presence in all our lives.

One that would not disappear simply because we looked in the other direction.

8

"*Do you mean* to go to tea with us, Papa?"

Clarissa's high-pitched voice danced down the stairs ahead of her to the gloomy entry hall below where her father stood. His dark face was caught in the muted light that fell from the transom, but the shadows could not be chased from his eyes. He looked remote and oddly uncomfortable in both waistcoat and frockcoat, and a black satin bow tie was knotted tightly about his neck. But no one could have accused him of not taking the proper care with his attire.

His decision to accompany us had been made just that morning, and then only because the day was drab and cloudy. He feared the fog might roll across the moor and shroud the lane and the Hall by late afternoon, making our return difficult and possibly dangerous.

He waited until she had reached his side, and clasped her hand within his own. "I fear I must. Bastian is an able driver. But there are some responsibilities I will trust to no one but myself."

His words were directed to her, but his gaze met mine, and there was a warmth to his eyes that flustered me. I averted my eyes and busied myself at the mirror retying the sash of my bonnet.

Unwittingly, Clarissa added to my embarrassment. "What a pity your new dresses are not made up. But I think you are still every bit as pretty as Miss Pengelley, don't you, Papa?"

There was a long pause and, if I had not come to know something of his character, I might have supposed him at a loss for a polite or appropriate answer. Instead, I knew he deliberately prolonged my discomfort for the sake of his own amusement. I struggled to hide my annoyance.

At last, he took pity on me. "Prettier—or would be if only she would not scowl."

"Scowl! Of all the—" I remembered Clarissa and gritted my teeth. "It is this wretched bonnet. It simply refuses to be tied correctly."

"Would you like my help?" he asked, his voice suddenly sweet. "I used to be quite a hand at helping ladies straighten their garments."

"I would not think of imposing on you. You are already doing us far too great a service by agreeing to be our escort. Besides, it is done."

"But the bow looks just the same as when we came downstairs," Clarissa said.

The color on my cheeks heightened. "Nonsense. It's fuller and . . . and—"

"And the brim more forward," Lord Wolfeburne said.

Clarissa shrugged, but she accepted our judgment. "And doesn't Papa look handsome?" she demanded of me.

I gave him a quick glance, but that was more than long enough to see the laughter in his eyes. "Every inch the gentleman . . . the well-dressed gentleman." I corrected myself, letting his lordship know that my approval was intended for his attire and not his behavior.

What I had intended as a reproach failed to do more than arouse a soft chuckle. Still, it was a relatively congenial—and, I hoped, auspicious—beginning to our afternoon. Neither Lord Wolfeburne's dress nor his manners could be faulted, and I prayed he would continue in this fashion, at least for that while that we tarried in Sir Ronald's home.

Even as the thought occurred to me, I had the horrible feeling he would not.

Sir Ronald's house lay five miles to the east, and his daughter had not quite rightly insisted they were our closest neighbors. There were numerous small stone-hedged farms between the two estates, where flocks of sheep and a few dairy cows grazed. Children clambered on gates to watch us pass, and Clarissa waved at each one of them, her eyes bright and a smile quick upon her lips.

Her happiness vanished at the sight of a rag doll, clasped in the hands of a dark-haired child. "Matilda," she cried. "I forgot Matilda."

"She will be waiting for you when we get back," her father said, with a typically male disregard for the importance of dolls.

I put my arm around Clarissa's shoulders and gave her a squeeze. "Matilda will understand, and we will not be gone long."

"Do you think she will be frightened without me?"

"She has Mrs. Pendarves to keep her company."

"But if the fog comes—"

"Then Mary will close the curtains, and Wilkins will let out the dogs," her father said, coming at last to some understanding of her distress.

"There, you see," I added. "She will be perfectly safe."

Clarissa nodded, but some of her happiness was gone.

We reached Pengelley House shortly before the appointed hour. It was a two-story stone structure, sheltered from the moors by a cluster of elms and wide-spreading oaks. The house appeared to me cheerful and . . . I hesitated, at first unable to identify the sensation that enveloped me. Then the word I sought popped into my thoughts.

Safe.

It enjoyed a serenity that was absent from Wolfeburne Hall.

To make matters worse, the normality of the one place only underscored the distressing undercurrents prevalent in the other. I glanced down at Clarissa with misgiving. Would she, too, mark the difference between this home and her own. To my relief, she was busy smoothing the creases from her muslin dress and checking the ties of her own bonnet.

The housekeeper ushered us into a lavish drawing room. Two Grecian statues had been set into niches on either side of the pink marble fireplace. A three-tiered, crystal chandelier hung over a rosewood table, and armchairs, upholstered in a soft pink brocade, ringed the edges of the room.

Four of these chairs were occupied, for we were not the only guests. Two couples, one of Sir Ronald's generation and the other nearer my own age, turned their heads in our direction. There was a marked look of curiosity and a hint of apprehension on their faces.

Miss Pengelley rose from the bench of a spindly legged harpsichord and hastened to greet us. "Father will be down in a minute," she told us. "I'm afraid he will not be hurried for any reason. You must forgive his rudeness." She bestowed a sweet and somewhat nervous smile on Lord Wolfeburne. "I am so glad you decided to come, milord."

"It was most kind of you to invite me."

There was a thinly hidden edge to his tone, and I glanced at him doubtfully. It was my anxious hope that only I heard anything amiss in his tone.

His gaze met mine, and my thoughts must have been plain upon my face. "Are you unwell?" he asked.

"Of course not."

"I thought perhaps the carriage ride was too much for you. You seem unsettled."

"Not at all, milord."

"Something else, then?"

"Nothing, milord." Nothing but his own behavior, a fact he fully appreciated.

"Perhaps you had better come and sit down," Miss Pengelley said, all concern for me, but her relief at being able to remove her attention from Lord Wolfeburne was plain.

I thought her a kind young woman, someone who worried more about the troubles of others than about herself, and I pitied her for the burden she had offered to shoulder. Encouraging Lord Wolfeburne to reenter society would be like leading a wild beast through a garden party. She would find herself badly outmatched if he chose to be difficult.

Before I could take my seat, there were introductions that had to be made. The elderly couple, a Mr. and Mrs. Drewe, were close friends of Sir Ronald and at least nodding acquaintances of Lord Wolfeburne. Both were stout, with florid cheeks and hearty smiles that lost some of their warmth and confidence when they were bestowed upon Lord Wolfeburne.

The second gentleman was their nephew, the Honorable Edward Treffery. He was a soft-spoken man, given to polishing his spectacles on a checked handkerchief whenever he grew flustered. That seemed to be often.

He was accompanied by his wife Ramona, a dark, sloe-eyed woman who showed signs of the Spanish blood that was prevalent among the Cornish people. Despite heavy features, she was unquestionably striking.

Her gaze fastened on Clarissa. "What a lovely daughter you have, Lord Wolfeburne. It is a shame we do not see more of you both."

There was an awkward silence in which Mr. Drewe cleared his throat. It was Clarissa who saved us by announcing that Mrs. Treffery was the most beautiful lady she had ever seen. There was a round of laughter, and we settled into our chairs with relief. Only Lord Wolfeburne appeared wholly at ease with the tension in the room.

A cane grated on the walnut flooring, and Sir Ronald limped into the room. Having only seen him seated in his carriage, I had not realized that he needed assistance to walk, although his bad leg seemed to give him little trouble. Despite his uneven gait, he marched through the drawing room with a soldier's bearing.

He paused in the middle of the room. "So you've come, have you, Wolfeburne? It was my contention you would not."

His lordship acknowledged his host with a nod of his head so slight as to be almost derogatory. "Sir Ronald. When have I ever done as was expected?"

"Never," he retorted in a booming voice. "To your own disservice."

"Father, really. Do come and sit down before you persuade our guests that you are completely without manners."

"There's nothing the matter with *my* manners."

Despite his objections, he allowed his daughter to make him comfortable in one of the wing chairs and accepted several cushions for his back. She lifted a crocheted shawl to throw across his legs, but he gave her a look of utter disdain.

"Good Lord. Get away with you. I'm neither an invalid nor in my dotage. Fool woman. As bad as her mother."

"In fact, you seem in very good health, Sir Ronald," Lord Wolfeburne said.

"Good enough," he said. "And yourself?"

Lord Wolfeburne's gaze rested on me for less than an instant. "Better than I deserve."

"Hmmph. That's true enough, I'd wager. Sarah, ring for tea."

She hesitated. "I thought we might talk for a while, Father. It's still early."

"Do as you're told, girl." He brandished his cane at her. "I'm too old to be polite when I'm hungry."

"Really, Father. The way you talk, one would think you were sixty or more."

Nevertheless, she did as she was bid, and I was relieved to know we would have more than each other's remarks to occupy our attention. Sir Ronald had made his disapproval of Lord Wolfeburne obvious, and I wondered how long his criticisms would be tolerated.

Probably only until they ceased to amuse his lordship.

But throughout tea, Lord Wolfeburne could not have been more charming. He complimented all the ladies present on their attire, discussed hunting and fishing with the gentlemen, and generally put everyone at ease. His geniality was marred only by the occasional wicked smile he flashed in my direction.

It was nothing more than a game to him. And, for the moment, it pleased him to be amenable. Too easily that could change. Sublimely ignorant of his erratic moods, Sir Ronald's guests were quickly won over.

Mrs. Drewe recovered her broad smile and throaty voice and suggested he attend a dinner they were giving next month. Her words dropped to a murmur. "I doubt that any of us fully appreciated how deeply you suffered after your wife's death. I hope you will let us make amends now that you are more yourself."

Mrs. Treffery leaned forward to rest her hand intimately on his coat sleeve. "Indeed, you must. We would not hear of your refusing." She withdrew her hand before anyone could accuse her of behaving in an unseemly fashion.

"As I recall, his behavior before his marriage left a great deal to be desired." Sir Ronald's statement flustered everyone but the very person he had intended to upset.

Miss Pengelley did her best to smooth over the awkward moments and make certain we were all comfortable.

She was often aware of our needs before we were aware of them ourselves, and had even unpacked several of her old dolls from her attic trunks for Clarissa to play with when she was finished with her tea.

Hearing this, Clarissa's large eyes clouded with dismay. Miss Pengelley turned to me questioningly.

My puzzlement vanished as quickly as it had come. "I don't think Matilda would mind if you played with them," I told Clarissa. "Probably, she will want to hear all about them when you get home."

She happily accepted my reassurance.

"You have a way with her," Miss Pengelley said after Clarissa had slipped from the table. There was a hint of wistfulness in her eyes and the tone of her voice.

I smiled. "No more than yourself. It was very thoughtful of you to think of the dolls."

"I have always liked children," she said.

Liked them and wanted her own, apparently.

What a good wife she would make Lord Wolfeburne, I thought with a start. And it would do him good if someone were to nudge him in that direction.

Again, I suffered through a siege of conflicting emotions that made no sense to me. First came a rush of relief. It was as though, by knowing he might remarry, I had escaped some danger. But that was followed by a sharp and deep sadness, as if I had also suffered some great loss. But why I should be saddened by the thought of his remarrying, I did not know.

That, or I deliberately chose not to know.

I forced my unruly thoughts back to Miss Pengelley. She was a gentlewoman in the true sense of the word. Nothing in her behavior or her timid remarks to Lord

Wolfeburne suggested she had anything more on her mind than offering him her support and friendship. But she handled her difficult father with tact and patience, and was the kind of person who would see only the good in others, no matter what their faults. Then, too, her obvious love for children made her an excellent choice, for Clarissa badly needed a mother. She would be good for them both, and I wondered that he had not already thought the same.

Perhaps if they saw each other more often, he would.

"A very good man, the late Lord Wolfeburne," Sir Ronald said, and I realized he was speaking to me.

My gaze dropped to my hands. "I cannot think of a single occasion when he behaved less than correctly."

"Yes," Lord Wolfeburne murmured. "That was certainly Henry. I doubt that the idea of impropriety ever crossed his mind."

"Indeed, it would not have," I said, convinced that the man had lacked the necessary imagination. Still, I did not dare look up lest I catch sight of his lordship's amused face and give way to laughter.

Mr. Drewe reached over and patted my hand. "Although we saw little of him after his marriage, I remember him fondly. His is a great loss, I'm sure Sir Ronald didn't mean to remind you."

"You need not worry about Miss Lane," Lord Wolfeburne told him. "I have great faith in her ability to put those memories behind her."

"Of course, she will," Sir Ronald said. "First time I laid eyes on her, I could see she was a sensible young woman. Didn't I say so, Sarah?"

"Yes, Father."

"Lady Clarissa is lucky to have her at the Hall. And so

are you, Wolfeburne. Henry gave her a good upbringing. Always could rely on him. No-nonsense kind of man. Not like you."

"Not at all," he said pleasantly.

"More's the pity."

"You are right in thinking Lord Wolfeburne quite different from his brother," I said hastily. "But I have found him to have many admirable traits of his own."

Miss Pengelley nodded. "Of course, he does. Really, Father. I know you were fond of the late Lord Wolfeburne, but you cannot expect everyone to be alike. Just think what a dull world this would be if we were."

"Dull? A man who can be trusted is not dull." He banged his cane on the floor. "Still, maybe the responsibility of a title and estates will do you some good. Might make a man of you."

"Have you forgotten? I have always had the responsibility of the estates," his lordship said with a mildness that made my stomach muscles tighten.

"That's right, Father. Ever since the death of poor Mr. Morrison. Shall I pour some more tea, Mr. Drewe?"

"Ever since he got sent down from Oxford, you mean."

My head turned sharply toward Sir Ronald. What had he said? Expelled from Oxford? But that would have been shortly before he came to London, when I had seen nothing but goodness in his character. Could I, in my childish admiration for him have been deceived as to his nature? Was that why he and his brother had argued? And why had there been nothing said afterward? I could not imagine the late Lord Wolfeburne failing to voice his disapproval of his brother's conduct to all who would listen. It was simply unlike him.

"All water under the bridge, Sir Ronald," the Honorable Edward Treffery said, giving his spectacles a good polish.

Miss Pengelley nodded. "Really, Father. Please don't start that again. And pass the cakes to Miss Lane. Her plate is empty, and I'm sure she'd like another."

"Yes, please," I stammered.

"As would I," Mrs. Drewe added.

Sir Ronald's heavy brows drew together. "Let me tell you, if I had been sent down, I wouldn't have gone about bragging to everyone. Although, as I recall, you weren't so forthcoming about what you'd done to deserve expulsion. You would have done better to hang your head and done your level best to get readmitted. A man needs a good education. Some things may have changed since I was a young man, but that much is the same." He glanced at his daughter. "What did you say?" His gaze fell on the iced cakes. "Oh, yes. Glad to."

He lifted the plate, and I took one blindly and babbled something inane about how good they were. "You couldn't find better in London."

"Father insists upon keeping a good chef. Don't you, Father?"

"What? Oh, yes," he muttered. "Can't do much when you get older, but there's no need to go without decent food. Not until the teeth go, right?"

I joined in the polite laughter and gave Lord Wolfeburne a meaningful look, hoping he would do the same. My attempt to prod him roused nothing more than a faintly tolerant yawn, but I was grateful even for that. At least his determined good humor had not yet failed him. But less than an hour had passed, and the afternoon was deteriorating quickly.

Miss Pengelley turned to me and smiled bravely. "I was so pleased to learn of your arrival. Doublebois is a small village, and I rarely see anyone other than the parson's daughter, Miss Worsley. Have you met her? She is a very worthwhile person. Isn't she, Father?"

"Oh, admirable sort. Plain as pudding."

His daughter's cheeks colored and I quickly said, "Lord Wolfeburne also thinks highly of her. He had thought to ask her to give Clarissa her lessons. But that was before he realized I would be willing to come to Cornwall."

"Willing?" his lordship queried. "I would venture to say eager. Even insistent."

It was my turn to flush.

Surprisingly, it was Mrs. Treffery who covered my embarrassment. "Yes, Miss Worsley would make an excellent governess. I believe she tutors some of the village children, and her talents are quite wasted on them."

"But, of course, Lady Clarissa is much happier with you," Miss Pengelley added. "And we are very glad you came."

"Of course," Mrs. Treffery agreed.

Sir Ronald quickly tired of our inane chatter. Picking up the silver bell that stood near his daughter's elbow, he rang for the maid and told her to bring in a decanter of brandy.

"Your stomach has been bothering you all day," his daughter said.

He glared at her. "We've got guests, Sarah. As you've seen fit to remind me more than once. And I'm certain

Lord Wolfeburne is used to something stronger than tea in the afternoon. We will all need something to brace ourselves if you insist upon continuing this conversation."

Prompted by Sir Ronald, the subject wandered from Miss Worsley to an upcoming hunt. Mr. Drewe clapped Lord Wolfeburne on the back. "We'll expect you to attend, old man. And throw the next one. Your grandfather used to fill every room in the Hall during the season. You shall have to do the same."

"It's about time you took up some of your social obligations," Sir Ronald added, but his tone was noticeably less friendly.

The thought of noisy hunt-enthusiasts crowding the Hall made me smile. That would soon chase out the shadows and the oppressive darkness. Smugly satisfied with the turn the afternoon had taken, I glanced across at Lord Wolfeburne to see if he shared my sentiments.

He was sitting stiffly in his chair, his polite expression fixed to his face, and in answer to the remark he only nodded curtly.

Fortunately, Mrs. Drewe was an avid gardener, and she brought up the neutral subject of roses. When her hostess deplored her lack of success with her own bushes, she insisted upon dragging all of the ladies out into the gardens to give us the benefit of her advice. Clarissa skipped along beside us, having grown tired of the dolls. With some misgiving on my part, we left the men to their own interests.

We remained outside for some while, although both Miss Pengelley and I glanced uneasily toward the drawing room as the lecture rambled onward. It was only Clarissa's need to attend to personal needs that sent us back inside. Miss Pengelley insisted on taking care of her, and the rest of us returned to the drawing room without them.

My gaze went immediately to Lord Wolfeburne. He lounged in his chair, his legs stretched out before him, his bow tie loose and dangling about his neck.

His glass was half empty, much as it had been earlier, but I had no way of knowing how many glasses had been poured during our absence. Sir Ronald and his guests were plainly disgusted, but he stared at them through bleary and dispassionate eyes.

"Damn it, you've got responsibilities," Sir Ronald said, then noticed us in the doorway and fell silent.

But Lord Wolfeburne saw no need to let the discussion rest. "And to whom should I consider myself responsible?" he demanded, his words slurred.

"Why, your peers, of course." The stiffness of Mr. Drewe's posture seemed designed to compensate for his lordship's careless sprawl. "Drunkenness and rude manners were bad enough when you were a commoner, but you're titled now."

"And should that make a difference?"

"Of course, it does," the Honorable Edward Treffery said, fishing for his handkerchief. "You have a position to maintain. You degrade all your peers by your behavior."

"Nonsense. I am certain the locals are aware of your true worth."

Sir Ronald's cane banged across the arm of the sofa. "That's just the kind of remark I would have expected from you. You've no sense of propriety. Or responsibility. Not to your name or to your daughter."

Lord Wolfeburne's eyes narrowed. "My daughter is none of your concern."

"And less of yours, it would seem."

"Be careful, Sir Ronald. Or I shall forget that you are almost twice my age and incapable of anything more forceful than an insult."

The elderly man quivered with rage. "Do you dare to threaten me in my own home?"

"If you invite me here only to insult me then you must expect the worst."

"Damn you, sir," he said again, forgetting we were in attendance. "I will not have it."

"Your language, Sir Ronald." Lord Wolfeburne arched his eyebrows. "There are ladies present."

"You insufferable young upstart. Leave my home immediately or I shall be forced to—"

"To throw me out?" He smiled lazily. "I hardly think you capable. Not even with the help of these two gentlemen. But you are certainly welcome to try."

There was the sound of Clarissa's voice in the hallway, and the thought of her bursting in upon this unpleasant scene stirred me to act. "Please, Lord Wolfeburne. It is growing late and you said you wished to return before dark."

Clarissa entered before I had finished speaking. "Do we really have to go, Papa? I have had such fun."

He looked at her bright face and nodded slowly. "Yes. I fear it is time," he said, sounding a good deal more sober than he had done just a few minutes before.

What possessed the man? I already knew he withdrew into the semblance of drunkenness whenever he pleased, but why now? To allow himself the freedom of insulting his host as Sir Ronald had repeatedly insulted him? Or was this an act to draw attention to himself instead of some deeper problem? Either way, I could find no excuse for his behavior.

With some reluctance and greater confusion, since she had missed the argument, Miss Pengelley rang for our bonnets and mantles. "But we will see you again in the near future, I pray," she murmured.

Her father glared at her. "Lord Wolfeburne knows full well the extent of his welcome here. There is nothing else that needs to be said."

"And the same can be said of your welcome at Elmtree House," Mr. Drewe added.

Miss Pengelley glanced about her and her lips trembled. It was clear from the tone of both men's voices that Lord Wolfeburne would not be allowed to take one step through their doors. She started to protest, then glanced down at Clarissa. Wisely, she bit back her questions.

Mercifully, Bastian wasted no time bringing up the carriage. I did not draw a decent breath until we had passed between the gates. Then I sank back against the cushions. It was impossible to speak in Clarissa's presence, but the ride would be a respite during which I could gather my wits about me. Certainly, any hope there had been that Miss Pengelley might some day become Clarissa's mother was gone.

And once again I had to deal with my wayward emotions.

Lord Wolfeburne studied me with eyes half hidden beneath the brim of his hat and the mop of dark hair that had fallen across his brow. The defiance in his face, his unruly hair and careless posture, gave him the look of a spoiled and troublesome child. But closer observation revealed the twist to his lips and the darkness behind that heavy-lidded gaze. No child could have been capable of displaying such deep bitterness and misery.

Clarissa peered from the carriage, her cheeks pale. She seemed aware that something was amiss, for there was nothing beyond the carriage to capture her attention. Fog had drifted from the moor and spread over the fields to cloak the small farmhouses.

The horses plodded through the sodden gray afternoon, their ears pricking up at the barks of the farm dogs. The lane ahead of them was visible for several yards, but that distance dwindled the nearer we came to the Hall. At the crossroads, the horses nickered and came to an abrupt halt.

Bastian looked back over his shoulder. "They can't see where they're going, milord."

Lord Wolfeburne raised his head and squinted into the gloom, but the fog was too dense for sight to penetrate. He frowned, then catching my worried glance, shrugged. "It was to be expected. Otherwise I should not have come." His lips twisted into a disgruntled scowl. "It was foolish of me to have given my consent." He lifted a lantern from the floor of the carriage, one he had placed there only that morning for apparently just such an emergency. "You can, I pray, survive without my company for a short while?"

His eyes were mocking, but Clarissa tensed. "You will be careful, Papa?"

"The veritable soul of discretion," he told her. "And you, Miss Lane? No words of caution before I go?"

"None that would not be wasted," I retorted. "Besides, the fresh air is certain to do you good."

There was a flash of pain in his eyes, but he quickly smiled and tipped his hat. "Then, in good conscience, I shall leave you."

Thereafter, our progress was slow, for the horses demanded the attention of both men to be coaxed forward. Lord Wolfeburne handled the nervous animals with skill and competence, keeping a firm hold upon their harness and holding the lantern with a steady hand. Their repeated attempts to stop were met with unyielding resistance. After observing him for several minutes, I knew for a certainty that he was anything but drunk.

So I had been right. It had all been an act. But an act meant to serve what purpose?

Despite the struggling horses, we reached the Hall safely. Mrs. Pendarves threw open the door before we had descended from the carriage and called out to ask if we were all right.

"We are all safe enough," his lordship shouted back to her.

I bustled Clarissa into the Hall, my own thoughts momentarily forgotten in my haste to see her out of the damp air. Mrs. Pendarves promptly removed her from my grasp. "There's a hot bath waiting for you upstairs, young lady."

"I'll be right up to help you," I said.

The housekeeper shook her head. "I'll see to her. I've got a pot of hot tea in your sitting room. And his lordship will find a hot toddy in his study." Without waiting for thanks, she ushered Clarissa up the stairs.

I started to follow.

A firm hand fell upon my arm and held me back. I turned to meet Lord Wolfeburne's gaze. It was disturbing not so much for its intensity as for the longing and need that I saw there. Some of my irritation faded, and I felt a sudden sympathy for him, although he deserved none.

"Are you upset with me?" he asked in a soft voice that could not have carried beyond my ears.

"Would you expect me to feel otherwise?" I was determined to hold him accountable for his behavior despite the weakness in me that wanted desperately to understand and forgive him.

His hand tightened on my arm. "Was it so important to you that we remained on good terms with the Pengelleys? Sir Ronald is pompous and self-righteous, and his daughter too well-intentioned to be anything but a nuisance."

I gasped. "How can you speak so cruelly of her when she showed you nothing but kindness."

"I would wager she had already prepared my social calendar for the next twelvemonth."

"Nonsense. She was only trying to include you in activities that you have missed for several years."

"I can manage my own affairs without help from anyone."

"In the past, you have not proved yourself very capable." I knew I overstepped my bounds but was unable to bite back my retort.

There was a flicker of annoyance in his eyes, but his lips curved into a taunting smile. He brought his face nearer to mine. I could smell the brandy on his breath, saw the beginnings of a beard upon his jaw, and caught glints of gold in his dark irises. They shimmered in the glow of the gas lamps, and he held my gaze captive with the sheer force of his will.

"Now I have you to advise me, have I not?" he murmured.

I stiffened. "Mock me if you like, but your behavior today has done Clarissa no good."

"She is too young to care for balls."

"In a few years she will feel differently. And she needs to get out"—I started to say *of the Hall*, but stopped myself in time—"into society."

He rubbed his thumb against my arm, emphasizing the closeness of his person and the strength of the contact between us. "She has you for company. And her father, for what that is worth."

"She also needs a mother."

I stopped myself before I revealed the entirety of my thoughts on that matter, but I had already said too much. Lord Wolfeburne blinked with astonishment.

"Do you mean to say you have chosen a wife for me?" he demanded.

"O-of course not. B-but I could hardly fail to appreciate Miss Pengelley's qualities, and realize how much difference she, or someone like her, would make in your life."

"She would not suit my needs. Not in *any* fashion."

Deliberately, he surveyed me, his serious eyes filled with a meaning that made my throat tighten. Had I not been standing on the stair, my arm imprisoned in his grip, I would have edged backward from everything I read there.

Unable to escape, I attacked. "What about Clarissa's needs?"

"She has you, does she not?"

"I am only her governess."

"She seems content with the arrangement."

"She would not complain to you if she was not."

He glared at me and his grip slackened. "Enough. I see no reason to discuss the matter with you."

"Then I presume I have your permission to retire?" I pulled free of him, turned my back to him, and mounted the next stair.

"Jessamy," he called after me.

I turned.

"Do you mean to tell me it would please you to see me married to Miss Pengelley?"

I swallowed, knowing that the answer to his question was not a wholehearted yes. But I could hardly admit to that. "What pleases or does not please me is hardly the issue."

"You have not given me an answer."

"It was a foolish question and deserves to be ignored."

"You are not laughing."

"Pardon?"

"If my question is so foolish, then why are you not laughing?"

"Must you be so literal?" I demanded. "Not everything that is ridiculous is laughable."

There was the glimmer of a smile. "Nor, for that matter, is everything that seems ridiculous as nonsensical as one might believe."

"Now you are talking in riddles, and I am too tired to unravel them."

"Then we must finish this conversation another time."

"I cannot see that there is anything further that needs to be said."

"Do you not, Jessamy?"

"Certainly not!"

"How strange. It would seem to me that this conversation has only just begun."

9

After Lord Wolfeburne's shocking behavior at Pengelley House, I expected to see a return of the reckless and dissolute gentleman who had summoned me to the Hall. To my relief, I was wrong. Over the next few days he appeared more and more like the young man I remembered. His hair was neatly combed, his attire both correct and spotless, and his manner disarming. Nor did he make any attempt to bait me or reintroduce the subject of our last discussion.

Common sense warned me it was foolish to be misled by what was merely a different kind of performance, for all I wanted to believe that this mask was real, not pretense. But nothing at the Hall was as it appeared—least of all the man who was master there.

The purpose of his improved behavior was made clear to me the first evening we dined together. Throughout the silent meal, his manner was as stiff as his pointed standing collar. After the plates had been removed, he regarded me solemnly across the length of the dining room table.

"You have not, I hope, decided to accept my offer of assistance and look for another placement?"

"The thought had not even crossed my mind." Nor did it hold any appeal for me.

He relaxed, ever so slightly. "That is something I am glad to hear. Clarissa would suffer your loss more deeply than any loss she has suffered since her mother's death."

"Then set your mind at rest," I said calmly. "I am wholly content with my role here."

"As am I," he murmured.

My heartbeat quickened.

He removed his serviette from his lap, his movements suddenly brisk and officious. "I had supposed—" He stopped and shrugged. "No matter. Let me say only that I am glad to find myself mistaken."

"Actually, you have utterly convinced me that I am needed here," I said, grateful that he had rushed over that one soft remark.

"And that is important to you? To feel needed?"

"I would think that it is important to everybody to feel their services, and therefore they themselves, were necessary."

"More important even than enjoying a normal existence?"

"It would be preferable if one did not have to choose between the two," I replied.

His fingers drummed on the tablecloth, and candle-light flashed off his ring. "You have the irritating habit of avoiding my questions, Miss Lane. I expect a direct answer and will accept nothing less."

That statement, coming from someone who made concealment his way of life, deserved a withering response. But his question interested me. Certainly, I had never had a normal life. And for all that was amiss at the Hall, I had found a welcome and a place for myself there that I had found nowhere else. I would not lightly relinquish them.

"If I must sacrifice one for the other, then yes," I said. "I do think it more important to be needed. Even if that means foregoing the social niceties."

While I spoke, he studied me intently, listening not only to my words but marking how I said them. The instant I had finished, he flashed the familiar wicked grin that had been absent for several days.

"Then I shall not think it necessary to restrain myself. Instead, whenever I fall short of your expectations, I will make certain that I reemphasize your value to us."

It was the kind of distorted reasoning I had come to expect from him. I glared at him from across the rim of my glass. "Must you twist everything I say to your own advantage?"

"We are adversaries, are we not?" he asked cheerfully. "You must expect such behavior. *No quarter needed nor given.* Do you remember?"

"You have not let me forget."

His questions answered, he rang for dessert, although he satisfied himself with a glass of brandy. Between mouthfuls of gooseberry pie, I could not help glancing across the table at him and noticing how different he looked when he paid even a passing attention to his appearance. He was unquestionably handsome, his table manners were impeccable, and he had the bearing and confidence of a man used to being in authority.

Still, the dark side of his personality hovered about him. It was like seeing a double image, one ghostly and pale, the other vibrant and alive. Two starkly different personalities warring for the upper hand. And somewhere beneath lay a third—perhaps the only true personality of the three—manipulating both of the others whenever and however it pleased. How, I wondered, could such inner control result in such outer chaos?

Lord Wolfeburne waited until I had cleared my plate and emptied the last drops of elderflower wine from my glass. "If you are done, perhaps we could adjourn to my study. There was a book I wanted to loan you."

"Certainly, milord."

I brushed the crumbs from my lips and rose obediently.

His study, too, showed the effects of his recent attempts at self-improvement. I paused in the doorway to look around the room. The clutter and debris had disappeared, the shelves and tabletops had been recently dusted, and the carpet and cushions had been straightened. The dark oak wainscotting that ran around the walls had been polished, as had the brass fireplace fixtures that hung from the marble mantelpiece.

"I hardly recognize the place," I said teasingly. "One might make the mistake of thinking you a changed man."

"But you would not?"

"It is a mistake I have made before and shall not make a second time."

He beckoned for me to enter. Castor and Pollux rested their great heads on the brass railing that encircled the hearth. Neither thought my presence enough of a reason to disturb themselves. Reassured, I took a seat by the fire.

Lord Wolfeburne followed but did not take the opposite chair. He tended to look uncomfortable in chairs, I realized, save on those occasions he sprawled in apparent drunkenness. He was too restless even for those slight constraints.

He nudged one of the dogs' heads with his shoe and set his foot on the railing. His fingers twisted at his ring. "You are quite wrong," he said at last.

"Milord?"

"I am much altered from the individual you met upon arriving here. You yourself have changed me."

His face was all sincerity, but modesty did not allow me to admit such a possibility. More likely this was his method of letting me feel an importance I did not truly possess. I frowned. "It pleases you to tease me."

"It does. But, in this particular case, I am completely serious."

"I cannot see a difference. Merely a change in poses."

"Can you not?" He took a step nearer me. "Then you are not near enough to hear the beat of my heart or feel the warmth of the blood within my veins."

I regarded him warily. "I can hardly take credit for

that. Simply by dint of your being alive, you proved yourself to have both heartbeat and blood in your veins."

He shook his head. "I breathed." He took a breath. "I walked." He took another step toward me. "I went through all the motions of being alive. And yet I did not live."

He reached out for my hand, and I quickly pulled it from his reach. "Did you not say something about a book you wanted to show me?"

He sighed and dropped his hand. "Ah, yes. Let me fetch it for you."

He went to the bookcase and removed a thick volume which he brought to me. "You may, perhaps, recognize the title."

I read aloud. "*On the Origin of Species.* Charles Darwin. Yes, I have heard of his work. Last year, when it was published, there was an enormous stir in London." I opened the cover to discover it was a first edition. "How did you come by a copy? It was sold out on the day of issue."

"A friend of mine who knew my interests obtained it for me. I am much indebted to him. Have you read this, then?"

I shook my head. "Lady Wolfeburne would not permit what she called 'such an ungodly piece of writing' in her home."

"And do you share her opinion?"

"I can hardly discuss what I have never read. And though I have heard something of his ideas, I think word of mouth an unreliable source, at best."

"I fully agree. Perhaps, for my sake, you would give it

your attention. I would be interested in your opinion."

I glanced at him, expecting to see a mocking smile, but his face was sober and his gaze intent upon my face. So his request was sincerely made, although somewhat odd.

I shrugged. "If you wish. Although greater minds than mine have already been applied to the matter. I doubt that I will have anything noteworthy to add."

"Nevertheless, I would still be interested. If I learn nothing new about evolution, I will certainly discover something about you."

I found the possibility disquieting. It seemed he was not the only one who liked to keep his deepest self hidden and protected.

It was several days before we spoke again. They were quiet days. And still nights. The moon was full, its light unobscured by either clouds or fog, and it hovered in the sky, a pale imitator of the summer sun. It was an ideal opportunity for me to discover what set the dogs to howling, but, perversely, they remained silent. Once, I caught a glimpse of their prone bodies, stretched out upon the lawns, their heads lolling to the side. Both of them were totally given over to sleep.

Some watchdogs they, I thought with mild contempt.

But perhaps there was nothing to disturb their rest.

Clarissa appeared to benefit from the undisturbed hours. Her cheeks took on a pink glow, and her eyes were clearer and brighter. She laughed easily and more often, and did not complain when I steered her away from the ruins during our afternoon walks.

Our new dresses were finished and delivered. Clarissa accepted her walking dresses with little interest and was definitely more taken with the dresses that had been made up for me. They were bright and fashionable, and I felt a childish thrill of pleasure upon seeing them.

It was a feeling I promptly squashed. They had not, after all, been ordered with my pleasure in mind, but were merely intended to improve Clarissa's outlook. It would not be wise to regard them as symbols of a new and better life, lest I be rudely disappointed.

"What will you do with your old gowns?" Clarissa demanded, cocking her head and staring at my black taffeta with utter disapproval.

I smiled. Compared to the colorful creations laid out on my bed, the taffeta was, indeed, drab and disappointing. "I shall put all but one of them away," I told her. "There would not be enough room in the wardrobe otherwise."

She offered to help, but I suggested she change into one of her new walking dresses. There was no reason we couldn't go out on the moor that same afternoon. Good-naturedly, she scurried off to choose between the dark green and navy serge dresses that Mary had carried to her room.

I removed my mourning clothes from their hangers and replaced them with my new finery. That done, I pulled a straightback chair to the side of the wardrobe and clambered onto the seat to pull down my portmanteau. It slid forward easily and dropped to the floor with a thump.

I started to step down. With only one foot on the

floor, my hands still clasping the back of the chair, I came to an abrupt halt and stared in horror at the leather case.

It had been badly scarred. Someone, or something, had taken a knife and made four slashes across the top. They were deep cuts, made side by side, the middle two longer than the others, and they had passed through the thick leather completely.

Who would have done such a thing?

And why?

It was wanton destructiveness. That, or someone had deliberately tried to upset me, and I could think of no one who would have a reason to do such a thing.

I got on well with everyone at the Hall, even his lordship after a fashion. He seemed determined to be obliging should I decide to take my leave. Indeed, he seemed more afraid that I would stay against my wishes than leave in defiance of his.

Gingerly, I pulled at the leather. The case was completely ruined. I could store my dresses there, but only because they would go no further than the top of the wardrobe.

That gave rise to another possibility. Had Mrs. Pendarves, thwarted in her attempt to remove all avenues of escape, decided to destroy the case? I shook my head. It was impossible to picture that kind and thoughtful woman, knife clutched in her hand, savaging my poor case. Not even for Clarissa's sake.

Who then?

Mary?

Never. Unless she had first been instructed by Mrs. Pendarves, and I had already decried that notion.

Who was left for me to suspect? Wilkins? I had never

Join the
Timeless Romance Reader Service
and get four of today's
most exciting historical
romances free,
without obligation!

Imagine getting today's very best historical romances sent directly to your home — at a total savings of at least $2.00 a month. Now you can be among the first to be swept away by the latest from Candace Camp, Constance O'Banyon, Patricia Hagan, Parris Afton Bonds or Susan Wiggs. You get all that — and that's just the beginning.

Preview at home without obligation and save.

Each month, you'll receive four new romances to preview without obligation for 10 days. You'll pay the low subscriber price of just $4.00 per title — a total savings of at least $2.00 a month!

*Postage and handling is absolutely **free** and there is no minimum number of books you must buy. You may cancel your subscription at any time with no obligation.*

GET YOUR FOUR FREE BOOKS TODAY ($20.49 VALUE)

FILL IN THE ORDER FORM BELOW NOW!

YES! *I want to join the Timeless Romance Reader Service. Please send me my 4 FREE HarperMonogram historical romances. Then each month send me 4 new historical romances to preview without obligation for 10 days. I'll pay the low subscription price of $4.00 for every book I choose to keep – a total savings of at least $2.00 each month – and home delivery is free! I understand that I may return any title within 10 days without obligation and I may cancel this subscription at any time without obligation. There is no minimum number of books to purchase.*

NAME_____

ADDRESS _____

CITY_____STATE_____ZIP_____

TELEPHONE_____

SIGNATURE _____

(If under 18 parent or guardian must sign. Program, price, terms, and conditions subject to cancellation and change. Orders subject to acceptance by HarperMonogram.)

GET
4
FREE
BOOKS
(A $20.49 VALUE)

TIMELESS ROMANCE
READER SERVICE

120 Brighton Road
P.O. Box 5069
Clifton, NJ 07015-5069

seen him abovestairs, but certainly I could envision him capable of the deed if he had reason. Nor did he like me. But why, then, make my leaving harder than need be?

Sheer malice, perhaps? That, too, seemed unlikely. His lordship would only be angry with him if he discovered what he had done, and his own position would have been in jeopardy. A position that paid him more than he could possibly have earned elsewhere. As much as I would have liked to blame him before anyone else, his guilt seemed improbable.

Then who? There was only Clarissa left. Certainly, she had access to my rooms. Was her need to keep me there so great that she would destroy the portmanteau in the belief that it would prevent my leaving? To entertain such a thought would have been to believe her horribly disturbed.

I could not.

There had to be another answer.

I tried to recall the last time I had seen the case intact. That would have been when I had left it in the ditch near the crossroads. I strained my mind to recall the area. Had it been strewn with jagged stones? I remembered nothing but dirt and weeds.

But perhaps Davey had torn the case on the bed of the cart. Then, too, it had been stored in the attic for a week. Who was to say it had not lain against something sharp?

I wandered down the corridor in search of Mary, hoping to get answers to my questions. She was in the gallery, washing the windows, her face bright pink with the exertion.

"Anything wrong, miss?" she asked, catching sight of my face.

"Not really. It is just that my case is ripped and I wondered if you knew how?"

"Those awful gashes? Was like that when I took out your dresses. I supposed porter on train had been careless."

I shook my head. "Perhaps Davey would know. It was he who fetched my things from the crossroads, was it not?"

"Yes, miss. If 'ee's looking for him, 'ee'll find him in kitchen."

Davey was perched on one of the kitchen stools, blacking his lordship's boots, and I recognized him as the young man I had seen in the garden. Our short conversation left me little the wiser. He had, he claimed, found my case in its ravaged condition and supposed, as did Mary, that the accident had happened on the train.

"It couldn't have been stones, miss." He balanced the heavy boot in his hand. "'Tweren't the underside was torn."

It was, indeed, a mystery. But at least I knew that no one at the Hall was to blame. Some animal, possibly. The one who was killing the sheep. Perhaps even the dogs, although his lordship had insisted Castor and Pollux did not stray beyond the gates.

Further investigation had to be postponed. Clarissa met me on the stair, twirled about for me to approve of her new dress, and insisted we set off immediately. "See, I have brought Matilda." She waved the doll under my nose. "She has never gone walking on the moor and simply would not be left behind."

"And no wonder. She has missed out on one adventure this week. We must not think to deprive her of another."

The weather had been pleasant for several days, and there was no need to worry about either fog or rain. We had only to follow the tracks we found—some trampled down by people and sheep, others too narrow to have been made by anything larger than rabbits—and we would be safe from bogs. Then, too, I took care to keep the Hall in sight, a relatively simple matter since the tower could be seen for miles.

"And is Matilda enjoying herself?" I asked Clarissa while we strolled through the gorse and thick grass.

She nodded happily. "But she says she wants some purple flowers for her hair."

"Knapweed?" I asked. "Or does she mean the red campion because that has a purplish tinge?"

"As long as it is not thistles. She cannot abide thistles."

"Very wise of her."

I gazed down at the golden-haired doll. There was, as I had thought before, a knowing look in those blue eyes. I would have dearly loved to have been in her confidence.

"I used to have a doll," I told Clarissa, thinking she might like to hear the sad story of Meg. "Although she was a poor cousin to Matilda."

We strolled over the moor, the gorse catching at the hems of our dresses, and I told her my tale. Curlews cried above our heads, and bees buzzed past our ears, but mixed among the sights and sounds came the sounds and smells of the backstreets of London.

"And did you never go back for her?" Clarissa

asked me when I had done, her eyes wide with horror.

I shook my head. "Lady Wolfeburne did not understand. She gave me other dolls, dolls like Matilda. She meant well"—at the time, I added to myself, for that was before the birth of Annabelle—"but she didn't understand."

Clarissa bent over Matilda and whispered fervently, "I will never, ever leave you. No matter what. I swear!" she added, as though that settled the matter. "Matilda is my very best friend," she stated. "Except for my father. And now you, of course. But I can always talk to Matilda. Even about things I can't tell anybody else."

"I hope you will learn that you can talk to me just as you talk to her."

She squeezed my hand. "I know you are my friend, Jessamy. But I never have to think about what I say to Matilda. She can't tell tales, even if it is for my own good, because I'm the only one who understands her. She's mute, you see. Like Wilkins."

I stopped abruptly and stared down at her earnest face. The perfect confidante. Like Wilkins.

"Yes," I murmured. "Yes, I do see."

And why had I not seen before.

My conversation with Clarissa convinced me more than ever that there were secrets at the Hall that Lord Wolfeburne did not want repeated. That was something Wilkins could not do, accidentally or intentionally. And the man could neither read nor write. A curious lack for a man entrusted with a steward's responsibilities.

What was the secret Wilkins could not reveal? Somehow the ruins were involved. I was severely tempted to forget my promise and wander where I had been forbidden to go. But I could not explore them at night, in secret. Not with the dogs on guard. And should I step inside the walls during the daylight hours, he was almost certain to hear of my disobedience.

Had he meant what he'd said? That I would not spend another night beneath his roof if I disobeyed him?

I strongly suspected he had.

And what would happen to Clarissa if I was sent away?

It was not a chance I could take, whatever I wished to do.

And so my days—and nights—continued in the pattern that had been established. And whatever questions I had, they were forced to remain just that. Questions.

Each morning after awakening, and every evening before I retired, I stared out at the tower, watching and wondering. Perhaps if my hours had not been filled, I might have been unable to resist the temptation of going there, but I had other problems, and they were more deserving of my attention.

It behooved me to learn everything I could about Clarissa's childhood, in hopes of coming to a better understanding of her. She was a troubled child who locked everything inside her, and I needed to find what keys could be used to reach her. Something of her childhood, I already knew. And Mary willingly talked about the governesses who had preceded me, but she had nothing unexpected to add to my small store of knowledge.

All of them had been quiet, well-mannered young gentlewomen who had been utterly intimidated by their surroundings and their employer. Only Miss Osborne had been strong-minded and self-assured and, to all appearances, unafraid of Lord Wolfeburne. But not even she had challenged his orders—at least, not to his face. There had been her surreptitious feeding of the dogs.

Then, too, Mary was convinced—or chose to believe—that Miss Osborne's unflappable behavior had been mere posturing. But it was plain that the maid had disliked the woman and thought she had often overstepped her authority.

And none of that helped me with Clarissa.

Realizing I needed to look deeper into her past, I decided to ask Lord Wolfeburne to tell me something of his late wife. Such an improper question was almost certain to provoke him, but he searched for excuses to be provoked when none was provided him, and I had little to lose.

Nevertheless, I prepared with some care when the opportunity to speak with him was next presented. He had dined alone that evening and then, apparently tiring of his own company, told Mrs. Pendarves to have me join him in the drawing room.

"Please inform his lordship that I will be down shortly," I told her, and promptly set about attending to my appearance.

I was wearing the most attractive of the dresses that had been made for me, a sapphire watered silk with wide pagoda sleeves, full undersleeves of *broderie anglaise*, and a finely pleated skirt. It was my hair that needed attention. The constrained knot did not complement the dress's beauty. After several frustrating minutes of twisting my hair about into a chignon, I gave up the task as utterly impossible and hurried downstairs.

The drawing room at the Hall was not as lavish as that of the Pengelleys, perhaps because Lord Wolfeburne preferred his study, and the furnishings in this room had been given little attention. Some of the gilt finish was peeling from the cornices, and the pale blue brocade upholstery had worn on the arms of the sofa and the chairs. But one could still see remnants of its earlier beauty. The mantelpiece had been constructed from white marble and inset with carved figurines, and the chandelier was a mass of crystal pendants and hung with beaded crystal tassels.

Lord Wolfeburne lounged near the fire, one foot set across the other, a brandy glass forgotten in his hand. His gaze lifted from the flames when I entered, and he rose stiffly.

"Do you intend to make a habit of keeping me waiting?" he demanded.

"Forgive me, milord. I needed a few minutes to make myself presentable."

"Indeed?"

He scrutinized me from head to toe, marking the placement of each ribbon and curl. I squirmed beneath the brutal assessment, feeling entirely inadequate and conscious of each and every one of my failings. Then his face lifted, and he smiled.

"This time, you are forgiven. You are well worth the wait."

He bowed graciously and lifted my hand to his lips. The kiss barely brushed the back of my palm, and his fingers held mine lightly, but a burning heat seared through my flesh and up the length of my arm.

He smiled knowingly, fully aware of my discomfort. "Any man who saw you in that dress would fall in love with you. Immediately and completely." His voice and words were teasing, but the look in his eyes was not.

I felt a strong need to change the subject, and said firmly, "Your praise is entirely undeserved, milord. May I sit down?"

He regarded me for several long moments and then shrugged. "As you wish. And perhaps you are right. Your hair badly needs attention."

"I did try," I said, less discomfited by his criticism than by his compliments. "And only learned what I should have already known. I am who I am. It is too late for me to change."

"Come, now. One failure does not warrant a retreat."

"I pride myself on being a quick learner."

"And do you also pride yourself on looking beyond the obvious?"

"Milord?"

He shot me a hard look. "You cling to the past, Miss Lane. Do you never wonder why?"

I considered his accusation and promptly dismissed it as wholly inaccurate. "There is nothing about my past to which I would wish to cling."

He smiled faintly but let the matter drop.

He was in a relatively good mood and, save for a few

penetrating and questioning glances that disconcerted me and brought the color to my cheeks, I spent a pleasant evening in his company. After an hour or more of friendly verbal sparring in which he did not once reproach me, even when I was at my most forward, I had the courage to broach the subject uppermost on my mind.

"How did Clarissa's mother die, milord?" I asked. At his offended glare, I hastily tried to reassure him. "Do not think I ask out of idle curiosity. It is only that it would help me to understand your daughter better."

He considered this, mulling it over in his mind, his fingers once again twisting at his ring. "I suppose there is some merit to your claim. Although I find the subject an unpleasant one."

"Then, by all means, forgive my intrusion and we will say no more of the matter."

"No, no. Only bear with me, for I cannot recall her death without much shame and guilt."

A shadow descended on him. His entire person seemed to be composed of different shades of black, and the darkest hues were in the hard line of his lips and the deep pain in his eyes. Then he spoke, and his voice was darker still.

"If my wife had been fabric, Miss Lane, she would have been a delicate lace. I was a young man, captivated by her beauty and charm. All I thought of was my own happiness and delight in finding such a winsome lady for my wife." He shifted awkwardly in his chair. "We met nearly nine years ago, I had recently been disappointed in another matter—"

I caught my breath, and he broke off to stare at me questioningly.

"That would have been shortly after you had been sent down from Oxford," I mumbled.

"Nothing escapes you, does it? And Sir Ronald was kind enough to bring my juvenile failure to your attention."

"That is none of my concern, milord."

He shrugged. "It no longer matters, save for the brief mention it earns in this tale. And it was only one of several disappointments that I felt I suffered unjustly. But I was an ignorant boy who thought life had made me certain promises, and I expected them to be kept. You, of all people, will know this to be unreasonable. Life makes us no such promises, and those who look for them are doomed to disappointment."

I swallowed.

"But I digress. This tale concerns my past, not yours. I was convinced life owed me recompense, and I found that recompense on a trip to Truro in the person of Miss Miranda Fairbanks. She was everything I desired in a wife, and I did not stop to consider what would happen to her if I brought her to these unhallowed halls."

He paused to clear his throat, emotion choking off his words. I wanted to beg him to be silent and forget that I had ever asked that foolish question. But he was already gone from both sight and sound of me, struggling with his own inner demons, and there was nothing that anyone could have said or done to retrieve him.

After a long pause, he stirred. "A wiser man would

have put all thought of her from his mind. But I make no claim to wisdom. And at first, she was happy. Any changes in her personality were slight and gradual, and I failed to notice them. But after Clarissa's birth, she fell sick. She was bedeviled by nightmares. She unraveled before my eyes. And I, still every bit the fool, supposed that I could save her."

His fist crashed down upon the arm of the settee, and I jumped in my chair. "In trying, I sealed her fate forever."

"But what could you have done to hurt her?" I said in protest, finding my tongue once again in my possession.

"What did I do? I trusted her, Miss Lane. Trusted her with something that should never have been shared. I thought the truth would give her strength to face a hundred nameless fears.

"Instead, it robbed her of the one source of strength that remained to her. It robbed her of her confidence in me, and she surrendered to the next illness that overtook her."

His distress drenched the room, like moisture in the air before a downpour. The room was heavy with its weight. I roused myself to shake off the oppressive feeling, lest it also take possession of me.

"Surely, you are blaming yourself unfairly," I said gently. "What could you have told her that was so damaging?"

He lifted his head and gave me a black stare. "That, please God, you will never know, for I shall never tell another living creature. Only be aware that Clarissa is much like her mother, and I will not have her death upon my conscience. I have protected her as well as I am able, but your presence has done much more for her. Only continue as you have so far done, and she will be fine."

"I had no thought to do otherwise. But I will keep in mind what you have told me here this evening."

He nodded. "Good. I ask no more of you."

He dismissed me with a wave. It was as abrupt a dismissal as I had ever received from him, but I did not hold him accountable for his behavior. Clearly, he was distracted by the pain of his memories.

10

Our talk gave me some insights. It confirmed my suspicions that Lord Wolfeburne guarded some secret, a secret that had been shared with his wife at great cost. And it explained Clarissa's determination to hide her fears. She would not fail her father as her mother had done. There seemed to be nothing for me to do but remain vigilant and ever conscious of her inherited tendency to succumb to nerves. I was struck again by her need for fresh air and exercise, even above her need for lessons.

Our daily tramps upon the moor were happy, invigorating expeditions, and the days when Clarissa suggested we go and sit by the ruins became rarer and rarer. But while this pleased me, I found something else in her behavior to concern me. Not once did she ask why we didn't return to the Pengelleys or attend the hunt mentioned by the Drewes and the Trefferys. Her oversight bothered me, for it could only mean she had noticed the tension between her father and his neighbors.

But the lack of other society brought us closer together. For some while, I did not realize the extent of my progress. It was Clarissa herself who enlightened me.

We had taken a stroll on the moor. The sun was sinking in the sky, for we had set off later than usual, and there was a brisk breeze that battered at our skirts and brought the blood to our cheeks. The moor stretched around us in every direction, green and mysterious, and the entire landscape was set in motion by the breeze.

Clarissa had been dancing at my side, her head twisting left and right, her eyes quick to catch any sign of movement. Ahead of us, two grouse burst from the thicket of gorse and took flight. Their wings beat the air directly before us, and Clarissa gave a cry of delight.

"Look," she said. "One is smaller than the other. Do you think they could be like us?"

I laughed. "Perhaps. I suppose even young grouse must have to be taught by their elders. I wonder if they enjoy their schooling."

She nodded immediately. "It would be wicked of them if they did not. Besides, perhaps the little one is being taught by someone like you, Jessamy. They could not help but like their lessons, then."

"And if the pupil is as attentive as you, then the elder grouse must also be content."

She glanced up at me and smiled, an unguarded, happy smile. "You were telling the truth, weren't you, Jessamy?"

"Indeed, it is always my intention. But to what do you refer?"

"The day we met. You said you would not leave me. I did not believe you then, but I do now."

My stomach tightened, and I rested my hand upon her shoulder. "I am glad to hear you say so. You are as dear to me as any daughter of my own could be."

"And Matilda, too?" she demanded.

"I could hardly love you and not love her as well."

She nodded, satisfied.

For a while we walked in silence. The damp earth sank beneath our shoes, and the scent of gorse and heather was strong and tangy. Everything seemed more alive after a fall of rain, the scents stronger and the greens darker—a deep jade instead of mere green. Rabbits hopped in the undergrowth, and twice we caught sight of a pair of long ears before their owners darted to cover. The air shimmered before our eyes, bright with the lingering moisture.

It was, I decided, an exceptional day, both in beauty and for the sense of contentment that had suffused me. Even the thought of returning to the Hall and the darkness that gathered there could not spoil that moment.

It ended all too quickly when a man's cry hailed us from across the moor. I turned and glanced around but saw no one. A second cry echoed the first, and Clarissa tugged on my sleeve.

"There he is. By the rocks."

I followed her gaze and saw why I had not immediately spotted the man. He was not standing, but crouching. A second man sprawled on the grass, his head resting on a folded overcoat. Shotguns lay to one side of them, their barrels propped against the stones.

I took Clarissa's hand and we hurried toward them. Whatever doubts I had about approaching them while Clarissa was in my care were assuaged as we drew closer.

From the cut and quality of their clothes, they were clearly gentlemen.

"Thank goodness you happened this way," the first man said, as soon as he could be heard without shouting. He peered at me from beneath droopy eyebrows that gave him the appearance of a good-tempered spaniel. Apparently satisfied by what he saw, he indicated the man beside him with a nod of his head. "My friend's gun discharged accidentally and he shot himself in the calf."

The prostrate man groaned and mumbled, "Confounded bad luck."

His trouser leg was soaked in blood, and a piece of cloth had been tied above the knee to staunch the bleeding. I glanced at his face. It was pallid and damp with perspiration. Clearly, he needed the attention of a doctor, although his injury did not appear to be life-threatening.

"Wolfeburne Hall is a good mile off," I told the man who had hailed us. "But there is nowhere closer. Shall I fetch someone to help you?"

He shook his head. "Stanton can walk with help. We've gotten this far, but he could use a second shoulder if you're willing. Hate to leave him lying on this damp grass longer than is necessary while I go for help. And if a fog should come up, I might never find him." He cast a sad look across the moor.

"I'm willing and strong," I told him. "If you are certain he can walk."

In answer, Stanton pushed himself into a sitting position. He paused, then nodded at us to say he was ready. Together his friend and I helped him to his feet, and he draped his arms over our shoulders.

Fortunately, he was a small man, short and moderate of build, and his weight was not as great as I had feared. With Clarissa leading the way, we hobbled back to the Hall. Our progression was interrupted by long breaks for Mr. Stanton to catch his breath. His friend, Mr. Pernell, and I were equally glad of a rest.

It was late afternoon before we struggled through the main gates. Davey stood in the middle of the driveway, raking the gravel into a smooth surface. He pushed back his cap, blinked, and hurried to add his strength to ours. Hot, concerned, and thoroughly exhausted, we clattered through the front doors.

Our voices and Mr. Stanton's pained grunts drew Mrs. Pendarves from the front parlor, her tidy, small person introducing a note of calm into our bedraggled midst. In the dark corridor beyond, a door slammed and Lord Wolfeburne stalked out of the shadows.

"Mrs. Pendarves, what is the cause of this commotion?" he demanded.

His gaze traveled over her head to me. My appearance must have startled him, for his face blanched. I managed a weak smile and hastily brushed back the strands of hair that had fallen from the knot of hair at my nape.

Not much reassured, he searched next for Clarissa. She was alight with excitement and not at all dismayed by our adventure. Apparently satisfied that there could not be much amiss, his gaze swept over the two strangers in his entry hall. One wore a frank look of expectancy, and the other sprawled on the caned chair, his bloody leg stretched out before him.

Lord Wolfeburne's expression hardened. "Mrs. Pendarves, take Clarissa upstairs. I do not want her having nightmares for a week."

He turned to me, and all concern for my well-being had vanished. "I presume there is an explanation for this disturbance," he said, speaking to me as though I were a servant.

Mr. Pernell impatiently stepped between us. "This is hardly the time for explanations. My friend needs to be given somewhere to lie down. Immediately. And a doctor to attend to his leg."

Lord Wolfeburne acknowledged him with a contemptuous look. "He will not find one at Wolfeburne Hall. And if you are suggesting that this gentleman should remain here until he recovers, that is out of the question. We are unused to receiving guests and have no rooms available."

There was an audible intake of breath from the three of us grouped there. I was the first to regain my tongue. "They can use my suite. Mary can put a cot in Clarissa's room for me."

He scowled. "This is not your decision to make."

Mr. Pernell glanced at his friend's pained face, and his pale cheeks flushed a deep red. "Where is your decency, man? Under the circumstances, we have every right to demand your hospitality."

"I will not have my household thrown into disorder because of some fool's carelessness with a gun. If he has no more sense than to shoot himself in the leg, he deserves to be discomfited. *I* do not."

I gaped at him. Whatever I thought of Lord Wolfeburne's manners, I had never supposed his character had so far disintegrated that he would refuse aid to someone who was clearly in need. This was a side of him I did not know.

Lord Wolfeburne's gaze flickered in my direction, and something in my eyes must have betrayed my thoughts. "Confound it. This is my home, and I have the right to refuse admittance to whomsoever I choose. Nor should I be compelled to give any explanation."

"He needs a doctor, milord," I said, insistent. "In the exertion of crossing the moors, he has lost a good deal of blood."

"The nearest is in Doublebois."

"Bastian must be sent for him."

"Miss Lane, you are becoming a good deal more trouble than you are worth. May I remind you that your welcome here is tenuous, at best."

The warmth drained from my cheeks, and bands of steel tightened around my chest. Mr. Stanton struggled to rise, lost his balance, and dropped back heavily onto the chair. "It is not my wish to impose on you, milord. Were it possible for me to go elsewhere, I should do so willingly and gladly. But, in good conscience, you cannot refuse me."

"I can and I do."

"You are mad," he said in a thin, colorless voice. "Completely mad."

"More likely drunk," Mr. Pernell retorted. "I am acquainted with both your name and reputation. Be assured, if you throw us out, our tale will do you no credit."

Lord Wolfeburne tossed back his head and laughed. I had not heard that reckless laughter for many weeks, and the sound unsettled me as it had done on our first meeting. The two gentlemen beside me exchanged glances.

Lord Wolfeburne smiled genially. "If you are aware of my reputation, then you must realize that I could shoot both of you where you stand and sink no lower in my peers' regard. However, I will offer you the use of my coach and driver. But that is all you shall have from me." He nodded to Davey who had discreetly and hastily withdrawn to a dark corner. "Have Bastian bring the carriage round immediately."

The young man pulled on the brim of his cap and dashed out the door.

Lord Wolfeburne surveyed his guests. "This is the best I can do for you. Take it or leave it. Either way, the hour is growing late, and you will not remain beneath my roof tonight."

Mr. Pernell's eyebrows quivered. "You cannot seriously mean to make Stanton suffer more discomfort than he has already?"

"And why not? Perhaps it will teach him prudence."

The man stiffened, and his arms tensed at his sides, but Lord Wolfeburne was a head taller and a good fifteen years younger. Possibly coming to this same conclusion himself, Mr. Pernell made no attempt to strike him, but gave a derisive snort and said, "This is outrageous behavior for one gentleman to show another."

"If that is all that bothers you, then set your mind to rest. As you yourself pointed out, it is commonly known I am no gentleman."

"Nor do you seem to care."

"I do not."

Mr. Stanton chose that moment to push himself to his feet, displaying a strength I had not thought he possessed. "Enough, Pernell. Let us be gone. I would not stay a night beneath this monster's roof if my life depended on it."

"Nor I," his friend said fervently.

Lord Wolfeburne bowed. "Then we are in agreement. I beg you not to soil my carriage while it is in your possession. Blood is devilishly hard to remove from the upholstery."

"Of all the—" Mr. Pernell glared at him. "Good day, sir. And may God forgive you for your heartlessness."

"No doubt, He will. He is, after all, in the business of forgiveness, is He not?"

The door closed upon this sally, and the silence closed in upon us with a heaviness that made movement impossible. Lord Wolfeburne frowned at the closed door and the sounds that issued from the driveway. But his interest appeared to be pretense.

Several minutes passed, but neither of us spoke. Lord Wolfeburne refused to look at me, and his stance forbade conversation. Outside, wheels crunched through the recently raked gravel. There was the murmur of voices, and the carriage door slammed. His sole excuse for ignoring me gone, he turned and regarded me.

The passion had drained from his face, and looking at him was like looking upon the castle ruins. Whatever life had once existed there was long since gone; only the walls remained standing.

"How could you?" I demanded, genuinely bewildered. "You have not even the excuse of drunkenness to give in your defense."

"It seems I have shocked you at last, Miss Lane," he replied.

"Indeed, you have."

"Then I can only hope you will forestall such occurrences in the future by not representing my home as the last outpost of civilization, and thereby saving us both embarrassment."

I shook my head in wonderment. "I begin to believe you capable of neither embarrassment nor shame."

Something flashed deep within his eyes, a flicker of light that was immediately extinguished. "You need not give me an accounting of my failings. I am well aware of what they are supposed to be. And if I were not, it is hardly your place to inform me."

"Certainly someone should."

"You live in *my* home, Miss Lane. At *my* sufferance. You would be well advised to remember that."

He marched past me and, without either his coat or hat, stalked out the same door through which Mr. Stanton and his friend had just left. Stunned, I stared at the vacant space where he had so recently been standing. How could I have believed that something of his former self existed and could still be recalled?

He was beyond redemption.

Alone in my sitting room, I reconsidered that opinion. Surely he could not be a complete villain. I mulled over all that had happened since my arrival, but it was not until I compared his recent deplorable display with the scene at the Pengelleys that I discovered a pattern.

That earlier outburst had followed upon Mr. Drewe's suggestion that his lordship arrange a hunt at the Hall. At the time, there had been an odd look on his face, a look I had attributed to Sir Ronald's insult. Could it be that he was afraid to bring his peers into his home?

Who lived beneath his roof but servants? Each of them well paid to do as they were told, many of them too fearful to leave their beds at night. And besides them, a long line of governesses. Timid young women who would not dare question their employer. Only Miss Osborne had been different, and she had been more interested in getting a full night's sleep than in delving into the Hall's mysteries.

Lord Wolfeburne's peers were unlikely to be as reticent.

I rose and went to the windows. Nothing seemed amiss at the Hall. Did the answer lie in the ruins? If so, I would certainly incur his lordship's wrath by trespassing there. Yesterday, I would not have thought him capable of sending me away. Today, I was less certain.

I sighed. His attitude affected me more than I cared to admit. At some point, since arriving in Cornwall, my sense of autonomy had deserted me. And if I wanted to remain, if only for Clarissa's sake, I would do well to make peace with Lord Wolfeburne.

Resolved to do just that, I changed into the watered-silk dress that Lord Wolfeburne had admired and sat up in the front parlor until the hour grew late, hoping to hear him return. By midnight, he had yet to appear. Outside, the fog drew across the moon and doused its cold brilliance with a damp blanket. From the parlor window, the driveway, normally a stark white ribbon twisting across the dark lawn, disappeared into the spongy grayness a few steps from the front door.

He would not be back that night, I decided. For if the

driveway was difficult to discern, following the lane would be impossible. I doused the lamps in the parlor, save for the one needed to light my way to bed. That done, I left the room, shutting the door behind me.

In the corridor, all was quiet. Shadows flickered up and down the walls, leaping, dancing shadows that threatened with a dark menace. They were abetted by the omnipresent silence that seemed to have a life of its own. It was an unnatural silence, born of mustiness and age, emptiness and secrets, the kind that could only exist during the late hours of the night in an old and isolated house.

I paused in the entry hall, feeling a foolish dread at the thought of the long, silent walk awaiting me. The stairway gaped, black and still, snaking upward to the landing. That, too, was dark, and the stillness and the otherworldly feeling put me in mind of my first minutes at the Hall—of Clarissa's pale face peering between the railings of the banister. There and then, I half-believed in ghosts myself.

I set my foot upon the first stair. At that same instant, the dogs began to howl. Their cry arose from very near the front door, a quivering, fearful cry that obliterated silence with a noise that was yet more awful. It was unthinkable that mere dogs could give voice to that almost human wailing.

Then it occurred to me that Lord Wolfeburne might have returned. I drew back from the stairs, determined to look outside and see whatever could be seen, even to admit his lordship if it was he who approached. My steps echoed across the marble tile, firm and determined, although I could not have said I was filled with the same resolve. Nevertheless, I turned the key in the latch and reached for the doorknob. The brass fixture was cold and damp beneath my fingers, but it turned easily enough, and I threw open the door.

Castor and Pollux stood at the bottom of the steps, their teeth bared, and the hackles on their necks standing in stiff rows. The unearthly howls issued from their open mouths, and specks of saliva dripped from their teeth.

I stopped abruptly, fearing they might turn on me, but neither dog glanced in my direction. Their heads and gazes were fixed directly ahead of them. Hoping they had come to accept me, I took a step toward them.

"Castor. Pollux. Be quiet," I said firmly.

To my surprise, their howls stopped abruptly, but still they did not turn, but took to making low growls that came from deep within their throats.

"Lord Wolfeburne," I called. "Is that you?"

There was no answer but, a short distance ahead of me, I heard the crunching of gravel, as though beneath someone's feet. The sound was too near for anyone who stood there to have failed to hear my question. I lifted my lamp, trying to cast its light on whatever was hidden in the fog, and descended the steps. Upon reaching the driveway, I paused.

There was a startled grunt. A frightening silence followed. Then heavy footfalls retreated down the driveway, and whatever had been there was gone. I was left to question the accuracy of my senses.

But if I mistrusted my own ears, I could not doubt those of the dogs. Their growls came to an abrupt end, and they dropped to their haunches. Their jaws split into wide grins and Castor's tail thumped against the steps.

I hesitated to approach them. With the intruder gone, there was only one being to whom they could direct their attentions. And while they made no protest at my having left the Hall, I was not convinced they would permit me to walk past them and reenter the home they guarded.

As I stood there, the door opened. Wilkins stepped beneath the portico, lantern in hand. In my haste to discover the cause of the dogs' howls, I had forgotten he had been told to silence them whenever they cried at night. He was fully dressed, tweed overcoat draped over his shoulders and walking boots on his feet. I supposed he had let his duties wait until he was warmly clad, something I would have been wise to do, for the night was cold and damp.

I did not linger where I stood, but emerged from the fog, my lamp swinging at my side. I boldly strolled by the dogs who merely followed me with their eyes, accepting me without question. Wilkins gaped as though I were a ghost.

"Good evening," I said, pretending that we often met in this fashion. "I thought Lord Wolfeburne might have returned, but apparently I was wrong."

Having no other means to express himself, the steward glared. Gripping me by the shoulder, he hustled me into the Hall. After shutting and locking the door behind us, he removed the key and pocketed it.

"Lord Wolfeburne may yet return," I pointed out. "Someone will have to let him in, and that will be difficult if the key is gone. He will not think kindly of you if he is forced to linger on his own doorstep."

In answer, Wilkins motioned with his hand for me to

go upstairs. Since there was no reason to do otherwise, I said good-night and did as he had bidden me.

Morning came very early, and I dawdled over my breakfast. My sleep had been troubled by dreams of sharp-clawed animals that leapt out of the darkness to attack me. Such thoughts had not bothered me while I stood alone in the fog, and yet some part of me must have supposed myself in danger or I would not have been troubled by nightmares.

With a light sigh, I pushed back my chair. Clarissa would be waiting in the schoolroom. If I lingered much longer, she would think something amiss and come in search of an explanation. The thought had no sooner occurred to me than there was a knock on my door.

"Come in," I called in a cheerful voice, hoping to ward off any anxious questions.

Lord Wolfeburne stepped into my sitting room. He was wearing the same suit he had worn the previous afternoon, although it was both muddy and rumpled. Stubble darkened his jaw, and his hair was matted. Judging from the green stains on his cuffs, I surmised he had spent the night on the moor. My gaze was drawn to the haunted look in his eyes. They were dark with pain and hunger for solace.

"Are you all right?" I asked, too startled by his appearance to remember how deeply he'd hurt me.

"That is something only you can tell me," he said softly. "Have I destroyed myself completely in your eyes?"

I hesitated. He seemed desperate to make amends, but his moods changed quickly. I would not be misled a second time. Nevertheless, it was important that we come to some form of truce. I set my breakfast plates back onto the tray and stacked them neatly atop each other.

Eyes safely averted, I said, "It is I who must apologize, milord. It is not my place to judge you."

"But you have, nonetheless," he murmured.

"Nonsense."

"And found me lacking."

"I blame only myself."

"Can you not bring yourself to forgive me?"

"Really, milord. The matter is already forgotten." I refolded my linen serviette, following the same folds that the iron had made until it resumed the neat rectangular shape it had originally possessed.

Lord Wolfeburne remained just inside my door, neither approaching nor retreating. "I am deeply and utterly ashamed by those things I said to you."

"It was I who acted out of turn."

"I responded like a child who cut his own hand, then blamed the knife for having drawn his blood."

"You concern yourself unduly."

Unable to do more with my serviette, I set it aside and cast my gaze about for something else that might demand my attention. But Mary had completed her morning's tasks with a thoroughness that Mrs. Pendarves would have applauded.

He cleared his throat. "There are a few dying roses that could be removed from the vases. And you have only to glance in my direction to discover that the fringe on the carpet is decidedly askew."

"I imagine Mrs. Pendarves will replace the flowers." I

forced myself to lift my head and meet his gaze. "It is time I was in the schoolroom."

He lifted his arm and braced himself against the door-frame, making it impossible for me to pass. "I told Clarissa I required a moment of your time."

"Surely there is nothing more to be said?"

"You have not yet forgiven me."

I swallowed hard. "You were most unjust."

He nodded.

"And your words cruel."

"Undeservedly so."

"Is that all I am to have from you?" I searched his face. "There is to be no explanation?"

He frowned. "I can think of none that excuses my behavior."

"You must have had your reasons, such as they were."

"And you are determined to have them from me?"

"I must."

Tears brimmed in my eyes. How could I resume my part in our odd friendship while I believed his favor could be withdrawn at any moment? And for offenses that escaped my understanding?

Something of my feelings must have been conveyed to Lord Wolfeburne. He straightened and walked across the room to where I stood. His hand reached out to clasp mine in his strong grip. I trembled violently at his touch.

"Have you no notion of how deeply *you* wounded *me*?" he asked.

"I?"

"Indeed. Do you think, in all the commotion, I failed to see the disappointment in your face? Or escaped the painful knowledge that, in that instant, you viewed me as the same abhorrent creature who had disgusted his neighbors and acquaintances for more years than I care to remember?"

"But that is—"

He lifted a finger and compelled me to silence. "I have grown accustomed to their dislike and ill will, so accustomed that I hardly notice their curses and their insults. But I cannot make the same claim where you are concerned. You have retained a vision of me that I myself have forgotten. And for all my mockery, it pleases me to think that there is at least one being in this world who does not revile me."

"W-why that's nonsense. Clarissa adores you."

"Clarissa is a child and my daughter. She has no choice but to adore me. I am all she has."

There was, perhaps, some truth to this. And if his explanation did not account for all his faults, it allowed me to again believe that, whatever his moods or temper, my presence in his home was both important and necessary to him. Knowing that, I could not deny him the forgiveness he so desperately desired.

"I cannot say I fully understand," I said. "But certainly I can forgive you. All of us, at some time, have allowed anger to be our master."

His eyebrows arched, and the corners of his lips quivered. "Even you? You cannot mean me to believe something so incredible?"

Exasperated, I yanked my hand from his. The man was impossible. Having won my pardon, he had instantly deserted the field and redonned his favorite mask. He was as elusive as the fog that whirled and twisted outside his own windows.

"Tell me also why you drove those gentlemen from your home. And you may yet sweep aside all my doubts and restore to me that image of yourself you seem to cherish."

He shook his head. "You have heard all that I am willing to say. Only know that I did not act without cause. And if you will trust to my own estimation, then believe also that it was good and reasonable cause."

With those words he turned to leave, and I supposed that I would have to be satisfied with an explanation that was no explanation at all. If previous events had not already taught me he was guarding some secret, he would have found me harder to convince. Even so, I was not sure that his cause *was* good or reasonable. His statement only made me certain that there was, indeed, some motive for his behavior of which no one else was aware.

Save, perhaps, for Wilkins.

That thought prompted another memory.

"Please do not leave yet, milord," I cried after his retreating back. "There is something I must tell you."

11

He paused and nodded for me to continue.

"Last night, during your absence, the dogs started howling again. This time near the front door. By chance, I happened to be on my way upstairs, and I went outside to see if it was you."

His chin jerked up. "Did I not forbid you to leave the Hall at night? Suppose the dogs had turned on you."

"They did not, milord. Indeed, they were far too intent on something or someone who had trespassed on the estate to give my worthless person their attention."

"And what was that?" he asked, his face and voice suddenly guarded.

I shrugged. "I could not say. I thought I heard something walking across the gravel, but the fog was too thick for me to see. As soon as I held up my lamp, the creature bounded off."

"Another dog, do you think?"

"If so, then one that was near as large as Castor or Pollux. It had too heavy a tread to have been a smaller animal."

"I shall advise Wilkins to be more watchful." He frowned. "Where was the man? It is his duty to see to the dogs at night."

"I was up and dressed and by the front door. He was a few minutes in joining me. Too late, alas, to hear what I heard."

He gave me a severe look. "Luckily, there was no damage done, but you are not to disregard my orders. You gave me two promises upon entering my home, and I expect you to honor both of them."

"Yes, milord."

It was a mild reproach, lighter than I either expected or deserved, but the timing was fortuitous. Having settled our recent differences, I suspected he was not willing to scold me immediately thereafter.

"There is another matter, too," I added. "One that makes me think that it is not a large dog wandering about the moor, but something entirely different."

"Can I not be gone for a single night without your filling your free hours with matters that do not concern you?"

This time, his annoyance was plain, and there was something else I read in those dark eyes. An emotion that I had never before seen there.

Fear.

It was the one flaw he had always seemed to lack. For all he had once told me otherwise.

"As it happens, this matter does concern me. And I can hardly avoid using my mind. Unless you advocate severing my head from my body."

"I would not be the first Englishman to rid myself of a troublesome woman in that manner," he retorted. He softened his words with a smile. "All right. Tell me of what you speak, and I shall decide for myself if your conclusions have merit."

"As you wish. Only wait there for a minute."

I rose and swept into my bedroom. The portmanteau, now filled with my old dresses, was harder to pull from its resting place, but I was determined to display it for him. I emerged from the bedroom, dust spattering the backs of my hands, and tilted the bag for his perusal.

He stared, his features set in an impassionate mask that defied anyone to guess his thoughts. "And how did that occur?" he asked, his voice equally devoid of emotion.

"I do not know. Some animal clawed the leather while my luggage lay overnight beside the moor."

"More likely it was torn on the stones."

"There was nothing but weeds and dirt."

He shrugged. "Then Davey was careless in his handling. I shall speak with him."

"I have already done that. He insists he found the bag in this condition."

"Which is not to say he is not lying."

"Really, milord," I said. "I am not a fool. I am perfectly capable of assessing whether or not someone is telling me the truth." Indeed, I had caught *him* dissembling on more than one occasion.

He glared at me, and I was grateful for even that much of a response. His anger was infinitely preferable to that bland nothingness with which he confronted me.

"Then what, pray tell, is your conclusion?" he demanded. "I presume you have one."

"I do."

"And it is?"

"That the same creature who is killing the sheep also ripped my luggage. And since a dog's claws are not sharp enough nor capable of spreading this wide, it could not possibly be Castor or Pollux. Or any kind of wild dog."

He frowned and reviewed the damage. "Some kind of wild cat, do you think?"

"On Bodmin Moor?"

"As I recall, there was a traveling fair that passed through Doublebois some while ago. If one had escaped . . ."

"But surely they would have said something and made some effort to retrieve the animal."

"Not if they thought they might be responsible for any damages." He bestowed a smile on me, a remarkably pleased and genial smile. "Forgive me for speaking as I did. You may very well have found the answer. As for the case, I shall have Davey bring you down another. There is no point in keeping that one. It could not possibly be used again."

"Thank you, milord. But I do not expect to be traveling in the near future. There is no need to put him to any trouble."

"Nonsense. Of course you shall have a new bag. If only to keep the moths from your dresses." He nodded to where a fold of black taffeta poked beneath the torn leather.

I could recall a time when he would have been perfectly willing to feed my mourning dresses to the moths. But since it pleased him to be generous, I acquiesced.

Having promised to replace it, he took the savaged case from me. It was not until after he had left that I realized, in accepting his offer, I had also allowed him to remove the only evidence I had that such a creature existed.

Compared to the complicated relationship I had with her father, caring for Clarissa seemed almost simple. Her lessons proceeded well and her health steadily improved. She was becoming much more than a pupil to me. I dared not look upon her as a daughter, but slipped into the habit of regarding her as a little sister.

That, at least, was a role that could not be taken from me.

Each night, unless I was asked to dine downstairs, I read her stories and tucked her into bed myself. Often I remained until after she had fallen asleep. One night, thinking she might enjoy a glimpse of the full moon, I set my lamp on a small occasional table, lowered the wick, and went to draw back the curtains.

Clarissa leaped from her bed and thrust herself between me and the heavy folds of plum-colored velvet. "No, you must not. P-Papa would be upset."

My surprise at her dismay rather than her fragile weight held me back. "Whatever is the matter? I mean to do no more than let in the moonlight."

She shook her head violently. "No. You must not. Please, Jessamy."

"As you wish," I agreed, not willing to upset her further. "But tell me why you think your father would be bothered by something as insignificant as my opening your curtains."

I could feel her withdrawing from me. It was as if a

wall had descended between us, and I was not her beloved Jessamy but a stranger who must not, under any circumstances, be trusted. She would not even look me in the eye, but stared down at her fingers and twisted at the lacy edging of her sleeve.

"Clarissa?"

"All the curtains must be drawn at dusk and remain drawn until the sun rises," she said as though she were repeating some kind of catechism.

The remark was not at all unlike Mary's comments. But in superstitious and gullible Mary, they had made me choke back my amusement. Clarissa uttered them with a dread and conviction that made the goose bumps rise on my forearms and the hairs at my nape stiffen.

"That is simply to keep out the cold and damp," I said in response, determined to reintroduce a note of reality to our conversation. "Surely you have not been listening to Mary's tales?"

She shook her head.

"Then why would you attach any importance to such a simple matter?"

She said nothing.

I thought it foolish to press her. Whatever secret fear she held, I could only shake her trust in me by forcing an admission she was not ready to make. "Come," I told her. "You must get back into bed for the floor is cold and you have nothing on your feet."

I had not realized how seriously Clarissa took this matter of drawing the curtains at dusk. Clearly, she read more into the situation than existed. Despite her claims, I supposed the servants' fears had been instilled in her, and remembered again how aware children could be of the undercurrents that existed around them.

It was not a matter that could be dismissed.

The next morning, I ignored my breakfast tray and slipped downstairs to speak with Lord Wolfeburne. He had taken to rising earlier in the day, and often went to his study shortly after breakfast.

I found him seated at his desk, behind a neat stack of correspondence. He glanced up from the letter in his hand, his look faintly annoyed. He was properly attired in a suit that was somber but becoming. His hair was neatly combed to one side, and his face recently shaven. Nor could I help but notice that his fingernails had been trimmed and buffed to a shine. His eyes, too, seemed clearer, although they were darkened by a mild annoyance. It faded the instant he saw me.

"Miss Lane. I was not expecting you." His brows abruptly drew together. "Is everything all right?"

"For the most part, milord."

"Then to what am I indebted for this visit?"

Not long ago he would have assumed I had come to complain or protest. Which one of us, I wondered, had changed? Or was this merely a new manner he had of teasing me?

"May I sit down?" I asked, wanting to give myself a few seconds' reprieve.

He nodded.

I took the wing chair across from him, spread out the skirt of my dress, and lifted my gaze to his. As I had expected, he was watching me. Something in his eyes made my stomach flutter nervously, and I regretted having ignored my breakfast.

"It is good of you to speak with me," I said.

He chuckled. "I dare not refuse you, for I would almost certainly regret my rudeness."

"Really, milord."

"Forgive me," he said without a hint of remorse. "Please continue."

"Something has come to my attention, and I think it is a matter that deserves some thought."

He waited.

"It is this fuss over the curtains. Clarissa has come to believe there is something dreadful to be seen outside at night, and she is terrified. I think it would be wise if less importance was attached to the matter. Surely it is better that a few furnishings suffer, or more coal be added to the fires, than your daughter's fears be allowed to continue."

"And who told you that the curtains were drawn to keep out the damp?"

It was not the response I had expected. I stared at him. "As I recall, it was Mary. I imagine she was only repeating what she'd been told by Mrs. Pendarves."

"Of course. The ubiquitous Mrs. Pendarves." He leaned back in his chair. "She meant well, no doubt. The less said about the matter, the better. But, unfortunately, she misled you, however well meaning her intent."

"Then there is another reason?"

He nodded. "It is for Clarissa's sake the maids are sent about their business so promptly. Three years ago it was merely one more task added to their duties, no more or less important than any other."

"And then?"

"Something happened shortly after my wife's death. It was a period when Clarissa was most susceptible. Perhaps, that is *wh*y it happened. Another time she might not have been subject to wild fancies."

"What kind of fancies?"

He shrugged. "I am not entirely certain. She has never said much to anyone. What I know of the story, I will tell you as it was told to me."

His offer was as unexpected as his earlier reply. I had never known him to be forthcoming, and could only assume that, whatever had upset her, had no connection to his own secrets.

That, or he had begun to place his trust in me.

Lord Wolfeburne tapped his fingers on his desk, and his eyes clouded as he looked inward. "Clarissa was six. Her mother had died six months previously, and her most recent governess had packed her bags and fled my employ that same week. My daughter had been sitting in the servants' hall with Mrs. Pendarves, playing a game of cat's cradle. Mrs. Pendarves excused herself to tend to some trivial household disturbance and left Clarissa to amuse herself with Matilda."

He twisted at the wolf's-head ring on his fingers. "Minutes later, she screamed. It was not merely one short scream, you understand, but a series of screams that did not end even when Mrs. Pendarves and one of the maids rushed into the hall.

"Clarissa was sitting at the window, Matilda in her arms, and she was staring into the fog at something only she could see. Whatever it was had terrified her. She was hysterical. Even after they stopped her screams, she whimpered until the sleeping draught they gave her had taken effect."

"And did no one ever discover what had frightened her?"

He frowned and looked impatiently at the papers on his desk. "I told you, did I not, that there was nothing there?"

"Are you trying to say the child is a sensitive, milord?"

He stiffened. "Indeed, I am not. Table tapping and spirits are for spinsters. Women who receive too little attention from their families and have too little charity or intelligence to fill their empty hours with good works. She merely imagined something in the fog. Something that was not there."

"Why, then, do you draw the curtains?"

He scowled at me. "I should think the reason for that plain. If she has suffered from delusions once, she can suffer from them again. Clarissa was ill for a week afterward, then awakened with no memory of what had upset her. All she had acquired was a distaste for gazing into the fog. I do not want the incident repeated."

There was some kind of reasoning in this. Although not the kind I myself would have employed. Better, I thought, to prove to her that she had been mistaken than to support her doubts as he had done.

"Did you think to go outside and look around, milord?" I asked. "It might have been a sheep at the window."

"If I had been here, I would have done. Do you take me for a complete fool? Unfortunately, I had gone to Doublebois early that afternoon and had not yet returned."

I wondered if guilt was the reason for his annoyance. Likely, it was. Clarissa had only one parent to shelter her, which made his presence all the more important.

I sighed. "I have seen for myself that she possesses a

great deal of imagination. Matilda is very real to her, even at an age when many children lose interest in their dolls. And on our first meeting, she thought me a ghost."

"A ghost? You? There have been numerous timid creatures living beneath my roof these past few years, and any of *them* might have been mistaken for a ghost. They were all dull, gray wraiths with nary a life of their own save that life they assumed when they stepped through my portals."

I squirmed on my chair. "Really, milord. Must you always amuse yourself at my expense?"

He grinned, his irritation with me forgotten. "Indeed, it is hardly to be wondered at that Miss Osborne could disappear without our either noticing or remarking on her departure. I find it more curious the others did not simply disappear the moment we ceased to stare at them directly."

"You talk foolishness. And I—"

"But you, Miss Lane"—a wicked grin curved his lips and crinkled the corners of his eyes—"are the warm southern wind that chases spring across the land. Merely by your coming, you have stirred the dormant life within us. *Your* loss could not possibly be overlooked or ignored."

Despite his flippant tone, his eyes smoldered with unguarded hunger. I felt myself blush, and I was forced to avert my eyes. Even that did not stop him.

"Should you go," he continued, "it is we who will never be heard from again."

"We were talking of Clarissa, milord." My voice sounded unsteady and oddly high-pitched.

"Were we? I thought we had exhausted that subject."

"For the moment," I said. "But she will be waiting in the schoolroom for me, and I must go to her."

He sighed, leaned back in his chair, and watched me go.

I did not mention what I had learned to Clarissa. But late that night, after I had changed into my nightdress and unraveled my plaited knot, I pulled back the curtain and stared out at the night. There was a pale moon and a light fog, making vision possible for a short distance but blurring the shapes of the shrubs and trees. Everything was soft and hazy. It was like being entombed in clouds.

What had Clarissa seen?

Or what had she thought she'd seen?

How easy it was to see shapes in those thin, gracefully curving drifts. Curls of ghostly hair in their white lengths. Faces, both human and bestial.

I squinted and waited for the fog to twist into a recognizable shape. As I had expected, a figure began to form. It gradually emerged from the gray depths, moving toward me like someone walking across the lawns to stand not far from my window. I stared with interest, managing to make out the broad shoulders of a man, shoulders that I knew only too well.

Lord Wolfeburne.

Was I so preoccupied with him that I had only to relax for my mind to create his image? I blinked and opened my eyes wide.

The figure remained beneath my window.

He was blurred and indistinct, but I had no doubt he was real.

And his head was lifted to stare at me.

Was he walking alone with his demons? What other reason had he to come and stand beneath my rooms? On impulse, I undid the latch and pushed open the window. I leaned out, and thick lengths of blond hair fell about my face.

Pushing them back from my eyes, I called, "Lord Wolfeburne?"

The figure tensed.

"Lord Wolfeburne? Are you all right?"

He knew I saw him, but he did not answer. Could I have been wrong? Could it have been Wilkins? But the steward was a much smaller man. It might have been Bastian or Davey, but the first had narrow shoulders and the second was too slim.

Suddenly, I became very conscious of standing in a lighted window dressed only in my thin nightgown, with my hair undone. I pulled the window shut with a bang and let the curtain fall.

Nor did I look out upon the fog again that night.

It was several days before I saw Lord Wolfeburne again. Then, on my free afternoon, I went to the library to return several volumes I had borrowed for Clarissa's history studies, and found him there. He lifted his head from the map he was perusing, saw me hesitating in the doorway, and beckoned for me to join him.

It took only a few minutes for me to replace what I had taken and find the material I wanted for the next day's lessons. While I worked, his gaze followed me intently, never once leaving my face, and it became impossible to concentrate on what I was doing.

"I will not be more than a moment," I mumbled, hoping to distract either him or myself.

"But I wanted to speak with you," he said. "If you can spare me a few minutes."

I nodded warily, and he shifted the two high-backed, tufted armchairs that sat in the corners of the library so that they stood in close proximity, each facing the other. Beyond them, the mullioned windows looked out onto the lawns and the curved, gravel driveway, and purplish red roses batted against the panes.

It was a tranquil scene, but my stomach fluttered nervously. Would he mention standing below my rooms a few nights ago? I did not want to broach the subject if he chose to pretend he had not been there. Nor was I certain I wanted to hear the reasons for his odd vigil.

I settled onto the chair, trying to tell myself it was Clarissa he wished to discuss.

In fact, it was neither.

"I was wondering if you'd had a chance to look at the book I loaned you?" he asked when I had made myself comfortable, and he spoke with a poorly disguised intensity.

"I have been reading a little each evening," I said, wondering what it was about him that made him look different to me that day.

"And?"

"I have not progressed beyond the middle chapters, but what I have read was well thought out and the material provoking."

He stretched his legs out before him, propped his elbows on the arms of his chair, and peered at me from across his intertwined fingers. It was a casual pose, but not once did he lift his gaze from my face, and I did not make the mistake of thinking his interest merely polite.

"And do you think it possible that we have evolved from lower life forms?"

"Certainly, it is possible. But the idea is too foreign for me to accept easily."

He nodded, and his lips pursed thoughtfully. "And yet I am persuaded Darwin is right."

"And why is that, milord?"

He thought for a long while, making me wonder if he would answer at all. But finally, he spoke, picking his words carefully as though he wished to hide as much as he was willing to reveal.

"It is this . . . veneer we call civilized behavior. Less than a veneer, really, it is but the thinnest of veils. Rip it aside, intentionally or through some accident or misfortune, and what do you find?" His words pulsed with emotion. "Not a man as we profess a man to be. But something primitive and inhuman. A creature of passions and instinct, nothing more. I do not so much find it hard to believe that we have evolved from lesser life forms as I find it impossible to believe anything else."

Listening, I grew uneasy, for he, more than anyone, was like some primitive creature. Unbridled by convention. Scornful of society's mores. Acting on whatever impulse struck him. Was this the reason he supported Darwin's theories?

Finding it necessary to comment lest I betray my thoughts, I murmured, "The beast. The beast within us all."

"Then the notion does not shock you?"

Eyes bright, he leaned forward in his chair. His hand reached for mine and, unthinking, he stroked my fingers. Usually, it was his intention and desire to shock and unsettle, but on this occasion his gaze met mine with hope, an eagerness that convinced me he did not want to startle so much as find a sympathetic ear.

"But surely we are more than just our passions," I said, trying to ignore the familiarity in his touch. "Does not our intelligence lift us above the level of mere animal?"

"Even the most dangerous of animals can show intelligence and cunning."

I thought of my early years with Henrietta and remembered how nearly I had come to acting upon my murderous instincts. Pure chance had saved us both. Chance and that faculty that had let me translate experience into understanding.

"What of reason?" I demanded. "Can anyone who possesses the ability to reason ever be reduced to the sum of his passions? Surely the one must always rule the other. And if we have evolved over the eons, have not our reasoning abilities also evolved?"

His grip on my hand tightened. "What are you saying?"

"That w-whatever we might once have been, we are no longer," I stammered, finding his complete attention both heady and unnerving. "To regard ourselves as nothing more than what we were is to deny the entire theory of evolution."

He mused over what I had said. His handsome features appeared to be cut from smooth dark marble, and I was conscious of the sunlight flashing off the stones in his ring. It winked at me, distracting me and making concentration difficult. It was a strange discomfort. Had I been asked, at that moment, to depart his company, I would only have complied with great reluctance.

Lord Wolfeburne stirred and cleared his throat, and I started. "So you think that to believe in the existence of a primitive self is also to believe that self lost to ages past."

I nodded. "Surely, one line of thought must necessarily include the other."

"Perhaps." He frowned. "But I am less convinced than you. Look how easily man is roused to murder and warfare. You cannot tell me that he has progressed far from his beginnings."

Not so far that as a child I could not contemplate murder. Not so far that the dwellings of his early ancestors could not still be seen from the windows of his own home. Not so far that he could not sink into behaviors that marked him as unacceptable to genteel company, nor that I could feel safe in his presence when his dark moods were upon him.

I replied slowly, considering each word I spoke. "I doubt that I would find much that was recognizable in the Druids or the hut people. And yet if Darwin is accurate, thousands of years from now, those future peoples might find me far more akin to early man than to themselves."

A blanket of melancholy descended upon him, and he stared past me to some place far beyond that only he could see. The warmth had gone from his touch and the brightness from his eyes.

"I shall tell you how far we have come from ancient man." He lifted the hand he stroked and pulled me toward him. His voice was hushed, and his grim countenance was near enough to me that all else was blocked from my view.

"Less than a baby's step," he said thickly. "Less even than the distance traveled by the most discreet of whispers. We have not yet turned a page, nor finished a paragraph. Rather we have merely traveled from one word to the next. And there we hang, tentative and uncertain, as likely to be thrust backward into what we once were as driven forward into what we hope we may become."

I swallowed. What beast dwelled within his breast that made him view himself and all his race through such a darkling glass?

Part of me wished to deny everything he had said and insist that human nature was both noble and honorable. To say that it was our nature always to rise and improve upon ourselves. But honesty forced me to silence. Until I could erase my childhood memories, I could not meet his gaze and tell him he was wrong.

I reached out and laid my free hand on his sleeve. A muscle jumped beneath my fingers but, caught up in the intensity of the moment, I did not withdraw. "Surely there is as much reason to believe we can go forward as back. And whatever demons lie within us, threatening our grip upon civilized behavior, they can be exorcised. Of that much, I am certain."

"Exorcised? How? Do you intend to sprinkle me with holy water, or have the minister say prayers for my soul?"

"It is not to that kind of demon I refer. But rather to the dark sides of our natures. And if we are not strong enough to defeat them, then we must not fight alone, but turn to those who care enough to add their strength to ours."

He smiled faintly. "And do you mean to provide me with that support?"

"I would. If you would let me."

He stiffened and pulled away. "The battle is mine, Miss Lane. Do not tempt me with soft looks and gentle hands, for you would not thank me if I succumbed to your desire to save me. And, as it happens, I am stronger than you might believe. I might not win this fight, but nor shall I surrender."

12

Would I never understand him? We lived beneath the same roof, ate the same foods, passed each other in the hallways, sat in chairs that faced each other, and yet somehow we never truly touched.

To my confusion, he seemed to suffer that distance with even less tolerance than I. He sought out my company, often and regularly, needing me in a fashion I did not understand. And yet, just as determinedly, he thrust me away from him whenever he thought I drew too near.

I stood in a kind of no-man's-land, as I always had, it seemed, throughout my short life. Not truly wanted by those who had placed me there, yet compelled by them to remain. Before, I had always maintained my own walls—either through telling myself I did not care or by disliking those who held me in contempt with as much intensity as they disliked me.

But, at Wolfeburne Hall, there was a difference. Here, I was held in some favor. All the feelings I had held in check throughout my childhood struggled within me, eager to be released and bestowed on those who had shown me their approval.

But what then?

Was I to let myself care for a man as inconstant as the summer breezes? A man who was quicker to mock than he was to compliment?

I dared not.

He was not the only one who did not easily give his trust.

Instead, I lavished my affections on Clarissa where they were both needed and appreciated. Her father, too, made greater effort to spend more time with her, and my authority over her was lost the second she caught sight of him.

He emerged from his study one afternoon as we were returning from one of our walks, a mysterious smile upon his lips.

"Papa," she cried. Loose hair ribbons tumbling down her back, she threw herself at him and fastened her arms about his waist.

He did not attempt to disentangle himself, but pretended bewilderment. "And who is this?" he demanded of me. "Have I now taken to educating one of the farmer's children as well as my own daughter?"

She giggled with delight.

"Good heavens, but that giggle sounds familiar. Is that you beneath all that dirt, Clarissa?" He swung her up and kissed her on the cheek. She attempted to respond in kind, but he set her down in mock horror. "No, that is quite enough, you unnatural child. More of your attentions and I shall be forced to take a bath, and Mary will have more than enough to do fetching hot water for you."

"Oh, Papa. I cannot walk on the moor with Jessamy and keep my face clean."

"Why not? Miss Lane seems none the worse for the experience. Or is that a smudge of mud across her nose." He peered at me intently.

"Very likely," I said, dropping my gaze rather than face that fierce inspection. Somehow, I knew, he looked for something more than mere mud. Even though I looked at my feet, I could feel him watching me and sense his expectation.

It was unfair of him. Some things were within my power to give him, but he looked for a kind of companionship I could not provide. I was neither his social nor intellectual equal, and a proper union between us was unthinkable. Nor was I the sort of woman to consort with him outside of marriage. He did himself no good by pretending otherwise.

And that was something I, too, would be well advised to remember, I told myself.

I raised my eyes to discover Lord Wolfeburne's attention had returned to his daughter. He shooed her upstairs with the admonition to scrub herself thoroughly or he would refuse to acknowledge her as his.

I started to follow.

"Miss Lane," he said, calling me back.

"Yes, milord."

"Would you dine with me this evening?"

It was not an order but an invitation, the first he had ever issued. All the rest had been royal commands, leaving me no doubt that I had not the right to refuse. Was his altered behavior due to increased respect, or did he simply assume I would not refuse him? I hoped it was the former, but realized the latter was more likely.

And also the truth.

I nodded. "Thank you, milord. I would be delighted."

Supper passed pleasantly. For the all-too-brief period that we dined, our murky surroundings were transformed by a golden candlelit haze in which reality was cast into the background and dreams were brought to the fore. I could believe us two other people in a very different setting. Paris, perhaps. Or Rome. Somewhere where laughter came easily to one's lips, where sad memories evaporated beneath the warmth of endless sunshine, and where the night was not to be dreaded but anticipated with a secret pleasure.

Throughout the murmur of our conversation, the tinkle of crystal and silverware, Lord Wolfeburne retained that mysterious smile I had seen upon his face that afternoon.

I set down my fork and pushed my plate aside, satisfied in a way that could not be attributed to mere food.

"Are you done," he inquired, and in his voice was the first hint of impatience I had heard that evening.

I smiled and nodded. "It was an excellent supper, milord."

He brushed my compliments aside. "Shall we adjourn to the drawing room? There is something I would like to show you."

"If it pleases you, milord."

"Indeed, it does." His smile deepened.

A fire had been lit on the hearth, and the gaslights flickered from the wall sconces. I could see Mrs. Pendarves's touch in the carefully arranged roses, and the sensation of warmth and mellow sunlight flowed between the room we had just departed and the one we now entered.

I glanced around me, searching for something that would explain his lordship's behavior. But everything was in its usual place, all carefully dusted and tidied. I would not find my answers there. Then he cleared his throat, and my attention returned to him.

"I have a small gift for you," he said, smiling and withdrawing a packet from his coat pocket.

"Surely you have given me enough gifts," I said, protesting.

He put up a warning finger. "If you recall, you accepted the dresses as a *favor* to me. Besides, this is different. The dresses were a necessity. This is more personal."

I need hardly have told him that personal gifts should not be exchanged between us. He could not have been oblivious to the impropriety of his behavior. I frowned at the predicament in which he, through his generosity, had placed me.

"Come, Miss Lane," he admonished. "There is no point in donning your governess face with me. Save that for Clarissa when she has dropped her lesson book. I am not a schoolboy, and such tactics will no longer serve. More likely, I will only take great delight in provoking you further. Besides, it is foolish to refuse a gift you have not even unwrapped."

I sensed he was drawing me into a trap from which I would not be able to extricate myself. But he had phrased his words in such a manner as to make protest seem both futile and unreasonable. And that, I supposed, was exactly his intention.

With less grace than was polite, I accepted the packet he gave me and unfolded the tissue. Inside lay two delicately worked silver combs for a lady's hair. They were old and heavy and clearly valuable.

"I bought them for my wife. But she died without ever wearing them. I intended to give them to Clarissa when she grew older, but if you will accept them, it would please me more if they went to you. You may find you have greater success with your hair when supplied with the proper materials."

"But I could not poss—"

"Let me show you how they work. If you would allow me."

Not waiting for my permission, he reached up and pulled the pins from my braided knot. The heavy braid tumbled down my back, and he quickly unraveled the sections.

An embarrassed heat flared across my cheeks. "Milord, really. This is most—"

"I boast no expertise with a lady's hair. Mine is more of an amateur's fascination, but sometimes enthusiasm suffices where skill fails."

With deft and gentle fingers, he brushed my hair back from my brow and the sides of my face. My scalp tingled beneath his touch. If he had any notion of the effect his touch had upon me, he pretended not to notice, but gave his full attention to the task he had set for himself. For several long minutes he worked, humming softly beneath his breath, not minding that his subject stood before him, stiff and awkward and unable to find or catch her breath.

Then, holding my head still, he stepped back and studied his handiwork. Not once during his scrutiny did he look into my eyes or at my cheeks whose scarlet hue he could not have failed to note. Apparently satisfied, he took first one comb from my hand and then the other, and pressed them into place.

"A marked improvement," he pronounced. Holding me by the arm, he led me to the gilt-framed mirror that hung over the mantel and forced me to admire his efforts. His own face was reflected immediately above and behind my own, and my awareness of him intensified.

"Do you agree?" he asked.

I stared at myself and tried to forget that he did the same. He had fashioned my hair into a clumsy chignon, one that was less successful than my own attempts had been. But his efforts had much the same effect as my own. The severity he called "my governess look" had gone from my face. I looked younger, much nearer my true age, and I saw a vulnerability in my face that still startled and frightened me.

"Is something wrong?" he demanded, his sharp gaze catching that fleeting expression of fear and doubt.

I shook my head. The reasons for my panic escaped me. I only knew with absolute certainty that he was the cause for my turbulent emotions and the last person with whom I wanted to discuss them.

"It is just that I hardly recognize myself," I said.

An eyebrow arched, and I realized he had caught the lie. To my relief, he did not pounce on me and demand the truth. Instead, he nodded. "But age comes soon enough to us all. There is no reason to hasten the process as you seem to want to do. But you have not told me if you are pleased with the combs."

What answer could I give? To say no would be to be rude and ungrateful. To say yes . . . to say yes would be tantamount to accepting his gift. Something I simply must not do.

I lifted my gaze to his reflection in the looking glass. "I am much impressed with your handiwork, milord. And the combs are indescribably lovely—"

"I must correct you," he murmured, his lips close to my ear. "It is not the combs that are lovely. Rather it is yourself. My gift is mere ornamentation, but it pleases me to see you wear them, nonetheless."

"But, of course, you realize I cannot accept them."

"I realize no such thing."

He reached up and stroked the back of my head. His fingers drifted over the thick strands and brushed the back of my neck. I knew I should step away from him. That I should sharply remind him that such behavior was unacceptable, and I deserved and expected better treatment while I lived beneath his roof.

But I could not. There was something hypnotic and compelling in his gentle touch, in that dark gaze that was warm upon me, like summer sunshine flooding over a shadowed nook. Whatever he was, whatever dark secret tormented him, he had shown me greater kindness than I had ever known. He, alone, had treated me as a person worthy of respect, a person who possessed a heart that was essentially good, however humble and shabby my beginnings.

It was wrong of me, but my own need betrayed me. To have pushed him away from me at that moment would have been to deny myself the love and appreciation for which I had always hungered. I had not the strength.

Nor had I the inclination.

His fingers moved from the back of my neck to my throat. They rested there beneath my chin in a light grasp, and his thumb brushed thoughtfully along the line of my jaw until I was aware of no sensation other than that of his thumb and the tips of his fingers. The world around us seemed to fade into a dark blur, unimportant, more vague than any dream or fantasy.

And then a black wave of panic rose within me, and I could think of nothing but that I must escape. That I dared not remain one second longer in his embrace.

He must have seen my thoughts in my face, for his grip tightened on me and a strong arm wrapped around my waist and pulled me against him. Our bodies were no longer separated, not even by a gap so infinitesimal as to give but a passing nod to propriety. Instead, I could feel the length of him against me, the hardness of his muscular chest beneath that wholly respectable coat, the warmth of his body against mine. I was suffused with heat greater than that to be had from any fire.

"Let me go," I pleaded. "You must not do this."

He groaned. "You cannot be unaware of my feelings for you. You could not have avoided the subject with such deliberate intent had you truly remained in ignorance."

"If you knew that, then you had no right to ignore my wishes."

"I have every right."

"Do you think because I live beneath your roof, under your protection, that you may use me howsoever you will?"

"Good God! Do you truly think that of me?"

"What am I supposed to think?"

"That I need you and want you. That you are indispensable to me, and I cannot wait another day to claim you for my own. Nor can you make me believe that you do not care for me."

He laid his cheek against the side of my head and closed his eyes. Far from assuaging my fears, his gentleness inflamed them. Gripped by an irrational terror, I fought to free myself from his grasp. Instantly, he released me, and one of my flailing fists caught him a sound blow on his lower jaw.

I gasped at what I had done, but before I could speak a knock came on the door.

He stepped back as suddenly as if a wall of flame had shot up between us, and I knew not if it was because of my striking him or because of the awkward interruption. I sagged against the mantel and gasped for breath, although my distress was due more to my panic than any harm he had done me.

Lord Wolfeburne stepped to the far side of the hearth and waited until I had recovered myself. Then, with a dark look in his eyes, he said, "Enter."

The door opened, and Mrs. Pendarves walked into the room, a ledger in her hand, her loop of keys jingling at her waist. Her gaze fell on me and she looked surprised. I prayed it was only because she had not expected to find me there, and not because she had guessed what had so recently passed between us.

"Excuse me, milord," she said apologetically. "I thought Miss Lane had retired, and I brought the household accounts for you to see. But they can wait for another evening if you would prefer."

"It *is* time I retired, milord," I said, determined to grab at my chance to escape. "If you both will excuse me?"

He frowned, but could hardly make a protest.

Mrs. Pendarves nodded politely. "Good-night, Miss Lane. And if you don't mind my saying so, your hair looks lovely in a chignon."

So that was what she had noticed. Only guilt had led me to a different conclusion. "Good-night," I replied in a voice I did not recognize and sailed from the room, carried out on the wings of my own relief.

It was not until I reached the safety of my room and closed my door firmly behind me that I remembered the silver combs he had given me were still firmly planted in my hair. My scalp prickled beneath the feel of them. With a cry, I pulled them from my head and threw them on the bed. My vehemence, there, alone in my suite with no one to harm me, completely bewildered me.

I glared at the combs, as if they were to blame. They lay mutely on the counterpane. Incapable of hurting me, for all I seemed to fear them.

Slowly, my rapid heartbeat subsided to a more natural

pace, and reason returned. With it came a rush of embarrassment.

What had Lord Wolfeburne done to stir such panic and violence within me? It was not disgust for his person. I had always thought him handsome. Nor did I revile him for his character, for he was more wounded than willfully disagreeable. If anything, I pitied him for the torment he suffered. And on some levels, I respected him immensely, for he was intelligent—well-mannered, under normal circumstances—and he tried hard to be a good father to Clarissa.

In all, there seemed neither reason nor excuse for my behavior. Had I resented his advances, it would only have been necessary for me to tell him of my sentiments and call on him to behave like a gentleman.

And yet I knew that had he knocked upon my door at that moment, I would have been no calmer nor more reasonable in putting him from me.

I spent a restless night, and my mood had not improved by morning. Dread filled me at the thought of confronting Lord Wolfeburne, but sometime during that day I would have to return the combs to him.

I scowled at my reflection in the looking glass and savagely knotted my hair, pulling the curls back from my face with such force that my eyes widened and my scalp ached.

From the wardrobe, I chose the dress least becoming to my coloring, and was dissatisfied when even that failed to give me the look of authority I desired. It was too feminine, and the watered silk too delicate. But it was that or shake out the black twilled wool, and that would mean disregarding Clarissa's needs. I would have to make do with the dress I had on, and could only console myself by saying that the others would be worse.

I appeared in the schoolroom late and out of sorts. Clarissa was bent over her sketchbook, her childish lips pursed, a faint frown upon her brow. Her fingers gripped her charcoal, sliding it across the page in short, fast strokes.

"Good morning, Clarissa," I said. "Matilda."

I thought she had heard me come in, but at the sound of my voice, she jumped and flipped the pages of her sketchbook to cover her drawing.

"Do you not want to show me your work?" I asked, trying to appear only mildly interested. "It has never bothered you before."

She hesitated.

"There is no need if you would rather not."

The faint line on her forehead deepened. "It was Matilda's suggestion," she said reluctantly.

"Then you must ask Matilda if you may show your sketch to me."

I expected her to whisper in her doll's ear and pretend to listen, but she remained in her seat, swinging her legs beneath the table. Her eyes, so like her father's eyes, clouded with the signs of turmoil.

"Perhaps you would rather just tell me about your sketch," I said. "And I can imagine it on my own."

She shook her head, a hard, firm shake that surprised me, for she had never been an obstinate child. Immediately, she realized her adamant refusal might seem rude. "It is a secret," she explained. "One that only Matilda and I know. We promised each other we would never tell, but that was before we knew you, Jessamy."

I smiled. "And has Matilda told you that it would be all right to trust me?"

"She thought it would be all right if we drew you a picture. That is not really telling, is it?"

"No, not really," I said, certain that was what she wanted to hear.

Clarissa nodded. "That is what I thought. But . . ."

Unconsciously, she leaned in my direction. She wanted desperately to disclose something, and yet she had guarded some secret knowledge far too long to surrender it so easily to anyone. The strain caused by her struggles showed in her face and the nervous twisting of the charcoal in her fingers. In good conscience, I could not allow her to remain in such distress, knowing how easily her health could suffer.

"You can show me another time, when you are ready. Now you had better go and wash your hands before we start your lessons."

She nodded and left the schoolroom with a look of relief that reminded me of my own feelings when escaping the drawing room. I silently vowed not to place her in the same position again, no matter how much I thought she needed to confide in me.

It would have been an easy matter to take up her sketchbook and thumb through the pages, but to have done so would have been to betray her trust. What good would it do to better understand her if, in doing so, I committed an act that destroyed her faith in me?

Patience, I decided, was a virtue I did possess. Patience and determination.

Clarissa returned within a few minutes, her hands clean save for a faint gray line beneath her fingernails, and she settled into her chair and bade me a cheerful good morning as though it was the first time we had spoken.

Her behavior put me in mind of how she had failed to ask about the Pengelleys even once after our Sunday visit. This was the second time I had seen her forget what she did not choose to remember, and I found this tendency vaguely disconcerting. Surely it could only be harmful to her to deny what she could not confront.

But over the next few hours, Clarissa displayed a far greater attentiveness than I. Indeed, she must have been quite bewildered by the number of times I faltered in the middle of a sentence or failed to hear her questions.

"Are you not well, Jessamy?" she asked after I forgot again the point that I was making.

"Perfectly," I assured her.

"You do not look the same," she continued. "I thought so when you first came in, and now . . ."

"And now?"

"You seem . . ." She searched for a word that eluded her.

"Distracted," I said. "It means my thoughts are elsewhere."

She nodded.

"I suppose I am. But it is not a matter to concern you. And certainly I am not ill."

"I would not want you to get sick."

Was she remembering her mother? I smiled and tried to push my problems into the back of my mind. "You may set your mind at ease. I cannot remember the last time I fell ill with so much as a cold."

"And you would not think of leaving me?"

Her question stunned me. It had not occurred to me that she would assume that my altered behavior meant I had grown unhappy at the Hall. "Dearest Clarissa. Have I not promised I would never run away? That much you must believe."

"I thought you might be angry with me."

"For what possible reason?" I demanded, completely perplexed.

She sighed and her delicate shoulders dropped into a more natural line. Apparently, my confusion had made her realize that her suspicions, whatever they might have been, were untrue.

"If I were to be upset with you, for any reason," I added in my firmest voice, "I would come and talk with you, not run away."

Her eyes glistened, and I bent over her and kissed her cheek. "Now, let us have done with this nonsense. Mary will be bringing our luncheon, and she will think I have scolded you."

"And Papa will hear."

"And he will scold both of us."

She giggled at the notion. Clearly, he had never scolded her for anything.

"Whatever made you think I was upset with you?" I asked again, seeing the brightness had returned to her face.

She glanced down at the sketchbook, still lying on the table beside her slate. "I was going to show you. Really, I was."

"I know."

Her mouth formed a perfect circle, and then she smiled again, although her lower lip trembled. Then, with a quick motion, she grabbed up the sketchbook and thrust it into my hands. When I did not immediately respond, she reached up and began flipping the pages until she came to the one she wanted me to see.

I stared down at her drawing, trying to make sense of what I saw there. Clarissa's skill as an artist was limited, even for her nine years, but she had clearly drawn a window. It was tall and narrow, with lines that crossed each other like the wooden slats that held the light panes. To one side of the window were two figures, one clutching the other, and I determined they could only be Clarissa and her doll.

Then, what was beyond the window drew my attention. This was hardest of all to see, but it appeared to be a third figure of some sort. Man or woman, I could not tell. It was a lighter shade of gray than the first two figures, and drawn in flowing lines that barely suggested shape.

That shape it did suggest was quite horrible. There was a distortion that may have been due to her lack of skill, and yet again, it may not have been. The drawings of her and Matilda seemed properly formed. At least they did not give off this sense of menace that clung to the other.

"What is it?" I asked, hoping she would answer.

"Sometimes I have nightmares, and this is what I see." Her gaze was fixed to the page, and her face was stark white. "It is . . . it is my . . . my . . ."

She shuddered and ran out of the room.

13

There was a crash in the hall and the shattering of glass. I dropped the sketchbook and hurried out of the schoolroom. Mary was standing over a broken vase and a puddle of brown water, Michaelmas daisies scattered at her feet. She gaped at me, then turned toward Clarissa's bedroom.

"She bumped right into me, miss. It's not at all like 'er to be flighty."

"Never mind," I said. "Go and find something to clean up the mess. I'll see to Clarissa."

"Yes, miss."

Clarissa was bent over her washstand. Her back heaved, and the remains of her breakfast streamed into the basin. I hurried to her side and held her until the last spasm had passed. She lifted her face to me.

"Are you all right?" I asked.

She nodded weakly.

"I did not mean to upset you with my questions."

"I've had a tummy ache all morning."

I frowned. Perhaps more than the sketch had upset her. Both Davey and one of the downstairs maids had been ill with flu. I lay my hand across her brow. It was hot, and her face was flushed.

"I think we had better get you into bed."

I helped her change into her nightdress and settled her beneath the blankets. Silent and docile, she allowed me to tend to her. My mind was left free to wonder if her nightmares had been brought on by the flu or the reverse. Either way, deciding to confide in me had taken much courage. Had it also drained her last reserves of strength?

And what had she left unsaid? I considered her words. "*It is my . . .*"

Her mother? What else might she have seen that night when she had been only six? The night she had stared at the window of the servants' hall into the fog.

What could she have seen that she would have claimed as hers? Her governess? Her father? Neither would have given her a shock. And Lord Wolfeburne had been in Doublebois, had he not? I thought of the delicate, curving twists of fog and realized how easily they could have deceived a child into believing them to be a ghostly woman.

Mrs. Pendarves burst through the door, interrupting my thoughts. "Is the child ill?" she demanded. "Mary said she was not herself."

"I think she has a touch of the flu," I said. "If you would be so good as to remain with her for a few minutes, I will advise her father to send for the doctor."

I did not have to go far to find his lordship. Mary had gone straight from Mrs. Pendarves to his study, and we almost collided at the top of the stairs. He reached out a hand to steady me, and I was given a sharp reminder of his touch and those upsetting minutes I had endured the previous evening. I thought, for a moment, he shared my thoughts, but his first words told me otherwise.

"Is she all right?" he demanded.

I nodded.

"You should not have left her alone."

"She has Mrs. Pendarves for company. I was coming to find you. It would be wise to send for the doctor."

"I have already told Wilkins to send Bastian."

By his attitude, he suggested I should have assumed as much. He seemed very willing to find fault with me that morning. That, I supposed, was because he was disappointed in me for reasons that had nothing to do with Clarissa.

I gave him a critical look. There were dark circles beneath his eyes, and he had neglected to shave. Indeed, from his rumpled appearance, I supposed he had again spent the night stretched out on the settee in his study.

Seeing what I was about, he scowled. "Perhaps you should pay less attention to my appearance and show more concern for my daughter's health."

"Of course, milord. But I must ask for a few moments of your time. Something she said bears discussion. Can we speak in private?"

"Your sitting room?" he asked.

I started to suggest the schoolroom, then thought better of opposing him. "That will be fine, milord."

"I will join you there after I have looked in on Clarissa."

I preceded him down the corridor. All the while he followed me I could feel his gaze, and it took all my concentration to walk without tripping. He was like an ominous cloud at my back, a cloud that could burst into storm without warning. Even his tread had the hard sound of a thunderclap, and each step he took echoed up and down the corridor.

Desperate for any avenue of escape, I fled into the schoolroom. Clarissa's sketchbook lay on the floor where it had fallen. I picked it up and turned to the page she had shown me. Once again, I felt the chill that had shivered through me upon first glimpsing her artwork. Determined that she should not be upset again, I removed the page from the book and returned her other sketches to her desk.

I gazed down upon the sheet in my hand, upon the distorted figure forever captured in the window frame. I had the great desire to toss the horrid thing in the fire and let it burn, but some awful fascination prevented me. Instead, I returned to my sitting room and hid the page in the bottom of my desk drawer.

I had but a few minutes to regain my composure before Lord Wolfeburne knocked on my door. He entered, but made no attempt to sit next to me, taking instead the armchair across from the settee. His expression was no less forbidding, but all his interest was for his daughter and her welfare.

"This will not take long," I told him. "Then I will go and sit with her."

"There is no immediate need," he said stiffly. "Mrs. Pendarves has given her a sleeping draught. What was it you wanted to say?"

"Before she took ill, Clarissa was trying to tell me about her nightmares, nightmares prompted by what she saw in the fog on the evening you mentioned." I could have told him about the sketch, and yet something held me back.

He peered at me from atop his fingers, and once again my gaze fell on the massive gold wolf's head on his ring finger. "And did she succeed?"

I shook my head.

"But she said something?" he asked.

I hesitated, somehow knowing he would not like my answer. But, of course, I could not keep such a thing from him. "Before she became ill, she said, 'It was my . . . ,' but that was all. I think it likely she believes she saw her mother."

"That's impossible." He regarded me with complete disgust. "Do you expect me to believe in ghosts, Miss Lane?"

"I do not believe in them myself. But Clarissa does. And a child's imagination can play many tricks."

He considered this for a minute, then grudgingly nodded his head. "Forgive me. Whether she thought she saw a ghost or not, it is no fault of yours. But it disturbs me to think her capable of surrendering to such frightful delusions. I . . ."

"You fear you may lose her as you lost her mother," I said gently.

He furrowed his hair with his fingers. "She is all that is left to me, Miss Lane. I will not relinquish her."

I shuddered. It was a horrible thought.

He fell silent, and there was only the ticking of the clock on the mantel and the sounds of our own breathing. His fingers twisted idly at his ring, and I found myself counting the number of cabbage roses on the patterned carpet and struggling to speak the words I must say next.

"Milord—"

"Jessamy—"

We both spoke at the same instant and immediately broke off. I forced myself to continue before he had a chance to collect himself, for I knew anything he might say would make my task harder.

"Forgive me, milord, but there is something else that must be said. If you would wait but a moment."

I rose and fetched the combs from my dresser. Returning with them, I set them on the table beside him. "These are yours."

He glanced at them, but did not pick them up.

"I cannot possibly accept them," I added.

His lips flickered with a wry smile. "No. I suppose you cannot. Again, I must make you an apology. I have been too caught up in my own troubles to let myself admit to yours."

"Milord?"

"You are not the person I thought you were, Miss Lane." He held up his hand to forestall a protest. "Not that I think you deliberately misled me. It would be more accurate to say you don't truly know yourself."

"You speak in riddles," I said shortly, feeling that familiar wave of uneasiness spreading through me.

He sighed. "It's really very simple. In my preoccupation with my own difficulties, much about you has eluded me."

I straightened and held my hands in tight abeyance. "You can hardly be expected to be completely familiar with everybody in your employ, but I cannot see why that should concern you."

"I have mistaken your quiet reserve for strength—"

"That is—"

"—your control of your emotions for serenity—"

"You have no—"

"—and your hesitance for maidenly shyness." He paused to emphasize his words with a cool look that shredded the remains of my composure. "Last night"—he continued inexorably—"I realized my error."

I fought the urge to pat my hair and discover if the braided knot remained in place. "Admittedly, you startled me," I said in a tremulous voice.

"*Startled?* You were terrified. Give me your hand and I will run your fingers across the lump you raised upon my temple."

I yanked back my arm, bumping my elbow hard on the edge of the settee. "There is no need for that. My reaction was excessive, I agree. But under the circumstances, you could not have expected me to remain calm."

"My dear Jessamy." He shook his head and chuckled softly, but his eyes were deeply sad. "What did I do but hold you and tell you how much you meant to me? Hardly enough reason for complaint. Certainly, it failed to warrant the frenzy that possessed you."

"I am a governess in your employ. It is hardly suitable—"

"Nonsense. You know full well you are a great deal more to me than a mere governess. It pleases you to insist upon that relationship."

"That's ridiculous," I retorted, anger rising within me. "Why should I accept a subservient position in your household if I had a right to another? That would be sheer foolishness."

He regarded me with absolute conviction written in every line of his expression. "Because that lowly status lets you remain at a safe distance."

"From whom? You?"

"No. I imagine you could find other reasons to hold me off if that was your sole desire."

"Then from what? You make no sense."

"From life, Jessamy." He twisted the ring on his finger. "From life and happiness. From all that could be yours if you would only loosen the reins you hold on your emotions."

I shot to my feet, unable to sit still a moment longer and endure his attack. He was insufferable. I had always known him to be capable of arrogance, but he had truly overstepped his bounds. How had I ever thought highly of his intelligence? His opinions were all that could be expected of a man given to drunkenness.

I searched in vain for the words that would allow me to put him in his place, but I could think of none that suitably expressed my contempt. Indeed, the war of emotions inside me made speech impossible.

"What?" he asked. "No retort or set down?"

"Your comments are not worthy of retort," I said, finding my tongue at last. "You are talking nonsense."

"No, my love. Only consider your past and you will see that I am right." His voice dropped to a gentle murmur, and his dark eyes softened to a warm brown that invited my trust. "As a child, you were handed all your dreams and more besides, only to have them snatched from you in an abrupt and callous manner. It is hardly surprising you fear to risk your heart a second time. What you do not accept, no one can take from you."

"You refer to something that happened when I was a child. That was years ago. It could not possibly affect me now."

He rose and tried to approach me, but I hastily stepped beyond his reach. Sighing, he allowed me this small escape, but that was all he would allow. "A life-time is too brief a period to erase a painful memory from a sensitive heart. But fear of pain can always be conquered."

I glared at him. "You accuse me of cowardice. And yet you summoned me here solely because you admired my courage. There cannot be two of me in the same person, milord."

"Having the courage to face the dark alone when we are given no choice is not the same as choosing to make ourselves vulnerable to others."

He strode toward me. I flinched but could retreat no farther. Before I had time to draw a breath he caught my arm and propelled me into my bedroom. The sight of the recently made bed and its cheerful counterpane made me gasp. Surely, he did not intend—

I could not even permit myself the thought.

He stopped before the looking glass. I sagged against him with relief, but it was a short-lived respite. He pinioned my arms at my side and forced me to confront my reflection.

"Look at yourself," he said. "Your hair. The dress you donned this morning. You are once again the same person who first came to my door. Severe. Isolated. Untouchable. I am surprised you did not unpack one of your black dresses from the wardrobe."

To my great annoyance, I blushed.

He groaned and released me. "Dear God, Jessamy. Have I driven you all the way back into your cocoon? What prevented you from doing as you wanted? Some inner spark that cried out for life or merely a reluctance to remind Clarissa of death and mourning?"

My answer would only have added to his case against me. Feeling childishly stubborn, I set my mouth in a firm line and refused to answer his question.

My silence saved me nothing. He studied my face and took the answer he found there. "I cannot think you were too pleased at being thwarted," he said.

I swallowed hard. There could be no truth to his accusation. None at all. And if there was . . . But there could not be.

"Must you torment me?" I asked in a hoarse whisper.

"Good Lord, Jessamy." He pushed his long fingers through his hair. "Do you think it is my wish to hurt you? On the contrary. I want you to let go. To seize happiness where it is offered."

"Then you have no need for concern. I am happy with my life at Wolfeburne Hall and have been since I arrived."

"It is a false happiness, at best, my love. A governess has no life of her own. Only a place in someone else's home, teaching someone else's children, eating someone else's food off someone else's plates. Life goes on all around, her but she plays her role offstage."

"I am content with that. As are many women."

"Are you? There may be no real losses, but one day you will awaken to discover you have also sacrificed all hopes of true reward. You cannot mean to tell me that is what you want for yourself?"

I was beyond answering that question. With raised chin and squared shoulders, I turned and confronted him. He had no right to treat me in this manner. If I had nothing else, I had my dignity and a right to be treated respectfully. "I will not listen to another—"

"You will because you must." His anger rushed over me in a hard, cold wave. "Because if you run from me today, then I will corner you tomorrow, and again the day after. I will not let you rest until you hear me out."

There was a wild, fanatical brightness in his eyes, and his agitation had caused his hair to fall across his brow. He threw it back with a toss of his head, and his expression dared me to defy him.

What choice had I? Leaving him to follow if that was his wish, I returned to my sitting room. His footsteps echoed at my back. I resumed my place on the settee, all the while telling myself that nothing he said could possibly affect me.

Lord Wolfeburne stood at the windows, and his shadow blocked even that drab, gray light that pressed at the panes. He did not immediately speak. With my hands folded quietly in my lap, my eyes staring directly in front of me, I nodded my willingness to listen to whatever else he had to say.

"I shall take the combs," he said quietly. "But only to look after them for you until you are ready to wear them."

"That I shall not do."

"When I gave them to you, I had no notion of how fitting a gift they made. As I did with them, you have wrapped your passions in tissue and locked them in a deep drawer. Open your heart, Jessamy. Open yourself to happiness before it's too late."

My knuckles were white. I stared at them with interest and noted how the blood pulsed in the distended veins that ran along the backs of my hands. From somewhere far in the distance, Lord Wolfeburne's voice battered at me.

"It may be selfish to ask this of you. I, too, meant never to risk loving again. But you are different from other women I have known. If there is any possibility of my finding happiness, I know it lies with you." His gaze rested on me.

"Are you done?" I demanded.

"Fear is a terrible thing, Jessamy. It whittles away at you until all that is good in you atrophies and dies, and only the husk of what you once were remains. No one knows that better than I."

"Then you are hardly the person to lecture me."

"There is a difference between us. I fear for the safety of those I love. There is nothing I can do to ease my burden without risking the health and happiness of those around me. But you, my dear Jessamy, fear only for yourself."

"I am not your dear Jessamy," I cried. "And how dare you chastise me. You who are given to drunken tempers and . . . and rude manners that make you unwelcome in the homes of your peers. You have no right to criticize others. No right at all. Nor will I listen to another word, however you threaten me."

Ignoring his startled face, I jumped up and ran from the room. He called after me, but I did not stop. If there was no sanctuary to be had while I remained on his estate, then I would find my escape elsewhere. Praying he would not follow, I rushed down the stairs, pushed open one of the double doors, and fled the Hall.

I ran until it hurt to take a breath and my legs ached with the unaccustomed strain. I ran until nothing could be seen of the Hall or the ruins but the topmost stones of that single bleak tower. I ran until I found myself in the middle of a vast and wild expanse with nothing but rocks and grass for company.

There, exhausted, I dropped to my knees.

I did not have to return. Somewhere, in the distance, lay Doublebois and the railway station that would take me to London. To the northwest was Bodmin. Who knew what work might be had there? And scattered nearby were any number of small farms where I might find someone to take me in for a few days until I could make other arrangements.

I was not entirely without resources. Lady Wolfeburne would not help me, but Miss Pengelley and Sir Ronald would behave differently. An image of their attractive, peaceful home shimmered in my mind.

Slowly, the tightness that had banded my chest since midday loosened and fell away, and I enjoyed the first real breath of air I had drawn that afternoon. The breeze whipped my skirt about and dragged my hair from the knot at my neck. It stirred the blood in my veins and made me feel alive, truly alive.

My sense of relief faded quickly. Something of Lord Wolfeburne's words echoed in my ears, and I frowned. Was there really something wrong with me that I could feel safe only there? Where there was no one and nothing to intrude upon me? Was it only where life had receded to its lowest ebb that I could shake loose my hair from its pins and let go my defenses?

And what would happen to Clarissa if I deserted her? Would she be fated to struggle through her childhood with only Miss Worsley and Mrs. Pendarves for support? Her fragile strength further undermined by my broken promises?

And somewhere in the darkest reaches of my mind another question nagged at me. If I left, what would become of *him*?

What would become of me?

I stayed away from the Hall well beyond my usual hour, locked in a battle with my thoughts and memories, oblivious to the darkening skies and forgetful of the shortening of the days. Nor did I notice the encroaching fog, until I glanced up and realized with a start that I could no longer see the familiar gray stones. Everything around me was slowly fading, as though a magician had waved a gray veil over the countryside, whispered some mysterious incantation, and was deftly dispensing with all that had once been solid and immovable.

I scrambled to my feet, knowing I dared not linger a moment longer. As it was, it would be getting dark before I could reach the gateposts of the Hall. If I was to stay, then I was determined not to fall afoul of Lord Wolfeburne for yet another reason.

I set off. My feet moved forward at a pace that was a near run. Only my fear of stumbling over a rock persuaded me to show some caution, and it was nearly dusk before I reached the front doors and hurried inside.

Mrs. Pendarves's normally smooth brow was creased with lines, and she peered down at me from the upstairs landing. "Goodness, there you are. You'd better go to the study and tell his lordship you're back. He's in quite a state. A few minutes later, and he would have sent out a search party."

"Surely it is not as bad as all that?" I asked, shedding my damp coat and pulling off my gloves. "I am not that much later than usual."

She shrugged. "I told him as much. And that you had a head on your shoulders, but he would think the worst."

Of the things I least wanted to do, talking to Lord Wolfeburne headed the list. I hoped that I could keep the conversation brief.

The door to the study stood open, and a fire crackled and hissed on the hearth. I could see someone moving inside the room, for shadows played against the wall. I tapped gingerly on the door and was rewarded with a curt order to enter.

I stuck my head through the opening, intending to go no further. Lord Wolfeburne was pulling on his overcoat, his movements abrupt and jerky. There was a tearing noise, and I suspected that in his haste and carelessness, he had torn the lining. Nor was he alone. Wilkins was standing near the desk, a tight line to his lips, lanterns swinging from either hand. Castor and Pollux crouched at their feet, both dogs tensed for their master's command. From the sense of urgency in the room, one would have supposed I was thought dead, or badly injured.

"Forgive me, milord," I said.

Both men's heads jerked in my direction.

"Mrs. Pendarves said you were unduly worried and asked me to let you know I had returned." I spoke matter of factly, trying to show him by my voice and behavior that any concerns for my welfare had been unnecessary and excessive.

Lord Wolfeburne's outraged glare deflated any hopes I might have had of restoring him to reason. "Do you have any notion of the hour?" he demanded.

"I believe it is nigh on six o'clock."

At that precise moment, the clock on the mantel began to chime the hour, proving me correct. The coincidence was unfortunate, for it added a jocular note to my reply that I had not intended.

"Wilkins, you may return to your duties," he said, biting off his words. "Miss Lane, if you would be so good as to honor me with your company for a few minutes."

I debated the wisdom of making a hurried apology and begging to be allowed to return after I had removed my damp attire. A second glance at his expression convinced me his irritation would only increase if he were forced to wait on my return.

Wilkins held open the door for me to enter, and his lips curved into a smirk. He had been put to some discomfort on my account on more than one occasion, I supposed, and was pleased to see me get my comeuppance. As soon as I had done as I was bid, he left. The door closed behind him with a bang.

Lord Wolfeburne's attack was immediate. "How dare you throw my household into an uproar with your foolishness!" he cried, without giving me a chance to speak or sit down.

"Mrs. Pendarves did not seem much upset," I said, feeling a swell of resentment. "And the hour of my return is not that much later than usual. One and a half hours, at most. And I was not accompanied by Clarissa."

"Who lies upstairs this very moment, pestering the maids to tell her of your whereabouts and send you to her the moment you return."

I felt a pang of guilt, then realized that was exactly what he had intended. "You told me she had been given a sleeping draught. I assumed she would not awaken until late this evening. And if she is upset, no doubt it is because you have conveyed your fears to her."

"And why should I not be fearful? Between the fog and your own inexperience, you could have come to great harm."

I bristled beneath his fury. There was no reason for him to react in this fashion. Any fears he may have had for my well-being were wholly irrational, and I was determined not to let him abuse me for his own foolishness.

"I may have stayed later than I had intended, but I was never out of sight of the Hall. And it will still be light enough to see for another hour. You had only to look outside your window to realize I would have no difficulty in returning."

"And how was I to know—"

He stopped in the middle of his sentence and glared at me again.

"How were you to know what?"

He continued to glare at me a moment longer. Then his anger faded and he sank into his chair. His head dropped forward onto his hands and his shoulders sagged.

"Dear God, Jessamy. How was I to know you meant to return?"

"Surely you did not think I had run away?"

He lifted his head. "And why not? You ran from me last night, did you not?"

"But only to my own suite."

"You could hardly have gone farther at that hour. I hoped this morning to make you realize the cause for your panic and forestall any such occurrence. You have never shied from any other battle. I assumed that, given some time alone, you would not shy from this one either. Only tell me you had no thought of leaving."

I could not. Escape had beckoned to me. I would have liked nothing better than to have run and run forever, to have left the Hall and all of the demands it placed on me.

That he placed on me.

He stared at me in the silence. "Then I was not wrong?"

"Perhaps not entirely. Running away would have been easier than returning, but I could not do that to Clarissa."

"Nor to me?"

I said nothing.

"Nor to me?" he demanded.

I stared at him, enveloped in a heavy overcoat that covered him from jawline to the tops of his boots. Above the collar, his face was a pale triangle. There was an unexpected gauntness to the hollows beneath his cheekbones and, intense and watchful, his gaze fixed on me.

It was a hungry face, the face of a predator who was no stranger to deprivation. The face of an animal who knew that to miss a kill was to starve, possibly to die.

But his was a different kind of hunger, a need beyond that of mere food and drink. I recognized that need with a certainty that could only exist in someone who shared a similar need, who knew that to be lonely was worse than to be poorly clothed and improperly fed.

I shut my eyes and stifled a groan. But already I was lost. For if I doubted whether I had the courage to answer his need, I did not suppose for an instant that I could continue to deny my own.

I felt his arm encircle me, support me, and I sagged into his embrace. My face pressed against his thick overcoat, I mumbled, "No. Nor to you."

14

He did not press me beyond that one admission. There was no need. That he had broached my defenses was clear to both of us. The knowledge was reflected in his lightness of step, the glow in his eyes when he gazed upon me, the warmth in his voice whenever we spoke.

For all of that, he was in no hurry to rush me into greater intimacy, but allowed me to adjust and accept the emotions that flooded through me at the most unaccountable moments. It was as though, having thrown open the gates, they had become impossible to close.

At his insistence, I began to call him Trystan when we were alone. At first, I feared I might slip and call him by his first name in the presence of others. As the days passed, I discovered the reverse was more often true. It was his title that came most easily to my lips, and he was forced to point out my omission on several occasions.

"I believe you use my title as yet another shield to protect you," he said after I had mistakenly called him *milord* four times in but a single hour. His voice was soft and even, but noticeably controlled.

"Forgive me, mi . . . Trystan."

He shook his head, but his lips twitched.

Save for that, it was a peaceful period. Clarissa recovered quickly from the flu, but knowing the fervor with which she attacked her lessons, I insisted her studies be suspended for a good two weeks. Instead, I read aloud to her in my sitting room or told her stories of her cousin Annabelle, and we took longer and longer walks upon the moor.

One morning in November, upon arising to discover the sun shining, I decided it would be a good day to take a picnic luncheon and visit the beehive hut circles that were to be found upon Brown Gelly. It rose to the north of the Hall, a rounded and bare tor that swelled gently above the moor.

It was a fair walk, nigh on three miles, and not one I would have chosen to make in an afternoon or on a hot day. But Clarissa's strength had returned, and it was emotional and mental strain, not physical exercise, I wanted her to avoid.

She clapped her hands at my suggestion. "It would not be too far. Miss Osborne visited them when she was here. She walked there and back on one of her afternoons off, and said she spent a good two hours exploring the huts."

"Admirable woman," I replied. "But I think we will content ourselves with something less demanding."

And once again I was reminded of Miss Osborne and forced to wonder where she might have gone.

Together, Clarissa and I strolled across the moor, breaking our easy pace to sip from the bottles of ginger beer Mrs. Pendarves had packed in our picnic basket. Off in the distance, we saw two sheep pulling at the tufts of withered grass beneath their hooves.

Clarissa contemplated them from her perch on a flat stone. Idly swinging her feet beneath her skirt, she asked, "Do you think they're lonely?"

"I expect there are other sheep about," I told her, my head resting on that same rock, my gaze upon the cloud-speckled sky that stretched above me.

"But perhaps the other sheep don't like them and never come to visit."

I raised my head and looked at her, but she averted her eyes. "If nothing else, they have each other," I said, trying to assure her.

"And do you think that is enough for them?"

"If there is no one else, then it must be. Perhaps, they are stronger friends because they need each other more."

She paused to consider this, then nodded. I hoped this would end the matter, but barely a minute passed before she jumped off the rock and knelt down at my side.

"What if something came to hurt them?" she demanded.

I smiled. "Then the farmer or his dogs would protect them."

"But what if it were the farmer who hurt them? Then what would they do?"

"Why would he do such a thing?" I was completely bewildered by the turn the conversation had taken. "He needs his sheep for wool and . . . and he cares about them very much."

"Perhaps he could not help himself. Perhaps he changed. Or something changed him."

"Nonsense! Farmers do not change."

"Are you certain?"

"Absolutely."

I sat up and packed the bottles back into the basket. The sooner we continued on our walk and left the sheep behind, the sooner Clarissa would forget her melancholic thoughts.

Or so I hoped. Certainly, *I* could not forget them. It seemed her thoughts had not been for the sheep but for her own predicament. Although she had never spoken of the matter, it must have bothered her greatly that we had seen nothing more of the Pengelleys and their friends.

But her fears about the farmer's changing made no sense to me, although she had said something similar the day we stood outside the ruins. Had she noted the recent changes in her father and supposed his interest in me meant that he had ceased to care for her.

If that were all, I could assure her he had not.

Clarissa broke into my thoughts. "Do you like living at the Hall, Jessamy?"

"I would not willingly live anywhere else," I replied, feeling a rush of happiness.

"Not even London?"

"Especially not London."

"I thought London was a wonderful place."

"Cornwall is much nicer."

"But Uncle Henry liked London so much he would not visit us. That is what my father said."

"I suppose we all have different tastes."

Her delicately arched brows drew together in a line, making her look like a childish, feminine version of her father. "I think he was mistaken."

"In preferring London? Yes, I think so, too."

She shook her head. "I mean Papa. I think he was mistaken about Uncle Henry."

"Do you?" I asked, amused by her serious face.

She nodded. "I think it was not London he loved. I think it was Wolfeburne Hall he hated."

To that, I had no ready response. But she was not the first child to wonder why the late Lord Wolfeburne had never visited his country estate. The same question had occurred to me almost ten years before.

I was grateful when we reached the slopes of Brown Gelly. Here, Clarissa would find something less troublesome to demand her attention. And, indeed, she did. For half an hour, she ran up and down the gentle, sloping tor, calling for me to hurry lest I fall too far behind.

"There is plenty of time to explore," I called, and persuaded her to sit long enough to enjoy the luncheon Mrs. Pendarves had packed for us.

She had given us cold pasties from the pantry, long meat and vegetable pies that the Cornish miners took into the mines. They made a filling meal, and Clarissa finished less than half of hers before she announced she could not eat another bite. This, however, did not stop her from downing half a bottle of ginger beer and two mince tarts.

"Goodness. It is just as well no one is around to watch you eat," I said. "They could not possibly think you a young lady."

"You have eaten *all* of your pasty," she noted with narrowed eyes. "And there were six mince tarts when we started and now there are only two remaining."

"But I am only a governess, and nobody regards us as being of any real importance."

I deliberately helped myself to one of the two remaining tarts and dispensed with it in two enormous bites. Clarissa fell back on the grass and lapsed into a fit of high-pitched giggles. Her laughter rang up and down the slopes, and I decided the reward of seeing her happy was well worth the slight loss to my dignity.

It appeared our day might yet be salvaged.

Judging by the height of the sun in the sky, it was not long past midday. Those clouds to be seen wafted far overhead, innocent, white puffs. Lazily, I dusted off our plates and packed them into the basket.

Clarissa curled up at my side, her gaze fixed on the sparrows that darted in and out of reach to grab at the crumbs. After several minutes, she yawned and asked, "May I go and look at the huts?"

I nodded. "But remain where I can see you."

She rose, startling the sparrows who fled to a safe distance, and turned and scampered across the slope to the circle of stone dwellings we had come to see. I folded up our serviettes, slipped them down the corners of the basket, and followed at a more sedate pace.

Stepping into the circle of beehive huts was like stepping two thousand years into the past. The essence of those long-ago peoples still clung to the place, as their granite dwellings still clung to the hillsides of Brown Gelly, as indistinct and intangible as the fog that hovered above the marshes. One had only to look through the corners of one's eyes to believe one caught sight of them slipping between the huts like vague shadows. Or look at their primitive village, intact and waiting for their return. I had the odd feeling that they had never truly left, but only walked away, for a few hours or a day, knowing they would be back to reclaim their homes.

A strange coldness seeped through me. I did not like this place. It may have been nothing but foolishness, but I could not rid myself of the conviction that we were trespassing on a world where we did not belong. I glanced about for Clarissa and saw her peering into the low doorway of one of the huts, her nose wrinkled in distaste, a faint frown upon her brow.

I did not summon her away immediately, lest she catch the uneasiness in my voice or note my sudden haste. Instead, I called and reminded her we could not linger, for we had a long walk back and the days had grown short. She acknowledged me with a wave, but her attention was elsewhere. Suddenly, without asking permission or giving any warning, she sank onto her hands and knees and crawled into the hut.

Her disappearance plunged me into the depths of an unreasoning terror.

"Clarissa!" I cried, but either she could not hear my call, or I could not hear her answer.

Oblivious to everything but my growing panic, I gathered up my skirt and ran across the grassy enclosure. The pins fell from my hair, and my braid uncoiled and thumped against my back. Despite my headlong rush, I had not covered half the distance when she screamed.

It began as a thin, frightened wail, rising like smoke

from the chimney hole of the hut. In the few seconds it took me to reach the narrow entrance, it grew in volume until the sounds echoed within the stone walls and billowed from every opening. Mixed with her terror was a faint odor that bothered me. It hammered out a warning in my distraught mind, demanding attention, but I could think only of Clarissa.

Heedless of my dress, I flung myself on the ground and began to crawl through the tunnellike entry. My shoulders brushed the stones. Tiny rocks scraped at my palms, and her cries swelled in my ears, until my eardrums vibrated beneath their painful onslaught. Here, too, the smell grew stronger and, to someone who had once lived above a butcher's shambles, there was now no mistaking the smell of rotting flesh.

Something had crawled inside this ancient dwelling and died. Recently died, or the stench would have been unbearable and impossible to mistake, even from outside the hut.

And then another possibility occurred to me.

Was the truth even more horrifying? Had some luckless creature been killed, either there or on the moor, and then been dragged inside the hut and hidden there? And did only the victim lay within, or was this the killer's lair?

With what was Clarissa confronted?

I emerged from the damp closeness of the tunnel into the living chamber. Pale sunlight filtered through the chimney hole in the ceiling, diluting the darkness into a dozen different shades of gray. Only Clarissa's screams retained that sense of inutterable blackness and blotted out all other sounds.

I did not attempt to make myself heard, but scrambled toward her, reaching out for her in an attempt to comfort her more quickly. She crouched with her back to me, unconscious of my presence, her gaze pointed ahead of her to something I could not yet see.

My fingers brushed her shoulder. Immediately, her cries ceased. Only the echoes continued, an eery imitation of her terror that, ever so slowly, faded into nothingness.

"Clarissa!" I said sharply, intentionally speaking over the last whispering sounds. "It's Jessamy. I'm here."

"*Here. Here. Here,*" the echoes teased from all directions.

She did not answer, but whimpered softly.

That gave rise to vague, mocking whispers that were more bloodcurdling than her screams. We might have been surrounded by spirits who had awakened from centuries of sleep and been stirred to ghostly protest.

Clarissa fell against me, her body limp. Even her skin felt unnatural, clammy and lifeless. And yet she had not fainted. I cradled her in my arms and, dreading what I might see, peered over the top of her head.

And gasped.

Swallowing the urge to shriek, I tightened my grip on Clarissa and rocked her back and forth. It took all my strength to keep my eyes from returning to what I had seen.

A dead sheep.

Worse than dead. The creature had been savagely attacked. Its head lolled backward and its throat had been ripped open. The body had been gutted, not by something sharp that made smooth cuts like a knife, but by a dull, uneven instrument that had made ragged tears. The sheep's entrails were strewn on the ground. Blood had splattered the springy curls of wool and had spilled onto the earthen floor in a deep, dark pool, and glassy eyes stared upward vacantly, their dull sheen caught in the light from the chimney hole.

No dog had done this.

Nothing human could have done this.

It was pure savagery, the likes of which I had never seen.

Somehow, I had to get Clarissa away. How I did not know, for she seemed incapable of movement. But under no circumstances could we remain there.

It was impossible to shove her through the tunnel. Nor was she in any shape to crawl by herself. In the end, all I could do was back out and pull her after me.

I took her hands in mine. They were wet and sticky, and slipped easily from my grasp. She lay on her back, neither helping nor struggling against me, her slight frame seeming much heavier than I would have supposed possible. I sighed with relief when I felt the first cool draft of air sweep across my legs, and tried not to remember that leaving the hut was the first and shortest part of the journey to come.

I emerged from the hut, and my gaze went to my hands. They were covered in blood. It was everywhere. On me. On Clarissa. Smeared across her green walking dress. I picked her up and carried her back to the picnic basket and the grassy slope where we had eaten our pasties. Only then did I pause to rub her hands and wrists clean with our serviettes, and do the same for my own.

Her face was absolutely, impossibly white. And, although her eyes were open, she seemed to see nothing. Taking the blanket we had been sitting upon, I wrapped it around her shoulders. That done, I lifted her again and cautiously made my way down the hill.

This was a much slower progression than we had made with Mr. Stanton. There had been two of us to support him, and he had been able to stand erect and walk. I slipped and stumbled over the grass, pausing to rest only when I could not take another step.

Around us, the sun swept westward with frightening haste, and the sky darkened to a cobalt blue. My arms and legs were numb, and only my fear of that thing that had killed the sheep made me keep walking. Indeed, as long as I was able to draw breath, I would not stop.

At last, I saw the tower of Wolfeburne Castle, and never had it seemed so welcoming. I judged the distance between us to be a mile, at most. My legs wobbled treacherously, but I forced myself to go on.

I had not taken more than three steps when I caught sight of a horse and rider and knew instantly that it was Trystan. He saw us at the same instant and spurred his horse into a gallop. It would only be a matter of minutes before he reached us. With a muttered prayer of thanks, I sank to the ground.

He bore down on us like a fusilier, and the sod flew up from beneath his horse's hooves. A short distance before he reached us, his hand tightened on the reins, and he swung from the saddle before his sweating mount had come to a halt.

"In God's name, what has happened to her?" he

demanded, his gaze fixed in horror on Clarissa's vacant and immobile face.

I gulped back the hysteria that threatened me now that the responsibility for her life was no longer in my hands. "There was a . . . a dead sheep in one of the huts."

"Good God!"

"It was . . . it was . . ."

He shook his head and glanced meaningfully at Clarissa. "There is no need to explain," he said, his voice brusque. "I have seen them for myself."

To my eyes, Clarissa appeared beyond hearing, but I realized he was right. Neither of us knew exactly what she understood in her semiconscious state.

"Can you ride, do you think?" he asked, lifting his daughter in his arms. "And hold on to Clarissa if I lead the horse? If not, I will carry her."

"I can manage," I told him.

After my tediously slow journey, the last mile rapidly fell behind us. Trystan took broad, loping strides, and his long legs ate away the distance. Every few seconds, he glanced over his shoulder to assure himself that I had not slipped in the saddle nor lost my hold upon Clarissa.

He need not have worried. I believed that, had I lost consciousness, still they would have had to pry my fingers from around her.

At the Hall, Bastian was dispatched for the doctor on the already saddled horse. Trystan dashed up the stairs, Clarissa in his arms, with Mrs. Pendarves and me a bare step behind him.

A good two hours passed before he and I descended again, and the strain of those hours showed in the tension in his face and the tightly drawn line of his lips.

Clarissa had been put to bed, and the doctor had done all that he could do for her. Little enough, as he said himself. She had suffered a severe shock, and there was no way to tell whether or not she would fully recover or measure how long that recovery would take. In all the time we fussed over her, the only word that had passed her lips was "Matilda." I tucked the doll into the crook of her arm, and only then would she accept a sleeping draught from her father. Afterward, she sank into a restless sleep.

The doctor had suggested that I, too, should have a sleeping draught and be put to bed, but I declined. I could not bear the thought of being unconscious if Clarissa should call out for me. Nor had I given Trystan a full accounting of our disastrous day, and I could see the questions in his eyes.

With a hand resting on my shoulder, he guided me into his study and settled me comfortably on the settee. Over my protests, he lifted my feet onto the cushions and covered me with a blanket. That done, he poured me a glass of brandy from the decanter and, ignoring my protests, pressed it into my hands.

"I am not suggesting that you make a habit of imbibing," he said. "Only that you sip this for your nerves."

I followed his instructions and soon found myself enveloped in a warm and pleasant drowsiness, from which the events of the day receded slightly from the forefront of my mind.

"Feeling better?" he asked.

I nodded.

"Then if you are able to tell me, I would like to know exactly what happened."

I stumbled through the story. It was impossible not to blame myself for having let her wander about without me at her side, even for having suggested we picnic on Brown Gelly, but Trystan refused to let me berate myself. Nor did he speak a single word of reproach.

While I talked, he perched on a footstool he had drawn up to the settee and stroked my head, gently brushing back the wisps of hair that fell across my brow. "You are not to blame," he murmured. "If there is fault to be found here, then that fault is mine."

"Yours?" I said weakly, unable to generate the indignation I would have felt were I not feeling the effects of the brandy. "But you did not take her there."

"Perhaps not. But I have kept her at the Hall since her mother's death. It was utter selfishness. I wanted to believe she was happy, because she was *my* happiness."

"She encouraged you in that belief."

The line of his lips hardened. "I believed her because she told me what I wanted to hear. She was the only pleasure I took from life, and I could not bring myself to send her away."

"Nor would she have been happy if you did. The child adores you."

"Given how I have failed her, I do not deserve her adoration." He swore with a savagery that frightened me, even in my brandy-induced stupor. "It is unconscionable to think what she has suffered for my sake. Why did I not send her to Henry when she was six?"

"Would you have had her suffer the loss of two parents at once?" I demanded, the pain of his torment rousing me to a semblance of my usual self. "By such an act you would have caused her greater suffering, not less."

"And that was what I told myself. But it was nothing more than an excuse to keep her with me. She would soon have transferred her affections to her aunt and uncle."

"What nonsense is this? You despised both of them, as well you should have done. They were vain and selfish people, incapable of loving anyone other than themselves. Clarissa would have shriveled and died had she been left in their care."

He searched my face. "Are you certain? After all, you would have been there."

"And what could I, more an outcast than member of that household, have done for her at fourteen? At best, through my attentions, I would have drawn down Henrietta's wrath upon her."

"Had she relations on her mother's side, I would have sent her there. But Henry was my only option."

"And that was no option at all."

He sighed. "My poor child. For all it appears otherwise, she was not born into an easy life. I can only pray she recovers with the rapidity the doctor expects."

I felt a flash of doubt but said nothing.

My emotions must have shown on my face, for he started. "What's wrong? Have you left something unsaid?"

There was no alternative but to answer him, although I dearly wished my thoughts could have remained in my possession alone. "I cannot be sure, but I fear her shock involves more than the horror of seeing the mutilated sheep," I said gently. "When we were walking to Brown Gelly, she saw two sheep that had wandered off from the herd, and she . . . she seemed to identify with them. With their solitary state. At the time, she worried they might come to harm, although I insisted they would not."

I deliberately excluded any mention of the farmer. Trystan had enough to occupy his thoughts without wondering why his daughter might suspect him capable of harming her. And, even now, I thought it likely that it was the loss of his love that had frightened her rather than her supposing him capable of doing her any physical damage. It was foolish to alarm him.

"I told her the farmer would protect them. I worry now that she viewed the savaged sheep rather differently than another child would have done."

"God forbid! I cannot think she can endure much more of this. We must both pray you are wrong."

I fervently agreed.

Trystan enclosed my hand in his. "I fear I have done you no kindness in bringing you here but only embroiled you in my own troubles."

"You need feel no guilt on my account. This is the only place I have known any real happiness."

"An elusive quality, happiness. It can be discovered in the strangest of circumstances. Certainly, I would not have thought to find mine in a coal cellar."

He bent his head, drawing it near to my own, and I realized with a start that he intended to kiss me. I felt the initial stages of panic, the urge to take flight or hide behind maidenly virtue.

You must not, I told myself. *You cannot run now, when*

he most needs your support. Not if you care, in any way, for him.

I stiffened but lifted my face to his. Suddenly, the study seemed suffocatingly close, and there was a rushing, roaring noise in my ears that drowned out the pop and hiss of the fire and the sounds of my own breathing. Ignoring everything, I closed my eyes.

And waited.

And was rewarded with the touch of his mouth upon mine.

His lips barely brushed my own with a light kiss. Impossibly light. Like being swept by thistledown, and my lips tingled in its wake. How, I wondered, could this prickly man be capable of such absolute and exquisite softness? Surely he hadn't kissed me at all.

I opened my eyes, convinced that he had not. There was a smile in his eyes, warm and unguarded. And while I searched his face, his gaze sought the answer to his own question. What that question might be was not difficult to fathom.

I smiled.

Satisfied that I had no objection, his arms encircled me, and he kissed me again, firmly, leaving no doubt in my mind that I had, indeed, been kissed. Undeniably and most emphatically. Then he rested his cheek against the side of my head, and his arms tightened around me.

I sighed and squirmed deeper into his embrace. There was a luxurious warmth to be taken from those strong arms. Each second we remained there I held my breath, certain that now it surely had to end. That now he would release me, and I would find myself alone once more, colder and sadder for knowing what life withheld from me.

The seconds were strung together, one to the next, until I gasped for breath.

"Are you all right?" he murmured.

I nodded.

"It is possible, I believe, to be held by someone, even to accept their kisses, and still take air into one's lungs." Although his tone was teasing, a thin edge of strain sharpened his words.

"It is my first kiss," I told him, pretending he had mistaken the cause of my discomfort. "I am not properly acquainted with the procedure."

"Do not pretend to me," he said with a strange urgency. "Anything but that, I beg you. If you wish me to stop, you have only to ask."

"I do not wish it of you."

With his forefinger, he traced a line upward from my neck, beneath my jaw, to the tip of my chin. Using only that one finger, he did not lift but rather guided my face to his. Then his mouth descended again, and those early kisses were but a prelude to the demand he now placed on me.

His hand slid upward and cupped the back of my head, capturing me and holding me there so that I could not escape him if I tried. With savage and relentless force, he pressed his lips to mine and devoured them with the hunger of a starving creature. I was swept forward on the crest of that assault, at once battered and exhilarated by its power.

Could anything be more wonderful than this?

Could any price be too great to pay?

Telling myself the answer to both my questions was no, I gave myself up to his kisses and returned them with a passion I had not known existed in me. And in the middle of that torrent of need and abandonment, we clung to each other, two lost souls rocked by the storms that assaulted Wolfeburne Hall.

15

It was Trystan who pulled away, and I let him go reluctantly, reproaching him with my eyes for his retreat.

"Forgive me, my love," he whispered. "But I think we can go no further without the services of a minister."

I gave a little gasp. "You mean to marry me?"

"Have I not told you that I thought happiness was still possible with you?"

"You made no mention of marriage."

"What did you suppose, then? That I would have you for my mistress?" He chuckled softly. "I believe I have convinced you that I am entirely lacking in decency."

"Indeed, you have not. Your behavior has, at times, confused me. But in the short while I have lived beneath your roof, you have displayed more kindness and decency toward me than I experienced in twelve years at Wolfeburne House." I smiled. "Were it not for my knowing I could trust you, I should not have let you persuade me to love you."

He frowned. "And is that why you love me? Because you trust me?"

"It is."

He regarded me soberly. "Tell me, my darling. Could you love and admire a man who was a liar?"

The combined intensity of his gaze and oddity of his question startled me into silence. It was a blessed loss of speech, for the response that automatically rose to my lips would have confirmed what he himself already believed. That no woman of high morals or intelligence could have loved such a man.

But that was no answer to give *him*, a man who donned masks as other men donned their shirts each morning, a man who held his peers at arm's length for some reason known only to himself. When I recovered my voice, I chose my words carefully. "We are all obliged to lie in some fashion. Sometimes, decency demands it of us, and—"

"I do not talk of polite, social pretenses. Could you love a man whose entire life was a lie? A man who was a complete and utter fraud? Whose every moment was designed to make him appear to be someone he was not?" He grabbed me by the shoulders and shook me as though he could shake the truth from me. "Tell me. Could you love such a man? No, of course you could not. Nor could any woman who was not a fool."

I swallowed. "If you lie, it is not without an honorable reason. I am convinced."

"Honor." He scoffed at the word. "Honor is a luxury, and I am a poor man. If I lie, it is of necessity. To survive. To guard what little I hold dear."

"Surely, that *is* honorable," I said, my mouth dry.

His wild laughter echoed through the room. "I thought that once. Or so I told myself."

"And any man of principle would agree."

He laughed again. "Perhaps. In theory, it is easy to believe in principles, even to let them shape your decisions. But faced by those decisions each morning upon arising, confronted by them every waking minute, and tormented by them each hour that he sleeps, a man is forced to question what driving force truly compels him. To ask himself if it is not honor but fear of public scrutiny and humiliation, as well as a desire for a semblance of a normal existence, that has shaped his decisions."

He paced the length of the room in broad strides, finally coming to a halt in front of the windows. He lifted the curtains and stared morosely into the bank of fog that had rolled across the grounds to press against the stone walls of the Hall. I took note of the angle of his head and the direction of his gaze. There was no question that he looked toward the ruins.

"What is it?" I whispered. "What is there about the castle that tortures you?"

He started and turned. "What nonsense is this? Can a man not look across his own estate without someone making false assumptions?"

"Do not treat me like a fool. Lie to the world if you must, but not to me. There is no need."

"You are hardly in a position to make that determination."

"For heaven's sake, tell me," I cried. "Give me that same trust that you demand of me."

"I cannot. Do not ask."

"There is a secret that casts a shadow over all of Wolfeburne Hall. And it lies in the ruins."

"What are you saying? You have given me your promise never to go there."

"Nor have I broken that promise, but I am begging you to tell me of your own volition."

"Never!"

His reply hung in the air, dividing us as no wall nor barricade could ever have done. Some deep, intuitive part of me dreaded that it would always remain there, no longer audible save to my own ears and his, yet still capable of keeping us apart. Capable of destroying any happiness we might hope to enjoy.

"Trystan—"

"Dear God, Jessamy!" he cried, turning on me in a fury. "I have no right to you or your kisses. I thought I could pretend otherwise, but it would seem I am not wholly without conscience."

"What cause have you to feel guilty? You do not hold me prisoner here. Nor force me into loving you against my will."

"That is not enough."

"But I *do* love you," I whispered, terribly frightened that he would vanish from my life while I, like a child catching at mist, would have to stand there and watch him slip, irretrievably, from my fingers.

He sighed and shook his head. "Go to bed, Jessamy. I have acted precipitously and now must give this matter greater consideration. But it is late, and we are both distressed. We can talk more in the morning."

He turned his back on me, precluding any attempt I might make to protest.

Unwillingly, I left him.

*   *   *

It was early when I awakened, sometime before dawn, although the leaden gray of the sky heralded the approach of morning. The coming day showed little promise. Yesterday evening's heavy fog still blanketed the countryside, and a strong wind rattled the windows in their casements.

I lay beneath my blankets, trying to view with clearer gaze the conversation Trystan and I had had in the study. What bedeviled him? And would he allow his demons to divide us now that we had so nearly come together?

And was I to return meekly to my life as an observer, that half-life to which I had been sentenced as a child?

It was not possible.

Trystan had awakened me, had breathed life into my being and fired my emotions. They tumbled inside me, pressing me to speak and act, to feel and demand a piece of life. Whatever ability I might have once had to ignore them or tramp them down had been destroyed.

I would not allow him to take from me what he had taught me to want.

From this decision I took a deep satisfaction. It allowed me to rise and face the coming day with confidence. Clarissa should not awaken to an empty room, lest she have the chance to dwell on the horrors of what she had seen. She, like her father, needed my newfound strength to recover, just as I needed their affections.

I dressed hastily and left my suite. The corridor was empty, and the curtains were still drawn over the windows in the gallery and at the far end of the wing. Nor would Mary make her first trip upstairs for nigh on half an hour.

There was a thin crack of light visible beneath Clarissa's door. I quietly entered and glanced around the room. A low flame flickered in one of the lamps on her night table, and Mrs. Pendarves lay asleep in the wing chair. Her head was flung back, her mouth was open, and her chest rose and fell in a regular rhythm.

I thought briefly of awakening her and sending her to her own bed, then decided that, once conscious, she would likely insist on beginning her morning duties. Better to let her rest. I turned my attention to the bed and discovered that Clarissa had been watching me, a faint smile upon her lips.

"Good morning, Jessamy," she whispered. "Is it morning already?"

I stared at her, and it was all I could do to hide my amazement. One would have thought it was a typical morning, both from her behavior and her appearance.

When I failed to speak, she added, "Mrs. Pendarves must have fallen asleep while she was reading to me, although I cannot remember the story. We must let her rest. You can help me dress if you like."

"It is still early," I said, finding my voice. "There is no need to get up quite yet."

"But I have been lying here for *ages*. And I am hungry and want my breakfast." She giggled. "My stomach makes such noises, I was certain it would disturb Mrs. Pendarves. Mary says a lady's stomach never growls. Is that true, Jessamy?"

I was spared the necessity of finding a suitable answer

to this question by Trystan's appearance at her door. His dark face peered into the room, and his surprise at finding me there and Clarissa awake and chatting showed.

"Good morning, Lord Wolfeburne," I said, the same odd brightness in my voice that had been present in Clarissa's greeting to me.

"Is everyone up early today?" she demanded. "How nice of you to come and see me, Papa. It is not my birthday, surely?"

"Not for another three months," he said, avoiding my gaze.

She nodded. "That's right. It is not like me to forget." She gasped. "Is it your birthday, Papa?"

"I am too old for birthdays."

"Jessamy?" she asked.

"Nor mine," I told her. "Goodness, we do not need to have birthdays to come to your room at an early hour. I came because I was awake and wanted company."

"As did I," Trystan said.

Clarissa considered this for a moment, and a faint glimmer of understanding came into her eyes. "Sometimes I do not like to be alone, either. But I have Matilda." She squeezed the doll in her arms. "Just as she has me. But she will share me with you both, if you like."

"Indeed, we would," I replied, choking back the emotions that welled within me lest they bewilder her.

Trystan only managed a nod.

There was a soft yawn from the wing chair, and Mrs. Pendarves opened her eyes. She blinked several times at us, then pulled herself to an upright position. Her hands promptly went to straighten her chignon, which had loosened during the night.

"Goodness," she murmured. "I didn't mean to fall asleep. Is the child—"

"She has already awakened," Trystan said, cutting off her question.

"And you will be wanting to go and tidy up," I added. "You need not worry about Clarissa, for I'll give her any help she needs this morning."

I hustled her from the room before she could say something she shouldn't. The elderly woman allowed herself to be swept along without further remark, apparently sensing that all was not as it should have been.

Once in the corridor, she turned to me and demanded, "Is she all right?"

"She seems to have forgotten everything," I said. "And I think we must be careful what we say until she decides to remember."

"God bless us. I hope she never does."

I frowned, not certain I agreed.

But it did appear that Clarissa had benefited from her memory lapse. She ate everything on her plate at breakfast, insisted upon being given her lessons, and clamored for a walk when I questioned the advisability of going out in the damp air. Throughout the day, she laughed often, chattered until I thought she must run short of words, and squirmed in her chair as if she were too full of high spirits to be still.

I gave a report of her behavior to Trystan that evening, soon after she had been sent to bed. Too tense to sit, he hovered near the fire and stared thoughtfully at the flames. Nor did he lift his gaze, either when he spoke to me or as he listened to what I had to say. He seemed determined to ignore me, however much he might be forced to listen to my words.

"It is as if yesterday never happened," I said, aching for his embrace and unable to keep the emotion from my voice. "I suppose we should not be surprised. It is not the first time she has forgotten what she does not choose to remember, but I thought the others lapses deliberate. This seems to be genuine."

"And her state of mind?" he asked in a flat tone.

"Seems good. Perhaps a trifle high-spirited, but nothing untoward in a child of her years."

"Then we have been blessed by a piece of good fortune I did not expect."

If so, he seemed anything but pleased.

"I am not so easily convinced of that," I said, hating myself for disappointing him.

He glanced up at last. "What else could it be? Surely you do not think it advisable for her to remember her terror."

"If I believed her capable of never remembering, in any fashion, I would feel as you feel."

I reveled in the feel of his gaze upon my face. I would say anything, speak on any topic that would help me keep his interest. But something in my eyes betrayed me. His lids lowered, and he shielded himself from me with a veil of dark lashes.

"I fear she has not rid herself of these memories, but merely suppressed them," I continued miserably. "They might return at any time, perhaps as nightmares when she sleeps, perhaps when something jogs the missing piece of her memory back into place."

"We cannot protect her from every eventuality," he said bitterly.

He lifted his head to stare in the mirror set above the hearth. His gaze rested, not upon his own reflection, but on something else that was captured in the glass. A muscle in his jaw jumped, and his back was hard and still.

In a thick voice, he added, "But nor do I see that we should deliberately force her to recall something which her mind has hidden from her."

"If we are there to help her remember, we might protect her from a second, and greater, shock."

"Or hurt her when there is no need," he replied. "No, we must say nothing. I am convinced of it."

"Was it not you who taught me that fears must be faced?" I asked softly.

He scowled. "You are not a child of nine."

In that, he was right. I was stronger and older than Clarissa. But I had already seen her grasping for an understanding of the isolation she and her father endured, long after all memory of the disastrous visit to the Pengelleys had supposedly vanished. How long could she ignore what we had seen inside that hut?

Unable to remain in my chair, I rose and started toward him. "Trystan—"

He turned as though struck. "Forgive me, Miss Lane. If this topic is exhausted, then I must leave you. There are papers that need my attention."

Without so much as glancing at my face, he stalked past me and out the door.

* * *

Clarissa and I spent the evening together, Trystan having insisted that I should not leave his daughter's side until we were certain she had fully recovered. I suspected he had other reasons for making this request of me, but whatever there was to be settled between us would have to wait. Clarissa's welfare was of first importance.

Clarissa and I ate a quiet supper and spent the rest of the evening in my sitting room, reading a few fairy tales. The clock on my mantel chimed eight o'clock moments after I had finished the third story. I closed the book and started to speak, but Clarissa hastily interrupted me with a question about my childhood.

Unwilling to insist she retire until she was ready, I pulled my chair closer to the fire and invited her to do the same. For over an hour, she plied me with questions about London and her cousin Annabelle.

"Is she very pretty?" she asked, when I fell silent.

I nodded.

"Will I be pretty, too?"

"You are already pretty."

Caught in the glow of the fire, her face appeared to have the rosy tinge of good health, but the unhappiness in her eyes was unmistakable. Idly, she picked up the poker and prodded at the hot coals.

"Sometimes," she murmured, ". . . sometimes I wish I could be cousin Annabelle and live in London."

There was little to wonder about in that. But she could not be allowed to surrender to her melancholy. "Your father is much nicer than your Uncle Henry ever was," I said. "I suspect even Annabelle would envy you his affection."

"Yes. No one could be better than Papa. Even if he . . ." Her words trailed into nothingness.

"Even if he . . . ?" I prompted.

She sighed heavily. "I love Papa, and . . . and he has always been kind and good to me, but . . ."

I waited.

". . . but he—"

She broke off, scrambled to her feet, and flung herself into my arms. "Oh, Jessamy," she cried, face pressed against my bosom, her back heaving. "Papa is not like other people, is he? He's so very different. But that does not make him bad, does it? He would never mean to hurt anybody, would he? Even if"—she gulped for air—"even if some . . . sometimes he did."

"Good heavens!" I exclaimed, hugging her to me. "Your father is not a monster. We may not always understand the reason for his moods, but that is no reason to think the worst of him. And if he is short-tempered on occasion, then it falls to us to double our efforts to appreciate his difficulties. How hard it must be to manage the affairs of the Hall, as well as the house in London, for he takes care of his brother's family as well as his own."

She gave another hiccupping sob and then quieted. I pulled her onto the cushions beside me, took out my handkerchief, and wiped her tear-streaked cheeks. She accepted my ministrations, lifting her face to be cleaned like a small child who knew that nothing more was expected of her but her immediate compliance.

I finished and gave her a careful look. "Are you feeling better?"

"Yes, thank you," she said in a small, polite voice.

I was not satisfied by her response. The way she behaved, I might have done nothing more than ask her if she would like a piece of cake or a second cup of tea. "Are you certain you are all right, Clarissa?" I demanded, determined she would not brush aside my question. "If you are still worried, in any fashion, then you must tell me."

She shook her head.

I persisted. "Do you know how much your father loves you?"

There was a slight sniff.

"Has he ever hurt you?" I asked her. "Or done anything to make you think he would ever hurt you?"

She gave this some consideration. Behind her dark eyes, the thoughts churned slowly in her mind. Faint lines ran across her brow. Then her eyes widened, as though she had been struck by some awareness that had hitherto escaped her.

"He has never hurt me," she announced. "Not once."

"Nor would that be his wish," I added.

She smiled, a completely happy smile. The first, I think, that I had ever seen from her.

"Is there nothing else you would like to tell me?" I asked.

She thought for a minute. Then, with the look of an adult addressing a child, she rested her hand reassuringly on mine. "I do not think he would ever hurt you either, Jessamy."

"No," I said in a faint voice. "I am certain he would not."

"May I go to bed now?" she asked, fighting a yawn. "It has been a long day and I am very sleepy."

"Certainly, if that is your wish." I was completely bewildered.

Just once, I would have liked to have a conversation with either Clarissa or her father that didn't make me feel as though I had walked in long after it had begun or been forced to excuse myself before it could conclude.

Soon afterward, I retired to my own bed, still having come to no real understanding of what troubled Clarissa. But at least she had gained some sense of peace from what had passed between us that evening.

Or so I thought.

In the middle of the night, I awakened. Lifting my head from my pillow, I listened for the howls of the dogs, believing it was they who had awakened me. Instead, a child's scream filtered beneath my door.

Clarissa.

I sprang out of bed and ran from my suite, not pausing to grab my night jacket or pull on my slippers. Her frightened cries burgeoned from her room and swelled through the corridor, although I doubted they carried beyond the second floor of the west wing. Convinced there was only me to hear her, I doubled my pace. Three steps brought me to her door. I gave the knob a sharp twist and plunged forward.

"J . . . Jessamy?" she asked, unable to see me in the darkness.

"It is I."

"Light the lamp," she pleaded.

This I did quickly. Holding it in the air, I let the glow fall across the bed and peered anxiously at her face. She was white and shaken. Her eyes glistened with tears, and her lower lip quivered. But she did not appear to have suffered any physical harm.

"What on earth is the matter?" I asked.

She swallowed. "I had a nightmare. It was . . . it was . . . oh, dear. I cannot remember." She sagged into the pillows at her back. "What is wrong with me, Jessamy?"

"There is nothing the matter with you."

Nor was there any doubt in my mind that her nightmare had been of the dead sheep. And that, I told myself, is what comes of our shutting our eyes and pretending nothing horrible had occurred. Not that Clarissa was to blame. She was only a child, struggling to cope with her terror as best as she knew how. But we, as adults, should not have allowed her to fight this battle alone. And by supporting her pretense, that was exactly what we did.

I was furious for having let myself be swayed against my better judgment. Clarissa needed to be allowed to remember. Not by herself, while she slept, but while she was awake and with someone she trusted.

"I think I know why you screamed," I said gently.

"Y-you do?" she asked, and mixed with her hesitance was a touch of genuine relief.

I nodded. "In your sleep, you recalled something that frightened you. Something you cannot recall during your waking hours."

"But how could I have forgotten?" she asked. "I have a good memory."

"I know you do. But some things we want to forget. Nor am I certain you should be reminded. No doubt, when you are ready, you will remember. Only do not think your imagination plays tricks on you, or feel you must hide from what you saw."

"Was there . . . blood?" she asked. "There was blood in my nightmare. It was all over my hands."

"Yes," I whispered. "But it was not your blood. And there was nothing there that could hurt you. Nor can it hurt you now." I wrapped her in my embrace and rocked her.

She shivered. "I'm scared, Jessamy."

"Sometimes, if we admit to those fears and face them, they lose their power over us."

She stared up at me, her face paler than that of the bisque doll that nestled against her pillow. "I am not a c-coward. Truly, I am not."

"I did not say you were. All of us have fears of one kind or another."

"Even you, Jessamy?"

"Yes. Even I."

"And do you face your fears, too?"

"I am trying."

"Is it hard?"

"Yes, but not nearly as hard as being afraid and not knowing why."

"Then I shall try. Really, I will."

It was early afternoon when I knocked on the door of Trystan's study. He could not be left in ignorance of my talk with Clarissa, lest he unwittingly confuse her by continuing his pretense. Nor could I fail to tell him that I had disobeyed his orders.

Over the dogs' barks, he called, "Enter."

I glanced down at the voluminous pink skirt of my dress, and brushed my fingers over the folds to smooth out any creases that might be there. Then I took a deep breath, and stepped into the room.

"Have you a moment, Lord Wolfeburne?" I asked, thinking it unwise to use his Christian name. He had made his intentions plain, and I had not gone there today to challenge him.

He raised his head and glanced at me from across a leather-bound ledger. Upon seeing it was I, his brow furrowed and he demanded, "Is it important? I am extremely busy."

"I must speak with you about Clarissa."

"If that is all, I can spare you a minute."

He set the ledger down and rose from his chair. Behind him, the curtains were pulled back, and the light from the windows, although not bright, captured him in silhouette and threw his face into shadow. This was undoubtedly what he had intended, for he stood there, motioning for me to sit down, but making no move to do the same himself.

"She had a nightmare last night," I said, finding it horribly difficult to talk to a man whose expressions and reactions were impossible to see. "She was most upset, and I thought it unwise to keep the truth from her."

He said nothing.

Unable to keep looking at him, I let my gaze drop to my hands where they rested in my lap. It remained there until I had given him a full account of what had transpired. "I hope you are not angry with me," I finished. "Although I know this was not what you wanted."

He tapped his fingers on the edge of his desk before he spoke, an impatient rap that convinced me he was, indeed, angry. Then he released the breath he had been holding. "No. I cannot be angry with you. You did what you thought best, and you may very well be right. Certainly, I do not want her troubled by nightmares whenever she falls asleep. That can do her no good."

"That was my feeling, also."

"I had hoped . . ."

"Milord?"

"In a few years, she will be ready for a finishing school. Then there would be no reason for her not to spend a holiday with her aunt in London. She might find a man she wishes to marry and never need to return to this place. There is such a short while we need to protect her."

"A good six years, milord. And that is a long while to keep anyone in ignorance. Particularly an intelligent child like Clarissa."

He nodded. "More and more I become convinced she must be sent away from here."

"Might you yourself not take her to London?"

"I cannot leave here."

"But why not? Your brother saw no reason to remain here."

"And by ignoring his responsibilities, he forced me to shoulder them. I will not shirk them now that they are truly mine."

I started to protest, when I saw a splash of bright color outside the windows. It immediately drew my gaze. Clarissa had left the Hall and, with Matilda in her arms, was walking determinedly toward the ruins.

From the stiff position of her chin and the grim expression on her face, I knew immediately she meant to go inside.

"Clarissa!" I cried and pointed to her.

Lord Wolfeburne turned to look, but I could not wait. I gathered up my skirts and ran from the study, knowing I must stop her before she reached the stone walls. I had not gone many steps beyond the front door before I heard footsteps behind me. A moment later, Lord Wolfeburne brushed past me, his long legs devouring in one stride the same distance I covered in two.

Clarissa reached the arched stone entry and paused. She seemed in a kind of trance, similar to that mesmerized state I had noted on a previous occasion. Before she could prepare herself to go farther, Trystan descended and swooped her up in his arms. She cried out in alarm and dropped Matilda.

"Do not fear," he said. "You have come to no harm."

His voice brought her back to herself, and she looked up at her father, a faint look of surprise on her face.

"Did I not tell you the ruins were unsafe?" he demanded. "Why ever would you go there against my bidding?"

She swallowed. "Jessamy said we should face our fears and they would go away, Papa. And I have always been afraid of the castle."

"With good reason, you senseless little fool. It would take only one falling stone to crush that pretty skull of yours."

By now I had reached them. Every word of their conversation had carried across the empty lawns to me, and I was appalled at what my thoughtlessness had nearly done. "I had no notion—"

"I believe the suggestion was originally mine," Trystan said, interrupting me. "As I have always known, it is unwise to say anything to you that I might regret hearing again in a different context."

"Forgive me, milord."

He looked from me to Clarissa, who appeared content to remain in his arms. "No harm is done. Let us go back to the Hall."

"Matilda," she cried, suddenly struggling to free herself from her father's grip. "I cannot leave her."

"I will find Matilda," I said. "She cannot have fallen far."

"And you and I will go back to my study," Trystan said in his severest voice. "There are some things that must be made clear to you."

"I will be along shortly," I called.

I glanced around and caught a glimpse of white ruffles peeping from behind one of the stones that was embedded in the thick grass. Stepping cautiously, I walked to the far side. Matilda lay directly before my feet, face downward. I bent to pick her up and something snapped beneath my feet.

Immediately, I thought with horror that one of her hands had been crushed beneath my shoe. Then, with relief, I realized that her arm was lying at her side, almost covered by the folds of her muslin dress. I could not possibly have damaged her.

I stepped back and bent down to see what I had broken. Shards of rose-colored glass were scattered across the ground. I picked up several and cast about for more. Something shiny caught my gaze.

Whatever it was, it had become wedged beneath one of the stones and was difficult to pull free. At last, I succeeded and stared down at the piece of metal lying in my palm. It was a piece of brass, bent and twisted, but easily recognizable as what had once been the fittings of a table lamp.

16

I studied the crumpled brass and fragments of glass. Something stirred uneasily in my memory. But why? Had I seen that same lamp somewhere in the Hall?

Mentally, I scanned the various rooms with which I was familiar. Gaslights were in use downstairs, save perhaps in the servants' quarters where I had never been. Upstairs, I had only entered the west wing. This was far too decorative a piece for the schoolroom. Nor did it fit with Clarissa's bedroom decor. That left only my own suite and—

I gasped. Mary had told me a rose-colored lamp was missing from the corner table in my sitting room. It had been in use during Miss Osborne's time, but the table had been empty when I arrived. Was this the one the maid had searched for but failed to find? I had a strong feeling it was.

If so, who could have brought it here?

Clarissa? Mary? Mrs. Pendarves? All had access to those rooms. But if they'd wanted a lamp, there would have been others nearer at hand. There seemed to be only one logical answer.

Miss Osborne.

I was convinced it had to have been she. With this lamp, all of her odd behaviors fell into place like a jigsaw puzzle that had already taken shape and only needed the crucial pieces to form a picture.

Plain, unimaginative Miss Osborne. Too practical and matter-of-fact to loose her passions on a man. They had been reserved for higher, more scholarly pursuits. Archaeology had been her true love.

And she had been fascinated by the ruins.

What must she have suffered, looking out her windows upon the ruins of a medieval castle each morning and knowing it was denied to her?

One thought led to another. Had she fed the dogs with the intention of secretly coming here one night, not of running away as we had all supposed? Miss Osborne had scornfully denied being afraid of the dogs' howls. Mary had thought this pretense, but she had disliked the woman. Miss Osborne may have been exactly the kind of person she represented herself to be.

"And what happened to you?" I asked aloud.

Did she stumble and drop the lamp, then fear to return to the Hall lest her carelessness betray her activities? Or, without the lamp to light her path, had she lost her way in the fog and wandered out onto the moor?

I tried to imagine Miss Osborne tripping over an enormous chunk of granite that poked two feet above the grass but failed. What I knew of her made that seem quite impossible. Her sensible dress, the neatly turned cuffs, her manner toward Mary and Clarissa, even her archaeological background told me she was both careful and exacting.

Not the kind of woman given to careless accidents.

What, then, could have caused her to drop the lamp? Had something startled her? I peered into the depths of the ruins. What secret was contained therein? Something dangerous? A wild animal capable of ravaging a leather portmanteau and terrifying two enormous dogs? What would she have met if she'd passed beneath that archway, carrying only a lamp? Even Wilkins supported a pitchfork during his daily forays.

Had she fled from some frightening sight, forgotten the stones in her fear, and dropped the lamp? If so, would she not have run directly to the Hall? Instead, she'd disappeared without a trace. She had not departed from Doublebois Station. Could it be that she had not departed at all?

Could it be that she had been attacked and killed?

I searched the area, hunting for some clue. I did not know what might have remained after the passage of seven months. The rain could easily have washed all traces of blood from the rocks. The wind could have blown away pieces of torn clothing.

But what could have carried away the body of a full-grown, large-boned woman?

I scrutinized every square foot of ground near the castle entry, but found nothing that did not belong there. Still, Trystan needed to be made aware of my discovery. Whatever he had previously thought, now he would have to make an inquiry into Miss Osborne's disappearance.

I suspected he would not be at all pleased.

With the doll in one hand and the shards of glass in

the other, I went to his study. Clarissa was just departing, her ringlets drooping about her face, a moist sheen to her eyes. I put the hand that carried the pieces of broken lamp behind my skirt, afraid she might recognize them and question me. I need not have worried.

"You found Matilda," she cried, and some of her unhappiness faded. She opened her arms to receive her doll.

"She is not at all hurt," I assured her. "But there are a few grass stains on her dress."

Clarissa fussed over and scolded her, like a mother bird whose chick had tried to leave the nest before its wing feathers had fully grown. "I had better go and find another for her to wear," she said at last. "Matilda does hate to be dirty." She leaned forward and whispered to me, "Papa has told me I am to go upstairs and remain there. Nor am I to leave the Hall unless either you or he accompanies me. I have never known him to be so upset. Although he did not raise his voice," she said in an attempt to be fair.

"The fault is more mine than yours. But no matter what I said, I did not mean you to put yourself in danger."

"But I had to go . . . or I would never know if—"

"There you are." The door of the study banged shut, and I looked up to see Trystan standing in the corridor. Traces of a scowl were still evident upon his face, but he seemed much relieved to find me there. "I was just coming to look for you."

"There was no need, milord."

Deliberately ignoring my remark, he turned to his daughter. "Did I not send you to your room, Clarissa?"

"Yes, Papa."

"Then do not dawdle with Miss Lane."

"Yes, Papa." She turned to me and asked, "Will you come up soon, Jessamy? And talk to . . . to us? Matilda hates to be punished."

"As soon as I am able."

She gave me a grateful smile and fled.

Trystan cleared his throat. "And now, if you would be so good, Miss Lane. You and I must also come to some kind of understanding. I will not have this happening again."

"Of course, milord."

He stepped back to let me precede him into the study. In that narrow corridor it was impossible to pass without brushing against him. He flinched, but his features remained determinedly fixed into a stern mask that forbade intimate remarks. He need not have feared intimate remarks from me. There were more pressing matters that needed our attention.

The study was comfortably warm. It seemed strange to think that I had been in this same room a scant half-hour before, engrossed in conversation with him. So much had happened since then, it was like looking back to a different era.

What a difference a few shards of glass could make.

Trystan watched me take my seat, then leaned against the edge of his desk. Tension emanated from his stiff stance, and he looked down at me, at once remote and severe.

Giving me no chance to speak, he said, "I made it plain to Clarissa that she is not to go near the ruins again—for any reason."

I found it difficult to look at him and keep my thoughts collected. "I know you are upset. But she was only trying to rid herself of the terrors that have plagued her for many years."

"Some terrors are well founded. They should not be ignored."

"Although I do not think that your keeping secrets does her health any good, in this, you may be right. Look what I have found." Hand trembling, I showed him the shards of rose glass.

"What is that?"

"It used to be a lamp. A lamp that sat on the table in my sitting room, although it was not *my* sitting room then."

"Then whose? It is not your habit to talk in riddles." He bristled with impatience, an impatience that I believe was born of the fear that I might be leading him in a direction he did not wish to go.

I lifted my chin and reproached him with my eyes. "Nor was that my intention. It disappeared sometime before my arrival. I believe Miss Osborne was the last to have the use of it."

"You are saying *she* did the damage?" He pushed himself away from his desk and turned his back to me as though he had already lost interest. "Why should this be any concern of mine? One lamp more or less will not ruin me."

"I found the pieces while I was looking for Matilda. Do you not wonder how a lamp that sat in Miss Osborne's sitting room came to be laying broken outside the castle walls?"

A shudder passed down the length of his body, and

the color blanched from the back of his neck. He turned in a fury. "Damn the woman. She could not have gone there."

"I am convinced she did. Her father was an archaeologist, and she worked with him until his death. She desperately wanted to view the ruins. Which, of course, you would not allow."

If he'd intended to avoid touching me, that intention was forgotten. Trystan crossed the room and took one of the pieces from my hand. His fingers brushed my palm, but only I was aware. Lost in thought, he turned it over and over. But no matter how many times he looked, and how many times he held the glass to the light, it remained exactly what I had told him it was.

"I suppose you could not be mistaken?"

"Nothing else makes sense. I think she fed the dogs with the intention of going there unobserved one night."

"So you did discover the solution to that mystery, did you?" he said with a sad smile. "Have you more answers for me?"

"I think we can no longer assume that Miss Osborne left the Hall of her own free will."

He arched a brow. "Can we not?"

"Surely you must agree she has met with foul play."

"No, whatever I think, it is not that."

I stared at him. "But suppose . . . suppose she met with the same fate as that poor sheep."

"I think it unlikely."

"You cannot make that assumption. There must be an investigation."

He shuddered from head to toe, and then seemed to transform from human flesh to hard, implacable marble.

Only his eyes showed signs of life, and they burned within their sockets. He was a cornered animal, ready to fight for his life.

"Would you have me ask the local authorities to Wolfeburne Hall and invite them to pry wheresoever they will? I will not hear of it."

"You cannot pretend there is nothing wrong," I said in protest, determined that he should see reason. "Her whereabouts must be discovered, if she still lives."

"I am convinced she does," he said in a cold voice that made me think he would not have cared if he was wrong. "But I will make some private inquiries, if it will set your mind at rest. And in return, you must give me your word never to speak of this matter to anyone."

"But—"

"Your word, Jessamy. Trust *me* to do what must be done."

"And if Miss Osborne cannot be found?"

"Let us face that eventuality if and when we come to it."

I swallowed. What was wrong with him? I fully believed that, had I not pressured him to do otherwise, he would simply have dismissed the matter. What kind of man had no thought for the well-being of those who had been in his employ? There was no reasonable excuse for such behavior. Nor did I believe him when he assured me Miss Osborne could have come to no harm. His reaction to my news had been too violent.

Or did he now lie to himself, telling himself what he wished to hear, and ignoring what his heart must have known?

"How long?" I demanded.

"What?"

"How long must you be allowed to search before you will admit I could be right?"

"Give me a month. If I have not unearthed something to prove her still among the living, then you may do as you see fit."

It was all the concession I was likely to wring from him, and I nodded.

"And until then, we will go on as before?" he asked.

As before? Did he mean as the friends we once were, or as the troubled strangers we had become? I looked at him questioningly, but he immediately fastened his attention on the heavy gold ring on his finger.

Miserable to the core of my being, I dropped my own gaze. "If that is your wish."

"It is. And there is something else."

I lifted my head.

"Keep an eye on Clarissa. I am not convinced she means to give up this notion of hers to see the castle. You have told her she can rid herself of all that most disturbs her by confronting her fears. I feel it is a notion that will not die easily."

"I will talk to her. I could never forgive myself if something untoward befell her."

"Then I shall worry less for knowing you are here."

"Trystan—"

"Please leave me, Miss Lane. If I am to fulfill my promise to you, then I have a letter to compose. And Clarissa is waiting," he added, forcing me to remember and keep my promise.

I rose and went to the door. There I paused. Turning

back to him, I asked, "What do you hide in the castle, Trystan?"

"I do not recall having said that I hide anything there."

"It is obvious you do."

"Leave me my secrets, Miss Lane. You would not like to know them."

"Could I dislike them any more than I dislike not knowing them?"

He raised his gaze to the ceiling. "You must, for you have no other choice."

There was no defeating him. It was madness to try. Turning again, I put my hand upon the doorknob.

"Can I trust you, Jessamy?" he whispered.

"You, too, have little choice, milord."

I found Clarissa sitting in the schoolroom, her chair pulled to the windows, her elbows resting on the ledge. She peered through the panes, her wistful gaze fixed on the castle ruins. I shut the door firmly, and she jumped.

"We are both in complete disgrace," I announced cheerfully.

Her eyes widened. "I did not mean to make Papa cross with you, Jessamy."

"Of course you did not. Nor must you blame yourself. It is my fault for saying something that led you into trouble. Your father was quite right in being displeased."

I managed to pretend a sincerity I did not truly feel. But whatever my feelings about the dangers of letting hidden truths taint and poison her daily life, she had to learn the need for caution. Who knew what might have befallen her if she had entered the ruins?

I took her by the hand and led her to the sofa. When we were both comfortable, I looked at her and tried to impress upon her with my eyes the importance of what I had to say. "Whatever I might feel advisable, it was never my wish or intention for you to go traipsing on unsafe ground. And I must ask for your promise that you will never do so again."

"I have already promised Papa."

"I wish you to give me that same promise."

"If I must."

She glanced at Matilda, heaved a sigh, and mumbled the words I wished to hear. But all the while she spoke, her gaze was downcast and her lower lip protruded. The doll in her lap stared up at me, silent but all too knowing. I wondered if either of us really trusted Clarissa to keep a promise that had been extracted from her.

"Remember, Clarissa," I said gently. "Your Papa only desires your safety. When I spoke to you as I did, advising you to face your fears, I meant only that you should not blot out those things you find upsetting. You cannot keep all the unpleasantness inside you, night and day, without great cost to your health and peace of mind. But under no circumstances are you to put yourself in jeopardy again. That is more foolish still."

"You have been listening to Papa," she said accusingly.

"Of course. I must. He is your father."

"When you first came here you would not have let him persuade you to his way of thinking." There was a reproach in her voice that told me I had failed her.

But how? By desiring her safety. "Your Papa loves you,

Clarissa. And he only does what he believes is in your best interests."

She sighed again. "Papa is the best father in the world. But I think he loves me a little too much. He wants me to be happy, like Miss Pengelley was as a little girl, or like cousin Annabelle. But neither of them grew up at Wolfeburne Hall, or had a father like Papa. He tries to pretend to me that nothing is wrong, but sometimes things happen and he cannot. Then I must forget. That, or disappoint him."

"And is it only pretense on your part?" I asked softly.

She shook her head. "It used to be that I could not really forget, although I tried very hard. Then I would pretend for Papa and he believed me. But then . . . then . . ." She gulped for air.

I dared not press her further. "You do not have to tell me, Clarissa. Not if it upsets you."

She nodded gratefully. "Papa thinks he must look after me, but he is the one who needs to be protected, Jessamy. And I try, for I love him, no matter what he does. And it gets easier and easier to forget, at least while I'm awake. But then I have dreams that frighten me, although I cannot say why, and I know I must not look outside at night, nor peer too deeply into the fog, nor listen too carefully when the dogs howl, for their howling reminds me that there is something I must not remember, so I do not, but I am always fearful that I might."

Her words came out in a long, unbroken stream that gushed from her with the force of pent-up spring water. They explained much, at least about her behavior. She had always tried to please Trystan, usually with a fervor and passion that disturbed me.

But, in this instance, her feelings could be turned to some advantage. "If it matters so much to you to please your Papa, do you see that you must do as he wishes and stay away from the ruins?"

"But he is wrong, Jessamy. You are the one who is right, although he has persuaded you to think otherwise. I have let him hide everything from me, and now he feels he must. You would not let him do that. You would make him see that you were not afraid of . . . of . . ."

"Clarissa, this cannot be good for you."

"He needs to know I love him, no matter what," she insisted, beyond hearing anything I said to her.

"But he does. That is clear to all of us. There is no need for proof."

She disagreed with a stubborn shake of her head. "He needs to see I can be truly brave. And I can be, Jessamy. I do not care what happens to me. Truly, I do not."

"If something bad happened to you, your Papa would care. He would care very much, indeed."

"But perhaps it will not." She lifted her head to look at me. "Perhaps I will be like Wilkins and come and go as I please."

"Wilkins is a grown man who understands his duties and the need for caution. Nor do I understand what you think would happen to him, save that a rock might tumble down and strike him."

Or that he might come upon something capable of savaging a sheep, I added to myself.

Clarissa blinked rapidly, warding off her own dark thoughts. "Children are often like their parents, aren't they, Jessamy? Sometimes I study my face in the looking glass, and I can see his face behind my own. It should please me to resemble Papa if I love him, and I know I do. Instead, I worry that we are so much alike, and don't know why I worry."

"There is no need for fear on that score. Your Papa is a very handsome man."

"And yet it frightens me."

She fell silent, and when she spoke again, it was of trivial matters. The need to make Annabelle a new dress now that her best muslin had been stained. The slow approach of the Christmas holidays. And an idle remark questioning the possible whereabouts of Miss Osborne during that season. I answered, with great discomfort, that we must say a prayer for her well-being and happiness.

"If you like," Clarissa said. "Although she thought little of either Papa or me when she left."

"But we cannot judge her when we do not know her reasons," I said in a governessy voice that bothered me and persuaded her to change the subject.

In all, our conversation left me unsatisfied and worried that Clarissa would willfully break her promises. Nor could I leave Trystan in ignorance of that possibility. With that in mind, I approached Mrs. Pendarves after supper and asked her to sit with Clarissa for an hour. Good soul that she was, she did not object.

I took with me Darwin's *On the Origin of Species*, which I had finished reading a few days earlier and had not yet returned to Trystan. Since it was one he kept in his study and not in the library, it gave me an added excuse for intruding upon him, as well as a way of reminding him that he valued my opinions and my companionship.

The study door stood open. Trystan caught sight of me and glowered from behind his desk. "Can we not speak on a later occasion?" he demanded. Conflicting emotions warred on his face.

"I think the sooner we talk the better, milord."

Unwillingly, he nodded for me to enter.

Castor and Pollux watched me enter with interest, but neither dog growled. Not even when I took the armchair across from the hearth where they lay, basking in the warmth of the fire. Since that night I had stepped outside and told them to be quiet, they seemed to accept me as someone in authority, and I was tempted to pet them to confirm my suspicions. Trystan's wary gaze on me convinced me to keep my hands in my lap. Something told me he would not be pleased to discover his watchdogs no longer intimidated me.

"Will you not join me by the fire, milord?" I asked.

He shook his head. "There is no need. This will not take long, I hope."

It was more a command than a question, and I acquiesced with a nod, although I was determined to make full use of every second he allowed me. Nor did my deception cause me any pangs of guilt, for the battle I intended to wage was as much in his behalf as in my own.

Quickly, I related my concern that Clarissa might yet be tempted to go again to the ruins. Of the rest of our conversation, I said nothing, for I still had not made sense of all she had said to me, save to realize that her eagerness to please her father was behind her memory problems. And to tell him that would be to add to his burdens.

While I spoke, I regarded him surreptitiously. There

was a resignation in his face, a forlorn look in his eyes that suggested he had already said farewell to any thought he'd had of marrying me. But I was less discouraged than I might have been, for he could not remove his gaze from me when he thought I did not notice.

He marked each movement of my head and hands. His gaze drifted over my face with the softness of a caress. And there was a pull between us that made me want to rise from my chair and walk straight into his arms. Only the knowledge that he would push me from him kept me rooted to the cushions.

When I had finished, he thanked me stiffly. "I will make it a habit to remove the keys from the latch each night before I retire. Wilkins and Mrs. Pendarves have keys of their own should they need them. And now I shall bid you good-night."

It was impossible to recognize in him the man who had taken me in his arms and kissed me, the man who had claimed he needed me. "A moment more, milord," I pleaded.

"What now, Miss Lane?" he asked in a strangled voice.

"We are alone, Trystan. Can you not call me Jessamy?"

"Damn!" His fist hit the desk. "You must forget all that. I am convinced life holds nothing for us beyond the roles we now play."

"How can you—"

"For God's sake, Jessamy. This is not what I want. If I thought there was any way for us to be together without your being hurt, you would not be able to rid yourself of me."

"Perhaps you are mistaken.

"I am not. If there is nothing else, please go." He bent over the neat pile of letters on his desk and rummaged through them as though searching for something he needed.

I swallowed. "I cannot go just yet. Not without first protesting an unfairness."

"Whose?"

"Yours, milord. Or more exactly Trystan Wolfeburne's"—he flinched when I spoke his name—"for it is he who has treated me cruelly."

"This is not the time for—"

"Indeed, it is."

"Forgive me, but I still have papers to—"

"I will never forgive you," I cried, rising from my chair and sweeping across the room to stand before him. "You have brought me into being only to discard me the moment my heart began to beat. Clearly, you have come to a decision without either consulting or advising me."

He glared up at me. "You are not in a position to know what is or is not best for you."

"And do you intend merely to dismiss me from your presence and your life with a wave of the hand and turn of the head? As though I was nothing more to you than some lackey who blacks your boots each night? Your behavior is unconscionable."

He came to his feet as though I had slapped him. "You think that is my wish?"

"I do not. If I did, I would not force myself upon you. Not for an instant. I could accept your disinterest with more aplomb than I can accept your wanting me and yet putting me from you to satisfy some foolish sense of honor."

"It is not for that reason, I assure you."

His eyes were nothing more than dark hollows, windows into his tortured soul, and I ached to comfort him. But some instinct warned me that, if I moved toward him, he would find the strength to deny himself what I had to offer.

"Tell me why you have come to this decision," I said. "And perhaps your reasoning will be enough to carry me through the years that lie ahead. Empty years if I cannot enjoy your love, for I do not doubt there will be no one else for me."

He avoided my gaze. "You cannot know that."

"I can." My fingernails bit into my palms. "I have learned much about myself these past few hours, and I do not think I am the kind of woman who could give her heart twice in one lifetime."

"You must not talk that way. You are young and beautiful. I will not be the only man to appreciate that beauty and want you for his own."

"Perhaps. Perhaps not. But what another man might feel for me has no bearing on what I could feel for him. At best, he would have to be satisfied with scraps of my heart. I would not feed such poor fare to a dog, let alone to a gentleman who had claimed to love me."

"Dear God, Jessamy!" He sank into his chair, and his head dropped to his hands. Knowing I had stirred some doubt within his heart, I tentatively reached out and laid my hand upon his arm. He stiffened and glanced down, staring at my fingers as though they were venomous snakes. Unable to take a breath, I waited for him to recoil. Then, with a soft groan, he covered my hand with his own. Our fingers intertwined and, for that moment, he was mine.

"I knew I would rue the day I brought you here," he said, solemnly contemplating my fingers. "I underestimated how greatly. Are you determined, then, to ignore me in this as you have done in all things since coming here?"

"Hardly *all* things, milord."

"In all matters of any importance."

Save that of trespassing in the ruins. I had yet to cross that line.

As if he read my thoughts, he drew his hand away and leaned back in his chair. His gaze fixed on some spot upon the wall, and he stared past me. Once again I had lost him to the darkness that ruled his days and nights. The shadows that played upon his face had no outward cause, but swirled from somewhere deep within, and a heavy gloom settled onto the study.

"It will do you no good, Jessamy," he said at last. "I am convinced of it."

"Surely the decision to take that chance should be mine?"

He shook his head. "I will not see you hurt through your attachment to me."

"Attachment? I would hardly use so light a term."

"Fondness, then."

"Nor even that."

"Call it what you will. Only know, as badly as I have used you, it is still preferable to what you wish of me."

"Is it not my right to choose my own fate?"

"You do not know what fate you choose."

"Nor do I care as long as we are together."

He shook his head. "Give me time to think, Jessamy. I cannot give you an answer immediately."

"Then I will leave you, milord."

But only for now.

At the door, I suddenly remembered the book in my hand. "Forgive me, milord. I meant to return this to you, also."

He came and took the volume. It had been some while since we had spoken of the subject of evolution, and there had been other books I had borrowed from his library. He glanced at the cover unsuspecting.

Immediately upon seeing what he held, he laughed. Harsh, drunken laughter, although but a moment before I would have sworn he was sober. It fell about my ears like jagged glass, shredding the delicate link we had forged. Then he flung the book across the room. It hit the wall and thudded to the floor.

"My poor, dear Jessamy," he said, while the room still echoed with the sound. "You beg me to decide in your favor, then produce the very argument that must convince me to refuse you."

17

The dogs howled again that night, but they did not wake me. I was incapable of sleep. The memory of Trystan's last words and the look in his eyes persuaded me I had lost the battle for his love, but how or why remained unclear. The night's quiet had allowed my thoughts too free a rein, and I greeted the dogs' mournful cries with a sense of relief.

That relief was quickly replaced with guilt. Clarissa had confessed to a fear of the dogs' cries that went deeper than I had realized and each second the howls continued must only add to her distress.

I left my bed, pulled on my night jacket and slippers, and lit the lamp. The tiny flame illuminated the room with a yellow glow that flickered across the walls. In the corridor, I paused, halted by a noise from the gallery.

"Lord Wolfeburne?" I called, wondering if it was he.

My question met with silence.

I hesitated, convinced that I had heard something, but the meager glow from my lamp fell short of the gallery. It was draped in shadow, and for all my straining I could see nothing. I had only my ears to tell me that someone either lurked in that blackness or had recently departed this wing.

But now was not the moment to discover who.

I tapped on Clarissa's door, knowing she would be expecting me, but not wanting to startle her. It swung open at my touch, and I realized it had not been properly shut. Immediately, I grew concerned.

Entering, I said, "It's Jessamy. Are you all right?"

She did not answer.

I raised my lamp and the light spilled across her bed. It was empty. I gasped and searched the room but she was gone.

But where? To the ruins?

And had that been Clarissa in the gallery?

If so, she could not be far ahead of me. Calling out her name, I ran from her room and hastened down the corridor. All the while, I prayed silently that Trystan had remembered to remove the keys from the latches.

I scanned the gallery, but did not linger there. It, too, was empty. Instead, I went directly to the landing and swept down the stairs. My nightgown billowed out behind me, and my slippers slapped against my feet, but the sounds could not be heard above the noise of the dogs.

They were very near the house, as they had been that evening I stepped outside searching for Trystan. And just like that night, I had outstripped Wilkins and reached the entry hall before him. The double doors were shut, but that, in itself, was not enough to convince me Clarissa had not left the Hall. My hand went straight to the doorknob.

It refused to turn and the key was gone.

I felt weak with relief. She could not have slipped outside from here. And if Trystan had removed the key from this latch, he would most certainly have pocketed them all. There was some measure of relief to be had from that knowledge.

"Clarissa," I called again, not expecting an answer.

Nor did I receive one.

Wherever she was, she was determined to see her plan through without interference. And she had already decided that I had been swayed to her father's way of thinking. I could not expect her to reveal her hiding place voluntarily.

Where would she go if she could not get outside? Although I did not know her whereabouts, I knew her intentions. She was determined to face those things which most frightened her. Where would that have led her?

Instantly, the answer came to me.

She had gone to the servants' hall.

I was not entirely certain where to find that room, but knew it lay off the kitchen. Certainly, it was a start. Wilkins, had he appeared, could have given me the assistance I needed, but he had not yet stirred from his suite.

I set off through the Hall on my own, knowing there was no time to waste.

The shadows retreated at my approach, chased back to the corners only to reemerge after I had passed and resume their rightful places. The faint smell of must grew stronger. In the front and upstairs rooms it was reduced by the maids' constant cleaning and the pervasive fragrance of roses or dried lavender. But the servants' wing received less attention, and the odor seemed to have seeped into the wainscotting.

It gave me an odd feeling to be traipsing through the dark, narrow passageway. Nothing was familiar or friendly, and I felt strangely vulnerable. It was a ridiculous notion, for I knew there could be nothing to harm me in this wing. Had there been, Mary would certainly have told me, and her fears had all been reserved for the fog and the night.

And whatever was to be found there.

I passed beneath an archway and into the high-ceilinged kitchen. The odor of age and must faded beneath culinary aromas that had amassed in layers over the decades and centuries that Wolfeburne Hall had stood. The cries of the dogs were louder there, still sounding through the night, unabated.

I glanced around. There were two other passages, both lined with doors, leading off the kitchen. In the middle of one shone a faint line of light. Praying that I had found Clarissa, I hurried to discover its source.

Softly, I pushed open the door. The room was filled with a variety of overstuffed chairs and sofas, and a low-burning oil lamp stood on a heavy deal dining table that stretched down the middle of the room. My gaze went to the windows.

The curtains had been pulled back, and Clarissa stood with her face pressed against the panes. She stood on tiptoes, and the soles of her bare feet showed beneath the hem of her nightgown. Her back was to me, but the light of my candle was reflected in the glass and she could not have failed to be aware of my presence. Still, she did not turn nor glance over her shoulder.

"Clarissa, you should not have come here," I said in a soft voice. "You know your father would not approve."

She gave a slight nod.

"You must be freezing." The fire had long since died on the hearth.

"I cannot leave yet, Jessamy," she said, and there was a note of desperation in her voice. "Please do not make me."

Outside the window the dogs' howls were moving in our direction, coming nearer with every second that passed, and I did not want her to be standing there when they reached us. My gaze fell on a blanket that lay across the back of one of the armchairs, and I picked it up and shook out the folds.

"Clarissa, come and put this about your shoulders." I was determined to draw her from her position without alerting her to my own fears.

She sighed and turned. "Please, Jessamy. I promised I would not go to the ruins, but I did not promise I would not look out the windows at night. But when Papa hears of this, he will tell me to remain in my bed after I have been sent there."

"As indeed he should."

The howls grew louder. They echoed through the fog and through the walls where they filled the hall with sound. The air quivered with the reverberations. Determinedly, I held up the blanket for her to step beneath and nodded to her to do as she was told.

"Oh, Jessamy."

She sighed, but she had always been a well-behaved child, and it was not in her nature to display outright disobedience. Dragging her feet, she pulled herself away from the windows and allowed me to drape her with the blanket. I could feel her tremble beneath the thick wool.

"See what you have done to yourself," I said, briskly scolding her as though she had simply gone out in the rain without her coat. "You will be lucky if you do not catch a cold. Really, Clarissa. You are nine years old and must begin to show more sense."

I had to raise my voice to a shout to be heard above the dogs. Were it not for the fog blotting out the moon and stars, I had no doubt I would have been able to see them. But it was thick and dense, and the Hall was buried within its depths. They would have had to press their noses to the glass for me to have seen them. Suddenly, their howls ceased.

God bless Wilkins.

"We had better get you upstairs to bed," I told her. "If your Papa goes upstairs and finds you gone, he will be frantic."

I drew her away and she followed without resistance. With each step we took, her shivering grew more pronounced, and I realized that, her plans thwarted, she had become aware of her surroundings and the coldness of the Hall. Her teeth chattered, and she clung to me for greater warmth.

There was a light in the passage that had not been there a few minutes earlier, and when we emerged it was to discover Mrs. Pendarves standing there.

"Oh my dear life," she said. "I had a feeling something wasn't quite right. What are you doing down here? And at this late hour?"

"Explanations must wait for a better time," I answered. "Clarissa has nothing on her feet and she is freezing."

"Goodness, child. Whatever were you thinking of? Bring her into my room. I have the fire going."

She took Clarissa by the shoulder and hurried her down the hall. I started to follow, then stopped. The lamp Clarissa had lit in the parlor still burned, and the curtains had not been drawn. I did not want her escapade to become generally known amongst the household staff. If Mary was any example, they were already too willing to believe the worst of Wolfeburne Hall.

After telling Mrs. Pendarves I would be along directly, I returned to the parlor. All was quiet. This incident could have come to a far less fortunate conclusion. Thanking God it had not, I went to the windows and reached for the curtain pull.

There was a faint ripple in the fog directly outside the windows. I dropped my hand and stared. The lamp bounced a yellow halo of light against the wall of fog, lifting the blackness to shades of leaden gray. Something dark moved within those gray depths.

I watched, unable to move or speak. The dark center of the fog began to take shape. I saw the outline of a head and shoulders and realized that, whoever stood there, could not have been more than a scant foot from the windows.

Suddenly a man's face pressed against the glass. It was a savage countenance, more bestial than human. Matted black hair fell across his brow, and he stared at me, hungrily, consuming me with his gaze.

My breath caught in my throat, and I raised my hand to my mouth to stifle the scream that gurgled in my throat. Who—or what—stared at me? Even as I asked myself that question, I realized there was something strangely familiar about the face. Some passion within those dark eyes that I recognized. It was the same look I had seen only a few hours before in the eyes of—

I gasped.

"Lord Wolfeburne."

There was a flash of comprehension in those eyes, and I knew he had heard me.

And acknowledged his name.

And then he was gone.

The fog drew over the windows where he had been standing, wiping away all trace of him. Only my horror and dread remained to tell me he had really stood there. In all, he could not have stayed more than an instant, although it had seemed much longer.

I backed away from the glass and sank into the nearest chair, my heart thumping against my ribs. What had I seen? *Trystan?* It simply was not possible. Nothing in this world could change a man so completely.

The thought brought me to my feet with a start.

Was that what Clarissa had tried to ask when she spoke of change and of places that could change people? I shuddered. But what else could she have meant?

Suddenly all her fears made sense. She had seen the same face I had seen, recognized the features I had recognized, and later tried to draw them for me. I had supposed she had discerned a female image in the fog, but her words had only been, "I saw my . . ." She had been speaking of her *father*. Whenever the dogs howled, she feared for the creature they chased, for some part of her remembered and worried that Trystan could be hurt.

And I?

What had I said to him? That I should be allowed to

choose my own fate. That I did not care what that fate might be. Instead, upon learning the truth, I had gaped in horror and barely stifled my screams.

And seeing my dread of him, he'd fled.

I pushed myself up from the chair. My legs trembled beneath me and my palms were moist, but I drew strength from my conviction that he loved and would not hurt me. Even Clarissa had come to that conclusion. Some part of me knew her to be right.

I had to go after him.

First I had to contend with the problem of getting outside, but that was easily solved. Mrs. Pendarves had a set of keys. Her door stood ajar, just far enough to allow a crack of light to escape. I tapped on the door to summon her.

She answered promptly. Inside, Clarissa was huddled next to the hearth, her head drooping against the pillows, her eyelids heavy. A quilt had been thrown atop the blanket I'd given her and woolen slippers pulled onto her feet. I relaxed, knowing she had no immediate need of me.

"I have only come to ask you to take care of Clarissa for a while longer," I whispered. "And to borrow your key to the kitchen door."

"Whatever for?"

"Please do not ask me any questions," I said, imploring her. "There is something I must do."

"There is a key in the latch." Her brow creased. "But it's cold outside, and you aren't properly dressed."

"I will be all right. But I must have your key. Lord Wolfeburne will have removed the other."

"Why ever would he have done that? He never has before."

Her curiosity and surprise grew with each remark I made, and I became increasingly conscious that precious moments were slipping away from me. If I was to find Trystan while he was still near the house, I needed to hurry.

Mrs. Pendarves must have noted the urgency in my stance and expression. She shook her head, not fully approving of my intentions, but nor was she going to prevent me from doing what I had to do. She bustled off to fetch the key and returned a few seconds later. In her hands she also carried a heavy woolen shawl.

"You'd better put this about your shoulders."

"Thank you."

I did as she had bidden and then accepted the key. For the wave of gratitude I felt, it might have been made of solid gold and encrusted with precious gems. In less than a minute, I was headed back down the passage, lamp in one hand and iron key gripped firmly in the other.

The latch was old and stiff to turn, and my trembling fingers added to the difficulty of the task. But this, too, was accomplished, and I stepped out into the November night. Even beneath the shawl, I shivered and the damp ground soaked through my thin slippers.

Ignoring the chill, I took a deep breath and called out, "Lord Wolfeburne!"

My voice bounced off the fog and echoed about my head. My cry did not, as I had expected, start the dogs barking. I could only suppose that their familiarity with my scent and the sound of my voice meant that I had ceased to be considered a possible threat to the Hall.

Or perhaps they were, as Clarissa had always insisted, sweet-tempered animals and no threat to anyone save

Lord Wolfeburne himself. And then only on those occasions that he ceased to be recognizable as himself, even to those faithful creatures who had been trained to meet his commands.

The ruins were invisible behind a thick, gray wadding of fog that snaked and squirmed before my eyes. It was a dreadful fog that had come off the moors that night to lie about like some live and sentient entity. An evil concoction whose intent was to hide and conceal those creatures who could not bear the light of day. Its design, its entire reason for being, was to ward off those of us who dared trespass where we did not belong.

It stood between me and those ruins that Trystan must have made his lair. But if I set off walking due west, I could hardly fail to stumble across the fallen stones. And, should it be that I happened to miss them, it would only be to meet up with the tall hedge that edged the lawns and kept the moor at bay.

I did not run, but chose my steps carefully, waiting until I had walked some distance from the servants' wing before raising my voice again to call, "Lord Wolfeburne!" I repeated the cry again and again, increasing my volume until it seemed no one who did not lie in bed with their ears firmly plugged could have failed to hear me.

Once, I nearly called out Trystan, but stopped, hampered by the restrictions he himself had set. Although given what I had recently learned, my reticence seemed pointless. We had strayed far beyond the reach of drawing-room society and proper English manners.

At the thought, I smothered a burst of hysterical laughter.

My control over myself was tenuous. The emotions

rose and fell within me, each being replaced as quickly as they had come. I might have been on a see-saw or a child's roundabout. The world around me was a dark blur, while I was possessed with a frantic and wild exhilaration, knowing that disaster was my nearest companion.

It was a wonder that Trystan had held on to even the remnants of his sanity. What kind of existence had he been forced to lead? He had tried desperately to hide his secret from his peers and the members of his household, even his own family, with only Wilkins for support.

And before him, had he had the support of his father and Mr. Morrison? Was that why the one had ended the hunts and balls that had been "all the rage," and the other had been possessed of "a melancholic disposition"?

And what about Oxford? Had something come to light during his days there and caused his expulsion? Had some savaged animal been discovered and a search for its killer instituted? Had his elder brother feared the worst and demanded that he return to Cornwall? That would explain their quarrel.

There was no question in my mind that it was he who had killed the sheep. No wonder he paid the farmers without protest.

But what of the hapless Miss Osborne? Had she come upon him in the ruins and fled, dropping her lamp when she stumbled over the stones? Had her fear driven her far from the Hall, never to return? Or had Trystan murdered her? Was that why he did not wish to summon the authorities? To save himself? Or did he really believe himself incapable of harming anyone, in any guise?

Dear Lord, let that be the case.

Out of nowhere, there was a flapping noise, like that

of loose fabric slapping against someone's legs. It came from somewhere beyond me in the fog, and my questions came to an abrupt end.

Warily, I lifted my lamp. "Lord Wolfeburne?"

Silence.

"Lord Wolfeburne?" I called, louder than before.

"Jessamy?" the answer came. And in a voice I recognized.

But Trystan sounded far away, lost deep within the fog, and I ceased to wonder why he had not heard me calling him. Doubtless my voice sounded as muffled and faint to him as his did to me. But I knew we could not be far from each other. My senses told me I was not alone.

"Here," I called and stepped forward again, moving toward the flapping sounds, for they seemed to carry better than our cries. My toes stubbed against a large stone, startling me and almost making me drop the lamp, and I knew the castle rose within mere yards of me. But my progress had gained me nothing. The noises moved away from me faster than I could reach them.

It seemed he ran from me and, knowing the ruins far better than I, eluded me with ease. I stopped and sank down onto one of the stones. Unless he retreated into the castle I had no hope of catching him.

The second I ceased to follow, the noises stopped.

And then advanced toward me, only to stop again.

His breathing sounded in my ears as plainly as my own, like a dog heaving with exertion. I looked up, bracing myself not to show fear, but could see nothing beyond the small circle of light cast by my lamp. "Lord Wolfeburne?" I asked again, speaking louder than necessary, lest my natural voice dwindle to a hoarse whisper.

He made no answer. Nor did he approach me.

Not far away the dogs began to bark, an eager bark, not the fearful howls that always issued from them, and I suspected they had the comfort and support of Wilkins. They seemed to move in my direction, but it was difficult to tell.

Fearing they would be upon us in minutes, I lifted the lamp. The circle widened by inches, but I heard the sound of retreating footsteps and saw nothing more than a shadow slipping into the fog. Safely enveloped in its embrace, he paused again.

Was the idea of my seeing him in this condition abhorrent to him?

I lowered the wick until the flame was little more than a red glow. As the light receded, he crept toward me. Less than an arm's length from me, a figure took shape. The same figure I had seen below my bedroom window and through the panes of glass in the servants' hall. There was the semblance of the man I loved in that figure, but nothing more. And all about him was an odor that reminded me of a caged bear I had once seen at a fair.

It took all my strength not to shrink from him, for the body was less like that of a man than were his facial features. The shoulders were massive and hulking. He walked with a stoop, his long arms hanging before him. His hands were like claws, the nails long and curving. A glint of light flashed from his gnarled fingers, and my gaze came to rest upon a wolf's-head ring.

Trembling from head to toe, I stood. "Lord Wolfeburne," I whispered, unable to say more.

He grunted and reached for me. Those clawlike hands

fastened around my arm, cutting through the shawl and the thin cotton of my nightgown, and he pulled me to him. We were near enough that the smell of him filled my nostrils and made me choke.

Dear Lord! What had I done in summoning him?

He was a good foot taller than me, but because of his stoop, our faces were nearly on a level. He peered into my eyes, and with his free hand he caught at my loose braids and yanked them. Still, I felt certain he did not mean to hurt me for there was a tenderness to his rough touch. And in his eyes, barely visible beneath a swath of matted hair, I saw that same sad hunger that made my heart ache.

Not far from us, Castor and Pollux let out a howl. His grip on me tightened and his nails cut deeper, gouging into my flesh. I tried to pull away, but my efforts only incited him to greater force, and his fingernails raked down my arm, shredding both shawl and sleeve. With no thought for the damage he did to me, he dragged me over the stones and toward the ruins.

Unable to swallow my fear, I screamed.

"Jessamy!" Again, Trystan's voice cut through the fog, rising above the dogs' howls, and carrying across the lawns to where I struggled in the arms of a creature I had supposed to be him.

But was not.

I screamed a second time, lost to everything but the terror that flooded me. Then the dogs were upon us, their hackles bristling, their teeth bared. They separated and darted to either side of the creature, trapping him between them and cutting off his escape. Still clutching me in his arms, he snarled at them and twisted from side to side, searching for an escape. But whenever he tried to take a step, they darted at him and drove him back.

Behind them, a soft halo of light appeared, swinging to and fro in the fog. It rapidly grew brighter, and within seconds Trystan appeared, lantern in hand and Wilkins at his back. The expression on his face was one of stark terror. He lifted the lantern and plunged toward us.

The creature flung up his hands to cover his eyes, releasing me, and I ran into Trystan's arms.

He embraced me and released a ragged breath. "Dear God, Jessamy. Are you all right?"

I nodded, but could not speak.

"Thank God. If Wilkins had not heard you calling and fetched me . . ."

He stopped, unable to speak his fears aloud. With one arm, he held me to him, pressing me to him with all his strength. I sagged against him, clinging desperately and gulping for the air that seemed to have fled my lungs.

Trystan's nearness and his protective embrace gave me the strength I needed to recover my composure. At last I dared to look over my shoulder, to the wall of the ruins where the creature was crouched between two fallen rocks, his arm still flung over his eyes.

I shuddered.

Trystan hugged me even tighter. "You need have no fear. He has lived in the darkness of the ruins all his life, and the light terrifies him."

"What is he?" I demanded.

"What, indeed? Come, Arthur." He addressed the hulking brute. "Stand and let me introduce you."

It snarled, but did not move.

"What? Proper introductions will not suit you? Your

manners would be deplored throughout all of Cornwall. And I doubt you would even be received in London. No matter. I shall do the honors, however undeserving you may be.

"Miss Jessamy Lane, may I present to you my brother: Arthur, *Lord Wolfeburne*."

18

I gasped. It could not be.

Trystan's hold on me tightened and, inexorably, he finished what he had begun. "Arthur is my father's eldest son. The true heir to the Wolfeburne title and estates."

I stared in disbelief at the creature he called his brother, a creature more animal than human save for that disconcerting face that was so similar to Trystan's. "It is not possible," I murmured, as much to myself as to him.

He managed a short, bitter laugh. "Unfortunately, it is not only possible, it is an actuality. Come, let us go back to the Hall and leave him in peace."

"But—"

He could not mean to leave that creature there, free to go wherever he wished the instant the dogs and the lanterns were gone. Who knew what atrocities he would commit?

But that was exactly what Trystan intended. Over my protests, he guided me away from the fallen stones and that pitiful being who had rightful claim to them.

Wilkins followed with the dogs, both of them whining and as reluctant to be dragged back to the Hall as I.

Trystan did not take me upstairs, nor even to his study, but to his private sitting room where hot coals burned in the grate. He pulled an armchair up to the edge of the hearth and ordered me to sit down and remove my wet slippers. Then he disappeared into an adjoining room.

I gladly did as I had been told, for now that I was safe I couldn't stop shivering.

Mrs. Pendarves's shawl hung around me in tatters, and the right sleeve of both my night jacket and gown were ripped from shoulders to cuffs. Dark splotches of blood stained the cotton. I shuddered, wondering what would have happened if Trystan had not appeared when he did.

"Thank God Wilkins heard me," I said, hearing his step in the doorway.

He returned to my side carrying a quilt that he gently tucked around me. "He has long been concerned that you were too headstrong for your own good. And his attempts to intimidate you met with resounding failure."

He looked at me in exasperation and I, thinking of both my behavior and how I had thought the worst of poor Wilkins, could not keep from flushing.

"Moreover"—he continued, seeing he had made his point—"I fear that, in calling me, you summoned Arthur, for he is well familiar with his title. Since my father's death, I have never failed to address him in any other fashion. Initially, it was to take some petty pleasure in reducing Henry to his true status, if only to myself. After his death, it served to remind me that I, too, was a fraud."

"But what is he?" I asked, suddenly filled with questions. It seemed impossible to believe the same man could have fathered both Trystan and the grotesque distortion of a human being he called his brother.

He stared into the fire. "That we may never know. Although it is my belief the answer can be found somewhere in Darwin's theory. I suspect he is a throwback to an earlier breed of man. Unevolved. More beast than human."

"And he lives in the ruins?"

"He sleeps in the dungeons by day. At night, or when the fog is thick, he roams the moor. It is there, I think, he truly belongs. On the moor and in the stone huts."

"And you let him go wherever he pleases?"

"Should I force him to live out his life in the dungeons? Like a felon or a caged animal in a zoo? He has committed no crime save for that of being different from the rest of us. Or should he be institutionalized and made to suffer the scrutiny of men like Darwin and Huxley? I could not countenance the notion."

He fetched a chair for himself, setting it near enough to mine so that, after sitting down, he was able to reach out and take my hand in his.

"And think what public knowledge of his existence would do to the Wolfeburne name and family." He gently stroked my fingers. "What future do you think there would be for Henrietta or Annabelle if this were known? Or for Clarissa when she grew old enough to wed? No, I could not in good conscience allow that."

"But surely he is dangerous? It must be he who is killing the sheep."

Trystan shrugged. "He is well fed, but I think he hunts

to remind himself he is a man and meant to be the master of this world."

"But are you not concerned that he might hurt someone?"

Trystan shook his head and smiled sadly. "Whatever he appears to be, he is not dangerous. It is only the sheep he attacks, them rarely, and I make certain that the farmers are reimbursed for their losses."

"But what if he came upon someone by chance?"

"He would run from them. He's like a wild animal, frightened of nineteenth-century man and anxious to avoid him. Sometimes he strays nearer the Hall than I would like—perhaps he has some sense that it is his—but Castor and Pollux have been trained to drive him off without harming him."

"And what of Miss Osborne? She must have gone to the ruins and come upon him."

"And fled," he said in agreement. "Tripping on the stones and dropping her lamp in her flight."

"And when the light was doused, would he not have followed her?"

He shook his head. "More likely he had already retreated to the safety of the dungeons."

"But why, if she escaped him, did she not run to the Hall?"

He considered my question, his gaze fixed upon the fire, his handsome features set in concentration. "I have a theory about people like Miss Osborne. Unimaginative and practical to the core of their being, they believe in nothing that is not solid and wholly compatible with their notion of reality."

To this, I could agree. "That was why she was not

bothered by the dogs and their howls, for the possibility that there could be anything more dreadful outside her windows than a rabbit or trespasser would not have occurred to her."

He nodded. "When people like that are confronted with something outside of their comprehension, their fear is complete and overwhelming. It forces them to question either their own sanity or their entire pattern of belief. Rational thought would have been impossible. I suspect she ran as far from here as she was able at that hour. Nor do I think, even when daylight came, she would have been willing to return."

"But how can you be certain he did not chase her when, only this evening, he came for me?"

"You called him, did you not? Or rather you called for Lord Wolfeburne, and he thought you called for him. Nor was this the first time the two of you had met. There was the evening I did not return."

"And the night he stood beneath my window and I called to him," I said, realizing that it must have been Arthur then. "At the time, I thought it was you."

"And you said nothing to me later?" he demanded.

"I thought you did not want me to know it was you who had been standing there."

"Good Lord." The heel of his fist hit the arm of his chair. "No wonder he has trespassed near the Hall so often of late."

"What are you saying?" I asked, fervently hoping he did not mean what I supposed.

"Have you no idea? You had only to look into his eyes tonight to guess at his emotions."

I swallowed hard. It *was* a look I had recognized. I

had seen the same hunger and need when Trystan looked at me. It was that expression that had convinced me it was he who had peered into the window of the servants' hall.

Trystan noted the changing expressions on my face and nodded grimly. "So you have guessed."

"But why?" I whispered.

"His reasons are all too easy for me to understand. Only think what life is like for him. Always alone. No one of his own kind to share his hours. Can you even begin to understand the kind of loneliness he must endure? God knows, I can. For all I wish I could not," he murmured in a voice so choked with emotion, it was hard to distinguish his words.

"Dear Lord!"

Trystan rose from his chair and went to the windows, although whatever images he saw had to have come from his own thoughts, for there was nothing to be seen save for his own reflection in the glass.

"I suppose you had better have the whole story," he said, talking to the night. "For now it dictates your life as well as my own."

He sighed. "When Arthur was born, my father withdrew from social affairs rather than risk having his son's birth and condition become known. In keeping his secret, he had the aid of Mr. Morrison, a good man whose family had been in the Wolfeburne employ for nearly two centuries. After my father's death, Mr. Morrison assumed all direct responsibility for the true heir, leaving Henry and me to do as we pleased. But when Mr. Morrison fell sick and his responsibilities became too great for him, he wrote to Henry, advising him to return to supervise the estate. By which he meant care for Arthur until a new steward could be found.

"Henry was disinclined to leave London. That is hardly to be wondered at, for he knew the distasteful life that awaited him and his family in Cornwall. Instead, he sent for me and insisted I put aside my schooling for the remainder of that year. It was supposed to be a temporary solution, but having succeeded in dropping the burden of our eldest brother into my hands, he promptly lost interest in the matter.

"Admittedly, it was not possible to find another steward like Mr. Morrison. There was always the risk that someone who had not spent a lifetime in service to the Wolfeburnes might be willing to turn his secret knowledge to a profit. And while Wilkins can be trusted after a fashion, he has not the education nor the intelligence to take real control of the estate."

"And so you were forced to remain here."

"And let it be said that I had been sent down rather than have to answer questions as to why I had not finished my schooling."

He had kept the Wolfeburne secret well. Kept it from everyone save those two people most precious to him—his wife and daughter. "Did you know it was Arthur whom Clarissa saw when she was six?" I asked.

His hand tightened on my fingers. "I thought as much. But she made no mention of what she had seen afterward, and I hoped she had either shut him from her thoughts or believed me when I told her it had been nothing but the fog and her own imagination."

"Why did you not tell her the truth?"

"What would you have had me do? Take her to the ruins and say, 'Clarissa, this is your uncle.' She was only six, and the shock of knowing the truth had killed her mother. My wife could not look at me without seeing his face, without thinking Arthur and I were similar in a fashion she dared not imagine. Her feeble health could not bear the strain."

"And yet what Clarissa imagined was much, much worse." I took a deep breath. "She believed him to be you, changed somehow by the ruins, but you nonetheless. And from other remarks she has made, I gather she worries that because she is your daughter and you are something alike, she, too, could be changed by entering the ruins."

His chin jerked upward. "Why did you not tell me this before?"

"Until I saw him myself, I did not guess. And she would not tell her doubts to anyone but Matilda. I think she dared not lest, by doing so, she cause you grief."

"Good Lord. Only six years old, and already she was protecting me." His eyes glistened with tears. After a long pause, he swallowed and managed to ask, "Are you certain of this?"

"There has been no opportunity to confirm my suspicions. But given her remarks and my own reaction—"

"Your own?"

When I saw him from the servants' hall, I was certain he was you."

"You saw him?" he demanded. "And yet still you walked outside?"

"I had to tell you that, whatever bewitched you, it made no difference to me. I could not love you any less."

He averted his face, and his lower jaw clenched while he struggled to master his emotions. "Good Lord," he murmured again. "I have, indeed, underestimated you. Although the knowledge comes too late for us."

"And why is that?" An unearthly coldness spread over me.

He groaned. "You must leave here, Jessamy. If there is one person in this world who could be harmed by Arthur, it is you. He hungers for you as I do, and has made one attempt to carry you off. Although he would not kill you, you might find that preferable to his claiming you as his mate."

I gasped at the thought.

Trystan nodded. "I will not let that happen. And sending you away will serve two purposes. Clarissa loves and trusts you, as do I. You must take her with you. I will see that you have monies to go to France where you can have some kind of normal life."

"Without you?"

"It must be."

He spoke with such finality, I did not phrase my protest in words, but rose and went to him. When he refused to turn, I put my arms about his waist and laid my cheek against his back. He stiffened, and I felt the muscles beneath me tighten. Determined not to let him pull away, I clasped my hands together.

"There must be another answer," I whispered. "One that will not separate us."

"If there is, I have yet to think of it," he muttered. "And it is not for want of trying."

"Surely Wilkins can see that he is well fed and make payment to any of the farmers who lose their sheep?"

"And if Arthur falls sick or fails to return to the dungeons one morning? There are a myriad of ways for matters to worsen, and Wilkins has neither the skills nor the intelligence to handle them."

"Is there no one else who can be trusted?"

"At the risk of ruining so many lives?" He shook his head.

I groaned. "I could not bring myself to believe that you lacked all sense of honor or responsibility. Now that I find you do not, I would wish it otherwise."

"No," he whispered. "You would not."

With some difficulty, he managed to turn and place his arms around me. I nestled within his embrace, trying to memorize the feel of his muscular arms as they drew against my back, the hardness of his chest, and the smell of his shaving soap. It was not enough. Not to breach the years and miles that would come between us. I lifted my face to his.

He kissed me. It was a hard, bruising kiss that expressed all his anger and frustrated desire, and I returned it with a passion and need equal to his own. My lips grew tender, and my mouth parted beneath the onslaught of his tongue. With his invasion came a rushing warmth that started at the apex of my thighs and flooded through me. My legs trembled, and I sagged against him, but his strength supported both of us.

At last, he tore away and gulped for air, allowing me to do the same. But this time there was no reproach in his eyes, for it was not uncertainty or fear that had made me forget to breathe. Nor was he the first to seek more kisses.

Reluctantly, he drew back and shook his head. "If you

do not leave me now, you will not be permitted to go before morning."

"Nor would that be my wish," I whispered.

"Jessamy, you cannot do this."

"Then you must drive me from your door, for I will not go willingly."

He tried to put me from him but failed, not for lack of strength but lack of will. No sooner had his hands locked about my arms than he pulled me to him, and his lips battered mine once more. I pressed my body against him wantonly, determined he would not ask me to leave a second time. I succeeded beyond my expectations.

He tensed from head to toe, and his breath came and went in rough gasps. Silently, he pulled the torn shawl from my shoulders. It slid from his hands and fell about my feet, forgotten before it reached the floor. His attention had already moved to the ribbons of my night jacket. He ripped at them impatiently until they fell apart, and drew it down over my shoulders to let it fall atop the shawl.

His dark face hovered above mine, and he gazed down at the torn sleeve of my nightgown. His lips twisted into a faint scowl, and his fingers brushed gently over the scratches on my arm. He left a trail of goose bumps in his wake, and my nipples hardened beneath my nightgown.

Trystan smiled and, dismissing my slight wounds, cupped my breasts and lifted them to his mouth. He sucked at them through the thin fabric. I moaned, not caring that I stood in the arms of a man who was not my husband or that I wore almost nothing.

And that little I wore was quickly removed. Without

a word of apology, Trystan reached for the neck of my gown and tore it from head to toe. I gasped but offered no objection. Smiling, he ripped at his shirt. The buttons popped free and scattered across the carpet.

He let his shirt hang open and fumbled with his belt. The firelight played over his chest, highlighting the ridges of hard muscle and glancing off the mat of dark hair. I squirmed within his grasp, wanting to feel him next to me and to mold the contours of my body to his.

His trousers and then his undergarments slid down his legs, and he stepped out of them and pressed his naked body against me. I shivered, feeling his manhood throb against my bare abdomen, enjoying a delight I had never experienced.

Free to explore me as he chose, Trystan's hands wandered down the length of my body. He paused to stroke my breasts and tease my nipples back into a hardened state, before his fingers swept over my stomach, causing my muscles to contract and making me gasp yet again.

He lingered lovingly at the juncture of my thighs, and his fingers slipped between my legs. I moaned softly, giving myself up to the pleasure I found in those smooth, demanding strokes, enjoying the sensation of moist warmth that spread from me. I had never guessed that there was such unbridled physical delight offered to mere mortals.

Then he drew back his fingers. I begged him not to stop, but Trystan had more than my happiness in mind. Cupping his hands beneath my buttocks, he lifted me up and told me to wrap my legs around his waist. I did as I was bid, and he supported me there for an instant.

Then slowly he lowered me onto that hard male part of him.

Inch by inch, he entered me, letting me slide over the length and breadth of him. I cried out but he would not be denied. Nor did he pause until I had absorbed all he had to offer.

I gazed up at him in wonder, and he smiled knowingly. Then he began to slide up and down inside of me, moving slowly at first, then thrusting harder and harder until I thought of nothing but the growing warmth and returning thrust for thrust. Suddenly, all the sensations ran together in a rush, and I threw back my head and cried aloud.

Weak, still tingling, I sagged against him. "Now you could not possibly send me away," I murmured, speaking my thoughts aloud.

His arms tightened around me. "Now I could not think of doing anything else," he replied grimly.

Clarissa was no less dismayed than I at the thought of leaving her Papa, although she hastened to assure me that it was not for lack of loving me. "But he needs me, Jessamy," she said. "What will he do if I am not here?"

She did not say *to protect him*, but I knew that was what she meant.

Indeed, I shared her concern. While his life was not endangered, his happiness and peace of mind were certainly at risk.

But Trystan had determined that we would go, and he was quick to make the arrangements. In barely a fortnight, tickets had been bought, travel arrangements had been made, and a house had been rented for us in Nice. Mrs. Pendarves had been told she would be accompanying us, along with Davey who would be needed to see to our array of luggage.

On the day of our departure, I watched Davey from the window. He toted our cases and trunks one by one to the waiting cart, entering and emerging from the low-lying fog that settled everywhere about the grounds. All too soon, he completed his tasks and set off with Wilkins in the cart for the station, leaving us to follow with Trystan.

A half hour passed, and Bastian brought the carriage to the front door. A few short minutes and we, too, would have to be on our way or risk missing the morning train.

I glanced around my suite, saying good-bye to the small rooms I had come to regard as home. There were tears in my eyes, although I knew they were more for the good-bye that had yet to come. It was not until that moment, when I looked at the empty wardrobe, that I really believed Trystan would let us go.

While I lingered there, Clarissa burst into my room. Her face was also streaked with tears, but her eyes were wide with fright and she gulped for air with every step she took. She flung herself into my arms and her small chest heaved.

"What's wrong?" I demanded.

"Matilda," she said when she could force the word from her mouth. "Matilda."

"Take a deep breath, and tell me what happened."

In a minute she had recovered enough to speak. "I went to the ruins."

"Clarissa!"

She stifled a sob. "I had to go, Jessamy. I thought if Papa could see I was not afraid, he would not send us away. I had to show him."

"You did not go in?" I asked, praying she had not.

"But I did. Into the Great Hall. And Matilda went with me because she wanted Papa to know she was not frightened either. But I was frightened, and I ran away."

"And I am very glad you did," I murmured.

"But I dropped Matilda," she said with a wail. "She's alone in the ruins, and I cannot leave her. Please go with me and fetch her. Do not make me leave her, Jessamy. I promised her I would not forget her like you forgot Meg."

I felt a wrench of pain at her words. No, whatever must be done, Matilda could not be deserted. "Your father will fetch her. I have only to go downstairs and ask him."

"No!" she wailed. "You must not tell Papa. Don't you see. He will know that not only did I break my promise to him but I failed him as well. Please, Jessamy. I trusted you. You must not say anything to him. Only come with me, and I will fetch Matilda myself."

Her distress was too great to ignore. "I will find Matilda," I told her. "But only if you promise to remain here until I return."

She nodded.

"This time you must not break your word, Clarissa."

"I will not, Jessamy," she said, contrite.

I told myself there was no reason for fear. It was morning. Arthur would be in the dungeons, and I would go no farther than the Great Hall. I slipped out of the house and walked resolutely toward the ruins. A drift of fog hovered above the grounds, but it would be gone by midday. Already there was a soft brightness where the winter sun filtered through the swaths of gray, and the bushes and trees around me were muted but easily visible. Arthur's eyes could not have stood even so gentle and suffused a light.

The gray stones of the castle towered above me. Taking a deep breath, I stepped beneath the forbidden archway and into the Great Hall. A few steps beyond the entry, I came to an abrupt halt. It was darker within the castle than I had expected. The walls shut out the wintry light, and swirls of fog drifted through the massive room. A few more feet and I would find it difficult to see.

I dared not continue. It would have been absolute foolishness. There was no question in my mind that Arthur could walk about the castle as he pleased in this darkness. I had no choice but to go back and fetch a lantern.

But that would necessitate explanations, probably to Trystan, who would be waiting impatiently. It would also take another five or ten minutes, and there was no more time to waste if we were to make our train. I hesitated, not wanting to fail Clarissa, but seeing no alternative.

I frowned and peered into the gloom. By chance, my gaze lit upon Matilda. She was lying only a few feet from me or I should not have seen her at all. But it was a simple matter to pick her up and leave. With a sigh of relief, I took another step.

Something rustled behind me.

Time seemed to stop. I turned and stared toward the archway. A few feet to one side was a hulking shadow. Arthur, Lord Wolfeburne, had already left his dungeons. Perhaps, earlier, he had heard Clarissa's soft steps and been drawn to the sounds. That, or he had seen no need to descend to the ruins' darkest depths until driven back by the day's full brightness.

I retreated a step. What was I to do? I could not possibly escape while he stood within a few steps of the only exit. Even as I thought this, he lumbered toward me, cautiously avoiding the muted gray semicircle that marked the main door, until he stood between me and that precious fall of light.

My breath came and went in short gasps. Now, there was no hope of escape. I edged backward, keeping my gaze fixed on the creature. It would not do to draw his attack by moving quickly or abruptly. He approached with similar caution and stealth, but his stride was longer than my own, and I knew it would not be long before he overtook me.

My next step brought me up against the wall, and I glanced behind me to see I could go no farther. I squinted into the darkness. A few yards to the left of me was another doorway, and a flight of steps wound upward to some unknown destination.

Into the tower, I guessed. Better to go there than the dungeons.

I slipped to the left and mounted the first step. Arthur followed, his pace slightly faster. I did not wait but, grabbing up my skirts, I turned and fled up the narrow steps.

Slits had been cut into the circular stone walls through which I could see the fog and the soft green lawns. But they only tantalized me with a freedom that could not be gained. A child could not have squeezed through those tiny openings. I did not waste precious seconds in attempting the impossible, but hurried on.

Partway up, I came to a landing. A wooden door had been set into the wall, and an iron loop dangled invitingly. I pulled hard, but the door didn't budge. Fighting down my terror, I pressed my full length against the oaken planks, all to no avail.

Below, a heavy tread scraped the stones, and I knew that to remain meant to risk being captured. I shuddered at the thought of what would happen to me, for there was no longer any doubt in my mind as to the nature of relationships between men and women.

I hastened up the next flight of stairs, seeking another door and praying the next one would not be locked. My prayers were answered, but not as I had hoped. On the second landing was an open archway, for the door had rotted from its hinges. I peered inside. It was dark, and the window slits were no wider than those I had already passed. Nor was there anywhere in that small chamber to hide.

I lifted my skirts and ran up the third flight of steps. To my dismay, it brought me to the last and topmost landing. I glanced around wildly. Directly to my right was yet another door. It was solid, not rotted like the one below. If only it opened, I might yet escape my pursuer. Hoping to lock myself into the chamber, I silently prayed it would open, and pushed. Hinges creaking, it swung inward. I thanked God and took a step toward the cavernous darkness.

And came to a shuddering stop.

Clarissa's voice echoed in my thoughts. The tower had a room with no floor. Would it not be the topmost room? I braced myself in the doorway and gingerly slid my foot toward the blackness that awaited me. A mere six inches into the room the floor dropped away from my foot.

I gasped and drew back.

Behind me something scratched against the step.

I screamed and ran down the remaining length of passageway. It came to an abrupt end, and a stone wall loomed above me. Heavy timbers, what appeared to be fallen rafters, had been propped against the stones. I dislodged two of the lighter ones and managed to squeeze into the small, triangular space between them and the wall. Thinking it a poor hiding place, I crouched down and flattened myself against the stones. If I was lucky, my pursuer would lack the intelligence to see what I had done.

Arthur loomed on the landing. Immediately, with the instinct of a hunter, his gaze fixed on me. Still, he hesitated and his eyes pleaded with me for something I could not possibly give him.

I screamed again for Trystan, all the while knowing I could not be heard through the thick walls. It was no more use than screaming in a nightmare, when one opens one's mouth only to realize that no sounds would come forth.

I fell silent and stared at him, noting his haunting facial likeness to Trystan and the coarse hairs of his body that was more ape than human. Then I realized with a start that more than fear enabled me to see him so distinctly. It was brighter in the passage than it had been in either the Great Hall or on the tower stairs.

I looked up. Where the planks had been disturbed, thin rays of sunlight filtered through the cracks. At this height, we were above the fog. I frantically began shoving the debris aside, struggling to uncover the window slit. The last rotting timber crashed to the stones and splintered, and a wintry sunshine flooded down around me.

I sagged against the stones. I could not move from where I stood, but nor could he come any closer. Soon Clarissa would have to tell someone of my whereabouts, and they would search for me. And as long as the sky remained clear above the tower, Arthur would not hurt me.

Fifteen minutes passed and I waited there, frightened but relatively safe. Every few minutes I would hear the rasping of claws against stone, and I knew that he, too, remained, hoping for clouds to draw across the sun as I hoped for Trystan. Twice the light dimmed, only to brighten again almost immediately. Then I heard a strong voice cry out my name.

"Trystan!" I called. "I am up here."

There was the sound of running steps, and then the glow of a lantern was added to the sunlight. The landing was flooded with a welcome brightness.

The creature snarled and his head twisted from side to side. His eyes sought out the only patch of blackness in that entire length of passageway. With one hand shielding his eyes, he leapt for safety.

I screamed for him to stop.

If he understood, it was too late for him to halt his headlong rush. He plunged through the open doorway and was gone. Seconds later there was an awful thud.

I rose and ran sobbing into Trystan's open arms.

* * *

Clarissa and I delayed our trip to Nice, and when we went, we did not go alone. Trystan, Lord Wolfeburne, accompanied us, as it befitted a groom to accompany his bride on their honeymoon. Nor were we in any hurry to return to Wolfeburne Hall, for though it no longer held any dark secrets, neither did it hold pleasant memories for any of us.

And there was only one postscript to our story. It came in a batch of mail that was forwarded to us, and was written by the investigator Trystan had hired to trace Miss Osborne.

He had located her in Truro, at the home of one of her father's contemporaries. When he inquired after her, he learned she had arrived on the man's doorstep, feverish and distraught, and had remained beneath his roof until she recovered her health. How she had gotten there remained a mystery.

But during her recovery, she managed to make herself indispensable to the gentleman in question. Not long after she regained her health—in direct contradiction to Mary's prediction—he married her. According to the investigator, the match, while not of a romantic nature, seemed ideally suited to the needs of both parties.

"Ah!" Trystan lifted his head and smiled complacently at me over the page. "One final remark. The ex–Miss Osborne hopes that Lord Wolfeburne will see fit to forward her belongings."

"The gall of the woman," I said, thinking of the excessive number of times I had concerned myself with her welfare. "Does she not make even so much as an apology?"

"Not that it would appear. And yet," he said, his dark eyes dancing with amusement, "given my satisfaction with her successor, I am not moved to complain."

COMING NEXT MONTH

ORCHIDS IN MOONLIGHT by Patricia Hagan

Bestselling author Patricia Hagan weaves a mesmerizing tale set in the untamed West. Determined to leave Kansas and join her father in San Francisco, vivacious Jamie Chandler stowed away on the wagon train led by handsome Cord Austin—a man who didn't want any company. Cord was furious when he discovered her, but by then it was too late to turn back. It was also too late to turn back the passion between them.

TEARS OF JADE by Leigh Riker

Twenty years after Jay Barron was classified as MIA in Vietnam, Quinn Tyler is still haunted by the feeling that he is still alive. When a twist of fate brings her face-to-face with businessman Welles Blackburn, a man who looks like Jay, Quinn is consumed by her need for answers that could put her life back together again, or tear it apart forever.

FIREBRAND by Kathy Lynn Emerson

Her power to see into the past could have cost Ellen Allyn her life if she had not fled London and its superstitious inhabitants in 1632. Only handsome Jamie Mainwaring accepted Ellen's strange ability and appreciated her for herself. But was his love true, or did he simply intend to use her powers to help him find fortune in the New World?

CHARADE by Christina Hamlett

Obsessed with her father's mysterious death, Maggie Price investigates her father's last employer, Derek Channing. From the first day she arrives at Derek's private island fortress in the Puget Sound, Maggie can't deny her powerful attraction to the handsome millionaire. But she is troubled by questions he won't answer, and fears that he has buried something more sinister than she can imagine.

THE TRYSTING MOON by Deborah Satinwood

She was an Irish patriot whose heart beat for justice during the reign of George III. Never did Lark Ballinter dream that it would beat even faster for an enemy to her cause—the golden-haired aristocratic Lord Christopher Cavanaugh. A powerfully moving tale of love and loyalty.

CONQUERED BY HIS KISS by Donna Valentino

Norman Lady Maria de Courson had to strike a bargain with Saxon warrior Rothgar of Langwald in order to save her brother's newly granted manor from the rebellious villagers. But when their agreement was sweetened by their firelit passion in the frozen forest, they faced a love that held danger for them both.

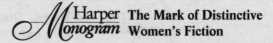 **Harper Monogram** **The Mark of Distinctive Women's Fiction**

If you would like to receive a HarperPaperbacks catalog, please send your name and address plus $1.00 postage/handling to:

HarperPaperbacks Catalog Request
10 East 53rd St.
New York, NY 10022

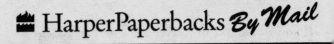

YESTERDAY'S SHADOWS
by Marianne Willman

Bettany Howard was a young orphan traveling west searching for the father who left her years ago. Wolf Star was a Cheyenne brave who longed to know who abandoned him—a white child with a jeweled talisman. Fate decreed they'd meet and try to seize the passion promised. 0-06-104044-4

MIDNIGHT ROSE by Patricia Hagan

From the rolling plantations of Richmond to the underground slave movement of Philadelphia, Erin Sterling and Ryan Youngblood would pursue their wild, breathless passion and finally surrender to the promise of a bold and unexpected love. 0-06-104023-1

WINTER TAPESTRY
by Kathy Lynn Emerson

Cordell vows to revenge the murder of her father. Roger Allington is honor bound to protect his friend's daughter but has no liking for her reckless ways. Yet his heart tells him he must pursue this beauty through a maze of plots to win her love and ignite their smoldering passion. 0-06-100220-8